RAVE REVIEWS FOR PATRICIA GAFFNEY!

THIEF OF HEARTS

"Ms. Gaffney delivers a knockout with the one-two punch of action-packed adventure and heart-pumping romance."

—Nora Roberts

"A stunning gem of a book that establishes Patricia Gaffney as Leisure's new star. She takes the ordinary and makes it shine."

—*Romantic Times*

SWEET TREASON

"This poignant, touching love story has enough adventure, romance, history and memorable characters to please readers. I foresee a wonderful future for this bright new star!"

—*Romantic Times*

"The action is non-stop, the writing at times reminiscent of Kathleen Woodiwiss. One of the better historicals to come out recently."

—*Rendezvous*

MOMENT OF TRUTH

"Why should I believe you?" Anna asked.

"Why should you?" Brodie leaned one hand against the rough wooden mantel behind her head, trapping her with his body in front, the fire behind. "How about for old time's sake? Or out of respect for your husband. Nick the upright, Nick the perfect."

He lifted his hand and rested it on top of her shoulder. "If he was so good, Annie, how could his brother be so bad? Hm?" With a little tug, her pulled her chemise down over her arm, baring her shoulder.

Anna held herself statue-still, not breathing, daring him. His hard mouth softened. There was a light in his pale eyes she'd never seen; he looked nothing at all like Nicholas to her in the second before he bent and put his lips on the naked place he'd made on her shoulder. Her eyes dimmed and closed, and she could hear her heartbeat in her ears. "Don't," she said, then felt the wetness of his tongue, lightly rasping, his lips softly sucking. "Oh, don't." He raised his head. His mouth glistened and his breathing was uneven. She'd been wrong; the moment of danger wasn't over, it was just starting. It was now.

Other *Leisure* books by Patricia Gaffney:
FORTUNE'S LADY
THIEF OF HEARTS
LILY
ANOTHER EDEN
SWEET TREASON

Thief Of Hearts

Patricia Gaffney

LEISURE BOOKS NEW YORK CITY

This book is for Mike Gaffney:
my brother, my friend, my fairest critic.

A LEISURE BOOK®

April 2000

Published by
Dorchester Publishing Co., Inc.
276 Fifth Avenue
New York, NY 10001

ISBN 0-8439-4803-5

Printed in the United States of America.

PART ONE

1

April 14, 1862 Bristol

"Don't seem fair, does it, mate? I was so drunk, I don't even remember bashin' the bastard's brains in. Didn't even know his name. What about you? Eh? Oh, I was forgettin'—you're *innocent*, you didn't kill *nobody*. Ain't that right?"

Brodie stared back at his cellmate's skeptical leer without smiling, and presently Shooter shrugged and went back to picking lice out of his beard. Through the horizontal slit in the stone wall, Brodie could see a section of cloud drifting past like a slow-moving turret. A thunderstorm was coming.

"Kinda peculiar, though," Shooter resumed after a minute, reaching out with the hand that wasn't shackled to squash a fat, lumbering bug on the damp floor between them. "Ain't it? I mean, you wakin' up next to a stone-dead whore, blood everywhere, and no idea in the world how she got that way. I'd say that was damn peculiar."

"Shut up, Shooter," Brodie said, without much

hope. He put his head back against the oozing wall and shut his eyes. The sounds of dripping water and muffled weeping came to him through the grate in the iron door.

"Can't blame a judge for not swallowing that, you ask me. Specially since you knew 'er, and her bein' in the family way and all—Ow!" Shooter grabbed his shin, scooted backward, and commenced to curse.

Brodie always felt bad after kicking Shooter. His cellmate couldn't fight back; his legs were too short to reach across the four and a half feet of straw-covered dirt that separated them. But regret was a cheap price to pay for the relief silence brought, and he'd reconciled himself to paying it as often as he had to.

Which shouldn't be too much longer, things being what they were. He would be dead in three days, and Shooter—Brodie's head jerked up. Oh, Christ, today was the day they were hanging Shooter. His pale eyes widened on the thin, still-whining figure huddled in front of him. How old was Shooter? Forty? Fifty? Hard to tell with that grizzled beard and all the filth on him. Brodie had almost gotten over being angry that he himself would die before he was thirty, but it still rankled that he wasn't going to die at sea. He'd always thought he would die at sea.

"You got any family, Shooter?" he asked, almost gently.

"Nah." He thought for a second. "How the hell do I know?" Then, "Nah," more positively. "You?"

It was on the tip of Brodie's tongue to say no, the answer he'd given for the last fourteen years to anybody who'd bothered to ask. But what was the point? What difference did it make now? "I've got a brother," he said slowly. The words sounded strange, new. "His name's Nick. And I might have a father."

"You *might* have a father?" The small black eyes registered paltry interest.

Brodie rested his chin on one updrawn knee, shifting his left arm slightly to take some weight off the raw flesh of his manacled wrist. "I mean he might still be alive. I don't know. I haven't seen him since I was six."

"Yeah? What's *his* name?"

Brodie smiled. "His name is Regis Gunne. He's the seventh Earl of Battiscombe." He joined in Shooter's harsh laughter until his cellmate's guffaws turned into the wet choking sounds that were coming more frequently these days. "You all right, Shooter?"

"Yeah." He wiped spittle from his chin and rested the side of his sweating face against the wall. "What the hell difference does it make?"

Brodie had no answer. They fell silent, and he began to regret his thoughtless overture to Shooter, however well-meant. It had unlocked a door, one he'd closed a long time ago and sworn never to open again. But he had, of course, from time to time. He'd even seen Nick twice. He hadn't deliberately thought of his father, though, nor said his name out loud in fourteen years.

But Brodie was going to die in three days. He had a sailor's awe of eternity; he'd seen its evidence spread out before him a thousand times in the sea and the sky and in the vastness of time. Still, something earthbound in him worried that this was it, that if he failed now to reconcile himself to the circumstances of his life and his family, his flesh would rot and his bones turn to dust, with no second chance anywhere, anytime, to try again.

But it was so hard. Too hard. A man couldn't give up a lifetime of resentment just because it was time to die. And as for his father, he was convinced his resentment was deserved. With Nick it was different. With Nick—

There was a rattle at the lock and the iron door squealed open, revealing two guards in the threshold. A priest hovered behind them. Brodie glanced at Shooter. They scrambled to their feet at the same moment.

Shooter began to cry. One of the guards unshackled his wrist from the wall while the other took hold of his free arm. When his knees buckled, they had to drag him toward the door. Brodie pressed back against the cold stone, not wanting to watch, unable to look away. All at once Shooter broke free, but instead of running he dropped to his knees again, then to his side, and wrapped himself up in a fetal ball. The sounds coming out of his mouth were horrible. One of the guards kicked him, and after a few seconds the other joined in. The priest kept his eyes on his prayerbook.

Brodie hardly knew he was yelling Shooter's name until the condemned man looked up at him, his face twisted in agony. "What's your name?" Brodie shouted, his free hand stretched out toward him. "What's your real name? Your *real name*, man!"

The guards paused. Shooter clambered up on his elbow, licking blood from his lower lip and holding his middle. He stared at Brodie until the film of fear over his eyes lifted a little. He whispered. "Jonathan."

"Jonathan what?"

"Shoot. My name's Jonathan Shoot."

Brodie held his arm out farther. "Good-bye, Jonathan."

One of the guards muttered a warning, but neither tried to stop Shooter when he staggered to his knees, then his feet, and gave Brodie his hand. The clasp was wet and shaky, but it got firmer the longer it went on. "I'll see you in hell, I reckon," Shooter got out, his voice trembling but his chin jutting in a brave imitation of his old bantam rooster style.

Brodie squeezed his fingers tighter and tried to smile. "Aye, I reckon you will. God bless you, Jonathan."

Tears flooded Shooter's eyes again, but he blinked them away. "God bless *you*—" But the guards were sick of it now and bundled their prisoner out of the cell with rough hands. "Give 'em hell, mate—" was the last Brodie heard, the voice full of desperate courage, before the door clanged shut and a terrible silence muted the room.

Brodie stared at the empty wrist iron dangling from the stone wall in front of him and shuddered. He'd felt like hanging Shooter himself a few times in the week and a half they'd been locked up together. He'd have given all he had to have him back now.

A new despair descended, worse than anything he'd felt before. All his life he'd taken things as they came, with a sailor's prosaic conviction that death operated on its own schedule and that worrying about it wasted a man's time. But life had turned ugly on him. The old complaisance wasn't a comfort any longer. Someone had murdered Mary and the child she carried—not his, but what difference did that make?—and he would be put to death for it the day after tomorrow. He had no philosophy, knew of no system that could make sense of this atrocity. The priest had told him it was God's will, a piety that had filled him with black, baffled rage. He felt it now, and brought his fist back to smash against the wall he was shackled to. Again, again. And now his boot, kicking the unyielding stone with vicious futility, over and over until the pain and his own weakness forced him to stop and he sank to his knees, panting.

His pale blue gaze went to the window again. The sky was almost black; he could hear thunder in the distance, moving closer. "Shooter's going out in style," he said out loud, then flinched. Jesus, was he going to start talking to himself? He settled back against the wall and closed his eyes. What if he did? To sink into babbling, slavering madness would be a mercy right now.

But no such luck. His mind was as clear as lake water. Already he was thinking again of his family. One of the deepest regrets of his life—and he had many—was that he'd never looked up his father and told him what he thought of him. Had Nick found him yet, he wondered, and ingratiated himself to him? If so, they deserved each other.

But what did they think of him? Anguish lay behind that question; he could scarcely face it. His family didn't know him. If they thought of him at all, if they believed anything, they must believe that Mary Sloane was a dockside whore and that he had killed her.

Brodie put his head down and watched tears spatter on the floor between his shoes. Rain beat in through the open window, soaking the wet stone floor. Outside the door he could hear the guard coming, dispensing the prisoners' dinners. How many more meals would he get before they hanged him? He counted. Five. He'd eaten a lot of bad food in one ship's galley or another, but he'd never eaten anything as putrid as the slop they served in the Bristol gaol. His stomach rumbled. He was starving. He knew he would eat all five of his meals, and then he would die.

2

"Mrs. Balfour!"

Anna looked up, startled, and caught sight of her own smiling, wide-eyed gaze in the mirror. I look *pretty*, she thought wonderingly, before she called out in answer, "Yes, Mr. Balfour?"

"Are you ever coming out? The champagne's going flat. You've been in there for hours."

The smile widened. "Nicholas, it's been five minutes! Give me five more, and I'll be ready." She heard a mock groan, and giggled. In the mirror, she saw that she was blushing.

Giggling? Blushing? Could this flushed and foolishly grinning young woman really be Anna Jourdaine Balfour? She leaned closer and peered at herself, as if to make certain. In truth, she'd have given a great deal to know what her husband of six and a half hours saw to love in that face. Healthy skin, perhaps, with no bumps or blotches. Pretty hair, she hoped, a sort of reddish-blonde color. And once someone had told her her eyes were "interesting," whatever that meant; to her they just looked brown. But beyond these dubious assets she could see nothing special about herself, nothing at all. She sighed, giving up, and then smiled again. After all, what did it matter? To her it would always be a mystery, but the deliciously incontrovertible fact was that Nicholas must see something in her, because he'd married her!

She closed her eyes and wrapped her arms around herself, savoring it. She was *married*. She, Anna Constance St. Claire Jourdaine, bookish and not beautiful, serious—some said humorless, but she disagreed with that—and level-headed to a fault, with really quite little to recommend her except the enormous fortune she would one day inherit—she was not after all, despite her own inner certainty and the countless predictions of friends and family to the contrary, going to die an old maid. But the most wondrous, the most miraculous part of this prodigious piece of good luck wasn't even the fact of her marriage, it was *who* she had married: the handsomest, smartest, most exciting man in the world, the man with whom she'd been in love since she was sixteen—the incomparably wonderful Nicholas Balfour!

And he loved her, too. He must, for this morning he'd told her he couldn't possibly wait three more weeks for the formal wedding her aunt had been planning for months, he had to marry her now, *today*. His impatience thrilled her, it was so uncharacteristic of him. Their elopement must be the most impulsive act of his life. It most certainly was of hers.

And now she had everything. In the space of six months, she'd gone from a lonely, semi-invalid spinster with unrealistic dreams of someday designing passenger ships, to a silly, laughing bride whose new husband not only allowed but actually encouraged her to participate in her family's shipbuilding business—which he would take over himself now that her father was so ill.

"Anna, I'm lighting the fire. Are you hurrying?"

"I am!" With a last awed look at herself, she turned away from the bureau and crossed to the cane chair on which Aiden O'Dunne had deposited her traveling bag. For the first time she noticed the white carnation stuck upright in the handle. How very sweet, and how like Aiden to put it there for her. When debating who should stand up for the groom, she and Nicholas had easily chosen Aiden, for one, because he was not only Jourdaine Shipbuilding's attorney but a dear family friend. For the second, Anna had suggested her cousin Stephen—for propriety's sake, to give their sudden elopement at least the *appearance* of having the family's blessing. But Nicholas had argued that Stephen would disapprove of their haste so thoroughly, he might give them away to Anna's aunt or even her father, ill as he was. So—without much enthusiasm on her part—they'd asked Neil Vaughn instead, Nicholas's new friend. He was no friend of Anna's, but at least he'd been sober during the quick ceremony in Reverend Bury's best parlor this afternoon, and even at the gay, intimate dinner at Aiden's house afterward. At least she thought he'd been sober; with Neil, it was sometimes hard to tell.

For herself, she'd told only two people: her cousin Jenny and her friend Milly. Milly had wept with happiness and immediately offered to be matron of honor. But Jenny had pleaded a migraine and begged off from the ceremony. Now Anna wondered if the headache was real. With all her heart, she hoped it was. Until a year ago Jenny and Nicholas had kept company, in a casual way. But when Anna's brother had died, Nicholas had comforted her and they'd fallen in love—or rather, he'd fallen in love: Anna had loved him since the day they'd met, eight years ago in her father's shipyard. The idea that Jenny's heart might be broken made her ache with pity and distress—but truly, *truly* she didn't think it was so! Her beautiful cousin could have any man she wanted with the crook of one finger, and she'd entertained *dozens* of suitors during the months Nicholas and Anna had been engaged. Jenny was fond of Nicholas, that was all. She was sure of it.

"Anna Jourdaine Balfour?"

"I'm coming!"

Anna moved to the wide tester bed in the center of the room, bare floorboards creaking with each footfall, and tossed her nightgown across the worn coverlet. The lamplight was mercifully dim, obscuring the dust and cobwebs in every corner, the dinginess of the plaster walls and the uncurtained window. The tiny two-room cottage was an unlikely choice for their wedding night, perhaps, and she didn't doubt that Aunt Charlotte would be doubly scandalized when she learned of it. But Nicholas had wanted secrecy as well as privacy, so that no one could interfere with their honeymoon escape to Italy tomorrow morning. He'd borrowed the cottage, five miles east of the city and in the middle of nowhere, from a bachelor acquaintance. Anna's home was a Liverpool mansion, but tonight this room didn't seem a bit damp or gloomy or untidy. In fact, it was the loveliest room she'd ever seen.

But her fingers were not quite steady as she began to undo the hooks down the front of her corset. She muttered the vilest curse she knew— "Blast!" No doubt it was a flaw in her character, but she hated being new at anything. And she hated this nervousness she could suddenly feel, like hungry mouths nibbling at her insides, turning her arms and legs watery with weakness. It was because she didn't *know*. If she *knew* what was going to happen—that is, something beyond the bare, unnerving fundamentals of the thing she and Nicholas were about to do—surely she would be reassured. Oh, why hadn't she asked Milly? Her friend would've explained everything, in the kindest possible way, provoking the least amount of embarrassment. But she'd been too timid. The thought of asking Aunt Charlotte had never entered her head. This total ignorance was outrageous, she saw now, even if in it she was no different from any other unmarried lady of her class. But tonight it struck her as a conspiracy.

She slipped her arms into the sleeves of her linen cambric nightdress and pulled it over her head. The gown was long-sleeved, high-necked, and very full. But she was naked underneath, and she'd never in her life felt so defenseless. Would Nicholas hurt her? Not deliberately, she was sure. But there was a medical book in her father's library, hidden in an obscure alcove on a top shelf, and she'd long ago devoured every word in it that related even remotely to human reproduction. It said that men derived pleasure from coupling and women did not. In fact, it stated explicitly that for a woman to experience passion during intercourse was a disturbing abnormality that ought not to be left untreated.

She could grasp the rudiments of the act well enough to understand why it might be painful; it was this unspoken insinuation that it was also degrading that puzzled and distressed her. A great deal of money had been lavished on her education and it had not gone to waste: she was intelligent, accomplished, and most important, a proper young lady. It could never have been said that in her entire life she had behaved toward the opposite sex with anything but irreproachable propriety. Yet on the seven occasions when Nicholas had kissed her during their six-month-long engagement, not once had she felt degraded.

She reached for her dressing gown at the moment Nicholas called to her, with a flattering touch of real impatience this time, "Anna, must I come in there and get you?"

"No, I'm—"

"Now, who in the world—?"

She heard it at the same time he did, a brisk knock at the outer door. Padding to the bedroom door, she opened it a crack and peeped out. Who could it possibly be? Aiden again? Neil, playing a trick—?

She saw her husband take a startled step back as a tall man in a mask shoved his way inside the cottage. "Who are you?" Nicholas had time to ask. Anna threw the door open wide. She saw no weapon, but an instinct made her scream. The man hoisted his arm high and slashed it down in a fast chopping arc. She screamed again, clutching at her hair. Nicholas made a sighing sound, then dropped to his knees and toppled over backwards.

The thick black hilt of a knife jutted from the center of his chest.

Primitive fear rooted her in place, her back pressed against the wall. Her breath caught in the top of her lungs and her throat closed in impotent panic, choking off more screams. The masked man peered at her—she could see his eyes behind two slits in the brown wool that covered his face. Time stopped. His gloved hands clenched and unclenched; she could sense his uncertainty as clearly as if he'd spoken it. At last a noise in the open door released them from their staring, speechless trance, and he whirled away from her.

"Bloody 'ell!" shouted a giant of a man in a checked coat.

The murderer backed slowly toward the fireplace, and Anna saw his purpose just before he reached down and seized the iron poker. The giant advanced on him, huge fists raised, no fear in his wide, vacant face. He stopped four feet away. The masked man glanced at the open door, feinted toward it, then abruptly lunged with the poker, landing a stunning blow to the big man's collarbone and making him stagger. The murderer scurried around him.

Anna saw that he was going to escape. Without a thought, she stumbled between him and the door. The poker jerked high in the air again and she cried out, flinging up her hands. Too late! She heard a rush of air and felt a crushing impact against her temple. Blinding light, as if her head were blowing up. A stench like burning in her nostrils. Then nothing.

3

Rain thudded in solid, heavy drops against the porthole glass, blearing the already-obscure view of churning whitecaps, black troughs of water, and bilious sky. The oil lamp that swung overhead from a hook barely illuminated the cabin, although it was midday. The room contained only one cot, a chair, and a small wooden chest. A woman lay on the cot; small and frail-looking, she appeared to be sleeping. A man leaned against the porthole. With hands stuffed into the pockets of his pinstriped frock coat, he stared out at the gray, liquid vista without seeing.

His pleasantly ordinary face was pale, unshaven, and marked with lines of distress. He wore his black hair parted in the middle, his graying sidewhiskers short and neat. He turned at a sound from the bed; but the sleeper had only sighed, and slept on. His troubled brown eyes softened as he watched her. With a quick shake of the head,

Aiden O'Dunne dropped his gaze and trod softly past the cot to the other side of the cabin.

Two trunks rested on the floor at opposite sides of the door. He opened one, saw the feminine apparel inside, and immediately closed it. He went to the other. Working swiftly, he searched the contents with dogged thoroughness, even testing the satin lining at the bottom for loose stitches. Among the clothes and toiletries were two small books, both guides for travelers to the Continent. He shook them lightly by their spines, but nothing fluttered from their pages. He thumbed through them rapidly. The second, *An Englishman's Guide to Rome*, had pen notations jotted on the inside back cover. O'Dunne scanned the markings, then slowly stood up.

He carried the book to the chair beside the bed and dropped down into it. His face was grim, his mild eyes bleak with worry. After a moment he put his head in his hands and stared between his shoes at the floor.

There was a rattle at the door, and O'Dunne sprang up from his chair at the moment it opened. A tall, stoop-shouldered man swayed with the motion of the ship for a minute in the threshold, then moved inside and shut the door behind him. "Find something?"

O'Dunne started to shake his head, making a deprecatory gesture at the book he still held in his hand. "It's nothing, just some—"

"Let me see."

He hesitated a fraction of a second, then handed the book to the other man. "It's some scribblings, probably just—"

"This is it." Roger Dietz leaned against the door and stared hard at the hand-written message on the inside back cover. "Exactly what we've been looking for." When he glanced up, his faded gray eyes glittered with excitement. "This is it."

"How can you be so sure? It's abbreviated, cryptic—it could mean anything."

"Don't be stupid, it couldn't be any plainer." Dietz's craggy face softened. "Sorry. I know he was your friend and this is hard for you. But there's no doubt—"

There was a low moan from the bed, and O'Dunne broke in hotly, "Never mind that, she needs a doctor! You've already as good as kidnapped her. If anything happens to—"

"She'll be all right, O'Dunne, I've told you. She'll regain full consciousness any time now."

"That's what you said hours ago. She hasn't a strong constitution to begin with, and this storm isn't doing her any good. If it gets worse—"

"Go up on deck," Dietz interrupted crisply. "You need some fresh air. Or else see to the prisoner—give Flowers a break. Mrs. Balfour will be fine. I've had some experience—"

"Aiden?" Anna tried to lift her head from the pillow, failed, and put a shaky hand over her eyes to shield them from the dim lantern light. "Are you here?"

O'Dunne hurried to the cot and perched gingerly on its edge. "I'm here, my dear. How do you feel? You're going to be fine now."

The light didn't seem quite so piercing. She pulled her hand away and squinted up at him. "What's happened, what is this place? Is it a boat?" She knew it was—but how could it be?

A man she'd never seen before loomed up behind Aiden's shoulder. "You're on a government-requisitioned sailing ship, Mrs. Balfour, en route to France," he said.

None of those words made any sense; they sounded like gibberish. She gazed blankly at the stranger for a few more seconds, then back at Aiden.

He took one of her hands. "Do you remember what happened?"

She closed her eyes in fierce concentration; then her face cleared and she smiled sweetly. "I'm married. Where's Nicholas?" Aiden paled and looked away. Her smile wavered. "What's happened? I don't remember. What's wrong with me?"

"Anna—"

"Your husband is dead, ma'am," the stranger said quietly. "He was stabbed to death by the same man who knocked you unconscious."

She felt no despair, only bewilderment and disbelief, and yet tears sprang to her eyes. "No," she said positively, pushing back with her elbows to sit up straighter. "Nicholas? Oh no, that can't —Aiden? Who is this man? What's happened?"

O'Dunne's face was grim and miserable. "I'm so sorry, my dear, but it's true. Nick's been killed."

She tried to laugh, then clutched at her temples when a shocking spasm of pain sliced through her brain like a dull razor. If only she could think! "I don't believe you," she said. "Why are you saying that? Where is he?"

"Listen to me." Aiden pressed her back to the pillow and she lay with her eyes tightly closed, hating and dreading the sad, gentle sound of his voice. "Nicholas is dead. I'm so very sorry. You were married two days ago. Do you remember? Afterward, you went to Nick's friend's cottage. A man came. He wore a mask. He killed Nick and he tried to kill you. You've been unconscious since then."

Nicholas, dead. Dead. She covered her face with her hands, pressed them against her eye sockets. If it was true, she wanted to be dead too. She muttered thick, garbled words of grief and denial into her palms as her mind teetered between incredulity and anguish.

"One of my men was outside, ma'am, watching the house. He tried to stop it but he was too late. The killer left his mark on him, too."

She dragged her hands away, and both men flinched at the sight of her face. She couldn't speak at all now; her enormous eyes asked the question.

"My name is Roger Dietz. I'm employed in a confidential capacity in the Ministry. We've had your husband under surveillance for six months because we—"

"Dietz, for God's sake—"

"Because," the tall man continued steadily, "we suspected him of selling Jourdaine-built ships to the American Confederacy."

Gibberish again. Her head was splitting. "Selling Jourdaine ships . . . to the Confederacy." She swallowed. "I don't understand." Tears trickled down her cheeks.

"Do you have to go into this now? She's ill, she needs to rest. I won't let you do this."

Dietz sighed, half in sympathy, half in exasperation. "Very well. I'll spell Flowers with the prisoner for a while." He braced one arm against the wall as the ship gave a sudden lurch. "I'm very sorry for all this, Mrs. Balfour," he said, sounding uncomfortable. He looked as if he might say more, but the moment passed and he only cleared his throat and muttered, "I'll come back in a little while," before he turned and left the cabin.

Selling Jourdaine ships to the Confederacy, Anna's brain repeated as she stared past Aiden at the closed door. Nicholas? What nonsense. It was false and absurd, an impossibility—and so must his "death" be. All of it must be a mistake. "Aiden," she said hastily, batting away a cup he was holding toward her, "this is insane, Nicholas isn't dead. Something's wrong, you've misinterpreted it, he can't possibly—"

"It's true, Anna. It's true."

His conviction infuriated her. "Damn you, did you see his body?"

He shut his eyes and nodded, and all the fight went out of her. A merciful emptiness descended. Minutes passed. She was dimly conscious that Aiden still sat beside her, that the sea was growing rougher. Once he spoke, urging her to eat. The very thought brought her to the brink of nausea. He held a cup to her lips again and said something in his stern, lawyer's voice; she gave up and swallowed a mouthful of cold, bitter tea, shuddering afterward.

"Now try to sleep. Does your head hurt?"

"I couldn't sleep. Tell me everything."

"Anna—"

"You must." Her voice sounded dull, exhausted. "While that man is gone. Who is he?"

"He's who he says he is. Do you remember Nick's death?"

"No," she said quickly. And suddenly fresh tears streaked down her face as the blessed numbness retreated. The pain of her loss was physical, a deep hurting of the heart. For a few seconds she confronted the fathomless, infuriating enigma of death, the dark truth that two days ago Nicholas had lived and today he was gone. *Gone.* She tried to feel it, to understand it; but such bottomless agony assaulted her, she had to let it go. Emptiness was excruciating, but it was endurable. And already she was grieving for herself, not Nicholas— *her* loneliness, *her* loss, not the ineffable tragedy of his extinction. That was unbearable.

She took a shuddery breath and reached for Aiden. Their arms curled around each other and they clung together. Her weeping turned to harsh, choking sobs, and he held her tighter. He murmured to her and patted her hair, letting her cry, not trying to make her stop.

Finally she pulled away to wipe her face with the edge of the sheet. After a moment she thought to straighten the collar of her nightgown, button the top button. Were there no other women on this ship? How had she gotten here? Who had been taking care of her?

"Sleep now," Aiden said, and started to rise.

She reached for his wrist and held on. "No, don't go, tell me what's happened. Yes! I want you to tell me. Please, please, I have to know."

He heaved a bleak, hopeless sigh. "I wish we had more time," she thought he murmured. Then, "How long have we known each other?"

She blinked in perplexity, but answered after a second's thought, "Since I was ten. Fourteen years."

"Fourteen years. Do you trust me?"

"Yes, of course. Of course I do." She hadn't any doubt of it.

"Good. Because I'm going to tell you something you didn't know, something . . . that will hurt you. And then I must ask you to do something that will be very, very hard."

Her stomach tightened with new dread. But she did trust Aiden. "Tell me."

"Six months ago I was approached by this man Dietz, along with two other men, lawyers for the ministry. Do you remember the incident in March of the *Oreto*?"

She nodded warily. A ship from a rival Liverpool shipyard had steamed out of the Mersey, ostensibly bound for the port of its new European owner. Instead it had sailed to Nassau, been outfitted for war, and metamorphosed as the cruiser *Florida* in the Confederate navy. An illegal operation, since it violated England's careful neutrality in the American Civil War, but highly profitable to the shipbuilders who had arranged it. The English government denied any knowledge, but the Union side suspected a conspiracy. "But that had nothing to do with Jourdaine Shipbuilding, that was—"

"No, but these men came to me to explore the possibility that the same thing was *going* to happen at Jourdaine. Again."

"Again?"

"They believe our ship *Ariel* went the same way last year."

"But that's absurd, we—"

"And they wanted to find out if a certain new ship of ours was really meant for sale to the Dutch, or if it was intended for another Confederate captain, to be armed secretly with guns and supplies in Naples and then used as a cruiser in the war."

Anna's thoughts were hopelessly scattered. "The Dutch? Are you talking about the *Morning Star*?" Jourdaine had launched the trim merchantman only five days ago from the Liverpool docks, bound for Amsterdam. O'Dunne nodded. "But how ridiculous! We would *know*."

"Would we?"

"*Nicholas* would've known. It couldn't be, it's impossible."

Pain flickered behind his eyes before he shifted his gaze to the blanket between them. "Nicholas would have known, yes. As the one responsible for coordinating the delivery of new ships to new owners, he would've known."

"Perhaps you had better say straight out what you mean," Anna said steadily. But the pain in her temples was rocketing out of control.

"I told the government men that if such a thing were going on, it must be without the knowledge of Thomas Jourdaine, Sr."

"Of course."

"I told them your father is a scrupulously honest man, and that in any case he has no need for quick money. I told them he would never help the South in the war, legally or illegally, because he's been violently antislavery and vocally pro-Union for years. They believed me." He looked away again. "And so they turned their attention to the second in command."

"No," Anna declared, with no hesitation. "It's a mistake. Nicholas would not have done it, wouldn't have had anything to do with something like this. For what? Money? He has—he had no need of it once he married me. What would be his reason?"

"None—now. But the ship must've been contracted for months ago, before your brother died, before you and Nick became engaged. There would be an enormous profit from an arrangement like this with the South's navy. He could've used the money then, before he discovered a way to make his fortune."

"A way to—" Anna went ice-cold, then burning hot with anger. "How dare you," she whispered, hazel eyes flashing fire.

O'Dunne stood up and pushed his fingers through his hair, ruining the neat center part. He did her the kindness of not looking at her while he delivered his next news. "These agents, Anna, they . . . investigated Nick's background. They discovered it was fabricated. He wasn't a clergyman's son; he never went to school in Wales or in England. They have no idea who he was, but there was no Balfour family in the Irish town he claimed was his birthplace. He made it all up."

She felt as if all the blood in her body had stopped circulating. "But we've known him for years," she got out, hands fluttering weakly. "It's impossible, it's some awful mistake." Her mind was in chaos, her skull was throbbing, she couldn't think. She retreated to the ultimate question: "Aiden, *who killed him?*"

"I don't know. I can only think it was Northern agents, spies for the Union who had the same suspicion we did and chose this way to stop it."

"No, I don't believe that."

"I didn't want to either. When these men told me what they suspected, I was as incredulous as you. I told them I *wouldn't* believe it until I'd seen evidence with my own eyes. And so—that was the job they gave me. To watch Nick as closely as I could without attracting his suspicion. To go over his books, to monitor his contacts in the yard, to—"

"To spy on him!"

He looked down, shamefaced.

"And what did you find?" she asked coldly.

"Nothing. Nothing at all."

Her smile was triumphant. But she put her hand over her heart, for before he'd answered, it had seemed to stop beating, and now she felt almost faint with relief.

"But Dietz wasn't satisfied. He thinks Nick insisted that you and he elope as soon as he found out the *Morning Star* would be ready to launch three weeks early."

"Why?"

"So he could meet the ship and its captain—a man named Greeley—in Naples, after she'd been refitted for war. And so he could get the money for her he was still owed."

"It's a lie!" The pain was excruciating now. Her mouth was dry; the nausea had returned. "It's a lie. You don't believe it, do you? You were his friend! Oh, God, I can't think, I can't think—"

"Anna, you're ill," he said, not answering her question. "This has been too much. I'll tell you the rest later."

So there was more. She was too exhausted to stop him this time when he got up to go. "Who is the 'prisoner'?" she managed to ask before he opened the door. He shook his head mutely. She flung a hand out. "Where is this ship going?"

He looked embarrassed now, glancing away. "To France. After that you're to go to Italy, to the villa you and Nick leased for the honeymoon." She could only stare. With a last helpless, miserable glance back, Aiden opened the door and went out.

4

"Mwuh," shuddered Billy Flowers, his head between his knees. A sudden lurch of the ship shoved his huge frame against the bulkhead behind him and he swore, holding his sore collarbone protectively. "Oh, bloody bleedin' 'ell . . ."

"What kind of ship is this, Billy?" asked Brodie, to distract him.

"Wot d'you mean, wot koind? It's a blinkin' boat, that's wot."

"How many masts? I couldn't see in the dark when they put me on."

"'Ow the 'ell do I know? I didn't count the beggars. Mwuh," he said again, holding his diaphragm and going even greener as a fresh roll almost tipped him off his bunk.

The same roll wrenched Brodie's wrist painfully against the manacle chained to the headrail of his cot, reminding him with nasty irony of the similarity of his circumstances now and two days ago.

He'd thought Dietz and O'Dunne were liberating
him, but there wasn't a hell of a lot of difference
between being chained to a wall in prison with
Shooter and being chained to a bunk in a ship's
cabin with Billy Flowers.

Not altogether true—there was one important
difference. Tomorrow he wasn't going to hang.

The door opened and O'Dunne stumbled in.
"Where's Dietz?"

"On deck," said Billy.

"You look terrible. Go on up yourself."

"Thanks, guv." Billy heaved himself up, made a
grab for his checked coat, and lurched out, swallowing rapidly.

The lawyer sank down on Billy's bunk. "It's
getting worse."

"We're at the mouth of the Channel—the cur-
rents are always hell here. Don't worry, we'll get
past it." O'Dunne sent him an odd look, one he
was getting used to. The lawyer was surprised
every time Brodie said something that sounded
halfway human. "Unlock this wrist iron, will you?
I'm starting to bleed."

"You know I can't."

"Come on, O'Dunne. Where the hell would I
escape to?"

The next moment, the sea pitched violently and
Brodie winced as his chafed wrist jerked hard
against cold iron. The ship righted itself and
O'Dunne gazed at him speculatively across the
small space of floor that separated them. He got
up, took a key from his waistcoat pocket, and
unlocked the padlock around the headrail. "Give
me your other hand." Brodie obeyed. They exchanged a silent, loaded stare during the five-

second interval in which he was, technically, free. O'Dunne looped the chain around his other wrist and snapped the lock between two links, leaving about sixteen inches of slack chain between his bound hands.

"Thanks."

O'Dunne collapsed back on his bunk. He rubbed his neck wearily, and after a minute he lay down. Brodie stretched hugely, then reached into his pocket for a cigarette. O'Dunne heard the scraping of the lucifer match. "Nick didn't smoke," he snapped.

Brodie crossed his booted feet and leaned back against the headrail, savoring the rich bite of the tobacco on his tongue and in his lungs. "That so?" he asked mildly.

"Who gave it to you? Billy? You'll have to get rid of it."

Brodie puffed stolidly, not answering. O'Dunne stared at him a moment longer, then shifted impatiently and returned his gaze to the ceiling.

Brodie studied him. O'Dunne was pleasant-looking when he smiled, with mild brown eyes that crinkled at the corners, but so far Brodie hadn't seen him do much smiling. He'd guess he was about thirty-seven or thirty-eight years old. Like most sailors, Brodie distrusted lawyers, but he had to admit O'Dunne seemed decent enough. Being upright and humorless was probably a good thing in a lawyer, anyway. "So," he said conversationally. "You still haven't told me about my 'wife.' What's she like?"

O'Dunne went stiff. "You'll meet Mrs. Balfour soon enough. She's a lady, and that's all you need to know."

"Uh-oh." He didn't like the sound of that. "Bit

of a mudfish, eh?" Frosty silence. Brodie sighed and slid down lower on his backbone. "Just my luck. One month of freedom left, two at the most, and I must spend it with a bleedin' shovelhead."

"Listen to me," O'Dunne bristled, sitting up on one elbow, "you'll keep a civil tongue where Mrs. Balfour is concerned, is that clear? If you so much as *look* at her in a way I don't fancy, you'll find yourself back in Bristol so fast your brain will spin."

Brodie rubbed his beard, brows raised curiously. "That so?"

"Yes, that's so. You'll be watched all the time; there'll never be any occasion for you to be alone with her. And I want your promise right now that you'll treat her with nothing but respect and courtesy at all times."

"Seems like you want a powerful lot of promises out of me, Mr. O'Dunne." He was thinking of the one he'd had to make before they would let him out of prison—that he wouldn't try to escape; that at the end of this bizarre affair he would go docilely back to gaol and rot there for the rest of his life.

"Well?"

"What's in it for me?" Brodie asked, feeling perverse. "You and I know that whoever killed Nick will likely have another go, this time at me. So you're not really much of a savior, are you? Fact is, you're more like the devil leading me down another sinkhole to hell."

"Your promise," he repeated, scowling.

Brodie crushed his cigarette out against the wall, leaving an ash-blackened circle. "Treat her with respect? Sure. My solemn oath. Shouldn't be that hard, the lady being such a hedgehog."

O'Dunne's lips tightened with anger. "I've seen you before, you know."

Brodie looked across at him, interested. "When?"

"A year ago. The Liverpool docks."

He went still. "That was you with Nick?" He kept his voice studiously neutral. The lawyer nodded. Brodie turned away and stared straight ahead.

He recalled that day, the last he'd seen his brother alive, as clearly as if it were this morning. Nick had looked so good. Silk shirt, fancy suit, tie with a pearl stickpin in it. Even carried a goddamn walking stick. When he'd seen him, a simple, flooding gladness had washed over Brodie. Without a thought for his tattered seaman's clothes, he'd walked right up to him and stuck out his hand.

Nick had gone white at first, then red. He'd started to smile—to this day Brodie would swear he'd started to smile—and then his face had closed up. "Sir, I don't know you," he'd murmured, in a voice Brodie would never forget. And then he'd walked away. The man with him had cast two curious looks back before they'd turned a corner and disappeared.

Brodie unclenched his hands and took a long, deep breath. The pain he felt because Nick was dead was worse than anything, worse than his own agony while he'd waited in prison to die. It was as if *he* had been killed, as if *he* were the one who'd been knifed to death in the dead of night, before the horrified eyes of the woman he'd just married, just made love to. He sat up straight, stiff with violent, pent-up emotion, and squeezed his eyes shut, one hand massaging his forehead. "Did he ever tell you who I was?"

O'Dunne hesitated, then said, "Yes."

Relief coursed through him. So Nick had told one person he had a brother. He hadn't known until this moment how important that was to him. "Were you good friends?"

Again O'Dunne pondered his answer. "Yes."

"What did he say about me?"

"He said you'd swindled your father out of his life savings and disappeared when you were fourteen years old."

All the air went out of him; he felt as if he'd been kicked in the chest. "Son of a . . ." He scrubbed his face with his hand and let out a short, bitter laugh. Then he turned his face to the wall, blind to everything, and didn't speak again.

After a time, he didn't know how long, he heard O'Dunne's slow, even breathing; when he looked over, he saw that the lawyer was asleep.

Moving quietly, he stood up. God, it felt good to stretch. The ship rolled; he absorbed the motion with expert effortlessness, knees flexed, body swaying. The thud of his boots was silent beneath the noise of wind and waves. He opened the door and stepped outside.

Besides the galley, there were four cabins below, he saw quickly. All he wanted was a walk, a chance to stretch his cramped legs. He'd eaten and slept a good deal in the two days since his release from prison, but he still felt a strange core of weakness, as if something deep inside hadn't healed yet. He was halfway to the ladder, his only thought to pace a few times between it and his cabin, when he heard the clang of footsteps, descending. Damn! A sailor's gumboots appeared in the companionway. The cabin door beside him was closed. Was it locked? No. He pushed it open, passed inside, and closed it behind him.

And halted, back against the door, frozen motionless. By the light of one oil lantern he saw a girl, lying in a bunk along the cabin's right wall. For a long time he just stared, almost in disbelief, because the sight was so incongruous—he could count on the fingers of one hand the times he'd sailed a ship with a woman aboard. Then the truth dawned on him: This girl was Nick's wife. Nick's widow.

He went closer, holding the slack chain in his hands to silence it. She was small, hardly bigger than a child. Was she sick? Her face was almost as white as the pillow. She had reddish hair, or maybe light brown—the light was too dim to see. He remembered her name was Anna. Her delicate eyelids fluttered, and for a second he thought she would wake. But she didn't, and he realized she was dreaming.

He should go, it was wrong to watch her like this; her face looked naked, too exposed, he ought to leave her alone. A tiny smile played at the corners of her mouth, and the sweetness of it pushed back his resolve. How pretty she was. He stared, entranced, until her smile faded and a little cry—of fear?—sounded deep in her throat. Nothing after that, no expression except the fragile flickering of her lashes, but he worried for her. He went nearer, hovered over her. *Don't be afraid, Anna*, he thought.

She was walking in a field of lilies. The sun shone bright and hot, but the lilies were cool, icy-white, and luscious. Nicholas was holding her hand, walk-

*ing beside her. She felt lit up inside with happiness.
He stopped once and turned her in his arms, kissing
her with reverence and passion. Then they set off
again across the cool white lilies.*

*From all around them came a sound that fright-
ened her. There was nothing to see but distance, but
from somewhere a harsh braying whine was growing louder, scaring her, making her skin feel vulnerable. She wanted Nicholas to stop and turn around,
to run back with her across the pale lily field, but he
wouldn't stop. She saw a rent in the clouds over
their heads, and the nose of a knife blade slicing
through. The howling whine was like a saw, deafen-
ing now as the blade descended.*

*She opened her mouth to scream. A low-pitched,
fierce, commanding sound issued from her throat,
louder than the whine, louder than anything she'd
ever heard. The very air turned to sound and
swirled with strong, vibrant color. Her lungs felt
empty and purified. Without surprise, she watched
the blade turn to silver smoke and dissolve among
the clouds. Nicholas came toward her, his eyes
shining with gratitude and love.*

She awoke, and he was there. Kneeling beside
her, his eyes so intent, his face so dear. She
reached up to him with both arms, and he came to
her. Something between a moan and a sob trembled in her throat as she clung to him, holding
herself against him. *Nicholas. Oh, my dear.* Her
heart ached with the fullness of her love. She
tightened her arms around him, shuddering with
relief and gladness, and lifted her mouth for his
kiss.

Afterward, Brodie would think back to that
moment, that instant in time when he should have
let her go, and he would remember why it had

been impossible. It wasn't because she was lovely, or because her body under her thin gown was supple and delicate and exciting, or because the fragrance of her soft hair beguiled him. What made him return her yearning embrace and kiss her with such tenderness was simply that she wanted it so. Her need was a tangible thing, urgent and poignant. Like her arms it encircled him, bound him to her. He could not resist it.

Anna opened her eyes when the kiss was over, and something prickled across her skin, an impossible intimation. Her mouth tried to form a word. "You . . ." came out in a whisper, all but inaudible. His shining eyes were all she could see clearly in the lamplight. His hands moved restlessly on her shoulders and she heard a clink of metal— again, but this was the first time the sound registered. Something cold and heavy lay across her breasts. He straightened slowly and took his hands away. She saw the chain.

There was a breathless moment while Brodie's soul felt naked and he waited for her to revile him. Her lips moved uncertainly and he closed his eyes, lost to everything except regret. Then something rebellious stirred in him, and before she could speak he pressed her back against the pillow and kissed her again.

Bewilderment paralyzed her. Wide-eyed, she let him do it, while her mind struggled and flailed. This wasn't—this couldn't be—"Anna," he murmured against her lips. His voice!

The pressure of her palms against his chest was light, ambiguous; Brodie ignored it. His tongue found the delicate line where her lips met and probed it with slow and exquisite gentleness. She quivered in his arms, poised on the baffling edge between outrage and acceptance. Then her mouth opened, and he rejoiced. Their tongues touched in a shy greeting. They forgot to breathe; their hearts thudded heavily in unison. He nibbled at her top lip and pulled it into his mouth, tasting her velvet warmth. Now their tongues circled more boldly, sliding sensuously, craftily holding still. He stroked his fingers along her soft throat and she made a purring sound that vibrated against his hand, making him smile. The dreamlike intimacy of the kiss grew more urgent. She was shaking, but no more so than he. The sensitive tips of her breasts pressed against his coarse linen shirt, melted into him. She sighed a long sigh into his mouth, holding his head, tasting him.

Brodie broke the kiss and sat up, surveying what he would need to do to get her undressed quickly. He had no scruples left, and his conscience was a functionless instrument buried under the crushing weight of need. He brought his hands to the button at the high neck of her gown, and her odd, amber-colored eyes, dreamy before, hardened with sudden intensity. Her head turned sideways on the pillow, restless and uncertain.

His hands froze. "You're hurt," he said wonderingly. "You've hurt your head."

The profound sympathy in his voice brought tears to her eyes. "Yes, I'm—but I'm all right now," she whispered. Her first words to him.

Her first words. She knew it as surely as she knew anything. He wasn't Nicholas.

Brodie saw the dreadful knowledge in her eyes. Before he could speak—and say what?—the door burst open and smashed against the bulkhead behind them. "'E's 'ere!" shouted Billy Flowers, his enormous body dwarfing the cabin. Brodie stood up slowly. O'Dunne and Dietz jostled each other through the doorway. Dietz muttered a harsh order and Flowers advanced.

The first blow of the giant fist caught Brodie on the cheekbone and hurled him against the opposite wall. He raised his arms to ward off the second, noting with relief that his shoulder wasn't broken, and that the cockney's hand was tangled harmlessly in the chain between his wrists. Bringing his hands together to make a club, Brodie swung out with all his strength. His fists connected with Billy's sternum, and he had the satisfaction of seeing him turn purple and stop breathing. But his victory was short. There was nowhere to go—the wall was at his back, the stolid giant blocked his way forward. A chain was an ugly weapon, but it was the only one he had. He swung it.

Flowers caught it like a lobbed tennis ball. One savage jerk dropped Brodie to his knees; one backhanded blow across the face made his ears ring. Or was that Anna screaming?

"Stop him! For God's sake—" O'Dunne was beside himself.

"That's enough!" barked Dietz, and like a well-trained attack dog Billy subsided. "Are you all right, Mrs. Balfour? Did this man hurt you?"

Anna didn't hear the question. Clutching the sheet to her bosom, trembling, intent, she stared at Brodie. She knew she was close to fainting, but she had to hear his answer. "Who are you?" she got out in a feeble whisper.

Brodie stumbled to his feet, ignoring Billy's feral warning growl. The chain rattled when he wiped blood from his mouth and pushed the hair out of his face. It was the accusation in her eyes that triggered the defensiveness—that and his own guilty conscience. He made her a shallow, mocking bow. "Pleased to make your acquaintance, Mrs. Balfour. My name's John Brodie. I'm Nick's twin." The shock in her eyes burst through the thin wall of his defiance like a fist.

Flowers gripped his arm with unexpected gentleness. He moved toward the door at a laggard's pace, unwilling to go. He turned back in the threshold to see her, one last time. O'Dunne hovered over her, patting and murmuring, blocking his view. But he thought he could hear her crying.

5

"Let me make sure I understand this," Anna said, the helplessness and anger inside turning her voice sarcastic. "You're suggesting that after we land in France, I travel by coach to Italy with Mr. Brodie, pretend to 'honeymoon' with him in Florence, then go to Rome and wait for him and Aiden while they find out in Naples if my husband was a criminal. Do I have that right, sir?"

"Anna—" Aiden began placatingly.

"You have it partly right," interrupted Dietz, folding his arms and returning her look of outrage with an impassive stare. "If you do your job well and Brodie turns out to be a good enough actor, we might use him in England too, to find out who at Jourdaine Shipbuilding was working on the scheme with your husband."

Anna shook her head slowly, eyes wide. The man's audacity amazed her. "Mr. Dietz, you take my breath away. What on earth makes you think I would agree to this insane plan?"

"Several things. For—"

"Especially when the solitary shred of 'evidence' of my husband's treachery that you've managed to find consists of a meaningless notation in the back of a book." She stalked to the bed and picked up the "incriminating" guidebook, turning the pages violently to the back cover. "'Greeley, B.N., 30th—#12, midnight.'" She gave a contemptuous laugh. "You say this proves Nicholas was to meet a man named Greeley at the Bay of Naples on May 30th at midnight. I say it proves nothing at all and you're grasping at straws."

"Perhaps you're not aware of all the things we've learned about your husband, ma'am."

"Perhaps you should tell me what they are, sir!" Her head throbbed dully. She pulled her robe more tightly around her shoulders, conscious of the impropriety of her situation—alone in a cramped ship's cabin in her nightclothes with two men—but she was past caring about propriety. The outlandishness of her circumstances rendered decorous behavior irrelevant; she felt as far removed from safe, soothing convention as if she were on another planet.

"I'm afraid I'm not at liberty to do that."

She let out her breath in a disdainful huff. "Why doesn't that surprise me, I wonder?"

"But I can tell you that we're virtually certain Mr. Balfour, or whatever his name was, was responsible for a similar scheme a number of months ago involving another Jourdaine vessel."

"That is absolutely preposterous."

Dietz ran his fingers through his short, graying hair and heaved a decisive-sounding sigh. "Ma'am, the government is determined to get to the bottom of this. I'm sorry to say it, but the alternative to your helping us is to shut your father's company down." She whirled on him and he held up a hand. "Naturally that would invite a scandal," he went on before she could interrupt. "And needless to say, it would also embarrass Queen Victoria, who knighted your father not six months ago for his years of devoted public service to his country. We're as anxious to avoid such a—"

"You can't do that," Anna cried, holding on to the back of the room's only chair for support. "Jourdaine Shipbuilding is a hundred and twenty years old—my great-great-grandfather built it from nothing! There are men who work for us now whose grandfathers and great-grandfathers worked there all of *their* lives. This is outrageous! Jourdaine is a good company, a principled company, you can't—"

"I'm sorry, but there's more at stake here than that, as I think you know. England's neutrality in the Civil War in America is in a precarious state. There are plenty of men in Parliament just waiting for a chance to enter the conflict on the South's side, and another English merchantman secretly converted to a Confederate warship is all it would take—the North has never believed in our government's claims of ignorance."

Anna flung away from him and began to pace back and forth across the tiny space between the bed and the door. Both men pressed backwards to give her more room; she wouldn't sit down and so they stood, backs against the wall, as uncomfortable with their stifling proximity as she. The storm was over; it had blown itself out in the night. Blue sea met blue sky on the distant horizon, and the light wind blowing in through the open porthole smelled clean and fresh.

"Mrs. Bal—"

"Mr. Dietz." She stopped pacing and faced him. She wanted no more of his well-reasoned arguments; her brain was still too sluggish to counter them. "Answer me this. How can you—or you, Aiden!—how can you stand there and ask me, in good conscience, to live on intimate terms for an indefinite length of time with a total stranger, a man you tell me is a murderer? Even assuming that I survived that ordeal, do you have any idea what would become of me if the slightest hint of such an arrangement ever became known? Do you have any conception of what my reputation would be worth? Or how it would hurt my family?"

"As to that, I've been given to understand that yours is not a particularly close or loving family," said Dietz.

Anna flashed a look of astonishment at Aiden; he had the grace to flush with embarrassment and turn away.

"But apart from that, O'Dunne will travel with you, and you'll be guarded at all times. You'll be safe, and so will your secret. No one but the three of us and Mr. Flowers, plus a few well-placed officials high in the Ministry—very high, I might say—will ever know. Anyway," he added, annoyed by her mutinous profile, "it's done. You're halfway to Italy—you're already 'compromised,' if you choose to look at it that way."

"You—you're saying I have no choice?"

"None that I can see." A moment passed and then his voice softened. "Try to look at it from our point of view. Concealing your husband's death is the only way to discover whether he really meant to sell the *Morning Star* to the South—something I should think you'd want to know as much as we do."

"He didn't!"

"In the second place, the government wants to learn who his contacts were among the Confederates so that they can be warned off or otherwise dealt with. Keeping him 'alive' would give us that opportunity."

"Rubbish!"

"And in the third place, since it's inconceivable to us that your husband acted alone, we're interested in finding out who at Jourdaine Shipbuilding might try to get in touch with Brodie while he's pretending to be Nick Balfour."

She made an inarticulate sound of frustration and fury and turned toward O'Dunne. "What have they done with Nicholas's body?" she demanded.

The lawyer looked startled. "They've buried him."

"Where? In an unmarked grave?"

He shifted uncomfortably. "Only for a little while, Anna. When this is over they'll arrange for his 'death.' He'll have a real burial then, as your husband."

Rebellion rose in her like bile. "I won't do it. I don't care about any of the consequences. What you're asking is monstrous—ghoulish. I won't do it!"

There was a protracted silence. Then Dietz said, "Very well. No one will force you."

"Thank you very much indeed."

"This will come as a bit of a blow to your brother-in-law."

"My—Mr. Brodie, you mean? That man is no relation to Nicholas," she declared illogically. "A man like that, he *deserves* to rot in prison for the rest of his life." She swung away, unwilling to let them see her flaming cheeks.

For the last twenty-four hours she'd been reliving her encounter with the detestable Mr. Brodie, struggling against memories that were graphic, accurate, and inescapable. Even now she flinched inwardly with mortification as she recalled who had initiated that unforgettable embrace, and exactly how it had felt. Squeezing her eyes shut and biting her knuckles did no good—the quick, breath-stealing pleasure she'd taken in his arms was an indelible memory, not to be willed away.

In the long hours before dawn she'd prayed that it had been a dream, a nightmare, but she'd had to face the bitter fact that it had happened. It seemed an unspeakable blasphemy, an obscene betrayal of Nicholas, yet it was real. The one thing she could not bring herself to face was the treachery of that instant when she'd known—God help her, she'd *known*—and still she had let him put his hands on her.

"Perhaps he should rot in prison," Dietz was saying; "that's what he would have done if you'd agreed to help us. As it is, he'll hang."

She turned around in slow motion. She had to wet her lips to speak, and even then her voice was only a whisper. "What?"

"I say, as it is—"

"You're lying. He agreed to your scheme, he kept his side of the bargain. You can't execute him now. You're saying that to manipulate me. It's despicable."

Dietz pushed away from the wall, preparing to leave. "I'm sorry. I assure you it's no bluff; fair or not, it's the simple truth. If you won't help us, Mr. Brodie will be taken back to Bristol and his original sentence will be carried out." He crossed to the door. "It's a difficult decision; I'm not unsympathetic to your plight, although it may look as if I am. I'll help you in any way I can. I give you my word that none of this will ever be publicly revealed. And your personal safety will be guaranteed at all times." He watched her for another minute, then opened the door and walked out.

She could only stare at the floor, mute and frozen. Her mind was in turmoil. Aiden was saying something, asking if she wanted him to stay. "No! This is your fault—you're the one who told that man Nicholas had a twin, *months* ago, when you were spying on him! If you'd stayed out of it—" She jerked away, ashamed. She'd never spoken to her friend like this before; it frightened her.

O'Dunne's voice was bleak and hopeless. "My dear, I wish to God I had."

"Oh, Aiden, I'm sorry, I'm sorry! I know none of this is your doing. I don't know what would've happened to me if you hadn't been here."

Awkward, he took her hand and held it. "I tried to talk Dietz out of this, believe me, but he wouldn't listen. I told him he was putting you at risk because of your health."

"My health? Do you mean my head?"

"No, or not only that. I mean your general constitution, your—well-being."

She put a hand over her chest unconsciously,

then laughed without any humor. "I wish I had thought to tell him that. But there's nothing wrong with me anymore, Aiden, you know that."

"I know everyone hopes it's true." He smiled his gentle smile. "What will you do?"

"I don't know." All of her choices were unthinkable. "But I'll tell you one thing," she said fiercely. "If I agree to take part in this ridiculous plan, it will be to clear Nicholas's name, not prove his guilt!"

"Billy, my boy, what are you doing in there?"

"Well, wot th' bloody 'ell d'you think I'm doin'?"

A fair question, considering Billy was sitting inside the privy. "Hurry it along, will you? We'll miss our supper at this rate."

Billy cursed in colorful cockney and Brodie smiled. The last thing he'd expected to feel was fondness for his bodyguard, but Flowers was a hard man to dislike. That is, once you got over the idea that he could—and would if he were told to—kill you with one blow from either of his gigantic paws. But he would do it without malice, maybe even with regret, and Brodie wasn't one to hold a man's occupation against him. Live and let live, he always said.

Besides, if he'd wanted to escape he could've done it by now—any day, in fact, since they'd landed in France more than a week ago. He could do it now, for that matter, while Billy sat in the jakes and he stood outside, hands free for once, waiting for him. But like a fool, he'd promised that he wouldn't. Up to now he'd never gone back on his word to anyone. His pale blue eyes narrowed in speculation as he considered that there was probably a first time for everything.

"I'm walking around to the front, Bill. Meet you there." Flowers muttered something and Brodie strode off, savoring the unexpected few minutes of freedom. It was a beautiful evening, soft and warm, and the sun was setting beyond a wide, dark valley in front of the *pension* in Reillanne where they would stay tonight. The clouds were that salmon-and-silver color he associated with inland sunsets in Europe, not like the ones in Australia, for instance, which were redder and more—

He halted, halfway to a rotting wooden fence that separated the inn yard from the adjacent pasture. His brother's widow stood beside the fence, staring at the brilliant sky. For the past nine days he'd seen her only from a distance, and never by herself. They rode in separate hired carriages, he and Billy in one, she and O'Dunne in another. But sometimes he would catch a glimpse of her in a hostel at night, taking her meal alone or with Aiden—he and Billy always ate in the kitchen. On the rare occasions when their eyes would meet, she'd always look away first, usually flushing, as though she found the sight of him indecent or disgusting. The thing she was best at was ignoring him, looking right through him as if he didn't exist. It would pique his temper—until he'd consider that it was probably no more than he deserved.

She hadn't seen him yet; he took the opportunity to stare at her, openly for once. Close up, she was even smaller than he'd remembered, and slighter. And her hair wasn't brown at all in the sun's slanted rays, it was red. A pale, soft, pretty shade of red that she was wearing in a sort of bun at the back of her neck. She'd changed from her brown traveling dress to a lilac-colored one, high-necked as usual, and she looked as neat and clean as a new penny. She held her hands behind her back, standing straight and proper in that upper-class-lady's posture he'd never seen her slacken. But what he could see of her face looked sad, not proud; he thought she might even be crying. An edge of sorrow moved through him with no warning. He'd wanted to speak to her for days, and yet, now when the chance was finally here, something held him back.

Then a rook flew up from a fallen log behind her, with a shrill caw and a whir of wings, and she turned. And saw him. She took off instantly, making a wide, rapid detour around him and heading for the inn.

He strode toward her, long legs easily eating up the distance between them, and caught her at the top of her panicky circuit. For a second he thought she would run, lift up her skirts and fly for safety like a scared schoolgirl; but the image of it must have seemed as ridiculous to her as it did to him, for she stopped instead, dead in her tracks, facing away from him. It was an effort to keep his arms at his sides when what he wanted to do was take her by the shoulder and spin her around. But it wasn't necessary; after a silent minute she pivoted in a half-circle to face him, stiff as a soldier on guard duty.

In the fading sunlight he saw that although she was small and delicate, she was anything but frail and had a lovely, woman's body. Her eyes were fine but odd, the color of coffee with cream. Her face was subtle; he felt he was looking at her but not yet really seeing her. If she was beautiful, it was an eccentric kind of beauty. He kept a safe, respectful distance. But now that he had her, he wasn't sure what to say.

Oh, God, he has Nick's hair, Anna thought disconcertedly. His eyes. The long, hawklike nose, with the same arrogant bump in the middle. High cheekbones, cheeks obscured by a soft beard, one shade lighter than the reddish-brown hair, exactly like Nicholas's. And the same wide mouth, thin-lipped and sensitive, hard without a smile, gentle with one.

The resemblance was unbearable. She felt pain that was deeper and more intense than anything she'd felt before, pain so harsh it frightened her. But she stayed where she was, and somehow she managed not to cry.

Directness always came easiest to Brodie. "I'm sorry for what happened that day on the ship. I know I shouldn't have kissed you. But you took me by surprise and I . . ." What? "Stopped using my head. I'm sorry." She just kept staring. "I didn't know you were hurt, you see, or I wouldn't have touched you. I'm sorry." Damn it, he would keep saying he was sorry until she said something back, opened her mouth and spoke words to him. So far she hadn't moved a muscle, only peered at him with her strange, startled eyes and held herself away from him as if long, poisonous spikes were sticking out of his body.

His voice. Dear God, his voice! She'd always loved the musical sound of it, the unique and intriguing pronunciation that was Welsh, Irish, and English all at once. She willed herself to keep her eyes open and focused on him, for if she closed them it would be exactly as if Nicholas were standing in front of her, speaking to her. In self-defense, she resurrected her fury toward *this* man, this hateful impostor. "Do you expect me to forgive you? I never will, and you can stew in it, Mr. Brodie. I don't care how sorry you are, it won't change what you did."

He stepped back. The last thing he'd expected was to have his apology thrown back in his face by this stiff-necked, pocket-sized harpy. "It won't change what you did either," he snapped. "Or did you forget that part? If Billy had come two minutes later, you'd have been back on your honeymoon, Mrs. Balfour. And you'd have loved it."

First she went white, then bright pink with embarrassment. Out of habit, he muttered a short, vulgar word, cursing himself, and she went even redder. She shrank back when he lifted a hand toward her, and he dropped it back to his side hopelessly. Without another word, she turned around and ran toward the inn. This time he didn't follow.

6

"Where's Flowers?" asked O'Dunne.

"Across the hall," said Anna.

"Guarding me," Brodie added helpfully. "That is, if he's awake."

They glared at him. He crossed his ankle over his knee and smiled blandly back across his steepled fingers. His bodyguard's unique ability to fall deeply asleep in seconds anywhere, any time, was a source of amusement to Brodie, of intense irritation to Anna and O'Dunne.

Dinner was over and they were in the deserted public room of the Reillanne *pension*, about to commence their first formal meeting. Which must've been O'Dunne's idea; Brodie couldn't imagine Mrs. *Balfour* suggesting it. She couldn't stand to be in the same room with him. The only thing his apology had accomplished was to limit his freedom of movement even further. O'Dunne had come out of the inn at the very moment she'd bolted toward it. He'd stopped her and they'd exchanged a few hasty words in the doorway. Brodie didn't know what she'd said to him, but he could guess. Because now his hands were chained together again, and Billy, looking sheepish, had told him they would stay that way. At all times. No exceptions.

He folded his arms across his chest as best he could, and his lips tightened as cold iron rubbed against the raw flesh of his wrists. It was a pain he ought to be used to by now, but he wasn't. Maybe because it didn't just hurt him, it made him mad. He narrowed his stare at Anna, and felt spiteful satisfaction when she quickly turned her back on him. He was finished feeling guilty about her. He knew it hurt her to look at him. He was sorry for that, but hell, it wasn't his fault he looked like his twin brother. It didn't give her the right to stare straight through him like he wasn't there, or as if he was a bucket of fish guts she'd stumbled over in her drawing room.

"Let's get this over with, Aiden," she said. She looked stiff as a staysail boom in her lilac dress, all buttoned up like somebody's maiden aunt. He wondered if she was wearing a corset. From the look of her bosom, high and immobile, he thought she probably was. Why did women do that? Especially women like her, whose bodies were small and delicate and already perfect. Now she was blushing again, turning that pretty apricot color. He hoped she was reading his mind, because he was deliberately remembering the day on the ship when she'd let him touch her, and the way she'd sighed, and exactly how her mouth had tasted.

He was through feeling guilty about that too.

She'd started it, after all. If he'd known she was sick he wouldn't have kissed her. Which was what he'd tried to tell her, for all the good it had done him. She'd told him to *stew* in it.

"In just a minute," O'Dunne said without looking up, still scribbling something.

She didn't like that. She wanted this meeting over and done with so she could get the hell out. She was pretending to be absorbed in some book, pretending she wasn't on pins and needles because Brodie was watching her. Oh, he had her rattled, all right. She rose, crossed to the far side of the room, and peered out the window, as if some fascinating phenomenon were going on out there in the pitch dark. He narrowed his stare, and it didn't surprise him at all when the back of her neck got red and she slowly turned around to face him. It was as if he'd willed it. She looked back at him boldly, and he realized she was trying to stare him down. He rubbed a forefinger softly along his upper lip and didn't blink. Her cheeks flamed. He smiled. Her eyes darkened and her face went statue-still. He could practically hear her telling herself not to look away. He had to tell himself not to laugh.

Then O'Dunne ruined it by getting up and signaling to her to join them. The relief on her face was comical as she returned.

"I felt it was time we three had a talk and established our mutual objectives," O'Dunne said in his lawyer's voice, thumbs in the armholes of his waistcoat, bouncing a little on his toes. "As I see it, our first objective is to establish Mr. Brodie as Nicholas Balfour. Now, in order to—"

"How did you get the name Brodie?" Anna interrupted.

She looked all feisty and brave, ready for battle now that O'Dunne was close by. He glanced at the lawyer. Hadn't he explained that to her yet? "I was born with it."

"You're lying."

His eyes narrowed; a muscle in his jaw jumped. "So you think your name is really Balfour"? he asked slowly, dangerously.

"It is!"

O'Dunne started sputtering about something. Brodie was on the verge of telling her the truth when something stopped him. Her smallness, maybe, or her stubborn chin. He'd already made her cry once. "Balls," he muttered, getting to his feet and going to stand by the empty fireplace.

O'Dunne bristled. "That's the last time I want to hear any cursing out of you, Brodie, is that clear? First, because there's a lady present, and second, because Nick never swore."

Anna frowned, puzzled. All he'd said was balls; was that a curse? "Balls"?

"Now. Our second objective is to—"

"Wait a minute," she broke in again. O'Dunne sighed. "We're not through with the first objective, Aiden. What exactly are you talking about?"

"Just what I said, we have to establish Brodie as Nick."

"Yes, but how? It's going to be a little more complicated than fooling a handful of servants at the villa in Florence. Nicholas and I were going to pursue several introductions in Rome, business contacts of Father's. And we would very probably have run into people we knew there."

"Yes, yes," agreed O'Dunne.

She gestured toward Brodie, who was staring at her sullenly. "How do you expect to pass this—

person—off as Nicholas? There's a resemblance, certainly. But anyone who knew Nicholas would know after speaking to this man for two minutes that he is *not Nicholas.*"

Brodie flushed. Unclenching one fist, he reached into his pocket and pulled out the tobacco pouch Billy had given him.

"I told you before, Brodie. No smoking."

Expressionless, he rolled a cigarette, licked it shut, struck a match on the brick hearth, and lit it. He inhaled a deep chestful and blew the smoke out with a defiant puff. A small thing, but it meant a lot to him.

"You'll have to stop eventually," O'Dunne said in a mild tone, backing off. "You're only making it harder on yourself." He looked at Anna again. "It's true, compared to Nick he does have a few rough edges—" he paused while she let out an unladylike snort—"but we've got more than three weeks before Rome and we'll spend that time sanding them off. I'll need your help with this, Anna."

"You don't need help," she snapped, "you need a miracle." Brodie scowled, smoking steadily. "Can you read, Mr. Brodie?"

He considered not answering. "Aye, I can read. And I can count up to ten if I use my fingers." He watched her lip curl unpleasantly. The air was thick with hostility. He moved to the old-fashioned casement window and flicked out his cigarette. Then he had an idea. He hawked up a big gob of spit and blew it out too, then turned back innocently. Mrs. Balfour went a mottled shade of pink and drew herself up, quivering with indignation.

"Aiden," she choked, "this will never work!"

"Now, now, let's—"

"Three weeks to make a gentleman out of *him*?" She pointed rudely. "Three years wouldn't be enough! It's impossible! He's a barbarian!"

Brodie reached inside his jacket to scratch his armpit. "Could be she's got a point, O'Dunne."

The lawyer drew an exasperated breath, annoyed with both of them. "That may be. But we're here to try, and that's what we're going to do. Anna, you agreed; it's too late to back out. It's not a question, at least for now, of turning Mr. Brodie into a gentleman. The immediate goal is to be ready by the thirtieth of May to convince someone named Greeley that this man is Nick." She started to speak, but he forestalled her with a raised hand. "I know you don't believe any such meeting is planned. I hope you're right, but we have to prepare for it all the same as if it were going to happen. It's the only way to prove or disprove Nick's complicity."

She could see his logic, but the plan still rankled. "Do you know anything at all about shipbuilding, Mr. Brodie?" she asked, her tone rich with sarcastic hopelessness.

"Not a bloody thing, Mrs. Balfour."

"Look here—" O'Dunne began.

"I mean a *bleedin'* thing."

Anna colored again. The occasions on which anyone had sworn in her presence were so few as to be beyond recollection. She thought of a dinner party she'd attended not long ago at which one of the guests, in an effort to avoid the forbidden word, had observed that the meat appeared "quite ensanguined."

O'Dunne made an impatient gesture. "Then you have a considerable amount of studying ahead of you. You'll never begin to be the expert Nick was, but that's not necessary. All you need is a grasp of the fundamentals, at least for the time being."

"What exactly was my brother an expert at?"

"Everything," Anna said before O'Dunne could open his mouth. "And if you lived to be two hundred years old, you couldn't come close to him in any way, Mr. Brodie. *In any way*." Silence while they glared at each other. She was thinking of their first meeting. So was he.

O'Dunne coughed. "Nick was Thomas Jourdaine's right hand after T.J. died."

"T.J.?"

"Mrs. Balfour's brother, Thomas Jourdaine, Jr."

To Anna's surprise, Brodie muttered something soft and sent her a look of genuine sympathy. His pale eyes went gentle and his hard mouth relaxed. She looked away in confusion. "When did it happen?" he asked quietly.

"A year ago. As I told you, Mrs. Balfour's father is ill, almost an invalid now, and most of the burden of running the company had fallen on Nick's shoulders."

"Didn't you tell me there was a cousin?"

"Stephen Meredith. He's second in command under Nick. He takes care of the administrative side of things, the internal housekeeping, so to speak. It was Nick who really ran the shipyard and dealt with the workers face to face."

"Did he design ships?"

"No, but he understood a marine architect's drawings and plans. He could read diagrams."

"He understood shipbuilding from beginning to end," Anna put in, her chin high with pride.

"There wasn't anything worth knowing about the building of ships that Nicholas didn't know."

"My, my," mused Brodie, "when do they canonize him?" He cocked a brow, watching her bristle. "Well, that's wonderful, it truly is, but I've got one question. If my brother knew everything there is to know about building ships, and if you're a lawyer, Mr. O'Dunne, and you're a . . ." he paused while Anna waited tensely, "a very lovely young lady," he finished, bowing fatuously— "how the hell am I supposed to find out what Nick knew about ships so I can fool people into thinking I'm him? Which one of you is going to teach me?"

"I am," said Anna flatly.

Brodie grinned. "You?"

"I."

He laughed out loud. The sound was so like Nicholas's laugh, her anger never surfaced and she stared, transfixed. "With all due respect, ma'am," he said when he was finished laughing, "I think our little plan is in deep trouble."

O'Dunne started to speak, but Anna's voice rose over his. "Do you, Mr. Brodie?"

"I do, ma'am. I humbly confess I do."

"If that's true," she said silkily, "then I suggest your immediate future is in deep trouble as well. I suggest that if 'our little plan' fails, you'll find yourself back in prison sooner than you expected. Sooner than you deserve, perhaps, although that seems impossible. In the meantime, you might start trying to remember all you've ever heard about sheer drawings and longitudinal framing and intercostal keelsons, Mr. Brodie. Think about the optimum distance between transverse bulkhead frames in a middle-class merchantship. Consider the difference between a rivet with a countersunk head, chipped flush, and one with a snap head and a conical neck. Aiden, have you finished with your 'objectives'?"

"I . . . no, I—"

"Well, I'm not able to listen to them any longer. I want to speak with you alone. Occupy yourself with something useful, Mr. Brodie. Read a book." She scooped up the one on the bar and threw it at him. Taken unawares, he barely caught it. She strode to the door and opened it. "Mr. Flowers!" Billy came. "Watch Mr. Brodie."

"Yes, ma'am."

"Come, Aiden."

O'Dunne threw Brodie a look that almost but not quite communicated masculine sympathy. Catching himself, he changed it to one of stern warning. "Stay here until I come back," he ordered, then hurried to catch up with Anna in the hall.

The moon was half-full; by its white light Anna avoided the larger ruts and obstacles in the dirt courtyard and picked her way past brush and hedges to the same fence from which she'd earlier watched the sunset. She paced while she waited for Aiden. When he joined her, she blurted out without preamble, "What can you be thinking of? Do you seriously believe this"—she held her arms out helplessly, unable to think of a word derisive enough—"this *scheme* can work?"

"Yes. I do."

"But you've seen him, you know what he's like—"

"He's a lot like Nick."

"He's nothing like him!" she denied hotly. "A

resemblance, nothing more! He's uncouth, ill-bred, vulgar. Did you see him—" she couldn't bring herself to say a word so indelicate as *spit*— "did you see what he did? He's impossible. A pagan!"

"I've spent some time with Mr. Brodie, and I say it can work. But not without your help."

She threw up her hands and resumed pacing. She was angry with Aiden, angry with Brodie, and angry with herself for agreeing to play any part at all in this absurd charade.

"I don't only mean teaching him the rudiments of shipbuilding or describing the *Morning Star* to him and that sort of thing," he went on mildly. "I mean the subtler details of impersonation. Things like . . . how Nick wore his hair or tied his cravat. Gestures he made, his walk, figures of speech he used. The sort of cologne he—" He broke off when Anna made a soft sound of pure frustration.

"But I don't *want* to teach him those things, those—personal habits." She faced him earnestly. "Have you thought about what this means? Have you considered what it will be like for me? Not just if something goes wrong and it becomes known, but how hard it will be, how painful?" She swallowed the lump in her throat and kept talking. "Aiden, I don't think you really understand. I can hardly bear to look at him," she admitted thickly. "He looks so much like him. Just now, when he laughed, I couldn't—" Her throat closed and she had to stop. She kept her face averted, not wanting him to see.

"Anna, my dear. It hurts me to see you this way. I don't know what to say." He patted her shoulder clumsily.

She had a sudden idea. "Why can't we say he's

sick? Cancel the trip to Rome entirely and say he's too ill to travel. That way we wouldn't have to meet anyone at all. We could wait in Florence until it's time to go to Naples for your rendezvous with the nonexistent Mr. Greeley. Even if there is such a person, we don't know he and Nicholas ever met. In fact, for all we know, Brodie's not necessary at all—*you* could impersonate Nicholas."

"You're right, as far as that goes. We don't know for certain that Greeley and Nick ever met. But as for me pretending to be Nick—I'm sorry, I'm not willing to take that chance."

She looked away, privately admitting that the risk was too great but unwilling to acknowledge it.

"Besides, Anna, you're forgetting one fact. Somewhere there's a man who believes Nick is dead because he thinks he killed him. We can't hope to draw him out if Brodie stays in Florence and Rome incognito."

"Draw him out?" she repeated stupidly.

"Of course. Brodie's a target. If he stays out of sight, the killer will make the natural assumption that we're only pretending he's alive, and won't bother to show his face. But if Brodie's out and about, looking, talking, and behaving exactly like Nick, the murderer will believe—because no other explanation will occur to him—that somehow Nick survived. Then, with any luck, he'll try again."

"With any luck—?" She blinked in disbelief. "Are you out of your mind? He could be killed. What are you thinking of? Does he know?"

"Does who know what?"

"Does Mr. Brodie know he's a 'target'?"

"Yes, of course."

She tried to absorb it. It made sense in a horrible way. Nicholas's brother was trading certain death by hanging for the possibility of it by assassination. But it seemed so ghastly, so cold-blooded, it made her shiver.

"Our dilemma," O'Dunne pursued, oblivious to her distress, "is that we don't know for certain that it was Union agents who killed Nick. But since no other possibility comes to mind—he had no enemies that we know of, at least none that hated him enough to kill him—there's no alternative."

"It couldn't have been. I will not believe it."

"Who, then?"

Her mouth opened, then closed. She scowled.

O'Dunne smiled tolerantly. "I understand your feelings about Mr. Lincoln, my dear, and your views on slavery and the war, but don't let your idealism blind you to the facts. War and idealism rarely exist simultaneously. That's hard for you to understand, I know, because you're a woman. Your temperament is too gentle to comprehend it."

Anna was so used to the condescension in his tone and his sentiments from the men of her acquaintance—her father, her cousin Stephen, even dear Nicholas—that it never occurred to her to take offense. She was still grappling with the enormity of the idea that Brodie was meant to decoy Nicholas's killer back out into the open. "What if he's killed?"

"What's that?"

She'd spoken so softly, he hadn't heard. "Nothing." She set the thought aside. It was too unwieldy.

"Listen to me, Anna. If you really can't go

through with it, we'll end this business with Brodie tonight and you can start for home tomorrow. None of this was my idea, I promise you. Dietz will just have to think of something else."

She stared up at the black sky, remembering what Mr. Dietz's alternatives were—to shut Jourdaine Shipbuilding down and send Mr. Brodie to his death. "And if I agree to it, what will happen when it's over?"

"When it's over, when Brodie's usefulness is at an end, we'll simply kill him off. You'll say that he—that Nicholas—died of a fever or in an accident, and you buried him in Italy. Brodie will go back to prison, and you'll resume your life in England as the widow you are. And no one will ever know the truth."

Anna shivered again, gripped by a cold, inscrutable emotion.

"I've spent the last two weeks with him, don't forget," Aiden continued gently. "I understand your reluctance to have anything to do with him, but honestly, he's not quite as bad as you think. I'm confident you're in no physical danger from him." Anna colored and looked away, remembering. "And I don't think he's a violent man."

"Not violent! But he murdered that woman, he—"

"He denies it."

She gaped, then shook her head in wonder. "I think you believe him. Aiden, I think you like him!"

"I don't like him! If it were up to me, he'd be dead and Nick would be alive!" He moved away from her to hide his emotion.

She followed, and touched his arm softly. Sometimes she forgot she wasn't the only one grieving for Nicholas. She thought of all she had lost, and of what it would be like if she went back to England now. The curious thought struck that she was less lonely here than at home. That was something else she would have to think about. In a little while. "Very well, Aiden, I will try. I'll try to get through the next few days with that man. But stay with me, will you? Mr. Flowers doesn't inspire a great deal of confidence as a bodyguard, does he?"

He turned back, smiling, and took her hands. "Everything will be all right, Anna, I promise." They started to walk back toward the inn. "But . . ."

"What?"

"Tomorrow I think we should all begin riding together. There's plenty of room in our carriage for four, and it's time Mr. Brodie got started with his lessons. After all, he's got a lot to learn about—what was it? Transverse bulkhead frames?"

She returned a wan smile for his benefit. "Oh, very well," she said on a tired sigh, resigning herself to it.

"Good girl. I admire you a great deal, you know. I think you're a very brave young lady."

"I'm not brave at all," she scoffed, putting her arm through his. "I think I must be mad."

7

"Wot're all these cross buggers niled t' the trees?" wondered Billy, pointing out the window as the heavy, lumbering *carosse de diligence* bumped and rattled over the rutted road. They'd crossed the Maritime Alps into Italy that morning; now they were moving through a dim and lonely wood, where it seemed the lowering trees were squeezing the carriage in a dark, gloomy vice. Their progress was slow, monotonous; the unending tedium had everyone on edge, even Billy.

When no one else answered his question, Brodie drawled matter-of-factly, "They mark the places where travelers like us got robbed and murdered by highwaymen." Three heads swiveled toward him, then quickly looked away. Anna made a soft, scornful noise and went back to staring out the window. "It's true," he insisted. "It says so right here in this book you gave me."

She nodded grimly, ruing that impulsive gesture. All day Mr. Brodie had been entertaining them with choice phrases translated from Italian that he'd gleaned from the guidebook she'd thrown at him last night. Phrases like "Oh, Lordy, my postilion has been struck by lightning," and "Alas, we are beset upon by wolves; some fine fellow do please dispel the noisy brutes."

"And have you found an appropriate deterrent to highwaymen in your phrase book, Mr. Brodie?" she asked coldly.

"Yes, ma'am. Two, in fact. *Chiami un vigile*, which means—"

"'Call a policeman.' That'll be a big help. Already I feel safer." She hated sarcasm; the man just seemed to drag it out of her. "And the second?"

"*Ecco, questa sì che è bella.*"

She frowned, puzzled.

"Wot's that?" asked Billy.

"That, Bill, is what they call an idiomatic expression."

"Wot's it mean?"

"It means 'Hullo, this is a rum go.'"

Brodie, Billy, and even Aiden chortled with merriment while Anna stared at them crossly. Mr. Brodie's sense of humor was lost on her. "If it's not putting you out in any way, perhaps you might turn your attention for a few minutes to something besides clever Italian sayings."

Brodie closed his guidebook and smiled across at her as she began to rummage around in the corner of her seat. Presently she brought out a flat, heavy-looking, wicker-covered object about sixteen inches square. It proved to be a writing case, a wondrous thing, a portable marvel, with velvet-covered receptacles for paper, pens, a tiny ink bottle, wafers, sealing wax, envelopes, and postage stamps. The neatness, the finicky efficiency of it almost made him laugh: it was so exactly the sort of contraption she would own.

She looked up and sent him a quelling glance, as if reading his mind. "I thought we would begin very simply," she opened, not meaning to sound patronizing but unconsciously adopting the tone of a rather stern schoolmistress, "and sketch the primary buildings and structures of the Liverpool division of Jourdaine Shipbuilding. I like to think we've a model shipyard; once you understand the rudiments of our operation, you should have a rough but sound grasp of shipbuilding in general, for we build everything from clippers to cargo steamers."

"Which do you like better?"

"I beg your pardon?"

"Clippers or steamers. Which do you like better?"

She thought for a moment. "I have no actual preference. Each has its use, steam for reliability, sail for economy. As for speed, they're roughly equal now, but that will change as propellor and engine technology improve. There will always be resistance to steam, but that comes from people who possess more nostalgia than practicality."

"Oh, aye, and we couldn't have that."

She smiled minimally. "Ah, I perceive you're one of the die-hards, Mr. Brodie. Let me guess. You talk of 'leaving the sea and going into steam,' and you call coal 'bought wind.' You deplore the end of the sailing era because that's when men were men and ships were ships, and now it's nothing but noisy engines and ship's firemen and great propellors spoiling a good four-master's sailing qualities." He said nothing, and she raised her eyebrows. "Well?" Fleetingly she wondered why she wanted to provoke him.

She'd succeeded, if the bunching of the muscles in his jaw was any indication. But his voice betrayed nothing but friendly disagreement. "Well, now, there's a bit of truth in what you say, Mrs. *Balfour*. A man who signs away for voyage after voyage in sailing ships gets to like the life, if only because he knows no other. But when he quits sail and goes into steam, all he's really trading is one filthy, cramped forecastle for another. Instead of eating the slops from the galley of his undermanned windjammer, he gets to eat the slops that come out of the galley of his undermanned steamer. The voyages are shorter, the pitiful pay's a bit more regular, and there's less shanghaiing. And a steamer has a boiler room where he can dry his clothes every once in a while. But that's about it, Mrs. *Balfour*. He's still got the same drink-crazed captain, the same number of senseless floggings, the same mad, bucko mates who would slit his throat over a chicken bone." He leaned forward. "To my mind, ma'am, it's mostly romantic ladies and gentlemen who talk about the glories of life at sea, the same ones who order their meals in bed whenever the ship rolls two degrees."

Anna's lips tightened. Obviously he thought she was one of those who idealized a seaman's life, and it was galling to admit he was partly right. She knew a great deal about ships but very little about the lot of the men who sailed them, and it was a lapse in her education she'd never even considered, much less lamented, until this moment. Brodie was watching her with a bland look, eye-

brows raised in what she suspected was a parody
of her own expression a moment ago. It annoyed
her.

"How old were you when you first went to sea,
Mr. Brodie?"

"Fourteen."

"And you're what, now, twenty-eight? Twenty-
nine?"

Brodie smiled thinly. She knew exactly how old
he was. The question revealed how hard it was for
her even now to acknowledge that he was any
blood kin to her precious Nicholas. "Twenty-eight,
ma'am."

"Twenty-eight. Fourteen years at sea. And yet
Aiden tells me you'd only just received your chief
mate's certificate before you were . . . arrested."
She said the last word with great delicacy, as if it
were slightly foreign, slightly vulgar. "That's a bit
unusual, isn't it? I believe the average length of
time it takes an able seaman to become even a
master on, for example, a thousand-ton merchantship is more on the order of seven years.
Why did it take you so long, I wonder?" From the
corner of her eye she saw Aiden shift restlessly
beside her. No doubt he thought she was baiting
Mr. Brodie. But she didn't care. Among other
things, she was sick of the tone of his voice when
he called her "Mrs. *Balfour*."

The sly innocence of her tone piqued Brodie's
temper. "Well, now, a fine lady like yourself
probably doesn't know that there's two ways for a
man to reach the poop on most vessels. One's
through the hawsepipe and the other's through the
stern windows."

It was irritating to admit she hadn't the slightest
idea what he was talking about, especially since

she knew he was using his idiotic sailor's jargon on purpose to baffle her. "You've made your point," she said stonily. "Would you mind translating that now?"

He smiled. "The poop's the officers' quarters. A man—"

"I know that."

He made her a little mock-congratulatory bow from his seat. "A man with a rich, influential family reaches it through the stern windows; without it, we say he squeezes into it through the hawsepipe. A hawsepipe—"

"I know what a hawsepipe is, too," she snapped. "How very interesting. I confess I'm struck most by the *convenience* of the excuse. But never mind, let's begin our lesson. I sense we have a very long way to go."

Brodie sat back, expressionless. It was a convenient excuse, but he'd have taken a dozen lashes before admitting it to Mrs. *Balfour*. A truer reason for the slowness of his professional progress was that until a few years ago he hadn't given a damn whether he had a command of his own or not. He'd been a raw, swaggering sailor given to brawling and defying orders, then suffering the inevitable punishment afterward with arrogance and noisy bravado. He was older now, and not as angry. Time had sobered him a trifle. Getting his mate's certificate had seemed like a beginning, the start of his real life.

Then someone killed Mary, and everything went to hell.

He could see that Anna was enjoying herself now. Her sketch of Jourdaine's shipyards had gotten away from her; she had to add another sheet of paper to the first to make room for the rest of the docks. She was explaining what was what in her incredibly refined, upper-class accent; but her voice was so musical, so sweet, really, he found himself not minding. He glanced over at O'Dunne; the lawyer returned a cool stare. Billy Flowers had rested his head against the side of the coach and gone to sleep. Anna was pointing at something and explaining it to him. He squinted and bent forward awkwardly, pretending he couldn't see from so far away. "Should we switch?" he asked O'Dunne, all innocence.

"Oh. Certainly." The lawyer got up and the two men changed places, Brodie's chain rattling as he flopped down beside Anna with a satisfied sigh.

She reared away as if she smelled a two-day mackerel, her back poker-straight, shoulders rigid. That riled him. He clasped his hands and leaned over the writing case, studying the diagram intently, making sure the side of his thigh brushed hers. He heard her draw a startled breath and felt her go even stiffer. "What's this?" he asked, pointing, rattling. She had to shift toward him to see. He turned his head at that moment, and the tips of their noses touched. She went that pretty apricot color he was growing fond of, and he sat back, smiling.

The lesson progressed. Anna began to lose some of her tension after a while, although Mr. Brodie's constant and, she suspected, deliberate nearness kept her from relaxing completely. It grew warm in the carriage, and she had a bad moment when, with some difficulty, he unbuttoned the full sleeves of his linen shirt and rolled them up to his elbows. The sight of so much muscular forearm and reddish-brown hair had the peculiar effect of temporarily emptying her mind. She didn't think she'd ever seen Nicholas's bare arms in all the years she'd known him. No, she was sure of it; she'd have remembered. "A gentleman doesn't roll up his sleeves in the presence of a lady," she almost admonished Brodie. But that was for another lesson; she didn't want to overload him with new information on his first day.

"You say Jourdaine builds everything," he said after she'd described the facility with which they forged their own iron to make stems and stern frames. "Will it continue to, or do you think you'll specialize in one kind of ship someday?"

It was an interesting question; Mr. Brodie had no idea how interesting. Not quite understanding the motives for her own candor, she confided her dream. "It was my hope that we would begin to concentrate on a new line of passenger ships, an intercontinental fleet of luxury liners that would sail between Europe and America. And sail them ourselves instead of selling them on contract to an independent shipping line. Now that's not likely to happen."

"Why not?"

She regarded him gravely. "Because Nicholas is dead. And because Stephen is only interested in building warships." *We can't lose*, she recalled her cousin insisting, for there was always a war somewhere, whether England was fighting it or not. His cynicism repelled her, but her father saw his point. Business was business. Without Nicholas to support her, she foresaw Jourdaine going in exactly the direction Stephen wanted it to.

"But the company is still your father's, isn't it?" asked Brodie.

"Yes."

"And when he's gone it'll be yours, won't it?"

"Yes."

"Then I don't understand. Why can't you build what you want?"

Anna laughed softly. "Mr. Brodie, your naïveté is charming, if a bit breathtaking. The answer, in a word, is because I'm a woman."

"So?"

It wasn't naïveté, she decided, it was stupidity. She shook her head impatiently, dismissing the subject, and began to explain the difference between knees, breasthooks, and crutches in longitudinal framing.

The afternoon lengthened, grew warmer. O'Dunne fell asleep with his chin on his chest. Billy Flowers snored delicately. In the middle of a dissertation on wave troughs and their impact on keel design, Anna caught Brodie in a yawn. She laid down her pen.

"Perhaps that's enough for today," she announced magnanimously.

"Oh, don't stop on my account. This is fascinating."

She suspected he was being facetious. "Where were you born, Mr. Brodie?" she asked abruptly, surprising both of them.

"Didn't Nick tell you that?"

"I'm asking you."

"What did *he* say?"

She didn't answer, merely waited.

Brodie sat back and crossed his long legs. "I'll tell you, but only on one condition. That you don't call me a liar afterward."

Anna flushed. "I apologize for that. I—"

"Apology accepted." He smiled; she didn't smile back. He was beginning to wonder if she had any sense of humor at all. "I was born in my father's house in the Vale of Clwydd, in Denbighshire. I lived there for six years, and then my mother and my brother and I moved to Llanuwchllyn, near Llyn Tegid and the Dyfrdwy. That's the River Dee to you."

"Wales," she said, just to be sure.

"Aye, Wales," he confirmed, laughing.

Not Ireland, then. She believed him. It meant Nicholas had lied. "Are your parents living?" she asked faintly.

"My mother's dead."

"Father?"

"Not dead. As far as I know." Or care, he added to himself.

Anna had so many questions, she didn't know where to begin. But to ask them would be to admit Nicholas had lied about *everything*, and she wasn't ready for that. "You and Nicholas, you . . . did grow up together, I suppose?" she asked without much hope.

"Aye, until we were fourteen. Then we took different paths, you might say."

His tone held bitterness, she noted. "And yet you both followed the sea. Or ships, at any rate."

"It's a curious thing, that. Llanuwchllyn is as inland as can be, but we both found work near the sea. I can't explain it. It wasn't something we talked about as children."

"They say . . ." she swallowed painfully, ". . . they say there's a special bond between twins." There, she'd admitted it. It was a beginning.

Brodie had an inkling how much the admission had cost her. He wanted to touch her, put his hand over her small one gripping the edge of the writing case, but he didn't dare. It would scare her to death. Instead he said, "Annie," very softly, the name coming to him quite naturally. "I'm sorry you're so sad."

Anna straightened her shoulders, composing herself, and made another concession. "It is possible my name is not really Balfour, that Nicholas . . . made it up. If it's hard for you to call me that, then I suppose you may call me Miss Jourdaine for the time being. It's—what I'm used to, after all. But I have not given you permission to call me by my Christian name, and certainly not by a silly nickname no one else has ever called me." In the middle of this speech she realized they were both speaking in low, nearly intimate tones, almost as though they were trying not to waken Aiden. The idea shocked her. She raised her voice to a more conversational level, but the lawyer slept on.

"No one?" asked Brodie, still in a murmur. "No sweetheart ever called you Annie? And it's such a pretty name."

"I've had no 'sweethearts,'" she said frostily, "except my husband."

And he probably called you "Miss Jourdaine" in bed on your wedding night, thought Brodie. He clucked his tongue in pretended surprise and sympathy. "None at all? Not even one?"

"None." His pitying tone annoyed her.

"Why do you spell Jourdaine with all those extra letters if you're just going to pronounce it 'Jordan'?" he wondered unexpectedly. "Why not spell it the way it sounds?"

For the first time since he'd met her, she laughed. It transformed her pale, solemn face in the most wonderful way, and the throaty, gurgling sound of it brought an instant smile to his lips. "That's a ridiculous question," she answered good-naturedly, "coming from a Welshman—a man who pronounces Clwyd as 'Cloo-id' and Rhuddlan as 'Rithlan.'"

Brodie grinned appreciatively, enjoying her game attempt at a Welsh accent. "You've been to Wales, I see."

"Oh yes, or to Llandudno, anyway. It's beautiful, and becoming quite a popular resort." She drew a quick breath. She was actually speaking to this man as if they were social acquaintances! She felt a sudden flash of disloyalty to her husband, and a hint of something else even more treacherous. She began to stopper her ink bottle and remove the nib from her pen.

"I've not been back since I left," Brodie said quietly, as though he hadn't noticed her withdrawal. "Llandudno's pretty, but someday you should see the valley of the Clwyd, with the hills of Flint rising up in the east and the gentle land all around you flecked with sheep and different-colored fields. I always meant to go back and see my mother's grave, but I never did." He left unspoken the thought that now he never would.

He didn't need to speak it. Anna's fingers halted in the act of folding her papers. With a shock, she realized she was beginning to see Mr. Brodie as a man, someone separate from Nicholas, not just his mirror image or an impostor pretending to be him. The thought both relieved and disturbed her. Living for several weeks in close quarters with this man would be less painful if his every word and gesture didn't remind her with such agonizing vividness of his brother. Yet she shrank from the inevitable humanizing that would also occur as she learned to know him, even understand him. Something warned her it would be safer to remain strangers.

"Lesson over?"

She started at the sound of Aiden's voice, and looked up with a tiny, inexplicable twinge of guilt. But how absurd; what had she to feel guilty about? "Yes, we've just finished. We accomplished quite a lot, I think," she said as she busied her hands with putting the rest of her things away in her case. "For the first day."

"Good timing. We seem to have arrived at our *pensione*."

"Oh. So we have."

So they had. With a small, appreciative smile for the irony of it, Anna watched Mr. Brodie shake his bodyguard awake. Aiden put the *diligence* step down and jumped out, turning back to help her, arms raised. She had to step past Brodie to get to the door. She gave Aiden her writing case, leaving him with only one hand to help her. There was an awkward moment when she felt gingerly for the step with her foot, one hand extended, the other clutching the door frame. All at once she felt Mr. Brodie's two big hands on either side of her waist, holding her steady. She found the step, took Aiden's arm, and made it to the ground without incident. The whole undertaking was over in seconds. And yet for long minutes afterward she was preoccupied with recollections of sensation, half-thoughts of how those ten fingers had felt, splayed wide against her ribcage, holding her still, pressing her tightly. With kindness, with—

consideration. And then she thought of something else, something that embittered the odd sweetness of the memory. She remembered that although she hadn't felt or heard it, between those two strong hands that had held her so securely was an ugly black chain.

8

At least it wasn't raining. Not pouring, anyway; not those black, nearly solid sheets of slanted water that had undermined the road and washed earth and stones down its steep face like coal down a chute. Rain fell almost gently now, and thunder was only a distant grumble beyond the farthest range of the Tuscan Apennines. But the damage was done: the rough track that had been the road was now a slick and dripping morass of churned-up mud and rocks, and the *diligence* was stuck in the middle of it.

"Ho!" shouted the driver, cracking his whip over the rumps of the two enormous oxen he'd hired to pull them out. The farmer who owned the beasts strained in front, hauling on their harnesses, feet braced in the mud. At the rear, Brodie and Billy Flowers heaved and groaned and pushed at the coach with all their strength. And at the side of the road, safely out of the way on a clean patch of damp moss, Anna and Aiden O'Dunne stood and watched from under their umbrellas.

Billy was a bigger man, a muscle-bound giant of a man, but Anna barely noticed him. Her attention was riveted on Brodie's leaner, neater physique. His hair was plastered to his head, his white shirt to his body. She responded to Aiden's comments in absent-minded monosyllables as she contemplated Brodie's long, handsome legs, the bunched muscles in his bare forearms, the powerful but elegant curve of his back. She could admit that it was a pleasure to watch him, openly for once, but told herself the enjoyment was merely aesthetic, the sort one takes when looking at sculptures in a museum. She had spent her life around men whose idea of strenuous physical exertion was riding to hounds, or perhaps batting in a spirited cricket match. Refined people who yet must make a living did so sitting behind desks— so she'd been taught. Mr. Brodie had made his living by sailing ships. That made him, by definition, the reverse of a gentleman.

For a few seconds she tried to imagine Nicholas helping to push a coach out of the mud. Impossible. He wouldn't have done it—he'd have stood there with her, like Aiden, and watched. Being a gentleman, he'd have thought it beneath him.

The coachman cracked his whip again and again; the sound was sharp over the shouts of the men and the harsh snorts of the tired animals. All at once one of the oxen stumbled. It fell to its knees and slid with greasy speed a foot backward in the mud, pulling its companion with it. The coach lurched. Brodie jumped back in time, but the wooden fender caught Billy Flowers with a sharp crack to the top of his bent head. He collapsed on his face in the dirt.

Anna cried out from behind her hands, positive that the carriage would roll back again and crush them both. The fallen ox was still on its knees despite the driver's lashing whip and the frantic shouts of the farmer. Brodie had Billy under the arms and was dragging his heavy, dead weight with excruciating slowness from under the coach. Anna cried, "Help him!" clutching Aiden's coat, pushing at him. The lawyer moved forward but then stopped, uncertain. Anna threw her soaked, pearl-colored parasol into a puddle and took two steps toward the struggling pair on the ground. But Brodie got one of Billy's lifeless arms around his shoulder at that moment. With a groan and three mighty strides he lugged him out of the ditch and up the shallow bank and then collapsed, at Anna's feet, on top of Billy's unconscious body.

Brodie rolled away and sat in the dirt, head bent, panting, arms dangling between his bent knees. Aiden and Anna hovered over Billy. "He's all right," Brodie managed to say, "just a bump on the canister." Finally he staggered to his feet. As he towered over them, large and wet and tired, all three came simultaneously to the same unsettling realization: Brodie's hands were free and his guard was unconscious.

He smiled, grinned, savoring their discomfort while he pondered what he could do to heighten it. O'Dunne was a tall man, but he was taller. The lawyer carried a pistol, but he could take it away from him. He put his hands on his hips, preparing to gloat—then whirled around toward the wet, crashing noise that sounded suddenly from behind them. Before any of them could react, three riders burst out of the trees and surrounded them.

"*Banditti*!" shouted the coachman as he sprang from the carriage seat to the mud and scampered into the woods on the other side, the farmer close behind.

Brodie and O'Dunne closed ranks, with Anna in the middle. The three men jumped from their mangy horses and called out in rapid Italian, waving pistols. They were rough, shabby, and mean-looking.

"What do they want?" asked O'Dunne, his hands high in the air.

"What the hell do you think they want?" Brodie growled. "Give 'em your money."

One of the robbers climbed agilely to the top of the coach and began hurling baggage to the ground. Another one opened it and stuffed what he wanted—jewelry, some of Aiden's clothes, Anna's shoes—into a sack. The third jabbered at them, pointing his gun.

"Money and jewelry," Anna translated, trying not to tremble. Without hesitating, she took off her jet earrings and brooch, her onyx ring, while the bandit made a search of Billy's inert form for valuables. O'Dunne handed over his wallet and pocket watch.

The robber shouted at Brodie. He held up his empty hands and said conversationally, "Sorry, you ugly son of a bitch. Nothing. *Niente*." He remembered a phrase. "*E molto seccante*."

The bandit cursed and shoved him in the chest. The one on the ground called to him, "Paulo!" and he went, but he kept his gun trained on Brodie.

"What did you say to him?" muttered O'Dunne. He looked terrified.

"I said, 'It is very annoying.'" Anna stared at

him incredulously. "You still have that pea shooter in your pocket, O'Dunne?"

"I've got it."

"Well, when do you think you might take it out and start potting at these bastards?"

"There are three of them! I think it's best if we—"

Paulo came back then, and O'Dunne closed his mouth. Anna noticed he was sweating. Unconsciously she moved closer to Brodie. Paulo called out to his friends and they remounted their horses, their bulging bags of loot slung across the saddles. She gasped when he reached out and pulled her to him by a handful of the front of her dress.

Brodie shouted a blasphemous curse and lunged. "Let her go!" The robber aimed the gun at his head and cocked it, grinning a gap-toothed grin, black eyes inviting. Brodie halted, fists clenched, knees flexed. "Shoot him," he grated through his teeth. "God damn it, O'Dunne, *shoot him.*"

The bandit backed up, one arm across Anna's chest, pulling her with him toward his horse. Her knees were buckling and she was afraid she couldn't obey when he ordered her into the saddle. He shoved her up roughly with a hand on her rump, then jumped up behind her and turned the horse.

O'Dunne wasn't going to shoot. In fury and disbelief, Brodie saw that there was one last chance. He sprang at the trotting horse, intending to grab the bandit's boot and unseat him. But Paulo saw, swung his gun, and fired. Brodie felt a fiery slash along his cheekbone and the side of his ear, and kept coming.

Anna screamed. The bandit fired again, but this time the gun only clicked. He jabbed his heels into the horse's sides and it bolted forward, smacking Brodie broadside in the head and chest and knocking him over backwards. Anna shrieked again, sure they were trampling him. Paulo hauled on the reins to turn the rearing horse and galloped into the trees.

Brodie staggered up, holding his side, wondering if his ribs were broken. O'Dunne hurried over to help him, but he shook him off. "Give me the gun," Brodie snarled.

"I can't, you—"

"Give it to me!" He seized him by the lapels and shook him. They stared at each other for long seconds, and then Brodie let go.

O'Dunne reached into his inside coat pocket and extracted the pistol.

Brodie swore foully. "You call this a gun?" A four-shooter, and he wasn't a very good shot. He pocketed it, though, and set off toward the horses that were tethered out of sight in the woods.

"What are you going to do?" The lawyer wrung his hands, watching as Brodie untied the biggest horse.

He surveyed the bridleless, saddleless animal. He'd been on horseback twice in his life, both times when he was a child. He led the horse to a rock and mounted it. "Get up on one of these and ride until you find somebody who can help us. Bring 'em back here and then follow our tracks. I'm going after Mrs. Balfour." O'Dunne just stared. "Do it!" he shouted, kicking the animal's sides and yanking on its mane to turn it, shoving O'Dunne out of the way in the process. Before he crashed into the wet underbrush, he looked back to see Aiden leading another horse over to the rock.

Following the hilly trail was easy; the sodden ground was pockmarked with hoofprints. He could even tell which horse Anna rode with Paulo because the indentations were deeper. The woods were thick, but he was on a path of sorts. Smaller ones ran across it at intervals, but the prints kept going straight. The hard part was keeping the damn horse on the trail with no bridle or stirrups. He leaned forward and held the animal's head straight with two hands on the halter to go forward, hauling on it to make it turn right or left. His progress was agonizingly slow, and it ate away at his nerves. He concentrated on forward movement to avoid thinking of what might be happening to her, now. Muttering curses out loud, he wiped the bloody rain from his face, barely aware of the icy burn from the bullet graze across his cheek.

He guessed he had gone about four miles when the woods began to thin out toward a flat, grassy plain. The prints disappeared, and he felt a rush of panic before spotting them again up ahead. They seemed to head straight across the meadow to the opposite forest, which ended abruptly at the foot of a low, craggy hill. He set out at a fast trot, zigzagging across the plain, swearing vilely at the horse as he bumped up and down, graceless but determined.

Three-quarters of the way across, he saw a cottage at the base of the hill, almost hidden in trees, three horses tied up outside. He jumped from his own horse, turned it around and gave it a hard slap, then dropped to the wet ground on all fours. Crawling, he made it to a low thicket within a hundred feet of the cottage and peered around, listening. A trickle of smoke drifted from the chimney. The horses were still saddled, and the implication of that froze his blood. He pulled Aiden's gun out of his belt and checked it. On a deep breath, he darted across open space to a cover of crumbling stone wall, pausing there again until he heard it—Anna's shrill "No!"

Forgetting caution, he made a wild dash for the cottage. Twenty feet away, he saw a man in the doorway. Without breaking stride, he aimed and fired. The man dropped. Brodie kept running, over him, through the door. He saw Anna huddled in the corner of the single room, her clothes strewn everywhere. To his left a gun fired; the bullet smashed into the wall behind him, splintering it. He whirled and shot, twice, and the second man fell. The third—Paulo—was scrabbling in the pockets of his discarded jacket, frantically searching for his pistol. Teeth bared, Brodie cocked, aimed, and waited. Paulo found his gun, turned— and crumpled as Brodie's bullet smacked into the center of his chest.

Brodie threw the empty pistol down and moved toward Anna, slowly, not wanting to frighten her, but hoping she wouldn't faint before he could get to her. She looked white enough for it. The bastards had gotten her down to her underwear, and he cursed their souls to hell, feeling a dark, primitive gladness that he'd killed them. "You're all right now," he said, just before he wrapped her in his arms.

She felt his warmth, the generosity of his body, and began to shake uncontrollably. Her throat worked as she swallowed down bitter tears and

held both fists over her chest, pressing hard to
relieve the deep pressure in her heart. The trembling worsened, and suddenly her knees gave way.
Brodie's arms tightened warmly, holding her
closer.

When he realized she really couldn't stand, he
scooped her up and carried her to the chair in
front of the just-kindled fire. He meant to seat her
in it, but her slender arms flexed in protest and she
wouldn't let go of his neck. So he sat down
himself, with her on his lap. He pushed close to the
fire to warm her feet and legs and chafed her bare
upper arm, holding her tightly. The smallness and
warmth of her helped to steady him, to lessen the
enormity of the realization that he'd just slain
three men. He murmured to her. The fragility of
her body called up something powerful in him,
something protective and carnal at the same time.
He tried to keep his hands soothing and impersonal, but there wasn't an inch of him that wasn't
intensely aware of her as a woman. He caught a
strand of her pretty hair, red-gold and candle-
bright in the glow of the fire, and drew it away
from her face. "It's all right now, Annie," he
whispered.

She was struggling, drowning emotionally between awful memories of near-disaster and almost
hysterical relief because it was over. She hadn't
cried or given in to her terror during the abduc-
tion; even when the man named Paulo had ripped
the clothes from her body, she'd felt more helpless
fury than panic. Now she was suffering the reaction, and could do nothing but clutch at Brodie's
shirtfront and let his low, calming voice slow her
blood.

In time her teeth stopped their incessant chat-

tering; her heartbeat thudded in a steady rhythm.
She felt the heat of the fire on her legs and became
aware of her condition, her state of undress.
Something held her immobile, though, locked
inside the hardness and security of his arms,
suffering with increasing pleasure the gentle hand
stroking her hair back from her face.

He held her away a little to see her and murmured, "Did they hurt you?"

She shook her head. She was grateful they were
facing the fire, unable to see the bodies, but she
knew they were there. She tried to reconcile this
man who held her so tenderly with the one who
had shot three people minutes ago, coldly, cleanly,
and without compunction. It wasn't possible. She
stifled a quick shiver—of cold or of fear?—and
stole a glance at him. "Your face!" she cried,
seeing the effects of his wound clearly for the first
time.

He touched his fingers to his cheekbone gingerly, noting it still oozed blood. But not much; it
wasn't serious. A little piece of his ear at the top
was gone for good, though. Luckily she hadn't
noticed that. "Might leave a scar," he said quietly.

After a few seconds she understood the implication. Nicholas had had no scar. If they met people
he had known, they would have to think of a way
to explain it. Suddenly the full burden of the risk
she'd undertaken returned like a sack of stones on
her shoulders, heavy and unavoidable. Mr. Brodie
had saved her, but he was not her friend. And this
peace between them was an illusion. In a matter of
weeks he would be sent back to prison. Where, for
all she knew, he belonged.

He felt the slight stiffening of her body and
sensed her subtle retreat. In self-defense, his sym-

pathy hardened, cooled. Extreme circumstances made strange allies, but the truce was over now. He stood up abruptly.

Her stockinged feet hit the floor with a slap and she gave a soft, startled cry. The air felt chilly and rude on her bare skin. Turning her back to him, she went closer to the fire, as close as she could get, in need of its warmth more than before. She heard a muffled scraping sound and guessed what it was. She didn't want to turn around but found herself doing it anyway, and watching in silent horror as he dragged two bodies, rumpled and ungainly in death, out of the cottage. When he returned, he was sweating from the exertion, but his face was pale and set.

He looked at her across the width of the room, taking note of the protective way she held herself, the careful impassivity of her features. "I've never killed anyone before," he said hoarsely, unwillingly. What did he care what she believed? To save himself, he sneered his next words. "But you don't believe that, do you, Mrs. Balfour?"

She didn't know what to say. She didn't know the answer to his question, and he frightened her. "Why should I?" she whispered. He moved toward her. She could hold her ground or step back and risk setting herself on fire. She stood still. How had she ever felt safe with this man?

"Why should you?" He leaned one hand against the rough wooden mantel behind her head, trapping her with his body in front, the fire behind. "How about for old time's sake? Or out of respect for your husband. Nick the upright, Nick the perfect." He lifted his hand and rested it on top of her shoulder. Her nostrils thinned and her light brown eyes turned fierce. "If he was so good,

Annie, how could his brother be so bad? Hm?"
With a little tug, he pulled her chemise down over
her arm, baring her shoulder.

Anna held herself statue-still, not breathing,
daring him. His hard mouth softened. There was a
light in his pale eyes she'd never seen; he looked
nothing at all like Nicholas to her in the second
before he bent and put his lips on the naked place
he'd made on her shoulder. Her eyes dimmed and
closed, and she could hear her heartbeat in her
ears. "Don't," she said, then felt the wetness of his
tongue, lightly rasping, his lips softly sucking.
"Oh, don't." He raised his head. His mouth
glistened and his breathing was uneven. She'd
been wrong; the moment of danger wasn't over, it
was just starting. It was now. She remembered
everything about his kiss, before, on the ship, and
felt capitulation surge slowly, giddily, in her limbs
and her abdomen. She shut her eyes to hide her
surrender, knowing her face betrayed her anyway.
Her mind closed on her only defense. "Nicholas
was upright," she said shakily. "He would not
have done this, not—taken advantage."

The fire in Brodie's eyes burned out slowly. He
didn't move, but she sensed his absolute withdrawal. "Ah, no," he said carefully, "not Nick.
Nick was a gentleman, through and through." He
reached out, and this time she couldn't repress a
quick, panicky gasp. He smiled and tugged her
shift up to cover her shoulder. He whispered.
"Either that, Annie, or he didn't want you half as
badly as I do." Her eyes flew to his face. "Get
dressed, O'Dunne should be here soon."

"Where—where did he go?"

"He went for help." He stepped back, away
from her.

Aiden went for help, she thought. And you came, and saved me. She watched him walk out the door and close it quietly behind him, leaving her alone. "Thank you," she said to the empty room.

Aiden, Billy Flowers, and two other men rode up a few minutes later. O'Dunne surveyed the corpses in front of the cottage, then strode past Brodie without speaking. Inside, he and Anna embraced. Brodie watched them from the doorway, his arms folded, face expressionless.

"My dear, are you all right?"

"Yes, I'm fine." But she was so tired.

"They didn't hurt you?"

"No, no. Aiden, who are those men?"

"From the village, a few miles from here. One speaks English. He said the men who robbed us are—were—brothers, that they've terrorized the area for months. Are you sure you're all right? They didn't—" He hesitated uncomfortably.

"No, I'm fine. They did nothing. Mr. Brodie—got here in time."

She turned, still holding Aiden's hand, at a noise in the doorway. Brodie was backing up slowly while Billy lumbered toward him, holding a length of chain. In the middle of the room they both stopped. Billy had a lump the size of a lemon in the center of his forehead, but seemed otherwise unaffected by his encounter with the back of the coach. He threw O'Dunne a questioning glance. "Wot d'you sigh, guv?"

For an instant Anna's eyes locked with Brodie's. He was waiting to see if she would protest. She knew it, and said nothing. Her fear of him had shifted; it came from another source now.

Brodie saw that she wouldn't speak, and he smiled a chilly, frightening smile. "It doesn't matter what he says, Billy, you won't chain me again. Not unless you kill me first."

Billy's jaw went slack. He looked back at O'Dunne for guidance. In that second Brodie made a grab for the chain, yanked it out of his huge hands, and slung it across the room into the fire.

"Bloody 'ell!" roared Billy. He started to lunge at Brodie, but Anna's hand shot out to clutch at his coat sleeve.

"Stop it, stop! Leave him alone!"

But it was Brodie who was spoiling for a fight—with all of them, it seemed. He stood with hands fisted, jaw jutting aggressively, anger crackling like live sparks in his eyes. "Try it," he taunted Billy, but his gaze was on Anna.

"Stop it!" she said again, to him this time. "Aiden." Her voice shook. "Mr. Brodie saved my life. You told me he's given his word that he won't try to escape, and I . . . believe him." She swallowed, her gaze fixed unblinkingly on Brodie's taut, dangerous face.

O'Dunne looked back and forth between them with wary interest, then cleared his throat. "Very well. In that case—"

But Brodie wouldn't make it easy for him. "I'm not asking for your permission, O'Dunne. I'm telling you."

Anna watched Aiden's eyes narrow in anger, and spoke quickly. "It scarcely matters, does it, since there's no longer any chain. What's to be done now?" She took the lawyer's arm and moved him forcibly toward the door. "Must we spend the night in this village you spoke of? Is there a constable's office nearby? Or—what would it be in Italian, a *questura*?"

At the door she risked a glance back. Brodie stood in the same defensive posture as before, and there was still anger in his eyes. But his hands were free. She sent him an almost-smile, her expression an ambiguous mix of gratitude and mistrust, and pulled Aiden the rest of the way outside.

9

May 4, 1862 Florence

In the milky-gray hour between night and day, Anna dreamed of flowers. Wakefulness pulled at her, but she resisted. The dream was pleasant, plotless; she wanted it to go on and on. But the relentlessly cheerful song of a cardinal pierced the dream-veil and she sat up, half-expecting to see the noisy bird perched on her night table. She was awake, and yet the barrier between dream and reality seemed tissue-thin because her room, though still dark and shuttered against the morning sun, was already fragrant with the delicate and delicious perfume of freesias. She put her feet on the cold stone floor and reacted to the mild shock as always, by scampering across the room to the long shuttered doors, flinging them open, and stepping with relief onto the sun-warmed boards of her wooden balcony.

The radiant beauty of Italy struck her each morning as if for the first time. All the clichés she'd ever heard about the *color*, the *light*, had turned out to be no more than the truth. It was impossible to describe—and she'd tried, often, in her journal. It had something to do with a transparent softness in the air, something rich and gentle and composed in the Italian scene; a mellow serenity; a nameless charm.

Casa di Fiori, house of flowers, was a miniature replica of a medieval castle, built a hundred years ago by a Florentine marchese. It had three floors, a ridiculous number of balconies and ledges, and a tower. Best of all, because it was built into the steep hillside, each floor was abundant in small gardens in different places and on different levels. Anna's third-floor balcony looked out over the highest garden, entered from the hall on the floor below. The Arno was not visible from here, but the flower-starred slope on its far side was brilliant in the early sunlight, with black cypresses cutting through the lushness like long, straight swords. Below her in the garden a Judas tree was in full pink flower, absurdly lovely, its wafting fragrance almost overpowering. A tiny breeze blew. Morning birds sang. Anna hugged herself, feeling washed through with light.

She turned away from the all but unbearable beauty and leaned her back against the railing. The sun flamed on her shoulders, warming her. Through the open doors she gazed into the cool dimness of her bedroom. She loved it too, the bareness of its white walls, the one small rug on the stone floor, the sparse old furniture. It wasn't the spacious "bridal suite" the servants had readied for Mr. and Mrs. Balfour—she couldn't have faced that. This room was tiny. Her bed was of black enameled iron, painted with bunches of gay flowers. Except for a tub of arum lilies by the door and a watercolor sketch of geraniums over the bed, there were no decorations. How different it was from her large, cluttered room at home in Liverpool. It was very odd, but at some deep, nearly unconscious level, and in spite of the circumstances under which she'd come, Anna was almost happy here.

It was hard to admit that one of the reasons she had fallen in so passively with Mr. Dietz's scheme was because she did not want to go home. She loved her family, truly she did, but the thought of grieving for Nicholas in her father's house, under the watchful eyes of her aunt and cousins, even her friends, had cowed her. She preferred being alone now, and she needed it. She was weary of her role as the dutiful daughter, the obedient niece, the unassuming cousin. She'd imagined her marriage beginning to change that role by allowing her some small measure of independence, a slight loosening of the restrictions she'd borne so submissively all her life. But that would not happen now, for she would never marry again. There would be no husband to encourage her efforts to define a life for herself outside rigid conventions or other people's expectations, and her fledgling attempts to contribute to the family business would doubtless come to nothing without the support of any male Jourdaine. She mourned that loss almost as much as she mourned Nicholas himself.

But guilt tormented her. What she was doing was selfish and dishonest. She ought to have gone home immediately and told her family everything. She'd never done anything like this before, it was completely out of character; the very strangeness of it shocked her. She thought of what might happen if the slightest hint of what she had done—denied and concealed her husband's death and taken up residence with a complete stranger who happened to be his convict brother—ever reached the staid ears of Liverpool society. She shuddered. It was not exaggerating to say that she would be ruined. Her father's wealth and respectability wouldn't be enough—her reputation would be shattered. But Mr. Dietz insisted there was no danger, swore the secret was secure, and told her not to worry. Aiden halfheartedly seconded him. Sometimes she wondered if they really understood the risk she was running. Because they were men, she suspected they did not.

She thought again of her father, and her guilt returned. He was very ill—what if he missed her? What if he needed her? Then she smiled a small, tight smile. He had his nurse all the time now; when Anna visited him in his room, he would look up from his book or his papers with one of two expressions: mild annoyance at the interruption, or mild puzzlement, as if for a moment he couldn't quite place her. No, she thought, almost resigned to it, her father wouldn't miss her. Neither would Aunt Charlotte. No one would, really, now that Nicholas was gone.

Abruptly she flung away from the railing and went back inside. After the brightness, she could barely see. She opened the wardrobe and searched through her gowns blindly, clutching one at random and pulling it out. She held it against herself while she stared at her dim reflection in the wardrobe mirror. She'd brought nothing black to wear on her wedding trip. Each day as she put on her green gown or her pink, her pale blue, even her white, she was seized with a fresh rush of guilt because she wasn't even mourning Nicholas properly. But that wasn't the worst. She turned from the mirror, shamefaced, and began to rummage in her bureau drawer for clean stockings. The worst was that sometimes she forgot to think about Nicholas at all. Sometimes, God help her, her mind seemed to be empty of any thoughts at all except about his brother.

The shipbuilding lessons were going unexpectedly well. Mr. Brodie was intelligent, she had to admit, and he already had a great deal of knowledge of the subject which he'd gleaned from experience at sea. Each day he listened to and grasped the rudiments of the operation at Jourdaine as quickly as she could explain them to him, and often their lessons ended early because she hadn't prepared enough material for them to cover. It was engine design that particularly interested him—which was unfortunate, because she knew much more about wood and metal fabrication. She'd sent Aiden into the city to procure books on the subject, but without success: they were all in Italian. Not that it mattered—Nicholas hadn't designed engines; Mr. Greeley, if he existed, would ask Brodie no questions on the subject—but the teacher in Anna hated to see anyone's natural curiosity stifled. Even Mr. Brodie's.

There was an edge of tension between them despite the success of the lessons, an aggravated double awareness that she found unnerving. She was scrupulously careful never to be alone with him, and yet she never felt truly safe in his presence. And that was strange, considering that a week ago he'd saved her from disaster at the hands of outlaw ruffians. Afterward he'd held her, comforted her, and she'd imagined he had a kind and compassionate heart. But if he did, she'd seen no evidence of it since then. On the contrary, sometimes she thought he was furious with her. But why? She sat down on the bed to draw on her stockings, remembering with reluctant accuracy the dangerous game they'd played—*he'd* played—in the cottage afterward, after he'd almost backed her into the fireplace. Was he angry now because she hadn't thrown herself at him out of gratitude for saving her, or—or because she found him irresistible? If so, he was even more arrogant than she'd thought. She sniffed, and pulled her petticoat over her head with a jerk.

Since that day, she'd treated him with cold, flawless propriety. She had an idea that her attitude irked him—which wouldn't have bothered her, would have pleased her, in fact, if his irritation had manifested itself in some other, some normal way. But his method of countering her frigid civility was to make fun of it. Subtly, without words, in ways she could hardly put her finger on. He accomplished it primarily by staring at her, bemused—amused—as though she were a fascinating example of some anomolous subspecies of female he'd only read about in books. And then as often as not his regard would change, and he would stare at her with frank, exaggeratedly sexual interest. That too was intended to disconcert, not flatter her, she knew, and it was intensely annoying to have to admit that it did. A great deal. She told herself she felt nothing but contempt for his games, which were childish in the extreme, craven ploys Nicholas would never have sunk to because he was a gentleman. But it was also true that as the drowsy, sun-drenched days dragged past, her unruly thoughts had begun to focus less on the sterling qualities of the honorable, upright husband she'd lost, and more and more on the devilish antics of his twin.

It shamed her. Confused her. Her reflection in the dressing table mirror was grim as she brushed out her hair and contemplated with deep chagrin the fact that already Mr. Brodie had taken more liberties with her than dear Nicholas had in all the years she'd known him, even during the six months of their engagement. And she'd *let* him. That was the worst—that was what galled! Mentally she groped for an excuse, something, anything that would mitigate the shame she felt because she'd not only allowed the man's advances, she'd responded to them.

In triumph, she located it. It exculpated her completely. The fact was, she hadn't been in her right mind. On both occasions when he'd touched her, she'd been in an extremely vulnerable state. Why, the first time she'd been asleep! Or nearly so. The second, she'd still been reeling from a brutal encounter with three would-be rapists. She hadn't known what she was doing. That was it. *She hadn't been herself.*

Satisfied, she stood up, buttoning her sleeves. She would lose no more sleep, waste no more time thinking about Mr. Brodie. She'd wasted enough time already worrying that she wasn't the decent, principled woman she'd always known herself to be. It was *he* who was entirely to blame. Any man who would try to exploit his brother's widow in a weak moment was a conscienceless, black-hearted villain. She despised him.

She smoothed her skirts, slipped into her shoes. Rearranged a hairpin and pinched her cheeks for color. Today she would tell him all about stanchions and deck girders. And nothing he could do—no mocking, exaggerated politeness, no thinly veiled double entendre, no hot, surreptitious glances at her bosom—would discompose her. Because she was impervious to him. He was boorish and offensive, and she was a lady. The wonder was how she'd ever let him affect her so strongly in the first place. But no more. Today was a new day.

"Mr. Brodie."

"Ma'am."

"Smelling the meat before consuming it is considered ill-bred."

Brodie squinted at the chunk of roast pork on the end of his fork. "Well, now, that may be," he conceded. "But where I'm from it's also considered a life-saving precaution."

"Not here, though, I think we can all rest assured," said Anna firmly. At least he was using his fork; Mr. Flowers took up all his food with his knife. She sighed dispiritedly. It was going to be a long three weeks. Mr. Brodie's table manners were neat but not polished, and definitely more practical than correct. "Bread, of course," she noted a moment later, "is broken off into small bits, rather than eaten whole in great bites."

She spoke in a general tone, looking at no one in particular, but Billy Flowers stopped dead with a giant mouthful of half-chewed biscuit and stared guiltily down at his plate. The evening wasn't going the way he'd hoped. This was the first time he and Brodie had been invited to eat with Mrs. Balfour and Mr. O'Dunne—before, they'd taken their meals in the kitchen—and he'd been looking forward to it all day. He'd taken special pains with his toilette, slicking his sand-colored hair back with oil and putting on a clean collar under his best plaid jacket. But he wasn't having any fun. Mrs. Balfour was smashing, tiptop, he was half in love with her, but tonight he wished she would shut up. Sit close to the table but don't lean your elbows on it, refrain from loud talking and laughing, use your napkin, not your handkerchief— Billy was so keyed up he couldn't taste his food anymore. He kept his eyes down and tried to look inconspicuous.

"It's rude to blow on one's soup and—" Anna laughed lightly—"of course one never *drinks* it; one spoons it up from the bowl and tries not to make slurping sounds."

Billy rose up from a near-crouch and wiped soup from his mouth with the back of his hand. He picked up his spoon surreptitiously, stared at it a moment in perplexity, then dunked it into his bowl. In an effort not to slurp, he put the whole spoon in his mouth, clanging it against his teeth and causing everyone to look at him. He belched nervously.

Brodie began to enjoy himself. Twenty years ago his mother had taught him and Nick all about table manners. Since then he'd gotten . . . a bit rusty. But compared to Billy, he ate like Prince Albert, and so poor Bill was getting most of the attention. Brodie sat on Anna's right, Billy across from him, O'Dunne on his other side. Everyone had changed clothes for dinner. Anna had on a gray gown of some soft-looking material, silk, he guessed, with darker gray stripes. He liked the way she was wearing her hair; it was softer tonight, coiled on top of her head instead of that bun thing in back she usually wore, and the candlelight was picking out the bright strands of copper and gold and—

"It's also rude to stare."

Brodie turned his slow gaze on O'Dunne, who had been silent up to now. Brodie had wondered a time or two before now if the lawyer was in love with the lady. He was protective enough of her, but Brodie couldn't tell if his devotion was because of love or friendship. He caught himself hoping it was the latter, then wondered why. What difference did it make? None, of course. It was only that Mrs. Balfour—he guessed he'd keep calling her that, it meant so damn much to her— had had a shock, and he knew, from his own very personal experience, that she was in a vulnerable state. He'd hate to see her snapped up by another man, even one as righteous and honorable as the lawyer, before she'd taken enough time to recover.

He swallowed another mouthful of pork and looked about for something to wash it down with. "Anything to drink around here besides this bug juice?" he asked, swishing the slice of lemon around in the little cup in front of his plate.

To his surprise, O'Dunne let out a bark of laughter and then looked across the table at Anna expectantly.

"That's the fingerbowl," she said matter-of-factly. "One doesn't drink it, one washes the tips of one's fingers in it after eating." She frowned at O'Dunne, who was still chuckling. "It's an understandable mistake, Aiden, and not really that funny. As it happens, the French gargle with it, although no English person would."

The lawyer sobered instantly.

"Mr. O'Dunne and I thought perhaps it would be best if you—that is, if we abstained from wine and spirits during the next few weeks."

Brodie loosened his grip on the bleeding goddamn "fingerbowl." "I see," he said, expressionless. Embarrassment and anger coiled around each other inside him. "Afraid I'll run amok if I'm given my daily rum ration, eh? Good thinking."

There was a moment of heavy silence. Anna rang the bell beside her plate. When the serving maid entered, Anna asked in her best schoolgirl's Italian for water and goblets, and the maid went away to get them.

Out of politeness, and because she found the tense, returning silence oppressive, she made an attempt at conversation. "What are meals like on board ship, Mr. Brodie?"

His look was cold. "Not much like the ones around here."

"No, I imagine not, but in what way? Could you be more specific?"

He sat back. Oh, he could be specific, all right. "Well, ma'am, on a sailing ship the big meal's at two o'clock. The men who aren't on watch gather around a big brass cooking pot in the forecastle. When the quartermaster gives the signal, we all pitch in with our knives and spoons, everybody after the biggest piece of meat."

She made a courteous humming sound and took a small bite of potato.

"This pot's also the center for all the practical jokes so dear to the hearts of us bored, simple minded sailors," he went on, warming to it. "The man who can slip an old sock or shoe into the soup is a great hero—to everyone but the cook, that is, who's apt to get fifteen lashes for gross negligence. Which the crew always attends with en--thusiasm, since they hate the cook and don't trust him. They think he's putting money meant for their pork and beans into his pocket. Which he usually is."

"What sort of food do they give you?" Anna asked faintly.

"Mostly hardtack, salt pork, and dried beans. You only get fresh meat in port. You can take along a few cows and kill them as you go, but they have to be kept on open deck and it's never long before they break their legs. Then you have to shoot them. You can keep chicken in coops on the sides, but in a small ship the decks are usually half-flooded, so the chickens either drown or get sick and die. Then it's risky to eat 'em."

"How . . . interesting."

"Sometimes there's cheese, but that gets to tasting pretty peculiar after a few days in the tropics. It won't kill you, but it can give you a mighty bad case of the runs."

Anna made a choking sound and laid down her fork.

"Ow, now, I 'ad that last monf," chimed in Billy around a mouthful of asparagus. "I et all of 'alf a bowl o' wot I thought was a foin mutton stew at Slattery's in Stite Street—in Soufampton; know it?" No one seemed to. "An' not 'alf an hour liter I've got the backdoor trots so bad I'm runnin' like a grey'ound fer the jikes. If I wasn't 'alf sick! I thought my insides would—"

Anna and O'Dunne rose to their feet simultaneously. Both were red in the face, the former from mortification, the latter from trying not to laugh. In a high voice Anna suggested they have coffee in the library and abruptly left the room, O'Dunne on her heels.

"Blow me, d'you think I said somefin' wrong, Jack?" fretted Billy, slipping a few biscuits in his pocket and clambering to his feet.

"No, no, never think it. You were a perfect gent."

"Truly? She went a bit green about the gills just then. Wot if I—"

"Nay, by no means. I think she likes you, Bill."

"Huh!" With great delicacy, Billy rinsed his sausage-sized digits in the fingerbowl and dried them on his napkin. "C'mon, mite, don't forget t' wash, ay?" And he waited until Brodie gave in, stuck his fingers in the damned fingerbowl, and wiped them on his trousers. "Likes me, ay? D'you really think so?"

"I'm sure of it. Why else would she go on and on at you about the butter knife and the salt cellar and the bloody salad fork? She's given up on me, see, but she still has hope for you."

"D'you think?"

Brodie guided him down the hall with a firm hand. "I haven't a doubt of it."

But no—Brodie's theory proved to be wishful thinking. Holding her coffee cup, paying but token attention to the conversation of the three seated men, Anna made a long, patient perusal of the library shelves and finally found what she was looking for. She carried a thick volume to the desk at the far end of the room and scanned its contents under the lamp with a practiced eye. She straightened. "Mr. Brodie."

He tried not to flinch. "Ma'am." She really should've been a schoolteacher.

"Would you come over here, please?"

O'Dunne and Billy sent him commiserating glances. He got up with the brave but temporizing movements of a boy about to be thrashed.

She came up to his collarbone. It was hard to imagine crossing her, though, she looked so strict, like a general all set to review the troops. Then he caught the merest hint of her perfume, a soft rose fragrance, and the aptness of the military metaphor crumbled. He sat on the edge of the desk, bringing their faces closer. "Have you got an improving book for me, Mrs. Balfour?" he asked softly, smiling.

"I do, Mr. Brodie. But I confess, I doubt if all the books in the British Museum could improve you."

"That hopeless, eh?"

"Beyond redemption." His eyes were lighter than Nicholas's, she noticed suddenly. The disparity was slight, but she noticed it. There was something faintly different about his smile, too. She glanced away uneasily and opened her book. "This is what's called an etiquette book," she said distinctly, as if speaking to someone not quite fluent in English. "If you can manage it, I think it might behoove you to have a look at the chapter on table manners. There's a section on topics appropriate for dinner conversation, too, which you should find rewarding."

"Ah." His smile widened. "Shall I pass it on to Billy when I'm done?"

"I don't think that's necessary," she answered, without a particle of humor.

In the lamplight he could see the tiny golden hairs on the side of her delicate neck. Her cheekbones were so fine and fragile, he wanted to touch them with his fingers to know what they felt like. Or with his tongue. Her unsmiling mouth was perfect, and he already knew exactly how it tasted. "What if I come upon some great big words I can't read?" he murmured. "Will you help me, Annie?"

Now she knew what was different about his smile. It had a gentleness Nicholas's hadn't. A sweetness. "I asked you not to call me that," she remembered to say after rather a long moment.

"But what if I can't remember? Annie's such a

pretty name. If you'd drop your guard just a little, it might even suit you."

Her chin went up. "What sort of name suits me is none of your concern, Mr. Brodie. And you would do well to—"

"Why don't you call me John?"

She stopped, taken off guard. He grinned, and his white, even teeth were a bright surprise against the darkness of his beard. "That," she said, "is out of the question."

"Why?"

"It just is." She closed the book with a snap and pushed it across the desk to him, signaling the end of the discussion.

"But why? I'm your dead husband's twin brother, Annie. Like it or not, we're related. I'm your closest non-blood kin." He tried to think of more ways to say it. "We Brodies have to stick together. I suppose I could call you 'Sis' if you don't like 'Annie.' Or—"

"*Will* you stop?" Her face was flushed, small fists curled, and she was standing in her drill instructor's posture again. "Our 'relationship,' Mr. Brodie, is a very tenuous and, thank God, a very temporary affair. I pray every moment that it will end soon. During its course, I must insist that you call me Mrs. Balfour and treat me with common decency and respect. Do I make myself clear?"

"You're wearing a corset, aren't you?"

Anna's mouth opened but no words came out. At home, such a question would have been unthinkable. Aunt Charlotte would not allow anyone to speak of even a bureau as having "drawers."

"It looks like you are, and I can't understand

why. You've got the prettiest little breasts, Annie. Why would you want to—"

Finally a sound came out, something between a squeak and a squeal. O'Dunne and Billy Flowers glanced over toward them. For reasons she didn't even try to understand, Anna lowered her voice so they couldn't hear. "Sir!" she hissed, purple-faced. "How dare you speak to me this way? Never, never say such things again!" In her agitation, she stamped her foot.

Brodie came off the desk and stood over her, hands in his pockets to keep her from running away. "Couldn't help myself, Annie," he said, speaking softly too. "I've been thinking about it all day. It seems like such a damn shame."

"No! No! You must not!" She took a step back, ready to bolt.

"Must not what? Think about your breasts?" He frowned sternly. "Now you're asking too much. I don't mind the shipbuilding lectures and the etiquette, but when you start telling me not to—"

Anna screamed very softly, pivoted, and ran out of the room.

O'Dunne jumped up and ran after her.

Brodie sat down at the desk and opened his new book. A lady never drinks more than two glasses of champagne, he read. When reprimanding a waiter, never mention his nationality. Don't gnaw on bones in public, nor bite corn off the cob, nor nibble melon from the rind. Don't even bother trying to eat an orange at the table.

He skipped a few pages.

Ah, here it was. Conversation at table should be cheerful and pleasant. Avoid discussions of sicknesses, sores, surgical operations, dreadful accidents, shocking cruelties, and horrible punishments. All allusions to dyspepsia, indigestion, and the like are vulgar and disgusting. The word "stomach" should never be uttered to anyone but your physician.

He was still chuckling to himself when O'Dunne returned a few minutes later. At first he didn't speak, only paced back and forth beside the desk in agitated silence. Brodie turned a page. Servants should not be allowed to remain up after the heads of the house have retired. And one always speaks of "retiring," never of "going to bed."

"What did you say to her?"

Brodie looked up. "What's that, your honor?" He'd taken to calling the lawyer that lately because it annoyed him.

O'Dunne repeated the question. "And don't say 'nothing,' because I know she's upset about something."

"What did she say?" he asked, interested.

O'Dunne's lips tightened in frustration. "Nothing," he admitted angrily. "She wouldn't talk." He came closer. "Listen to me, Brodie. You're treading on very thin ice. I told you before and I meant it—if you insult Mrs. Balfour or try to harm her in any way, you'll find your prison reprieve ending a great deal sooner than you expected. Do you hear me?"

Brodie was tired of insults and harsh words. He was a peaceable man, but his temper was provoked. He stood up. "I hear you. I hear you lying. You won't send me back to prison early because you're too eager to draw Nick's killer out again. You want to get him even more than you want to protect the lily-white honor of your precious Mrs.

Balfour. So take your threats and cram 'em, O'Dunne, and leave me the hell alone." He spun on his heel and walked out.

After a stunned second, O'Dunne said, "Flowers!" and jerked his head toward the door. Billy lumbered out after his charge.

10

"Hold still. Do you want me to cut your ear off?"

Brodie endeavored to hold still, despite the shorn hair inside his collar that was making his neck itch. But that wasn't the real reason he was squirming. The real reason was that Anna kept touching him. Turning his shoulder, holding his chin to move his head where she wanted it, folding his ear over so she could trim the hair behind it. And standing so close that he could see the pulse beating in her throat. Hear, sometimes even feel, her quiet breathing. Watch the shallow rise and fall of her breasts. Was this her way of paying him back for last night? If so, it was working. He was in an uncomfortable and embarrassing state of arousal, and if he hadn't known that such a cold-blooded, seductive ploy was beyond her, he'd have wagered she was doing it on purpose.

Yesterday she'd gotten a letter from someone

named Mrs. Middaugh, an acquaintance in Liverpool, who would be passing through Florence with
her family in a week and wanted to pay a visit.
Since then, efforts to turn him into Nick had
speeded up considerably.

"Is this short enough, Aiden?" she asked, glancing over at the lawyer, who was watching them
from the sofa.

He grunted. "A little more in back."

She obeyed, sliding the sleek, reddish-brown
hair through her fingers and trimming it carefully.
The gentleness of her touch filled Brodie with a
strange lassitude, enervating and urgent at the
same time. When she finished, she bent near and
blew the loose hairs from the back of his neck,
bringing goosebumps to the skin on his arms.
Damn it, she *had* to be doing it on purpose. He
breathed a sigh of relief when she finally laid the
scissors down and stood back to survey her handi-
work.

Evidently it didn't please her. She frowned,
arms folded, and regarded him first from one
angle and then another. She pursed her lips and
narrowed her eyes. Finally she shook her head.
"No."

"No?" said Brodie.

She ignored him. "Look at him, Aiden."

O'Dunne rose and went to stand beside her.
They studied him together. The lawyer shook his
head and frowned. "No," he agreed.

"No?" said Brodie.

They shook their heads in unison. "No," they
reiterated, in concert.

"Head has to come off, right?" he guessed,
trying to lighten the mood.

"It's not Nick. It just isn't Nick, even with the

new part on the right. I'm not sure why. Maybe the—"

"His eyes are lighter," Anna explained. "Not much but a little. His hair's lighter too. Just slightly."

"I think his skin's a little darker."

"He's thinner."

"The voice is the same, though."

"I think his hands are bigger."

"More muscular."

They stared at him with identical disappointed expressions, arms folded, and shook their heads again. Brodie stood it for as long as he could, then got to his feet.

"You're saying I don't look like my brother? After all this, after everything we've been through, you're telling me I don't look like Nick?"

"Of course you look like him," O'Dunne retorted. "You don't look exactly like him."

"There are subtle differences," Anna expanded. "Only someone who knew Nicholas very well would notice them."

"And even then, they'd never jump to the conclusion that this *isn't* Nick."

"No, no," she concurred, "they'd just think he looks funny."

Brodie glanced back and forth between them. "Funny? You give me a haircut and then tell me I look funny? Come on, Bill, let's go," he said abruptly to his bodyguard, who was sitting on the floor by the fireplace, playing with Domenico, the cat.

"Where do you think you're going?" demanded O'Dunne.

"Upstairs!" he hollered from the hallway.

"Well, guv?" Billy asked, preparing to go after

him. O'Dunne made a gesture of disgusted dismissal, and Billy trudged out.

"Well," said Anna faintly, staring at the empty doorway. "Well." She wasn't sure what had happened.

O'Dunne sat down again, unconcerned, and opened his newspaper. "Here's another piece on the Lancashire famine, Anna," he said presently. "It's getting worse."

"I read it. It frightens me." After a moment she went to sit beside him.

"In what way?"

"So many people in England are just looking for a reason to jump into the war in America. The cotton crisis provides them with a truly *noble* excuse to send English ships to break the Southern blockade. They can say they did it to save the Lancashire cotton workers from starving, when what they really want is to put a stop to this dreadful experiment in democracy."

O'Dunne stroked his sidewhiskers. "I think you're right. With the South winning, at least for now, it would take very little to push the government into an alliance. That's why it's important right now that we do nothing to antagonize the Union."

"Such as supply the Confederacy with warships," she said grimly.

"Precisely."

They fell silent. It was midday; from down the hall came the faint sounds of a servant laying the table for lunch. "I had a letter from Milly," Anna mentioned after a few minutes.

"Indeed? How is Mrs. Pollinax?"

"She's . . ." She hesitated, not sure how to

answer. "I guess she's fine. She sounded a little . . . under the weather, perhaps."

"She probably misses you."

She returned his smile noncommittally. Milly was more than under the weather, but Anna didn't feel at liberty to confide that news to Aiden. When Milly had married George Pollinax five years ago, it had seemed a heaven-made match to everyone who knew the handsome, dashing couple. It still did, to all but a tiny handful of Milly's closest friends, among whom Anna counted herself. George Pollinax was rich, didn't drink, and never gambled. But Milly's life with him had not been happy—Anna knew this from inference, not anything her friend had ever said explicitly—and her letter hinted that the situation had finally become intolerable.

This will come as a surprise to you, Anna, and I hope you will forgive me for being a great deal less than candid about my marriage for so many years. But you are the kind of person who sees nothing but good in everyone (except yourself), and I think I wanted to protect you from the truth about my life with George. Oh, how I wish you were here! There is so much I want to tell you, and I need your calm, sensible advice more than ever before. But how selfish of me to wish you were anywhere else except where you are. Has Prince Charming finally made you see the swan you really are, not the ugly duckling you've always thought you were? (I beg your pardon—I've mixed my fairy tale metaphors.) It's certainly time

someone did. I am so very glad for you,
Anna. No one in the world deserves happiness as much as you.

Ah, thought Anna, if only we were as good and
worthy as our dearest friends believed us to be.
She wanted to cry over Milly's letter. And she felt
so helpless. There was nothing she could do for her
friend in Italy. Almost worse was the knowledge
that, each day, she was deceiving Milly by not
telling her that Nicholas was dead. Bad enough
that she was keeping the secret from her family; it
seemed infinitely worse to keep it from Milly, her
kindest friend, her closest confidante. When she'd
agreed to the scheme she'd known it would be
hard, but she hadn't reckoned on this awful guilt.
Dishonesty in any form was not natural to her,
and the longer she kept silent about Nicholas, the
more she disliked herself. But she was trapped in
the lie now. She could see no way out.

A few minutes later, a movement in the doorway caught her eye. She looked up to see Billy
Flowers filling it with his massive frame, grinning
from ear to ear. "Shut yer eyes," he ordered
enigmatically.

"What's that?" said O'Dunne.

He recollected himself. "Shut yer eyes *please*."

The two on the sofa glanced at each other. After
a second's hesitation they obeyed. Presently they
heard the sound of footsteps on the stairs, in the
hall, and now in the room.

"Right, then," said Billy; "open up—*now*!"

They opened their eyes. Brodie stood a few feet
in front of the sofa, legs spread, hands in his
pockets in an attitude of aggressive nonchalance,

pretending he wasn't staring intently at Anna. His beard was gone.

"Ha!" O'Dunne jumped to his feet and went closer. He narrowed his eyes, examining Brodie's bare face with minute attention. "Yes. Yes, good thinking. I see what you're about." He turned to Anna. "Do you see? It makes sense. Clean-shaven, he looks completely different. Everyone will think the facial dissimilarities between him and Nick are because of the beard. Or the lack of it, rather. Good show!" he exclaimed, patting Brodie's arm once and smiling approval. "Don't you think so, Anna? I think it's a stroke of genius."

Anna nodded slowly, unable to look away from Brodie's face, while some unfathomable emotion tied her tongue. He certainly did look different; she admired Aiden's flair for understatement. She'd always thought he—she'd always thought *Nicholas*—was a handsome man, that his beard made him look distinguished, a little older than his years. But until now she'd never guessed at what an extraordinary face that beard had been hiding: hard-jawed and strong, with haughty, keen-edged cheekbones and a handsome, adamant chin; eloquent lips that seemed much more vulnerable now, though no less sensual, without whiskers to conceal them; and overall a vital, masculine symmetry that managed somehow to please and intimidate at the same time. She felt oddly comforted by the long, horizontal scar at the top of his left cheekbone: his solitary imperfection, it made him seem more human to her. Less godlike.

Brodie forced himself not to squirm under her grave and unblinking regard. It'll grow back, he told himself, as he'd been doing every few seconds for the last five minutes. Why didn't she say something? He hadn't thought it looked that bad. A little naked, maybe, but she'd get used to that, wouldn't she? Why didn't she say something? He narrowed his eyes grimly and managed to keep from glancing at his reflection in the mirror behind her, not asking himself why he gave a damn what Mrs. Balfour thought about him in the first place.

"It's . . ." Anna didn't know what to say.

"It'll grow back."

"No, no, it's . . ."

"It's what?" he demanded, coming closer and standing over her. "What?"

"It's . . ."

"It's a big improvement," O'Dunne supplied, taking Brodie's arm and beginning to lead him toward the door. "Come on, I want you to try on the new boots that came this morning." Brodie's feet were bigger than his brother's, and the lawyer had ordered new boots for him from a shoemaker in Florence. "Come on, there's just time before lunch."

Brodie let himself be pulled toward the door in a sideways, crablike fashion, still turned to Anna, still waiting for her judgment. "It's what?" he repeated at the threshold.

She held out an irresolute hand. "It's . . ."

"What?" he called back at the foot of the steps as O'Dunne pressed him onward. Halfway up, he thought he heard a faint voice from below saying, "It's . . ."

"Listen to this, Billy. A lady only takes the arm of her husband, her fiancé, or a family member.

And she never curtsies in the street, she bows. Got that?"

Billy grunted. Brodie's incessant quotes and readings were interrupting his mid-morning nap.

"When meeting on the street, always speak first to your milliner, your seamstress, or mantua-maker. Absolutely; that's democratic. Never say 'snooze' when you mean nap, 'pants' for panta-loons, 'gents' for gentlemen. And don't say an amusing anecdote is 'rich.' Wouldn't think of it." He turned a page. "Oh, say, listen to this."

Billy groaned and put the pillow over his face.

" 'An obvious withdrawal to attend to the neces-sities of nature, particularly after dinner, is indeli-cate. Endeavor to steal away unperceived.' *Listen* to this, Bill! And when you come back, 'let there be no adjusting of your clothes or replacing of your watch, to say whence you came.' " He guffawed gleefully. " 'Seem not aware of improper conversa-tion. Don't even *hear* a double entendre.' No indeed. And here's his final bit of advice for ladies: 'Dare to be prudish!' "

Anna came into the library at that moment. She paused for a second to listen to the rich, infectious sound of Brodie's laughter, which almost but not quite made her smile. "He ought to have included a piece of advice for you too, Mr. Brodie," she said, startling him. "Dare to try to behave like a normal human being."

Good Lord, thought Brodie, had she made a joke? He closed his book and stared. She looked so pretty, standing in a slant of morning sunlight in the doorway. She had on a flowered dress of pink and green and white, open in front, and under it another dress, he guessed it was, all white, with long sleeves down to the wrist. When the flowered dress opened, the white skirt underneath showed in the most wonderful, feminine way.

He got up from his chair and came toward her. She wasn't all buttoned up today, either; he could see all of her throat and even some of her chest, though the dress started just at the place where her breasts began their soft swell. Her hair was the color of safflower honey, with loose strands of gold brightening it, falling down around her face from a haphazard-looking knot on top of her head. "You look beautiful," he said truthfully, then savored the special treat of watching her cheeks turn that sweet, lovely apricot color.

All at once Anna gasped, and the color drained from her face. Brodie frowned and stepped closer. She put out an arm to fend him off, taking a backward step. "What are you wearing?" she said in an aghast whisper.

He glanced down at his new suit in bewilderment. O'Dunne had given it to him that morning. The fit was almost perfect, and he'd thought it looked all right. Sober, brown, a gent's—a *gentleman's* suit, he'd have said. "What's wrong with it?" He checked to make sure his fly was buttoned. "Too dull? Maybe a different tie—"

"That's Nicholas's suit!" She was mortified when scalding hot tears began to streak down her cheeks. "Damn you," she choked, backing out of the room. She began walking blindly down the hall to the front door. She heard Brodie mutter something to Billy Flowers, then heard footsteps behind her. She quickened her pace, but he caught her at the door.

His hand closed over hers on the knob and he loomed over her, a shadowy giant in the dim foyer. "Nick's dead," he said, his voice hoarse with emotion. "I loved him too, and I wish he was here instead of me. But he's gone." He gripped her shoulder with his other hand and made her face him. "I'm here. Me, John Brodie. I'm not his double and I'm not an impostor, I'm a man." He could feel her trembling under his fierce grip, and he let her go abruptly. When she fell back, he wrenched open the door and walked out into the blinding sunshine.

Anna waited a full ten seconds before following him. His strides were long and quick, he was almost out of sight already. "Mr. Brodie," she called. "Mr. Brodie!"

He glanced over his shoulder and saw her flying after him, holding her skirts, her heels clumsy on the rough gravel walk. She called out to him to stop, *please*, and he halted reluctantly.

Anna kept running, fearful he'd start away again, and by the time she reached him she was out of breath. It took a moment before she could speak. She put her hand over her heart, unaware of the sight she was to Brodie's hungry eyes, with her hair fallen down from its knot and tumbling around her shoulders, the faint dew of perspiration on her forehead, the agitated rise and fall of her bosom as she struggled to catch her breath. "Mr. Brodie," she got out, looking into his face with grave fervor, "I beg your pardon! What I said—please forgive me. It was unfair and unkind."

"Never mind," he said immediately. "Already forgotten."

She recalled he'd forgiven her once before, and just that easily, for calling him a liar. "You see, it's still so hard for me to believe he's really dead," she faltered. She felt she had to explain it all now.

"And that suit—Nicholas wore it the day he asked me to marry him." Her throat tightened, but this time she didn't cry. "It was stupid of me to say what I did. I wasn't thinking."

Now Brodie felt like apologizing to her. He took her gently by the arm and led her over the bumpy ground toward a coppice of laurel trees at the far end of the park. He felt her stiffen with surprise at first, then relax. Neither spoke until they were seated at opposite ends of a low bench under the trees, a safe expanse of cold stone between them. Then Brodie asked directly, "How long did you know Nick?"

"Eight years."

"What was he like?"

What a strange question. She answered as best she could, conscious of the irony—and perhaps the pain he felt—because she'd known his brother better than he had. "He was handsome," she began, then blushed and looked down. "A strong man. Ambitious. Determined to succeed."

"Did people like him? Did he have friends?"

"Yes," she said after a second's hesitation, "he had friends. Perhaps he wasn't universally liked by the men who worked for him, but I think that's understandable. He was their superior, after all, which isn't always a popular position. But certainly everyone respected him."

Brodie thought about the well-dressed, prosperous-looking gentleman who had shunned him on the Liverpool docks a year ago. He could see how a man like that might not be "universally liked." "Why did you love him?" he asked after a moment.

With scarcely a thought for the impropriety of

this conversation, Anna told the truth. "I think I fell in love with him the minute I saw him. I was sixteen. He was my father's new clerk. We met in the office in Liverpool one day, and I could hardly speak a word. Even afterward, for years, the only thing I could talk about with him was ships."

Bewitched, Brodie watched the way her mouth turned down at the corners just a little when she smiled, giving her face a sad, gentle look. She had an ambiguous smile, warm and cool at the same time, sweet but restrained, infinitely subtle. "Why?" he asked softly.

"Because I always felt so awkward and childish and stupid. And ugly. And he was so perfect, so charming and smart. And kind to me, of course, but with absolutely no idea of what I felt."

"And then?"

"Then . . . a year ago T.J., my brother, was killed in a fall from his horse. In Lincolnshire, at his fiancée's house."

"Were you and your brother close?" he asked when she hesitated.

"I loved him, but—no, we weren't very close. He was ten years older and saw me as . . . a bit of a nuisance. He and my father put up with me and my interest in Jourdaine with . . ." she paused again, weighing her words, "a certain amount of condescension." Which, she reflected, was not as bad as outright indifference—her father's attitude for the first fifteen years or so of her life. She was shrewd enough to recognize that her interest in shipbuilding had sprung originally from a desire to please him, to capture even a little of his stingy attention. It hadn't worked, not really, but over the years it had become its own reward. Ships were her passion—the only one she had thought she would be allowed, until the day Nicholas had asked her to marry him.

"But Nick was different," Brodie guessed, breaking in on her thoughts.

"Yes. He took me seriously, never patronized me. Sometimes he even askcd my opinion."

"And after your brother died?"

"Nicholas and T.J. had worked together for years, but never become great friends—or so I thought. So I was surprised when Nicholas came to me after the accident, needing comfort. I needed it too. And so—we consoled each other."

Brodie kept his expression blank, but something ugly occurred to him.

Anna's face was gentle, her eyes full of memories. "We began to spend time together outside the company." She laughed—"Actually speaking of things that had nothing to do with the building of ships."

"And you fell in love."

"He fell in love," she corrected lightly. "And six months after T.J.'s accident, he proposed marriage. In that suit." She found she could even smile about it now. It felt right, she realized, to be speaking to Mr. Brodie about his brother.

Brodie leaned back on his hands and looked up at the clouds, trying to conceive of his brother and this woman as a couple. He could picture them together physically—that part was easy. But when he tried to put Anna together in any other way with the man he believed Nick had become, the pieces didn't fit. Something was missing.

"At first my father objected. I think he'd thought of marrying me to a peer, some titled gentleman I'd met at my coming-out. But—I defied him!"

"For the first time?" Brodie ventured, though he was certain of the answer.

"Yes! I told him I was going to marry Nicholas, with or without his permission. He was so stunned, he gave in. Well, he didn't have anything against him except that he wasn't rich, and he was embarrassed to admit that. So he agreed."

"When did you lose your mother?" Brodie wondered.

"When I was four. She died in a fire."

They fell silent, thinking their separate thoughts. Out of nowhere slunk Dom, the cat. Ignoring Brodie, he heaved himself up on the bench, stalked into Anna's lap, curled himself into a hot, heavy ball, and began to purr. She patted his coarse fur helplessly, adjusting herself to his weight. She wondered at the things she'd seen fit to confide in Mr. Brodie, some of them things she'd never told anyone before. But was it really so surprising? Nicholas had died a sudden and horrible death, and afterward there had been no funeral, no burial, no opportunity to share her grief with friends and family. She had traveled to this strange new place and struggled by herself with the pain of her loss, and with the agony of suspicion and thoughts of betrayal. Aiden was an old friend, but even with him she felt constrained, unable to speak freely.

But with Mr. Brodie—at least today, at least for these minutes—she was at ease, and finally able to talk about Nicholas naturally. Healingly. With someone who had loved him too, for some sure instinct told her Brodie had loved his brother very much. Regardless of what had passed between him and her in the past or might in the future, she would always be grateful for this quiet, consoling present.

But the sympathy between them was only an illusion, and his next words betrayed it. "What will you do, how will you feel, if O'Dunne's right and Nick was stealing from your father's company?"

"He wasn't," she said stiffly. "Aiden's wrong. Nicholas would not have done such a thing."

Brodie said nothing, and wondered if she was as sure as she sounded.

His silence antagonized her. "Do you believe he would have?" She was fearful of the answer, but fully prepared to disregard it if it wasn't what she wanted to hear.

"I don't know," he said honestly. "Nick and I hadn't been friends for a long time, not since our mother died and we went different ways. I hope not. But . . ."

"But what?" she goaded.

He stared down at the ground between his shoes, forearms on his knees. "Nick was always dissatisfied, even when we were boys. Restless. And . . . he always wanted money." Because he believed he'd been cheated out of it, Brodie thought. Out of his "birthright," as he'd called it. "Let's say, I don't rule it out."

He heard the heavy thump of Dom hitting the ground, and looked up to see Anna on her feet. "I should've expected that from you," she said through her teeth. "The mystery is why I bothered to ask. You're the criminal in your family, not Nicholas! You're the one they would've hanged a month ago if it hadn't been for a miracle! Don't talk to me about my husband again, Mr. Brodie, don't even say his name. You're not—"

Brodie shot to his feet and strode toward her. Anna held her ground, but one look at his face told her she'd gone too far this time. He took her by the elbows and held on. The apprehension in her face pleased him. He was heartily sick of people telling him what he could do and what he could say, and he was especially tired of this woman's barely concealed contempt. He gave her a quick shake and brought his face down to her level.

"I'll talk about 'your husband' any damn time I want, you prune-faced, self-righteous scarecrow," he snarled, his nose an inch from hers. "Who the hell are you," he wanted to know, shaking her a second time, "telling me I can't say my brother's name? Take the stick out of your arse, Mrs. *Balfour*, and come down to earth with the rest of us."

Anna's wide eyes and open mouth made a triangle of dumbfounded circles. Five full seconds passed before she found her wits. Then she jerked out of Brodie's grip, spun around, and dashed into the trees behind her.

If she hadn't run, he wouldn't have chased her. But like an otherwise well-behaved dog, Brodie couldn't resist this fleeing cat. She scurried between laurel and fig trees, her colorful skirts beckoning to him like flirtatious flowers against the sober green of the rhododendrons. Her shoes handicapped her; he gained on her easily. When she looked back and saw how close he was, she let out a little shriek. The comical sound of it made him laugh out loud.

He caught her in a clearing of moss and violets. Seizing her arm, he stumbled in front of her, a maneuver that forced her to stop. She shoved against his chest with both hands and whirled around, preparing to bolt again. Two steps was all she got before he clutched her shoulder and she heard the awful sound of tearing cloth. She tried to scream, but she was out of breath and could utter only a pathetic, ineffective screech. Brodie tried to grab her again, to make her stand still—to put an end to this stupid scene between them. But she batted his hands away and kicked out at his shins.

It was her downfall. Their legs tangled, his unexpected reach for her arm unbalanced her, and she fell. Hard, on her behind, with him on top of her. For a second she lay stunned and motionless. Then she began to spit and sputter and struggle in earnest as his full weight pressed her into the earth and real panic set in. Her puny strength couldn't budge him; she gave up quickly and resorted to words, a more natural weapon.

"Get off me! Get *off*, you pig, you animal! Monster!"

He would have, was in the act of doing it, before she insulted him. After that, it would've taken a bomb to dislodge him. His hand landed by accident on the bare skin of her shoulder, and without a second's thought he slid it up inside her torn gown as far as he could, in front, until his fingers splayed across her chest. Anna gasped, gave up talking, and went back to flailing, her face a bright crimson, her straining arms and legs beginning to tremble from the shock.

Brodie began to enjoy the squirmy feel of her under him. The sight of his own fingers poking out of the top of her dress excited him. He tried to move his hand lower, but the narrowness of the armhole he'd stuck his wrist into prevented it.

He'd kiss her instead, he decided, and lowered his face to her throat. Her chin whipping around caught him on the temple with a sharp whack, and they both winced. Before she could turn away again he captured her mouth, but only for a second; her nails raking across the side of his neck made him jerk up and mutter foully.

Before she could scratch him again, he caught hold of her thin wrist and anchored it to the ground over her head. Slowly, deliberately, he withdrew his other hand from inside her dress. His eyes must have communicated his plans, for she started to writhe under him again. He smiled cvilly. She stopped breathing. Leering with triumph, he covered her right breast with his palm and stroked her seductively.

"Oh hell, Annie," he murmured after a few silent seconds. He couldn't feel a damn thing. "What the hell have you got on?" Disappointment swamped him. He squeezed the inert mound of whalebone and stuffing in his hand, to no effect, and swore again.

"If there is one small sp-spark of decency left in you, sir, you will let me go at once."

"Must not be any left," he told her, grinning. He tried to kiss her again, but her head swiveled sideways predictably. He had another idea. Watching her eyes, he worked one of his knees between hers, then the other, and slowly prized her legs open. Anna choked in disbelief, then moaned in utter despair as his widening thighs widened hers. He put his hand on her jaw and pulled her head around to face him. Her teeth were her last weapon. Just before his lips met hers, she dipped her chin and bit his softly caressing thumb as hard as she could.

"Ow!"

He rolled halfway off her, holding his throbbing thumb and watching as it reddened but didn't bleed. She seized her chance and wriggled out from under him, rolled to her belly, put one knee on the ground, and sprang up.

Brodie's arm shot out like a catapult. He captured her stockinged ankle in mid-step and she came crashing back to earth. For a panicky moment she couldn't catch her breath. His triumphant cackle sounded hellish in her ears.

"Not so fast, Mrs. *Balfour*," he grunted, dodging with difficulty the other foot she was trying to kick him in the head with. "Still a lot of unexplored territory here."

Screaming was futile; they were too far from the house for anyone to hear. She screamed anyway when she felt Brodie's two hands moving up her captive leg by slow inches, as if he were climbing a rope.

"I've seen less cloth on a six-masted schooner," he panted grimly, pushing more petticoats out of his way. He'd gotten as high as her garter when her free foot finally connected with something solid— his ear—and Anna rejoiced to hear his grunt of pain.

Her victory was brief. He whipped one hand out from under her skirts, his other still clutching her knee, and heaved himself up beside her. She strained away but couldn't prevent him from wrapping his free arm around her shoulders. When she tried to rear backwards, she found the intimate grip was unbreakable. Grinning at her, he located the back of her thigh with the hand that was still under her petticoats and rubbed it softly, slowly, up and down. They were both breathing hard, faces almost touching. Unable to resist, he reached higher until his fingers slid over the satin-soft swell of her bare bottom. The lovely warmth of her throbbed into his palm, made him want to keep his hand on her there forever. He buried his face in her neck and breathed in her fragrance, holding her close when tremors shuddered through her. "Annie," he whispered. He wanted to touch her so gently. He had to kiss her.

He pulled back to do it, and saw her face. Still and grim and defeated, eyes tightly closed, tears glittering on the lashes. The sensitive lips trembled, waiting, expecting the worst. He almost kissed her anyway, to soothe her—to show her it wouldn't kill her. He felt her frightened breath tremble on his cheek. When she opened her eyes, the wounded look in their strange golden depths finished him off. He took his hands from her, rolled away, and sat up.

Anna rested on her side for a few more seconds, hugging herself, trying to stop shaking. The urge to burst into loud sobs was so strong, she had to swallow repeatedly to conquer it. At length she sat up, to Brodie's left and behind him, and smoothed her skirts back down to her ankles. She could do nothing about her torn dress. There were scratches on the palms of her hands from when he'd tripped her. She blew on them a little, cupped them together gently, comforting herself. Her blood hummed in her ears. She felt weary beyond thought.

After a long moment she shifted her eyes to her tormenter. He no longer looked anything like Nicholas to her: he looked like himself. He sat with his elbows on his knees, face in his hands, in the attitude of one who feels either deep distress or deep disgust. But it no longer mattered to her what he felt. The important thing was that the energy to assault her seemed to have deserted him. She got to her feet slowly, as stiff as if she'd been kicked by a horse.

He heard the rustle of skirts and stood up too, though it was a moment before he faced her. Neither spoke. He felt an urge to reach out and brush the smudge of dirt from her chin. Her hair was loose, her tattered sleeve hanging halfway to the elbow. He took off his coat, Nicholas's coat, and made as if to put it over her shoulders. She flinched. He halted. He held it out to her across a distance of three feet and she took it, making sure their fingers didn't touch, and wrapped it around herself. She waited another moment, thinking he would speak, but he didn't. She made a wide half-circle around him and started through the trees toward the villa.

"Mrs. Balfour."

His voice was quiet; for once he said the name with no sarcastic inflection. She stopped and waited.

"There's no need for you to tell O'Dunne what happened here. I'll tell him myself."

She turned around to stare. "You'll what?" she whispered.

"I'll tell him myself. So you won't have to."

She closed her eyes briefly, swallowing. "You're that anxious to shame me, then? I don't understand you. What have I done to make you hate me so?"

It was Brodie's turn to stare. "You—Are you saying you don't want me to tell him? You don't want him to know?" She didn't answer. "I'm sorry," he said after a pause. "I didn't understand that it would embarrass you."

"No. I'm sure you didn't." Her voice held all the warmth of ice shards.

He deserved that, but it irritated him anyway. "Relax," he snapped, "your shameful secret's safe." He shoved his hands in his pockets. "And don't worry about anything . . . happening again, because it won't. I give you my word."

She gave a little strangled laugh, intended to sound derisive. "No, it won't. Not because of your worthless promise, but because if you ever put your hands on me again, you'll wish they'd never let you out of the Bristol gaol. That, Mr. Brodie, is my promise to you."

"That almost sounds like a dare," said Brodie, flashing a sudden smile.

She was afraid, she realized, to threaten him again. Afraid he would call her bluff. "I know why you attacked me," she whispered furiously. "You're jealous of your brother because he was everything you're not and never will be. Nicholas loved me and you wanted to ruin that, make it something dirty. You are petty and despicable, Mr. Brodie, and if you lived forever you could never be the man my husband was." She would have said more, longed to heap more insults on him, but his face—frozen in an expression of shock and vulnerability—finally stopped her. She sent him what she hoped was a shriveling look of disdain. Then she picked up her skirts, whirled, and disappeared into the trees.

11

"Aiden, don't go."

The words were out before she had any idea she was going to say them. O'Dunne looked up from the task of drawing on his gloves, surprise on his calm, kindly face. "What's that?"

Anna flushed. "Can't we say you're visiting, too? The Middaughs wouldn't think it strange. You could be passing through on your way someplace—"

"You know that's impossible. Dietz has sent letters from Scotland, ostensibly from me, telling everyone I'm visiting my ailing father."

"Yes, but the Middaughs—"

"Could easily hear of it, even though they don't know me. And then speak of it to people who do. Anna, the risk is too great."

Of course it was. She knew that. This was just last-minute nerves.

O'Dunne's voice sharpened. "You're not afraid

to be alone with him, are you? You won't *really* be alone, of course, but—"

"Certainly not." She picked up his hat from the hall table and fingered the brim, looking down.

"Has he done something? Said anything to make you—"

"No, no, of course not. I'd have told you if he had." She was grateful for the dimness in the foyer; it hid her guilty, crimson countenance. And yet it seemed impossible to her that Aiden could be oblivious to the almost palpable hostility that had existed between her and Brodie for the past week. There had been times when she'd hoped he would notice, and say something about it, so then *she* could say something and they could finally get this hateful situation out in the open! But she'd been too ashamed. Instead she'd been going through the motions of social civility with Mr. Brodie, feeling at all times as if she were on the verge of screaming.

The outlandishness of what had happened between them kept her from categorizing it. She had no place to put it in her experience, and no words with which to explain it to Aiden or anyone else. It was something she had to bear alone, conscious of a vast feeling of relief, of having avoided a truly dreadful fate, side by side with the most peculiar sense of anticlimax. For it had not escaped her notice that Mr. Brodie had touched her intimately, been on the verge of kissing her, and then drawn away when he'd found he didn't desire her after all. Thus along with everything else, she must live with the demoralizing realization that her feminity wasn't up to a common sailor's sexual standards. To anger and anguish, she could add humiliation.

O'Dunne took out his watch. He started to speak when there was a sound of footsteps on the stairs behind them. Anna turned around mechanically. Billy Flowers reached the last step with a house-shaking thump and stomped toward them. Behind him was Brodie. Anna pressed back against the wall instinctively.

"Sorry t' keep you whitin', guv."

"Never mind." O'Dunne took his hat from Anna's stiff fingers and fixed Brodie with a stern, unblinking eye. "We've been over everything that's expected of you tonight; I hope I don't have to go into all of it again."

"That makes two of us," Brodie agreed heartily.

"But I'll remind you of one thing, and I strongly suggest you take it to heart over the course of the next few hours."

"What might that be, your honor?"

O'Dunne frowned. "If you do, say, or even *think* anything disrespectful toward Mrs. Balfour tonight, I will learn of it, and I will take steps in reprisal against you that will make you very, very sorry. Do I make myself clear?"

"Clear as crystal." He flashed a quick glance at Anna, who was twisting her hands and staring straight ahead in a frozen way. "Mrs. Balfour's honor isn't in any danger from me tonight, and that's a promise."

"Good." The lawyer moved toward Anna and took one of her cold hands. "Are you sure you'll be all right?"

"Yes, of course. Perfectly." She forced a smile and patted his arm. "Now you'd better go; they'll be here soon."

O'Dunne nodded. He frowned one last warning

at Brodie and reached for the doorknob. "Let's go, Billy."

"Right you are." Billy squeezed past Anna, following Aiden. At the door he turned back. "Boo-wona sera, signora," he said carefully, then grinned. "And you, Jack—mind yer business tonight, ay? I might be closer than you think, watchin', like. Ay?" He clubbed Brodie on the shoulder with a friendly, bone-numbing blow and hulked out.

Almost before the door could close, Anna whirled around and hurried away down the hall. She was heading for the dining room, Brodie knew, where the soft clatter of silverware and crystal could be heard as the servants laid the table for dinner. She thought she'd be safe there. Moving more slowly, he followed.

In silence he watched her take a handful of forks from a drawer in the sideboard and count them. She wouldn't look at him, of course. He could stand on his head and she wouldn't look at him. Her delicate profile was cool, grave, and completely closed. There was no point in trying an apology; she would laugh at him, and he was weary of her scorn. Still, he had to say something.

"Billy's been practicing '*buona sera*' all day," he opened pleasantly, moving closer but not too close. She didn't respond. "I've been practicing something too. Want to hear it?"

"No."

"*Non è colpa mia, non ho fatto niente.* Want to know what it means?"

"No."

" 'It's not my fault, I didn't do anything.' " He chuckled, thinking she might join in. She didn't, and he remembered that in addition to everything else, she had no sense of humor.

"I've been learning a phrase myself," she mentioned a moment later, surprising him. "Would you care to hear it?"

"Sure."

"*Mi lasci stare.* It means *leave me alone.*"

His smile evaporated. He leaned against the wall, watching her hold water goblets up to the light and examine them—for what? bugs?—while she made a science of ignoring him. He thought again of apologizing, of blurting out that he was sorry he'd acted like an animal, it wasn't the way he'd ever treated a woman before, he couldn't understand now what the hell had gotten into him. But the inevitability of where that would get him—nowhere—stopped him again. He regretted his rashness now, his—impulsiveness, he'd call it. She'd call it callousness, but that meant a lack of feeling. He was guilty of many things where Mrs. Balfour was concerned, but lack of feeling sure as hell wasn't one of them.

"This is a salad fork, Mr. Brodie," she was saying in her schoolteacher's voice, holding one up. He had the distinct impression that had it been a pitchfork she'd have heaved it at him. "It's similar to a dessert fork, but the tines are slightly different. See?"

He tried another smile. "Don't worry, I won't disgrace you in front of your friends. I've been studying up, Annie. I know all kinds of things you don't think I know."

Her upper lip lifted in pure disdain.

"You don't believe me?" He cleared his throat. "Never pick your teeth in front of a witness. Don't drink your soup, don't throw bones on the table, and don't fold your napkin after eating." He beamed; she frowned, and began to fidget with the flower arrangement in the center of the table. "Actually rocking in a rocking chair has been discarded by genteel people, except when alone. The proper hours for morning visits are between two and five. With regard to ladies' clothing, a great variety of colors is more suitable in a carpet."

Was she smiling? He bent low, trying to see. She turned aside; he followed, hunched over, peering. Yes! The tiniest of smiles pulled at the corners of her lips, all the more beguiling because she was trying so hard to conquer it.

"Tuning a harp in public is very tedious for everyone," he went on recklessly. "Never allow a gentleman to take a ring off your finger to look at it, or unclasp your bracelet or—worst of all—inspect your brooch. Take your jewelry off *yourself* before letting a gentleman examine it. Never travel in white silk gloves, never—"

"Thank you, that's plenty." She spoke sternly, but the fleeting light in her eyes was good-humored for once. He hadn't known until now just how much he'd missed it. For a fraction of a second they smiled at each other; then she recollected herself and set about refolding all the napkins.

"So." He fingered a butter knife idly as he watched her. "What do I call these people? How well am I supposed to know them?"

Her reserve had recalcified; she spoke frostily. "You call Mr. Middaugh 'Edwin,' and the others Mrs. and Miss Middaugh and Mr. Trout. They're neighbors in Liverpool. Mr. Middaugh owns a number of match factories."

"Match factories, eh? Is he rich?"

"I suppose."

"Did Nick like these people?"

"Yes; especially Edwin."

"Do you like them?"

She hesitated. "I don't really know them. They moved in recently and they're more Aunt Charlotte's friends than mine. The only one you have to worry about is Mr. Middaugh; he and Nicholas belonged to the same businessman's club. Oh—after dinner, when you and Edwin are alone, give him a glass of claret, not port."

"Why?"

"Because he's a conservative."

Brodie blinked.

Anna felt herself flushing. "Liberals drink port, Tories drink claret," she explained reluctantly. "In general."

"Which did Nick drink?"

A pause. "Claret."

Brodie shook his head in wonder. "Who's Trout, again?" he asked a moment later.

"Mrs. Middaugh's father. He lives with them. I think he was in trade before he retired."

"'In trade'?"

"I believe he kept a shop."

"Ah." He went to the mirror over the sideboard, bent his knees to see himself, and fussed with his bow tie. "Are you sure men really wear these things?" She didn't answer. He brushed a hair from his sleeve and turned back. "Why are they late? You told them seven o'clock, didn't you?"

"Yes. Which means they won't arrive until about seven thirty-five," she explained shortly.

"Why?"

"Because it's fashionable."

"Why?"

She sighed. "It just is."

He pondered that for a minute. "How do you know these things? I mean, how do you all just *know* them, and for the rest of us it's a complete mystery? Is it written down somewhere? Is there a book?"

A quick, facetious retort died on her lips. He wasn't being sarcastic, she realized, he was genuinely bewildered. He expected her to tell him the truth, reveal some esoteric secret. "It's just . . . I don't know how to explain it. It's something one learns over time, from being around other people who know."

"So it's passed down?"

"I suppose it is, in a way. Not that it means anything. It's all made up, it's all arbitrary. It's nothing to . . . to feel envious of." Why was she trying to save his feelings? His next words silenced her.

"Nick knew, didn't he?" He stared down at his elegant blue suit, his face unreadable. "He'd have known exactly what to wear tonight. No one would've had to lay his clothes out for him, like he was a child." Anna went still with confusion. But suddenly he smiled, and his pale eyes, solemn before, brightened. "On the other hand, he wouldn't've been much help in a storm trying to rig a four-masted bark, would he?"

She let out a breath. Something softened inside her; something in her chest felt oddly swollen. "No," she agreed quietly. "I expect he'd only have been in the way."

"*Signora*, your guests. They arrive."

"*Grazie*, Daniella." Anna tilted up her chin and straightened her spine. She smoothed her hair in its pretty French twist and put her hands together at her waist in a natural-looking clasp.

But Brodie wasn't fooled. With a gentle half-smile, he came toward her. "Don't worry so much," he said lightly; "I promise I won't even spit on the floor." Her frown deepened, but he thought her lips might have twitched. "I won't say 'aye,' like you told me. And I'll call you Anna, not Annie." He took one of her cold, damp hands and rubbed the palm on his lapel, drying it. Before she could react, he gave her knuckles a quick kiss and took her arm. "Shall we go greet our guests?" As he led her out of the dining room and down the long hall toward the foyer, he murmured, "Now, remember, Annie," his mouth close to her ear, "because I'm going to be keeping my eye on you. A hostess's first duty is to the comfort and serenity of her guests. In addition, a genteel lady doesn't touch spirits, and she never drinks more than two glasses of champagne. . . ."

But a little while in the company of the Middaughs—husband, wife, daughter, and aged parent—would be enough to drive anyone to drink, he decided a few minutes later, no matter how genteel. He thought they were pulling his leg when he heard that the wife was Hypatia, the daughter, Constantia. Luckily formality was the order of the day, and he could avoid those mouthfuls with the handy expedient of Mrs. and Miss. Edwin shook his hand energetically and wanted to know where his beard had gone—and where had he gotten that scar? Why, he'd fallen on the ship coming over, he explained, in a storm. Nobody batted an eye. Mother and daughter joked that Anna appeared to have "gone native," by which he guessed they meant she was only wearing about half as many pounds of clothing as they were and wasn't quite as bell-shaped. Mr. Trout was a very old gentleman, silent and morose, a bit cowed, but he carried himself with great dignity. Brodie overheard Mrs. Middaugh whisper to Anna that she was sorry they'd had to bring him along, but there was no one at their hotel to watch him.

They decided to have drinks outside before dinner. Anna led the way, down an ancient flight of stone steps edged with periwinkles, under a wisteria-covered pergola to a terrace. They sat on black iron furniture under the peach and cherry and olive trees, blooming white and deep rose against delicate green. The sun was setting, but the hot smell of pine needles still sweetened the soft air.

Miss Middaugh, a languid, inert young lady who wore her blonde hair in a net at the back of her neck, roused herself to remark that she thought Nicholas and Anna's elopement quite the most romantic thing she'd ever heard of. She had on a tight-sleeved olive green dress with ball fringe and huge gatherings of cloth at the rear end. How did women sit in something like that? wondered Brodie; what the hell did it feel like?

Her mother's lips pursed in a thin, disapproving smile. "Indeed, yes, it was quite a surprise to everyone. Not least of all your dear aunt."

Anna longed to know Aunt Charlotte's reaction to her hasty marriage, but she dared not ask. Mrs. Middaugh was not a close friend; it would be unseemly to try to pump information from her. Anna had written several letters home—masterpieces of evasion and deception—but so far she'd received no replies.

"It's all my fault," Brodie said cheerfully, "I swept her off her feet. Wouldn't take no for an answer." She went stiff when he sat down on the arm of her chair and smiled down at her with husbandly affection. There was no room to move; try as she might, it was impossible to keep her arm from touching the side of his hard thigh. When he put his hand on her shoulder and gave it a loving squeeze, she almost jumped.

"How are the four of you enjoying Italy?" she blurted out.

"Tolerably well," answered Mrs. Middaugh, fanning herself. "It's not quite a *moral* country, is it?"

"The enjoyment of any foreign land is in direct proportion to one's ability to control the natives," said Edwin, folding his hands across his high-buttoned waistcoat and crossing his square-toed shoes at the ankles.

After a few seconds, Brodie realized he wasn't joking. "Control the natives, eh?" he prompted blandly.

"Yes, sir. Never pay them what they ask for anything, that's rule number one."

"What's rule number two?"

"Never try to speak their language. Puts you at a disadvantage, and they know it. Force 'em to speak English."

Brodie nodded slowly.

"Have you been to the Cascine yet?" Anna asked quickly, not wanting to hear rule number three, and the conversation took another turn. Brodie explained that he'd been a little under the weather, so they hadn't gotten out much to sightsee yet. As the minutes passed and the Middaughs showed no evidence of having any trouble at all believing he was Nick, he began to relax.

"We saw the Pope and his cortege in Rome," Constantia announced in a bored tone. "And once we took a donkey ride to look at the tombs in the Via Flaminia."

"I used to have a donkey," said Mr. Trout. They were his first words; Brodie had thought he was dozing. He lifted his grizzled neck out of his shoulders like a turtle and got an intent look in his bleary old eyes. Anna stopped herself from looking over her shoulder to see what he was staring at; she suspected it wasn't there. "His name was Charles," he said after a long, long moment. "Name was Charles. Charles was his—"

Mrs. Middaugh's violent throat-clearing made them all jump. "Yes, Papa," she said stridently, and began talking very loud and very fast. Anna and Brodie exchanged a quick, grave glance.

Brodie's mind wandered, became fixated on the mystery of whether the subtle fragrance of roses was coming from the garden or Anna's hair. The bare back of her neck was beautiful to him, a work of art. He thought of touching the small, delicate vertebrae that disappeared into the collar of her dress, of grazing the tiny golden hairs with the backs of his fingers. It was hard to believe that once he'd grabbed this fragile girl by the ankle, wrestled her to the ground, and then—*mauled* her. At the time it had struck him as a fine idea, and he still couldn't help thinking that part of it had been her fault. But now it all seemed preposterous. Impossible. What in the world had he been thinking of? Well, that was easy: he hadn't been thinking at all. Another organ besides his brain had been at work. It almost made him feel like the

barbarian she thought he was. A man didn't treat a
lady like that—and Anna was more of a lady than
any female he'd ever met. But something in him
wanted to peel away the genteel outer layer she
wore like a second skin, strip it off her and uncover
the woman who lived and breathed under it. She
was there, he knew it. He'd seen her twice,
touched her. Tasted her. He was beginning to
wonder if he was addicted to her.

The women were talking about someone they
knew, he missed the name. "It's sad, isn't it," said
Mrs. Middaugh, without noticeable sadness,
"when a woman of a certain age, *ni jeune, ni
jolie*"—she laughed lightly—"persists in making
a fool of herself. Don't you think so, Mrs. Balfour?"

Anna hummed something.

Not satisfied, Mrs. Middaugh offered proof.
"My dear, she made herself *cheap* in Carlisle Park
four Sundays ago by riding in a hansom cab with a
gentleman." She stabbed a stiff index finger into
her knee for emphasis. "A gentleman who was
neither her father nor her fiancé. *Unescorted*."

"Goodness," said Anna.

"But, Mother, that's not the worst," said
Constantia, with her first display of animation.
"When we paid a call on her—before the incident
in the park, needless to say—she served us *black*
tea, and she had the gaucheness to show us a
photograph album!" She laughed out loud; her
mother joined in.

Anna stole a glance at Brodie's intent look of
half-hidden bewilderment and murmured something faintly commiserating.

"Well, my dear," said Mrs. Middaugh, "what
can you expect? She keeps only three servants,

cook, housemaid, and parlormaid." She laughed again, and shrugged with humorous hopelessness. "So middle-class!"

"When you were in Rome," blurted Anna, "did you see—"

"Now, that's an interesting thing," Brodie interrupted, "this business of the classes. How would you, Mrs. Middaugh, define 'upper class'?"

Anna squirmed, exquisitely uncomfortable, but Mrs. Middaugh was happy to oblige. It was evidently a topic to which she'd given a good deal of thought. "The upper class?" She simpered with pleasure, closed her feather fan to signal her seriousness, and plunged in. "First, of course, there are the aristocracy and the gentry. Then, on roughly a par, there are the military, the clergy, and the bar. After that, your wealthy merchants, bankers, and Stock Exchange members. And finally, persons engaged in commerce on a large scale. The line is drawn at retailers, with whom one may never associate socially, regardless of personal fortune."

There was a silence following this pronouncement. All the Middaughs smiled at each other approvingly. Brodie stared at them with his chin in his hand, fascinated. Anna became aware that she was blushing. "Well!" she said in an unnaturally high voice. "Shall we go in to dinner?"

"This Irish problem, now, it's not so serious for you, Nick, because your labor force is skilled. But at my place it's becoming a real nuisance."

Brodie nodded politely. "How so, Edwin?" Which of these spoons did he eat his blinking soup with? This one was too small, this one was shaped like a leaf and had a "twig" for a handle, and this one was huge, a man could hardly get it in his mouth. He glanced down the long, candlelit table at Anna. She had her soup spoon poised in mid-air, brows raised, a very slight, conspiratorial smile in her eyes that warmed him to his bones.

"You can't get Irishmen to work like regular men, for one thing. They're a rowdy lot, hard to train, and impossible to manage."

"But they work cheap."

"They work for what they're worth," Middaugh retorted. "The dock workers are even worse. They live like animals and their slums are a city disgrace."

His wife nodded vigorously. "A *disgrace*."

The waiter was asking Brodie which wine he wanted, the Moselle or the hock. Was there some rule about it, depending on whether he'd eaten the white or the brown soup? Or whether he was a Tory or a Whig? A man or a woman? A Catholic or a Protestant? Anna's plate was too far away, he couldn't tell what color her soup was. Oh, hell. He pointed to a bottle at random. "Yes, but it's hard for the dock workers," he said mildly, sipping. "Their work comes in rushes and they've got to do it under pressure. They've got no steady, permanent jobs, so they have to put up with long periods of idleness and then sudden spurts of heavy labor. It's not an easy life."

Middaugh frowned at him in surprise.

"I wish they'd emigrate to Canada or Australia," said his wife, "if they can't find enough work here. Nobody's making them stay. I can remember when people felt safe in Scotland Road and the Exchange, but no one in his right mind would go there now." She shivered with delicate distaste.

"Do let's talk about something more pleasant."

"It's the natural inferiority of the blood," Middaugh pursued. "But what do you expect? When a race's overall intelligence level isn't much higher than—"

"I can have that beaver dress hat ready for you on Friday week, sir. Will that be satisfactory?"

The Middaughs froze for five full seconds. Then Mrs. Middaugh whispered, "*Papa*," her husband drained his glass in two loud swallows, and Constantia began to giggle into her napkin.

Mr. Trout seemed to be addressing Brodie. "Friday sounds fine," Brodie answered stoutly.

"Excellent. I can see you're a man of taste and style, sir. A good, sound beaver, with no cheap wool mixed in, now, that's a true gentleman's hat. Some would say a silk hat's a respectable hat, but I'm old-fashioned. Anyway, a silk hat's an *Italian* hat, isn't it? I mean to say, it's not English."

"No, sir," agreed Brodie. "Give me an honest English hat any day."

"There you are!"

"Papa, for the lord's sake." Mrs. Middaugh stared hopelessly at her plate.

"Eh? Eh?" The old man blinked at her, confused.

"Please, just be quiet."

Brodie frowned. What the hell was the matter with these people? They were embarrassed, all except Anna. Because the old gent was going a bit hollow in his cathedral? No, it was more than that. What really killed them was that he'd sold hats: he was a *retailer*. Now Mr. Trout was fingering his napkin in quiet puzzlement, glancing around the table under his thick white brows, wondering what he'd done wrong. "I had a silk hat once," Brodie said abruptly—and untruthfully. "It was a top hat. I was a lad of eighteen, and it was my first. Say what you will about fur, Mr. Trout, there's something about a tall, black silk hat sitting on top of a young man's head that makes him feel fine."

Mr. Trout beamed. "Well, now! That's true, sir. That's certainly true. That I can't deny."

After a tense and silent minute, Edwin Middaugh returned the conversation to the "Irish question," and Brodie addressed himself to it dutifully. He missed the look Anna sent him; if he'd caught it he wouldn't have understood it. It was a grave compound of surprise, gratitude, and admiration, shining through what looked suspiciously like a tear.

At last dinner was over. Anna rose, the Middaugh ladies with her, and Brodie got up to open the door for them—as she'd taught him to do that afternoon. As she passed in front of him he made a quick, private face of exaggerated panic, a moronic baring of the teeth and widening of the eyes that caused her to let out a sudden, unguarded laugh. She changed it to a cough immediately, and no one was the wiser. But her reaction tickled him so much, it gave him the heart to return to the table for the masculine claret, cigars, and conversation that were expected of him.

The gentlemen rejoined the ladies after the requisite fifteen-minute interval, and Anna was thankful. The Middaugh ladies' conversation had never enthralled her, and tonight it seemed particularly vapid. She searched Brodie's face for a sign of nervousness or anxiety, but found nothing except the same rapt puzzlement he'd exhibited earlier. More important, Edwin Middaugh seemed completely at ease in his company. She relaxed a trifle.

"Have you gentlemen been discussing all sorts of weighty subjects that would just confuse us silly females?" Mrs. Middaugh asked playfully.

Her husband took the question to heart. "It's true that a woman's brain is smaller in cubic content, which accounts for why she's not able to reason or generalize or pursue a connected line of thought as well as a man."

Brodie laughed, then broke off when it dawned on him that Edwin was serious.

Anna cleared her throat and started to say something, anything, when Constantia Middaugh suddenly let out a loud, horrified shriek. Everyone jumped and followed her pointing finger. Mr. Trout stared back, blinking sheepishly, as a dark, wet stain spread quickly across the velvet-upholstered chair on which he sat.

"Oh! Oh! I'm going to faint! I'm fainting!" promised Miss Middaugh, sinking back against the sofa cushion and covering her eyes.

Edwin jumped to his feet. "Oh, for the love of God," he said angrily.

Mrs. Middaugh clawed through her reticule for her vial of hartshorn while she made soft, semi-hysterical sounds of shame and distress.

Brodie realized Mr. Trout's family wasn't going to help him. He stood up. "Let's go upstairs, shall we?" he suggested mildly, jovially, touching his arm. "Clean you up a bit, what do you say?"

"Eh? Eh?"

Brodie helped him to stand. The Middaughs turned away as one from the sight of Mr. Trout's soaked trousers, the small puddle on the carpet under his chair. With a gentle arm around his shoulders, Brodie led him from the room. As they passed out of sight, Anna thought she heard him asking the old gentleman a question about hats.

When the Middaughs were gone, Brodie went directly to the liquor cabinet and poured himself a stiff brandy and soda. Next he went into the dining room and retrieved one of the cigars Edwin had left on the table. Anna had no heart to restrain him; if she'd smoked, she imagined she could use a cigar right now herself.

"Let's go outside, Annie. I need some air."

She turned without a word, and they walked out together. The moon was setting behind their backs. Wet grass flicked against their legs. The path wound under trellises, and trailing sprays of something sweet-smelling shook dewdrops on them. Starlight flickered over lilies on the pathsides. They came to a stone summer house, perched on the cliff behind the villa, overlooking the river, and stood in silence while Brodie smoked his cigar and took long draughts of his brandy.

After a few minutes, Anna said tentatively, "Thank you for taking care of Mr. Trout. It was—"

"Forget it." He faced her, his expression impatient. "First of all, just for a start, would you please explain to me what's wrong with showing people a photograph album when they come to visit you?"

"Nothing's wrong with it."

"Then why—"

"Some people think . . . it shows one isn't much accustomed to society if one amuses visitors during a formal call with albums and . . . family artistic efforts and pictures and . . . things."

"Why? What's wrong with it?"

"Nothing! I've just told you."

"Then why—"

"It's a rule of etiquette. That does not necessarily mean it's logical."

She was looking away toward the water; he thought she looked embarrassed. "Do you know what I think?" he asked.

"No." She dreaded to hear it.

"I think the purpose of all these 'rules of etiquette' is to keep the lower classes from getting into the upper. They're like this great shield that divides one class from the other. The stupider the rules are, the more complicated and idiotic, the better, because then the lower class will *never* figure them out." She turned around slowly. Pale moonlight barely illuminated her solemn face. "Well? What do you think?" he persisted when she didn't speak.

"I think . . ." She stopped; she felt the most peculiar mixture of melancholy, surprise, and resignation. "I think you're a very astute man, Mr. Brodie."

His frustration drifted away. She'd never given him a compliment before. He turned the words over in his mind, relishing them. A minute passed. "I wonder if Billy's out there somewhere right now," he mused, gazing across the walled, nearly invisible terrace that dropped away to the east, "watching to see that I don't make a run for it."

"Would you try?" she asked curiously.

He considered making a joke, but then he didn't. "No."

"Why?"

He sent her an odd smile. "Because I've given my promise."

She stared up at him. There were so many questions she longed to ask, but she had no idea how to begin. How curious, it suddenly seemed, that she hardly ever thought about the thing that should have been uppermost in her mind at all times—the terrible crime he'd almost hanged for committing. She thought of Mr. Brodie as many things, but rarely as a murderer. In fact, never. How very curious.

"See how bright Arcturus is tonight," he said, startling her, pointing.

"Where?"

"There. The Hunter and the Hounds. And Spica, the Virgin, under him."

She followed his pointing finger. "Can you steer a ship by the stars?"

"Aye—can. Yes."

She studied his upturned face. "You miss the sea, don't you? You love it."

"Love it?" He sent her another quizzical smile. "No, Annie, I'm like all sailors, I hate the sea. It's ships I love."

"I don't understand."

He faced her, but kept his hands on the stone railing. "A sailor goes off to sea when he's not much more than a child. His first voyage might last for three years, and after that he has no home, if he ever had one." His gaze shifted back to the star-flecked sky. "The life suits him. Money doesn't mean anything, and he's his own master. He doesn't own anything except his seabag and his tools. The things you want, the things you take for granted, mean nothing to him. He lives his life apart. His only enemy is the sea, because he knows it can kill him."

"He must be lonely sometimes."

"Sometimes."

"Doesn't he miss his home, his family?"

His voice hardened a fraction. "I told you, he doesn't have a home. His ship is all he has, and it's enough."

Anna shook her head slowly. "I don't understand," she said again. "The life sounds so hard, so . . . bleak."

"But there's beauty, too, and simplicity." He looked at his hands, and his voice went so soft, she could hardly hear him. "But I don't understand it either, Annie. Because sometimes I hate it, and I don't even know if I'll miss it."

She went perfectly still. The thought she'd successfully avoided for so long collided head-on with her defenses: in a little more than a week, as soon as their business in Naples was finished, Mr. Brodie would have to go back to prison. Of all the things she wanted to say to him now, she chose the safest. "But you love ships."

"Aye, I do."

"So do I."

They fell silent. Anna pondered the fact that they'd just sustained a long, personal conversation without resorting to harshness or insults or cheap innuendo. She valued this new closeness between them, how much she wouldn't let herself think. But common sense told her she was a fool. Nothing except pain could come from fostering a friendship between her and Brodie that would allow him to become real to her, a human being with feelings and needs and hopes just like any other man. But now the back of his wrist was brushing hers where their two hands held onto the railing, and that light, warm touch was becoming the focus of all her senses. She drew away, and felt inside a light, swift stab of regret.

"How did you like my friends?" she asked, needing to break in on this intimate stillness between them.

He stared down at her intently. "I'm glad you're not like them."

"Perhaps I am. Perhaps I'm exactly like them."

"No, you're nothing like them. Was Nick?"

She turned away. "He . . ." She didn't want to face the question, yet she knew he would not tolerate evasiveness. "Maybe he was, a little. In some ways. But he was ambitious, he wanted to pull himself up. I think that's an admirable quality in a man." She could hear her own defensiveness.

Brodie couldn't hear it. He was thinking that to her mind, he'd shown himself to be the kind of man who did not want to pull himself up. His brother had turned himself into a gentleman, while he'd run away to sea. Nick had gotten this woman to marry him, this woman who loved him so much she still couldn't let go of his memory, even though it was a false one. And Brodie was going to finish out the rest of his days moldering in a prison cell. He threw the half-smoked cigar to the ground and crushed it under his heel.

"I wonder where Aiden and Mr. Flowers are," she murmured.

"Are you afraid because we're alone?" His voice came out harsh, surprising her.

She faced him. "No," she answered honestly.

"Why not? Do you think you've 'tamed' me? Do you think you've turned me into a 'gentleman,' like Nick?"

The sneer in his voice bewildered her. She peered at him and didn't speak. When he came nearer she didn't move, not even when he stepped in close, so close she could feel his breath on her face. "Why are you angry?" she whispered.

"I want you to call me by my name," he said roughly.

"What?"

"My Christian name. Say it."

"I—Why?"

"Say it!" He didn't know why.

She swallowed. "I'll say it if you want me to. John."

His lips thinned. He wasn't satisfied. But now he knew what he wanted.

Anna knew, too. What shocked her was that the idea of kissing him didn't repel her. But she knew her duty. She put both hands on his chest and pushed. "Don't you dare," she said boldly, looking him in the eye.

"Don't dare what?"

"You know."

"What?"

She wouldn't say it; what if she were wrong? But he was laughing at her now, and that made her mad. "I want to go inside."

"Not yet. First I have to do something."

"What?"

He smiled. "You know."

He took her wrists and drew them around his neck as easily as if he were putting on his tie. She found herself held flush against him, tight, wrapped in his hard arms, with his lips nuzzling her hair. "I do not want you to do this." The words were muffled against his shoulder.

"Pretend it's Nick."

She pushed back, infuriated. But his mouth came down, hard and implacable, forcing her lips open. She grunted her unwilling anger through her teeth and pulled fiercely on his hair to make him stop, but he held on. She guessed that the pain she was causing him was only sharpening his determination, and let go.

A mistake. He made a noise in his throat and softened his ruthless hold, gentled his lips, and now he was tasting her. Stroking her lips, which began to tremble, with his tongue and sucking softly, intimately, at her mouth with his. She felt the identical surrender of the flesh she'd felt twice before in his arms, only this time it was worse because it was familiar and she wanted to know what happened after, what came next, how it would feel if he kept on and she didn't make him stop.

"Please, no," she whimpered, but the words were incomprehensible, uttered between the nothingness of her mouth and his. And he was speaking too, saying her name over and over, seducing her with the need she could hear in the blunt, aching sound of it. She forgot that he wasn't her husband, she forgot that he only wanted her because she was his brother's wife, and when his restless hands found her breast she didn't try to stop them.

"Lord God, it's a miracle," she thought he muttered, and guessed that he'd discovered that, for the first time in her adult life, she was without her corset. His fingers were so gentle, almost reverent, she wondered if he knew that no one had ever touched her this way before. "Ahh," she breathed on a long sigh of surprise—how intense this was, this pleasure! She swayed into him, eyes closed, hands clenching his shoulders, and let him kiss her and kiss her.

"You're lovely, Annie," he murmured against her lips, even as he wondered where this could possibly be leading. He sank one hand into the thick silkiness of her hair, and used the palm of the other to stroke against the tight little nipple he could feel through her gown. Her trembling acquiescence excited him unbearably and threatened to dispatch the last of his control, for he'd never wanted a woman this badly before. He ought to let her go. But he couldn't, not yet, it was impossible. He moved her backward until he had her against the rough stone pillar. Her eyes were like huge pools shimmering in the glow of the moon. He kissed her again until she moaned, and the helplessness of that sound of surrender buried what was left of his conscience. He understood now that she'd been dead wrong about his motives for wanting her. Nick had nothing to do with this, and spite was an emotion he was very far from feeling. His hands were clumsy with haste as he sought to open all the tiny jet buttons down the front of her dress without stopping the kiss. He felt wetness on his face, his lips, then his fingers. "Annie?" he whispered. "Why are you crying? Why?" He held her face in his hands and murmured to her, kissing her cheeks, her closed eyes.

His sweetness only made it worse. She took a ragged, trembly breath and turned aside, out of his arms. Now she couldn't stop, and she was sobbing. Some thick, insoluble pain inside was dissolving, lessening with each desperate gasp, and she couldn't stop. She felt his arms pressing her lightly back against his chest, stroking her, comforting.

"Don't cry anymore, I can't stand it," he

breathed against her hair, absorbing her long, shuddering tremors into his skin, hurting for her. "If you don't stop, I'll cry too. I mean it. I cry really loud; it would embarrass you to death."

She let out a wet snicker, then went back to weeping. He gave her his handkerchief, over her shoulder, and she buried her face in it.

"God, Annie, I'm sorry. Sorry for everything. I don't seem to be able to do anything but hurt you." But at least he understood now why she was crying. She wept for Nick, and because the pretending hadn't worked. And he wondered how, even for one second, he could have expected anything else. He squeezed his eyes shut against his own pain and held her. All he could be to her now was kind.

If Brodie thought he knew, Anna had no idea why she was weeping. It had to do with the death of something inside herself that had kept her safe from him until now. She felt overwhelmed with confusion and terrible, terrible guilt. The only thing she knew clearly was that she had better hide this new weakness in the darkest, deepest part of her heart and pray that he never discovered it. Because his ignorance of it was the only defense she had left.

She felt his hands drop away and heard him take a step back. "I won't do that anymore, so you don't have to worry." She folded her arms around herself, suddenly chilly. His voice was bleak and serious. "I mean it this time. I swear I won't touch you again, not even to tease you."

She stared up at the cold, impersonal stars. "Thank you" came out in a tight-throated, insincere whisper.

"I'll go inside now. Unless you'd rather go first, then I could—"

"No, it's all right, you—"

"I could wait here until you—"

"No, you go in. I'll come in a minute."

"Are you sure?"

"Yes."

Awkward silence.

"Well, then. Good night."

"Good night."

She heard him go past her, and pivoted when he would have come into her line of vision, because she didn't want to see him walk away. But the sound of his footsteps died slowly and then she was alone anyway, as alone as she'd ever been in her life.

12

May 28, 1862 Rome

"There's no need to come down; we can say good-bye to you here."

"No, Aiden, I want to. Just let me get my shawl. I—excuse me." Brodie was between her and the chair; she sidled around him nervously, glancing only for a second into his still, watchful face. She got her lace mantle from the back of the chair and then went ahead of him, O'Dunne, and Billy Flowers down the staircase to the ground floor of Casa Rosa, their new Roman villa. At the door to the dark, cobblestoned courtyard she paused. The *diligence* they'd hired stood ready by the gates, the big horses stamping. Rather than engage a coachman, the three men would take turns driving it themselves. It was nearly midnight. Barring mishaps, they would arrive in Naples the day after tomorrow.

"Well, Anna," said O'Dunne, taking her hands and smiling down at her. "We'll see you on Friday. Early in the morning, I should think. Enjoy Rome while we're gone, won't you?"

"Yes, I will." But she knew she would stay right here, waiting and worrying. Everything had been said; there was nothing left to do but kiss Aiden on the cheek and wish him godspeed. "You'll be careful, won't you? Not that anything's going to happen, but—"

"Yes, of course. Nothing will happen, and we'll take good care of ourselves. Now we'd best be off."

"Cheer-o, Mrs. Balfour," said Billy, making her a sort of bow. "Don't you worry about nuffing, I'll tyke care o' these two."

"Thank you, Mr. Flowers." Impulsively she reached for his hand. He muttered "Gor" or something like it, and blushed to the roots of his sandy hair.

Anna gazed into space for a second or two, empty-headed, composing her features. Then she faced Brodie. "Good-bye," she said levelly. Again she extended her hand. The sudden hard pressure of his fingers forced her to stop staring at his necktie and look into his eyes. They searched her face, and she grew afraid that he would see too much. And yet she didn't know herself what she was feeling at that moment.

"It doesn't do any good to worry," he said softly. "We'll find what we find."

"I'm not worried. You'll find nothing."

She watched the corners of his mouth curl in a smile that didn't quite reach his eyes. "My brother was a lucky son of a bitch," he murmured, for her ears only. "Good-bye, Annie." He let go of her hand and walked away.

The three men climbed into the coach, Aiden in the driver's seat, and a second later the heavy, ungainly-looking vehicle clattered out of the gate

in the high stone wall. A stoop-shouldered footman closed the iron doors behind them. Anna
waited in the doorway until she could hear nothing
but midnight silence. Then she turned and
climbed the stairs to the villa.

The drawing room on the main floor, the *piano
nobile*, was so richly furnished, it was difficult to
feel comfortable among all the objets d'art, an-
tique furniture, the priceless paintings and tapes-
tries. The house cost a fortune to lease, but Aiden
had taken it anyway, canceling the rooms in the
public pensione Nicholas had reserved in the
Piazza di Spagna, because of the villa's walled
privacy. Here there was no one but discreet and
well-paid servants to wonder why these inglesi
newlyweds had brought a friend along on their
honeymoon, or why the groom shared quarters
with a hulking cockney instead of his bride.

Anna sat down beside a beaded, tasseled lamp
and took up her book. Sleep, she knew, was
impossible. After a few minutes, she knew reading
was too. She'd told Brodie she wasn't worried, but
if he believed that he was a fool. They'd been in
Rome for three days, dining in trattorie, sightsee-
ing, looking at pictures in galleries—pretending to
be lovers, but always shadowed or accompanied
by Aiden or Billy Flowers. As the time drew closer
for Brodie's meeting with the mysterious "Greeley," her nerves had stretched tighter and tighter.
She'd demanded, wheedled, and finally begged
Aiden to let her go with them, but he was immovable. Nicholas wouldn't have taken her, he insisted;
he'd have left her in Rome, saying he had some
sort of business in Naples, and kept her as far away
from Greeley and the *Morning Star* as he possibly
could. Anna's answer, of course, was that it was all
nonsense, that all his precautions were pointless

because there was no meeting planned, no Jourdaine cruiser anchored outside the bay, and no illegal transfer of money and warship in the offing. O'Dunne had agreed that she was undoubtedly right, and gone right along with his plans.

She closed the book and held it against her chest, staring into space. Magdalena, the middle-aged woman who kept house for the absent conte who lived here during the season, poked her head in the door. "Permesso, signora, osso aiutarla?"

"No, grazie, Magdalena, I'm fine. Go to bed, why don't you. It's late."

"Sì, signora, for you too. Good night."

"Buona sera."

They smiled at each other. Each knew only a little of the other's language, but between them they managed to communicate very well.

Anna heaved a sigh and dropped her head back against the chair. She kept her eyes open, because so often when she closed them she saw Brodie's face. He'd been true to his promise, he'd kept his distance since the night of the Middaughs' visit. She thought of the moment when he'd told her of his intention, and of the bewildering flood of disappointment that had been her first reaction. Reason had returned since then, thank God; now she felt nothing but relief that he'd chosen to treat her the way a gentleman treats a lady. But honesty wouldn't let her hide forever from the truth that, at least for that one evening, she'd wanted very much for him to treat her the way a man treats a woman.

She stood and began to pace the Turkish carpet in front of a huge rococo desk. How foolish! How dangerous! Not to mention indecent, and against everything she'd been reared to believe was right and proper. More selfishly, she was afraid of the

pain that some hasty, furtive entanglement with
Mr. Brodie would cause after he went away—
which he would do, no matter what happened in
Naples, in a matter of days. For although he might
enter into such a liaison easily, she would not, and
she would suffer for it for the rest of her life. Thus
she was grateful to him for putting things right,
back into an honorable perspective. It was something she wasn't sure she, as extraordinary as it
seemed, would have been able to do.

But what an odd and shocking business it was.
She, Anna Jourdaine Balfour, actually in danger of
losing control of emotions she'd always kept in
such tight check, indeed, emotions she hadn't even
known she could feel, or at least not with this
intensity. But here honesty had its limits; with
unconscious haste she drew a curtain between
herself and the possibilities this acknowledgment
threatened to uncover. *Nicholas* had been her
lover. The only one she would ever have. Thoughts
of his brother dishonored him, dishonored her. It
was futile and stupid and perverse to allow un-
chaste fantasies to cloud the clarity of her judgment. She renounced them. She stood still in the
center of the room, hands clenched at her sides,
and made a vow. She would wait for Aiden and
Billy and Brodie to return with their empty news.
After that she would say good-bye to Mr. Brodie,
and she would never think of him again.

Eight bells. Midnight. He would be late, if there
was anything to be late for. The hollow sound of
another pair of footsteps came to him through the
fog. Brodie tensed, but the slight figure that mater-
ialized out of the mist was only that of a prostitute.
He shook his head at her suggestion, shook her
sharp fingers off his arm, and kept walking. The

lights were dim and infrequent on the ships, yachts, launches, and steamers docked in the berths to his right. To his left were the same dark, dingy warehouses and shuttered harbor offices that lined the wharves of every port he'd ever been in. Up ahead he could hear singing; seconds later a knot of drunken seamen wove harmlessly around him. Lights twinkled on the oily water close to the dock; farther out it was all swirling gray mist. He passed Pier 11 and slowed his steps. O'Dunne had said whoever was to meet him at midnight would be waiting at the twelfth.

The slip was dark. And empty. No—now he could see a dinghy tied up, ludicrously small in the wide berth. Brodie took out his tobacco and rolled a cigarette. If anybody asks, he thought dryly, Nick just took it up. Marriage drove him to it.

He blew smoke into the fog and thought of his brother's widow. If Nick turned out to have been a thief, he wondered who it would hurt more, himself or her. Ah, Annie, Annie. The game they were playing was almost over. Would she come with them when O'Dunne took him back to England, back to prison? Or would she stay in Italy and follow later, alone? Either way, only days remained of the time given to him to be with her. He crushed his cigarette out under his boot heel. How would they say he—Nick—had died? A fever? That was vague enough. They'd "buried" him in a Roman cemetery. The grieving widow would go home to the comfort of her loving family. But she wouldn't stay a widow for long, he'd wager. If her loveliness didn't snare a new husband quickly, her money would. Which of them had snared Nick?

Footsteps sounded behind him. He whirled. Two men, sailors. Moving quietly, unaggressively.

Brodie kept his hands in the open.

"Waiting for someone?" The accent was American.

He said one word. "Greeley."

The sailor nodded, satisfied, and began to untie the dinghy.

So it was all true. Brodie closed his eyes just for a second and let it wash over him, all the anger and regret.

The sailors rowed while he sat aft, watching the wharf recede. No stars tonight. When they were too far from shore to see the lights, one of the sailors lit a lantern and set it in the bottom of the boat, to illuminate the compass he opened and put next to it. Brodie wondered how far they had to row, but didn't ask.

Not far. Out of the mist to the port side soon came the muted dinging of a bell. The sailor who had lit the lantern called out a gruff hello. An answering call, close by, from the direction of the bell. Then he saw lights, and all at once they were alongside the great prow, so close he could see in the flickering lantern glow the faint, painted-over letters, N, R, O, M, as they rowed aft, toward the stern. No more *Morning Star*, then. What would she be in a few days, the *Savannah*? The *Charleston*, the *Baton Rouge*? He spat over the gunwale into the water.

When they were amidships, someone heaved a line down, then a rope ladder. The sailors maneuvered the dinghy close and tied up, knotting the painter through a ring in the big ship's counter. One of them nodded to Brodie, and he groped his way to the ladder and started to climb. They didn't follow. He hoped that meant his stay on board was intended to be short.

He saw that she was a square-rigged cruiser, fast

and long, so long they'd only been able to fit her with armor plating amidships and still keep her seaworthy; some eighty feet of her hull at either end was unprotected. Anna had told him she could do thirteen knots, more with her full suit of sails. He swung his legs over the rail and dropped to the deck. Two more seamen were waiting for him. Nobody spoke. He fell in line between them as they hustled him past the quarterdeck toward the main companionway hatch. By lantern light he could see her guns, or some of them. Reckoning quickly, he estimated twenty seven-inch smooth-bore muzzle-loaders, two smaller smooth-bores, and a couple of twenty-pound breech-loaders. The *Morning Star* was one dangerous merchantship.

Down the ladder they went, heels clanging on the iron rails. Single file, they traversed a narrow corridor to a closed door at the end. The seaman in front rapped on it with his knuckles. "Come in!" came from inside. Squeezing past the sailor, Brodie went in, and the door shut behind him.

He was afraid to say, "Hello, Greeley," to the man who got up from his desk and came toward him with an outstretched hand. What if Greeley was only the middleman, or what if he was sick in bed, or dead, and this was his replacement? Then he saw the insignia on the gray uniform, ending his dilemma. "Hello, Captain," he said, shaking hands.

"Mr. Balfour." The captain—Captain Greeley? —was a young man, younger than Brodie, but with thinning hair and a tired face. He didn't smile and he shook Brodie's hand with a noticeable lack of warmth. "I almost didn't recognize you without the beard."

Another question answered: Nick and this man had met. It must be Greeley. Brodie passed a hand

over his bare chin and made a wry expression.
"Bride's orders."

"Oh yes, I'd forgotten. You're on your honeymoon, aren't you?" There was an unpleasant barb
hidden behind the captain's aristocratic Southern
drawl. "Will you have a seat? Something to
drink?"

"No, thanks. I'd like to get this over with as
soon as possible." Whatever "this" was.

"Yes, I imagine you would." Captain Greeley's
lips curled faintly with distaste. He went to his
desk and opened a drawer, reached in with both
hands, and brought out a heavy canvas sack.
"You'll want to count it, I'm sure." He slung the
sack to the desk top and moved the lamp closer,
then stood back to make room for Brodie.

He went forward slowly, dreading what he
would find. But he already knew. He loosened the
drawstring and shook the contents—bundled Italian bank notes, thousands of them—onto the top
of the desk. For a long time he just stared. Ah,
Nick, he thought. He felt like crying. Damn you to
hell. Why did you go and do this? He began to stuff
the money back into the bag.

"Aren't you going to count it?"

"No." He pulled the string tight and turned to
face the surprised captain. "Anything else?" he
asked coldly.

Greeley sent him a narrow look, as if he were
reevaluating some preconception. "I guess not,"
he conceded finally. "But I'm surprised—I
thought you'd want to celebrate."

"Celebrate?"

"Like the last time. When we closed the bargain."

"Ah. Maybe another time."

"I doubt that there'll be another time."

"Why not?"

"We only got out of Majorca by the skin of our teeth, for one thing."

Majorca. So that's where they'd outfitted the *Morning Star* and turned her into an armored frigate. It was one of the things O'Dunne had wanted him to find out without asking.

"And for another, it's too risky now. Your government turned a blind eye at first; but now they're so afraid of antagonizing the Union, we can't trust them to stay out of our . . . private business arrangements anymore. So I expect we won't be seeing each other again, Mr. Balfour."

Brodie stepped forward. "Then I'll say goodbye." They shook hands, and he was struck again by the captain's ill-concealed antipathy. "You don't like me much, do you?"

Greeley raised thin brows. "Not much," he admitted after a moment's pause.

"Mind if I ask why?"

"Not at all. Let's say I've got a natural aversion to thieves."

"Thieves?" he repeated quietly. "But you're getting good value for your money, aren't you?"

"Oh, yes. But I wonder how much of the profits you'll end up sharing with your friend at Jourdaine Shipbuilding. I wouldn't put it past a man like you to cheat him, too."

A muscle jumped in Brodie's jaw as irrational anger spurted through him. It was only the mention of his "friend" that sobered him. If only he could ask, "Who? *Who* at Jourdaine was in this with Nick?" That was the other thing O'Dunne wanted him to find out. But he was damned if he could see a way to do it without giving himself away. So all he said was, "No honor among crooks, eh?" and went past Greeley to the door.

When he turned back, the captain was peering at him with the same look of faint puzzlement as before. "What are you going to call her?" he asked, his hand on the door handle.

"What's that?"

"The *Morning Star*. What's her new name?"

"Oh. The *Atlanta*."

Brodie smiled grimly. "Of course." He jerked open the door and went out.

His hurrying footsteps rang hollow on the wooden dock, and just for a moment he thought he heard others, behind him. He paused, listened. Nothing now. He hastened on, squinting through the worsening fog for a glimpse of Billy or O'Dunne. He stopped again. This time he heard them—footsteps that stopped a second after his did. He turned slowly, silently, one hand stealing to the money bag he'd put inside his shirt. He could see clearly for about twenty feet; after that it was all mist. Everything was quiet except for the rhythmic splash of waves against the pilings and, somewhere in the distance, the muffled pealing of a bell. Then, beyond the clear space, in the thick of the fog ahead of him, he heard a click. Recognition spun him around and let him get one step away before the shot fired and the bullet tore a scorching path between his arm and the wall of his chest. He staggered.

"Jack!"

It was Flowers' voice, in front of him. "Billy!" he shouted, running now. The huge cockney lurched out of the fog like a spouting whale, pistols in both hands. O'Dunne loomed up behind him. Shots exploded from everywhere. Brodie flexed his knees and dove head-first at a pile of hogsheads stacked in a doorway to his right. The mist closed in. Crouching, panting, he listened to the shooting and waited for the pain in his side to diminish. Then everything went still. The fog broke, and in the brief clarity he saw two bodies in front of him on the wet wharf. One moved, one lay still. He sprang up and went to the groaning man. Just as he reached him—it was O'Dunne—a bullet shrilled past his ear. He ducked, then scooped the lawyer up in his arms and dashed back into his doorway as the mist rolled in again.

When Brodie released him, O'Dunne's shoulders struck the door with a heavy thud. It opened. "Jesus God," prayed Brodie, and dragged the lawyer by the armpits over the threshold. They were in some kind of warehouse. "Where are you hit?"

"Leg." He held the hole in his thigh with both hands to stop the bleeding.

"Give me your gun," said Brodie.

"Why?"

"Billy."

"He's dead."

"You don't know! Give it to me."

O'Dunne started to hand over his pistol, but the violent crash of falling barrels outside flattened them both to the floor. There was a blinding blue flash from the doorway and Brodie heard wood splinter behind his head. He tried to dive behind some dark box to his left, but his legs were tangled up with O'Dunne's and he couldn't get free. His body jerked when another shot fired, this one closer, beside him, in his ear. This blue flash lit O'Dunne's wild-eyed face for an instant. Somebody in the doorway grunted, pitched forward, and fell.

Brodie scrambled up. "Are you hit again?"

"No," O'Dunne answered on a groan.

Kicking the lifeless body in the door out of his way, Brodie stumbled outside. Billy lay where he'd left him. His eyes were wide open; there was a black hole in his throat. Brodie reached for his wrist anyway. He dropped it and started up when a man ran past him, out of the fog and into it again, escaping. He stood, helpless, holding his side, and let him get away.

O'Dunne dragged himself out of the doorway, his wounded leg scraping behind. "See if Flowers has got anything on him that says who he is."

"Why?"

"Because we're leaving him."

Brodie stood still. "What?"

The lawyer lay on one hip, propping himself up with an elbow. "Listen. We can't take a dead man with us, and we can't leave him here to be identified. None of this is happening. Understand? We're not here, Billy's not here. There's no cruiser in the harbor called the *Morning Star*. Get his belongings off his body now, Brodie, and then help me into the coach. Do it!"

Brodie went closer and stood over him. "You're a cold son of a bitch, O'Dunne."

The lawyer passed a hand over his sweating face and slid onto his back. "Do it anyway," he said, staring up at the invisible sky.

Brodie did it.

13

Anna heard the *diligence* when it was still in the street, clattering over the wet cobblestones. It wasn't dawn yet, but she was wide awake and staring at the ceiling, thinking the baker's wagon was getting to market early this morning, when she heard it stop before the gates to the villa. Seconds later she heard the screech of iron as the gates opened. She sprang out of bed and ran to the window. Brodie! Leading the horses inside by the harness, and now running back to shut the gates. The front door was locked, she must hurry. She snatched up her robe and ran out, buttoning it on the way downstairs. A loud pounding started before she reached the bottom step. She dashed across the hall, jerked the bolt back, and dragged the door open.

"Hush! The servants—Aiden?" She smothered a scream as he fell forward in a dead faint, almost on top of her.

Brodie cursed and hauled him back up with one arm around his waist. "Help me, Annie, I can't lift him by myself."

Immediately she went to Aiden's other side and got his heavy arm around her neck. He muttered something, and she felt his body lose some of its limpness. He was already half-conscious and able to help himself a little. Somehow they got him up the stairs. "The sofa," she panted, and they stretched him out on the priceless gold brocade in his filthy, bloodstained clothes. "What happened? Is it his leg?" She knelt down and touched the lawyer's white, sweating forehead.

"Aye, his leg. He's not quite as bad as he looks. He's—"

"We must get a doctor."

"Well, he says—"

O'Dunne's eyelids flickered open. "No doctor," he croaked. "Don't need one."

"He's delirious. Rouse the stableman, tell him to fetch—"

"Listen to me." O'Dunne's hand on her wrist was like a strong claw. "Brodie took the bullet out, cleaned the wound. It's mending; I can feel it." Anna raised astonished eyes to Brodie, then looked back at Aiden. The lawyer's strident tone softened. "Anna, I'm sorry. Everything we were afraid of—it's turned out to be the truth. All of it." He glanced up. "Show her."

Wasn't there a gentler way to tell her than this? But Brodie unbuttoned his shirt with one hand, awkwardly, pulled out the fat canvas bag, and dropped it on the floor. The string tie loosened; the contents scattered.

They could only see the top of her head as she

stared down at the stacks of bank notes on the carpet beside her. One hand trailed over them with a skittish, dazed touch. The two men met each other's eyes in a quick exchange. Then Brodie went down on one knee beside her.

"Greeley's a Confederate captain," he said quietly. "They outfitted the *Morning Star* in Majorca, and now she's an armed and armored frigate called the *Atlanta*. Nick arranged it. There's someone else at Jourdaine in on it too, but I couldn't learn his name." Maybe O'Dunne's way, clean and fast, was kindest. He put his hand on her shoulder when she swayed, and left it there to finish his story. "Two men tried to shoot me as I was leaving the wharf. They got Aiden in the leg. Billy's dead."

Her hair was down, hiding her face. But tears splashed on the white-knuckled hands gripping each other in her lap. He stroked the back of her head softly, needing to comfort, wanting to cry with her. She never moved. Only when O'Dunne reached out and touched her arm did she look up and finally let them see her face. Then they had to look away.

Her voice came out thick and nasal from weeping. "I still think you need a doctor."

Brodie knew a coward's relief: she wasn't going to deal with it now. O'Dunne started to explain that all he needed was sleep, in a bed that wasn't rocking, and after that some hot food. Brodie wanted to stay; God knew, if he could've helped her with any of it, he would've stayed. But he suspected that his was the last face she cared to see right now. Then too, if he didn't lie down soon, he was going to pass out. He mumbled something about his room. Aiden's eyes were already closed;

Anna was busy taking off his shoes and stockings. Brodie walked out, and climbed the stairs to his room clutching the bannister, just as dawn broke.

Anna knocked softly, one ear pressed to the door panel.

"Come in!" called Brodie.

She strode in. "I thought you'd be sleeping."

"I was, then I—"

"Why didn't you tell me you were hurt?" She went to where he was sitting, in a chair beside a small table in the center of the room. Behind him the doors to a minuscule balcony over the courtyard stood open. In the bright afternoon sunlight, she could see him clearly. "I'd never have known if Aiden hadn't just told me. You look awful. When were you planning to mention it, right before you died? Or were you just going to leave a note?"

He grunted his amusement. "I'm not hurt bad, Annie. But I can't get my shirt off. Give me a hand, will you?"

She clucked her tongue, hiding worry and nerves behind irritation. She thought he meant he was too stiff to push his already-unbuttoned shirt over his shoulders; but when she started to do it for him, he let out a yelp and flinched away from her. She jumped and they both went white. "What? What—"

"It's stuck to my skin," he gritted through his teeth. "Here, and here." He straightened his left arm stiffly, revealing the bloody wounds in his bicep and side. "The bullet went straight through and out the front. It's just a graze, but when the blood dried, my—Annie?"

"I'm fine." She'd dropped into the chair next to his and was supporting her wobbly head in one hand, elbow on the table. There was a light knock at the open door.

"Signora?" It was Magdalena with a bowl of warm water and some strips of toweling. Anna motioned, and she brought them to the table. When the maid hesitated, Brodie glanced back and forth between the two women, brows raised in a question.

His skeptical faith in her nursing skills stiffened Anna's resolve. "Grazie, Magdalena," she said dismissively, and rose. "Come to the bed, Mr. Brodie."

A host of wonderful responses crowded his tongue, but he bit them all back and followed docilely.

They sat side by side. "Can you hold this?" She passed the bowl to him and he put it between his knees. "Raise your arm. Just a little. Does it hurt?" He made a noncommittal sound while she laid a water-soaked strip of towel on the tattered and bloody shirt covering the wound in his side. Waiting for it to saturate the cotton and loosen it from his flesh, she held very still, hardly breathing. The sight of his wide, hard chest, sun-browned and finely muscled, rendered her extraordinarily uncomfortable, in part because of the unreasonable longing she felt to touch him. Just touch him. Astonishing how much she wanted it. To slide her fingertips over the fascinating corrugation of ribs and muscles along his sides. Tangle them in the soft hairs in the center of his chest. Press them in gentle, narrowing circles around his hard little nipples . . .

"Try it now."

She took the towel away with a little guilty start. As gently as she could, she began to peel the bloody fibers from his side.

"Ow!"

"Don't be such a baby."

That would've irked him if he hadn't seen how pale she'd gone when she'd hurt him. "Rip it off all at once," he advised, stiff-lipped.

"No."

"Go ahead."

"No. It would bleed too much. I'm almost finished."

He hoped so. It wasn't a serious wound, but this slow peeling hurt like the devil.

"There, it's done. Now your arm."

They repeated the soaking process on the inside of his bicep. This time they spoke while they waited.

"Who shot you?"

"Don't know. O'Dunne says Union agents trying to stop Nick's deal."

"But they didn't even take the money."

"No. I went through the dead one's pockets. He was from Firenze."

"Florence! Do you think he followed you all the way to Rome and then to Naples?"

He shook his head, meaning he didn't know.

She swallowed and asked softly, "Did Mr. Flowers suffer?"

"Annie, no, he didn't. He never knew what hit him. I wanted to bring him back, but Aiden said we had to leave him." Rightly, he realized now, though it still struck him as cold-blooded.

The tears she blinked out of her eyes spilled down her cheeks. "I liked him very much," she whispered.

"He liked you, too."

"He did?"

"Yeah. He thought you were the best."

They fell silent, thinking of Billy. A minute later she pulled the soaked shirt away from the gash in his arm, then set about cleaning both wounds.

"Aiden said you saved his life."

Brodie made a dismissive gesture with his good arm. "No more than he saved mine."

"He said you could've left him there and taken the money."

He grunted. "Are you surprised that I didn't?"

She stopped what she was doing, but didn't look at him. She wasn't really thinking of what to say; the answer was clear and immediate. But something was happening in the air between them that frightened her.

"Well, are you?"

She looked into his eyes. "No, I'm not surprised." It was an admission of so much more than what he'd asked. And now was not the time to think of it, not now when it was time to wrap bandages around his arm and upper body, reaching around behind him to retrieve the strips of cloth, all but embracing him. She finished the task in silence and then began to put away the blood-red bowl of water and the dirty swabs she'd used. "You should rest now." She pushed him down to the pillow gently and began covering him with the sheet. "I'll tell Magdalena to bring you—"

"Annie, sit down, don't leave me yet. I have to tell you something."

His face was set and grim, the hand tugging on her wrist almost pleading. She should bring the chair over, she thought, but he was pulling her down beside him and holding on so tightly. "What is it?"

Abruptly he let her go, and scrubbed at his

unshaven face with his hand. He put the back of his arm over his forehead and stared at the ceiling for a long time. Then he gave a brief, unamused laugh and plunged in. "Since I've got you in a believing mood, I thought I'd tell you a story. It's short and ugly, and I don't really know why I want you to hear it. But I do."

"I'm listening."

She was, with her hands folded in her lap, back straight, prim as the schoolteacher she could've been. He felt like putting his hand on her knee and just holding it there while he told his tale. It would've comforted him a great deal, that slender knee under his palm. But of course he couldn't. He wasn't allowed to touch her at all.

"This story starts in Bristol, four months ago. I'd just gotten my mate's certificate and I was waiting for my new ship to finish loading. I'd been in port a week, and hired on with a skipper from Norway for a run to Melbourne for wool. I was putting up at a seamen's boardinghouse near the docks and spending time with an old friend of mine. A woman. Her name was Mary Sloane." He took his arm away and looked at Anna directly. "I'd known her for four years or more. When I'd happen to be in Bristol, I'd always look her up. We . . . we'd be lovers for a few days, a week, and then I'd go away, maybe not see her for a year. I gave her money when I had it, and I knew there were other men who did the same. If that makes her a whore, it's your word, not mine. To me she was a friend."

He was staring at her intently, not letting her look away. She felt called upon to say something. "I understand," was all she could think of, in a small voice. But it wasn't true.

"On my last night, we went to a tavern and had a few pints of ale. When we were leaving, a little boy caught up to us in the street. He said a 'gentleman' who admired Miss Sloane and wished Mr. Brodie well wanted him to give us a bottle of wine. I stuck it under my arm and gave the boy a penny. I remember teasing Mary about her secret admirer, though she swore she had no idea who it might be. In my room, we opened the bottle and drank about half a glass each while we lay in bed. After that I don't remember anything until morning."

Anna brought her clasped hands up to her chest and rested her chin on them, waiting.

"Someone was pounding at the door. I stumbled up, feeling like I'd been keel-hauled in the night. It was the landlady. She started yelling at me, something about the maid coming three times with our breakfast, and then she broke off all of a sudden and started screaming. I turned to look, and there was Mary in the bed, white as the sheet, and blood staining the pillow all around her head. Her throat was cut. My bloody razor lay on the bed beside her."

He watched her cover the lower half of her face with her hands. The amber eyes above her splayed fingers stared at him in horror. He drew a long, shuddering breath and finished. "There was no wine bottle in the room. Our glasses were half-full of cheap rum. No one believed me about the boy, and he was never found. Mary didn't have an enemy in the world. So there was only me."

Anna lowered her hands. "The child?" she got out.

So O'Dunne had told her that, too. "Not mine.

Mary was three months gone. I'd been on the other side of the world."

In the midst of everything else she was feeling, she was conscious of a fierce, unaccountable relief that Brodie's baby hadn't been murdered.

"All the months I was in prison, I kept asking myself why. Nothing was stolen—hell, there wasn't anything to steal in the first place. Everybody loved Mary; she was a good, gentle person. I kept thinking whoever had done it was doing it to *me*, not her. But why? I've had fights with men, plenty of them, especially when I was younger. But even then, none of those men was my enemy. They were just drunk, or mean, or both. I still don't have any answer."

He stared at her a moment longer, but her rigidly composed features weren't giving anything away. Except sorrow. He put his forearm over his eyes and spoke into the air. "Story's over. I think I could sleep now. Maybe the maid could bring me something to eat in a couple of hours."

Anna stood. She retrieved the bowl of water from the table and went to the door. She turned. "Mr. Brodie?"

He grunted.

"Why did you tell me?"

He pulled his arm away at that, but kept his gaze on the wall in front of him. "So you would believe me." He swallowed. "Do you?"

Her answer came easily. "Yes. I knew before you told me that you had never killed anyone." She saw him close his eyes tight, then turn to her stiffly on one elbow.

"You can't—Annie, you can't know what that means to me."

She had one more question. *Were you in love with her?* But the words wouldn't come. And then she began to fear they would come and that he would answer. Time passed. Somehow she broke the connection between their gazes and got out of the room.

"Aiden, how much longer?"

"I'm almost finished."

"That's what you said five minutes ago."

"Your interruptions don't speed things along."

That shut her up. She glanced at Brodie, wondering if he could possibly be as calm as he looked. His fate hung on the words in the message Aiden was decoding with such agonizing slowness. Would he ever finish? She didn't remember the message they'd sent two days ago taking this long to *encode,* and she'd even helped him with that, reading the letters he was to substitute from the paper he'd been given by Mr. Dietz before leaving England.

She went to the drawing room window and looked out, trying to compose herself. It was silly to worry about what the London telegram would say. After what Brodie had discovered in Naples, surely it was only reasonable that Mr. Dietz would want him to continue the impersonation in Liverpool. Someone at Jourdaine was a thief, after all, perhaps even a murderer, and Mr. Brodie was still the key to finding out who that person was. Sending him back to Bristol now when his job was only half-finished would be foolish and unreasonable—out of the question. That was what logic told her. Her emotions weren't listening, though, and she was almost shaking from a deep and puzzling premonition of disaster.

She caught herself setting off on a new round of pacing, and made a forced detour to the window seat. If she didn't stop, she'd wear a trough in the expensive rose-colored carpet. Brodie still had his nose in a book. As usual. This time it was *The Origin of Species*. She'd never known anyone who liked to read as much as he did. Once she'd asked him about it; he'd told her he'd been away from books for fourteen years and was making up for lost time. But how could he do it at a time like this? Didn't he understand what this telegram meant?

"I'm finished."

"Thank God." She stood and went to the desk where Aiden sat and clasped her hands behind her back. "Read it." She glanced over at Brodie on the sofa. He shut his book, but didn't stand.

O'Dunne cleared his throat. His lawyer's face was expressionless. "'Acknowledge report of A.O'D. 3 June—'"

"A-O-D?" interrupted Anna.

"That's me."

"Oh." Of course. "Sorry."

"'Acknowledge report of A.O'D. 3 June. Matter of M.S.—' that's the *Morning Star*—'under advisement. Take no further action. Request re. J.B. denied; proceed at once to Bristol. Acknowledge receipt.' It's signed, 'R.D.'"

O'Dunne lined the message up four-square with the desk top, his fingers patting its edges carefully, over and over. The silence expanded. At last he looked up. Anna blocked his view of Brodie. She hadn't moved; she stood stock-still, paralyzed. He got to his feet, took up his crutch, and hobbled around the desk toward Brodie. "I'm sorry, John," he murmured. "I don't know what else I could've done, what more I could've told them. If I could think of anything—"

"Forget it. It's not your fault, Aiden, you did all there was to do." He stood too, restless. "It's only what we expected, isn't it? Nothing's changed. For a few days I hoped for something different, but now that's gone. I'm no worse off than I was a month ago." He was staring at Anna's rigid back, hardly listening to his own words. "'Proceed at once,' they say. I can be ready any time. But what about your leg?"

"It's much better. I could go tomorrow or the next day."

Anna whirled around. "Tomorrow! Aiden, so soon! You—you're not well enough, you still have pain. Why risk hurting yourself again? If the wound should open or become infected—"

"The wound is mending perfectly, Anna. There's nothing to keep me here."

"Oh, but—"

"What's the point in dragging it out? All that's left is to arrange for Brodie's 'funeral,' and the authorities in London will take care of that. You'll stay in Rome until you hear from me—a matter of a week or two, no more. You'll be told when to write home of your husband's sudden death. Your cousin Stephen will probably come for you. I'll insist on coming with him. It'll be over within a month, Anna. Then you can go home."

Home. Her hand crept to her throat. Her shocked eyes darted to Brodie, away, back again. "This is—" She held out her arm, then let it drop to her side. *Monstrous* was the word she wanted to say. But she couldn't say it to Brodie, not now. Not ever. She had to get out of the room, quickly, before something terrible happened. What? Something, some admission or confession. "Excuse me," was all she could think of to say, and then she dashed past Brodie and Aiden and out the door, all but running for the stairs.

14

Morning. At last. The sleepless hours after midnight had crawled by with a sluggishness that left Anna feeling exhausted and unreal. Her body ached with fatigue, but it was a relief to be out of bed, not staring dry-eyed any longer at the brightening square of gray light around her window. She put on her robe and slippers and went down the hall to the lavatory. A modern wonder, it contained a bathtub and washstand with running water, hot or cold, and a water closet exactly like the one in her father's new Liverpool mansion. But it also had a mirror, and in its honest, unforgiving depths she could see the full extent of last night's damage. She didn't even look like herself. At least she hoped not. This person had blue circles under her eyes, a pale, sickly complexion, and a grim, white-lipped trap for a mouth. She rested her forearms on the shelf under the mirror and leaned in, punishing herself with a good, long look. "You look like hell."

The words were out before she'd known she was thinking them, and for a second she was shocked and astonished. Then her own widening eyes struck her as ridiculous, and she said it again. "Hell, Anna. You look like *hell*." A little smile tugged at her lips. Brodie would say something like that. Except he'd call her Annie, and then wait for her to blush. She watched in sick fascination as her eyes filled with tears. *Brodie*, she mouthed into the mirror. Then shook herself. She was tired; what else could explain this heavy sadness, this—morbidity? Surely not the knowledge that he was leaving. That she would never see him again. That he would spend the rest of his life in prison. Anna put her head in her hands and wept.

In her heart she knew the telegram she'd sent to London last night—unbeknownst to Aiden, needless to say—would do no good. If he couldn't persuade them, how could she? She'd told them nothing he hadn't already—that Mr. Brodie was brave, he was trustworthy, he'd brought the money back when he could have escaped with it and left Aiden to die. Even as she'd composed it, she'd known it was futile, and yet she couldn't have done *nothing*, sat back and passively waited for events to occur. When Brodie left, tomorrow or the next day or the day after, perhaps she would be comforted a little by the knowledge that she had done everything she could. But she didn't really think so.

Walking back to her room, just as she got to the door, she heard a noise and turned around. And there he was in a shaft of early sunlight streaming in the window over the landing. Shoeless and shirtless. Watching her, his blue eyes grave. When he moved toward her his bare feet were soundless on the floorboards. She thought again that his body was perfect, and waited, fiercely calm, for him to come. At the moment he reached her, they heard someone coming down the third-floor staircase—a servant, perhaps Magdalena, on her way to her morning chores. Without a word, Brodie opened Anna's door, pulled her inside, and closed it. And then, glancing at her to make sure she was watching, he locked it.

She tried to feel shock. She ought to gasp, cry out, "How dare you?" or even scream. But she only stood there, clutching at her dressing gown and staring hard at him, acknowledging the terrible inevitability of this moment. Still, when he reached for her, something old and ingrained made her say, "No!"

"Yes."

Already his hands were inside her robe, pushing it over her shoulders, trying to touch her skin under her nightgown. "Don't," she whimpered, arching away, pulling on his wrists.

He took her face in both hands, holding gently, but his voice broke. "He wants to go today, Annie. *Today.*"

"Oh, no. Oh, no."

He began to kiss the tears that trickled down her cheeks. Her hands went to his naked sides so naturally and she stroked him almost absent-mindedly, her senses concentrated on what he was doing with his tongue. She forgot to breathe, forgot to be sad, while his soft breath on her face awoke and renewed her like a blessing. "John Brodie," she sighed against his skin, hardly knowing what she said.

But he heard, and the words snuffed out his last

scruple even as they made his heart hammer in his chest. Her damned nightgown buttoned in back, and patience had never been his strong suit. Reaching around, he grabbed the two halves and ripped, sending buttons flying everywhere.

It was a mistake. Real fear routed the desire he'd seen for a few seconds in her face. But it only made him change tactics; not even fleetingly did he think of letting her go. He moved in slowly, giving her time, and put his lips on hers in a long, sweet, gentle kiss. He could feel the tremors under his hands along her delicate vertebrae, and he stroked her in soothing, skillful circles. She calmed. Her eyes closed and she let him nibble her lips apart while his hands slid lower. Her head went back against the door. When she sighed, he sleeked his wet tongue between her lips, then her teeth, and tickled the roof of her mouth.

She drew in her breath and held still for him. Very soon it was more than she could stand, and a soft, growling moan started somewhere in the back of her throat. He pressed closer, hot and reckless, inflamed by the helpless, almost tortured sounds she was making. She jumped when he slid his hands to her bare buttocks, but he only held her closer, kissed her harder, until she wilted. He wanted her defenseless, out of control. Watching her eyes, he reached down and pulled her thighs apart in back. He covered her shocked gasp with his mouth and pressed into her, needing her to feel how hard he was. With his tongue he coaxed her, seduced her, drunk with passion and his power over her. The bed was too far away, he would take her here on the floor. But no—he wanted to see her naked on the rumpled sheets. He had her nightgown bunched around her waist; with an impatient tug he got it down over her hips and lifted her in his arms in the same movement.

Stunned, Anna pressed back against his chest with weak hands, too beleaguered, her senses too besieged, to be sure what to say to him. "No" wasn't quite it. "Wait!" That was it, and she got it out just before he put her on her back and lay on top of her.

"Wait" wasn't in Brodie's lexicon at that moment. She was frightened, but he would make it all right. The thought of not having Annie, of not sinking now, this minute, with blind, drowned abandon into the core of her, froze his blood and hurt his heart. His need was physical, but also more. Joining with her was a violent, death-denying compulsion he couldn't explain and only dimly comprehended. She was his last chance. At what? Life, decency, humanity. Love. He had to have her.

The fact of her own nakedness was so shocking, it cleared Anna's brain of rational thought and left her with only alarm and aroused nerve endings. She was aware that Brodie was fumbling with his trousers. She had to make a decision. Quick. He sank down on his elbow to kiss her nipples, and then she thought she would delay making the decision; at the moment she hadn't enough resources. His soft, tugging lips made her groan. She hadn't known about this; this hadn't been in any of her father's books. She arched upward with her hips and his hand was there, right over her woman's place, urgent and inescapable. And searching, the fingers sleeking wetly inside, making her shift and writhe against his palm.

He took his hand away and she knew what was next. Last chance. She flexed her thighs together and pushed against his chest with all her strength. "Don't," she said clearly, looking him in the eye.

Something like amusement flickered across his taut face, as if she'd just told him a joke. He bent over and her arms collapsed weakly and foolishly between them. His kiss took her breath away while it told her, with great tenderness, to quit being silly. She tried one last time to stop him, by reaching down to cover herself with her hand. But she jerked it away when it encountered his enormous, prodding maleness, and he used the opportunity to part her legs again with his knees.

She was so small. He must go slowly, gently, conquer this need to bury himself in her at once. He kissed her closed eyelids and whispered her name against them. His arms tightened around her waist and he pushed higher. Her head went back and he nuzzled her throat, murmuring, moving in her.

Anna gritted her teeth and squeezed her eyes shut. So. This was intercourse. Dear God, it was as bad as she'd feared—worse. She felt angry and cheated, and hoped it would end soon. How long did it take? And whose idea had it been to make something that began so gloriously end in such sheer, grinding agony? Not God's; surely the devil's. At least it seemed to be finished; Brodie had stopped his painful thrusting and was staring at her with an expression that said he'd found it as horrifying as she. She turned her head to dry her tears on the pillow, ashamed to let him see she was a crybaby. "Is it over?" she sniffed, not able to look at him just yet.

"Oh, Jesus Christ God almighty. You're a virgin."

"I *was* a virgin," she corrected testily. "Would

you please get off me now? I can't breathe."

"Oh my God, Annie. Oh, no."

"Well, what difference does it make?" she panted, shoving at his body that had suddenly gone heavy and lifeless on her.

He scrambled to his knees with a groan and reached for her. "I didn't know, I swear. I thought you and Nick must've made love. Oh, baby——"

She wrenched her hands away and sat up, facing away from him, legs hanging over the side of the bed. It was stupid, but she couldn't make herself walk across the room and put on her robe because she didn't want him to see her naked. "Well, we didn't. Not that it's any of your business." She felt silly saying that to him, in bed, both of them stark naked, as if he'd made some impolite inquiry about her finances. But the lifelong habit of propriety was all that was getting her through these, the most uncomfortable minutes of her life, and she wasn't about to give it up.

They didn't? *They didn't?* His brother, thought Brodie, must've been a eunuch. He stared at her beautiful white back and thought of all he wanted to say to her. Where should he start? Apologies had never worked very well with her. But when he thought of how he must have hurt her, his heart twisted and he knew he had to try again.

"Annie." He put one finger on her spine, between her shoulder blades. She shuddered and dropped her head. "Annie, we——"

There was a soft knock at the door. Anna shot up like a geyser and Brodie made a grab for his pants. "Anna?" came Aiden O'Dunne's voice through the panel. "Are you awake?"

She threw a glance of sheer panic back at Brodie and crept forward, hugging herself. "Yes?" she quaked in a rising glissando.

O'Dunne's voice was subdued but excited. "I've got good news. A messenger just came with another telegram. Listen: 'Earlier decision set aside; ignore previous dispatch. Request re J.B. granted. Proceed to Liverpool, await further word.' Isn't it wonderful?"

Anna made a noise.

"Brodie's still asleep, I can't even rouse him. Hurry and come down, will you? We'll tell him together. All right?"

She got it out on the second try. "Yes."

They listened to the thumping sound of his crutch diminish and recede. An inner voice told Brodie that to fall back on the bed and roar with relieved laughter was not what was called for at this moment. He watched Anna stalk stiffly across the floor and retrieve her dressing gown, keeping her pretty backside to him, and thrust her arms in the sleeves with nervous, choppy movements. She knotted the sash around her waist as if she wanted to cut herself in two. Their tryst, he surmised, was over. He stood and pulled on his trousers, while part of his mind took in the bright smear of blood on the sheet he'd just vacated. She faced him, visibly pulling herself together, seeming about to make a speech.

"Mr. Brodie."

He knew he was in for it. Her withdrawal was a palpable thing, leaving him empty and hurting. Facetiousness came to his rescue. "Mrs. Balfour," he said in the same tone, making her a slight bow.

Her nostrils flared. "I feel the most terrible remorse for what I've done. I will pay for it the rest of my life with guilt and self-reproach." And it wasn't even any good, an irreverent voice inside reminded her. "But," she went on doggedly, "I won't accept the whole burden of responsibility. Much of this was your fault. You seduced me, and I will never forgive you for that."

Brodie put his hands on his hips. "It wasn't that hard to do," he pointed out ungallantly. "You wanted it too, almost as much as I did."

Scrupulous honesty wouldn't let her deny this insulting observation. "I may have 'wanted it,'" she retorted, lips thinning with distaste, "but only at first. It turned out to be just as disgusting as I had always heard."

That stung. "Only because it was your first time, for God's sake. Don't you know *anything*?"

She drew herself up. "I would expect you to say that! It's probably what all men say, to entice women to try the dreadful thing a second time!" He snorted. "In one way I'm grateful to you, Mr. Brodie, for solving the mystery: now I'll never waste another minute worrying or wondering what—" she could hardly get it out—"the marriage act is like."

Brodie muttered a curse and moved toward her, holding his arm out.

She jumped back. "Don't come near me or I'll scream!" He stopped and glowered. "Once you promised never to touch me again. Obviously your word is worthless. It seems we're going to be together in England for an indefinite length of time. I want no more of your promises, but I have one for you: If you ever put so much as a fingernail on my body again, I will tell Aiden you tried to rape me. *That* will send you back to prison fast enough!"

He folded his arms. "You know, Annie, you say a lot of things that sound to me like dares. It's lucky I'm a gentleman; otherwise—"

"Ha!"

"Otherwise I might have to take you up on them." He came closer. "You're bluffing anyway," he taunted. "You won't say anything about me to O'Dunne."

"That may have been true before, but no more!"

"No, you won't. You know why? Because ruining me would ruin you. Your precious reputation. Think about it." He smiled evilly.

"Villain!" she cried, seeing his point.

"Villain?" he repeated, exasperated. "Is that the best you can do? Can't you even say 'bastard'?"

"Get out."

"What about 'son of a bitch'? Can you say that?"

"Out!"

"Try. Honestly, you'd feel a lot better. That's one of your biggest problems, you know, not being able to *say* so many things. You use all these— what's the word? Euphemisms. Just now is a good example, when you said 'the marriage act.'" He grinned, then laughed. "Come on, Annie, let's call it by its name. We weren't engaged in the *marriage act*. What we were doing was—"

"Stop it! Get out! Now, you—" She ground her teeth with fury. He waited, his brows raised encouragingly. "Bastard!" Her hand went to her throat; tears swam in her eyes. "There," she whispered, "you've finally brought me down to your level. Are you satisfied?"

He closed the distance between them in two strides. She wouldn't allow herself to cringe, not even when he put his big hand on the side of her face and held it there so gently. "No, I'm not satisfied," he murmured, blue eyes blazing into hers. "But I will be. And so will you, sweet Annie. That's a promise I mean to keep." She sagged when he dropped his hand and moved to the door. "Hurry and put your clothes on," he said in his normal voice, his hand on the doorknob. "Remember? Aiden wants you to be there when he tells me the good news."

PART TWO

15

"I don't understand it. It makes no sense."

"What's that, my love?"

Anna ground her teeth, but kept her gaze focused through the carriage window on the gold stripe in the distance that was the Mersey at sunset. Brodie had hardly missed an opportunity to call her "my love" all day, not since they'd left Aiden at Southampton. "I don't understand," she enunciated, "why no one met us at the railway station."

"Maybe they didn't get the message. Or maybe they didn't feel like waiting after the train was two hours late."

Her shoulders moved in an irritable shrug. The Channel crossing last night had been rough and sleepless, they'd sat in a hot, noisy, overcrowded railway car all day, and she was in no mood for reasonable explanations about anything. She was exhausted and keyed up, and Brodie's unwavering chipperness had begun to get on her nerves. "Perhaps," she conceded tersely.

"'Perhaps,'" he repeated. "I always say 'maybe.' Which did Nick say?"

She considered. "'Perhaps,' I think. But probably both."

"'Perhaps,'" he said again, practicing.

"This is the street I live on." She began to straighten her flowered hat, patting the upswept hair at the back of her head.

Brodie whistled and craned his neck to see the tops of the four-story mansions lining both sides of the wide, tree-draped avenue. "Lucky girl, Mrs. Balfour. I've been to Liverpool plenty of times, but I was never this far inland."

Inland? She lived a mile up the hill from the river. But to a sailor, she supposed that might seem inland. Suddenly she sat up straight. "Oh, dear heaven."

"What?"

"Look."

"What?"

"All the carriages—that's my house—Aunt Charlotte's having a party! For us!"

Brodie cursed colorfully.

"Oh—*blast*!" Anna had begun to discover the satisfactions of swearing herself. They were tired, hungry, not at their best; she'd hoped to arrive in as low-key a manner as possible, attracting the least amount of attention, and confront the perils of impersonation in the morning. Oh, she could shake Aunt Charlotte for this! No doubt she'd thought of some social advantage, Anna guessed cynically; it wouldn't surprise her if some visiting duchess or viscount were in town.

"Well, love, it's too late to turn around and find

a hotel, so we might as well—" Brodie's eyes narrowed, his head jutted farther out the carriage window, and he lost his train of thought. "*That's* your *house*?"

"Yes. Now listen—"

His laugh cut her off. "No, seriously. That's the public library, isn't it?"

Distracted, Anna focused on the enormous red brick mansion she'd lived in for the last three years, taking note of the arched stone entranceway, dramatic peaked gables, functionless concrete pilasters. It hadn't struck her in precisely that way before, but now that he mentioned it its resemblance to a municipal building was undeniable—although she would deny it to Mr. Brodie with her dying breath. "How would you know what a public library looks like?" she snapped. "Now, listen to me. I don't know who my aunt may have invited, but most of them are sure to be people you're supposed to know. I've told you about most of them, but not all. Stay close to me and listen carefully; I'll try to say everyone's name before you have to speak. And for heaven's sake, say as little as possible. Pretend you're tired." Unconsciously she began to twist her fingers as her palms grew damp inside her gloves. She reminded herself that the Middaughs had had no trouble believing he was Nicholas; that ought to give her heart. Oh, but now he would be meeting dozens of people who had known Nicholas much better than they! The more she thought of it, the more nervous she grew. "Try to remember that a—a great deal depends on your credibility tonight," she told him. A very great deal; Mr. Brodie had no idea how much. Which was no doubt a very good thing.

The carriage came to a halt in front of Rosewood. Brodie knew it was "Rosewood" because the name was chiseled discreetly in one of the huge stone columns flanking a flagstone walk to the front steps. "Oh, I'll stay close to you, Annie," he said cheerfully as he helped her down to the curb, then kept his hands on her long after it was necessary. She reacted with inner violence, although her face remained a mask of composure. It was the first time he'd touched her since that horrible morning in Rome three weeks ago. The fact that the simple pressure of his fingers on her sides could take her breath away confirmed an awful, fatalistic suspicion she'd harbored in secret for twenty-one days. But she would not think about it now.

She spoke quietly, fearful that they were already being watched. "For the hundredth time, *Nicholas did not call me that*."

"He started to on the honeymoon. He started doing lots of new things on the honeymoon. Say, Annie, would you like me to carry you across the threshold?"

"Would you like me to kick you in the shins?" With a lurch of horror, she realized she had almost said "groin." She twisted out of his grip and started up the walk without him, not caring at the moment who saw what. Oh, he was impossible!

The front door swung open and the imposing figure of Aunt Charlotte stood four-square in the threshold. "You're late! We expected you hours ago."

"The train was late, Aunt Charlotte," Anna explained breathlessly, kissing her. "I see you invited a few friends in." She glanced over her aunt's shoulder at the people milling in the foyer and, behind them, the large drawing room.

"To welcome you home, dear. It's a surprise. Is your baggage still at the station? Nicholas," she exclaimed, allowing him to plant a peck on her florid cheek, "what did you do to your face? I would hardly have known you! Come in, come into the drawing room. I'd thought of an informal receiving line, just the two of you, but now it's so late—"

"Oh, no, please let's not," begged Anna. She took Brodie's hand and began to follow her aunt down the wide hall. Friends crowded around immediately, slowing their progress. "Edward, how are you? Mrs. Griffin, it's lovely to see you. Why, Esther Perkins, hello!" She named them all relentlessly, feeling foolish, and Brodie dutifully echoed her. Everyone exclaimed over his beardlessness, his fading scar, how much marriage seemed to agree with him.

Finally they reached the drawing room, where there were more guests and more greetings. A surprise wedding reception was the worst thing in the world that could have happened, but she'd have felt churlish saying so to Aunt Charlotte. By eloping she had, after all, cheated her aunt out of the opportunity to host one for her at the more conventional time—immediately after the ceremony. But what horrible timing for it now! She stole a glance at Brodie, and relaxed ever so slightly. She loathed admitting it, but when he wanted to he could be as charming as his brother. Still, it astonished her that people were accepting him so readily as Nicholas, for to her they hardly resembled each other at all anymore. Guests commented on his suntanned skin, and guessed that he'd spent much of his trip to Italy out of doors.

More than one observed that they hardly recognized him without his beard. It was working. Dear God, it was working! She wanted to laugh and cry at the same time. It was as if a balloon were inflating in her chest, filling her with a nerve-wracking combination of dread and euphoria.

Brodie felt the pressure of her hand in his and suppressed his own shiver of excitement. Christ almighty, it was working. At least for now. But what a powerful relief it was to know that, as long as all he had to do was grin like a fool and shake hands, everybody thought he was Nick. But God! what he wouldn't give right now for a cigarette.

"Jenny!" cried Anna.

But Brodie didn't need the name to know who this flame-haired girl hurling herself into Anna's arms was. He'd heard so much about Jenny, he felt as if she were *his* cousin. To him she gave a sisterly kiss on the cheek, and said what everyone else was saying—"Gracious, Nicholas, I hardly knew you!" She was lively and talkative and very pretty. She wore her shiny, reddish-orange hair loose and rather short, in a style that wasn't fashionable but was definitely attractive. Her pale yellow dress had a low, off-the-shoulder decolletage. She liked to shake her head flirtatiously, calling attention to her drop earrings. He watched her as she chattered excitedly to Anna, and soon he made a further observation, one he'd have bet money on: Jenny was the kind of girl who would let a man examine her brooch without taking it off first.

She backed up a step and slid her arm through that of the young man who'd been standing behind her. "Welcome home, newlyweds," he said in a bored voice and held a hand out to Brodie. He was tall, gaunt, and dissipated, and he smelled of drink.

"Hello, Neil," said Anna hurriedly.

Neil Vaughn, Brodie remembered, Nick's new friend. Anna didn't like him, though she'd never come straight out and said so. He had light, peculiar eyes that might've been blue once but now seemed bleached, perhaps from drink, to a cold, lifeless gray.

Is Jenny seeing Neil now? wondered Anna, eyeing their clasped arms. How odd, if so. Jenny was so vivacious, and Neil was—she didn't really know what Neil was. She wondered what Aunt Charlotte made of it. Neil was rich, she'd heard, but her aunt would require Jenny's successful suitor to have family connections as well as money. No one knew much about Neil Vaughn's family.

"So you finally came home."

She started at the sound of that stern, familiar voice, unsure as always whether the gruffness in it was feigned or not. "Papa," she said softly, rushing to him. Sir Thomas Jourdaine sat hunched in a wheeled chair, hands open limply on the blanket across his knees. She put her arms around his neck and gave him a long, gentle hug. Before it was over he batted her away, with a mixture of irritation and affection, and peered up at his new son-in-law. "Got tired of looking at statues, did you?" he said querulously, with a slight slur.

Brodie saw that the left side of his face was all but immobile when he spoke. "Yes, sir," he answered, taking Thomas's veiny old hand and holding it. Anna had said her father was ill, but he hadn't been prepared for this. He glanced at her;

she seemed disturbed at the sight of him, too. "It's good to be home, sir."

"You've got it all now, boy," the old man said cryptically, then explained. "Even my room. They've got me on the first floor now—turned my study into a bedroom, damned if they didn't."

"Papa," breathed Anna, shocked.

He waved her off. "Now it's you and Anna who'll run everything. Out with the old, in with the new." What started as a harsh laugh ended in a painful fit of coughing. Sir Thomas pulled a handkerchief from his sleeve and buried his mouth in it while Anna hovered over him, patting his shoulder, touching his back. Brodie stood by helplessly, filled with sympathy for this crusty old wreck of a man. Even so, another part of his mind couldn't help gloating over the thought of himself and Anna alone, together, in Thomas's old bedroom, tonight, as soon as this damned party was over.

"Will you be in to work tomorrow, do you think?" asked a man Brodie hadn't noticed until now. He was a younger version of Thomas, with the same brown eyes and determined mouth, but without the massive, bulging forehead that gave his uncle, even in his diminished condition, a look of bullish authority. Anna's hurried "Stephen" wasn't necessary; Brodie knew who he was. He watched her embrace her cousin quickly, noting little warmth between them.

"Tomorrow I think Anna and I will take some time to recover from our trip," Brodie said smoothly, shaking hands. "Aiden's due back from Scotland tomorrow, isn't he? I'll be in on Wednesday, Stephen. Bright and early."

Stephen Meredith nodded as his mouth tightened disapprovingly, and Brodie felt a faint but definite chill.

Thomas began to cough again. The heavyset, humorless-looking woman who had been standing behind his chair held a clean handkerchief to his purplish lips. "Sir Thomas will be retiring now," she announced with a darting look of challenge. Miss Fitch was her name, Brodie recalled. Anna couldn't stand her.

Anna hugged her father again—he hardly seemed to notice—and Miss Fitch wheeled him smartly from the room.

A gaggle of young women friends effectively surrounded her then, all talking at once, demanding to know everything about her wedding trip. Brodie wanted to hear her soft-spoken responses, but Cousin Stephen came and stood in front of him, blocking his view.

"If you're not coming in tomorrow, perhaps you could spare time now to answer a quick question."

"At your service," he said easily.

"They're laying the keel for that deepwater brig for the Norwegians tomorrow. How much hog spring do you want to allow for?"

Brodie stared, then blinked to keep his eyes from glazing over. Hog spring? He squeezed the bridge of his nose, squinting at the ceiling. "Let me see. Let's say . . ." *Hog spring*? What the hell was that? You "allowed" for it. Some compensating measurement, then. Could it be the natural sag of the keel before the ship was launched? What if it wasn't? He could feel his neck getting hot.

A ripple of feminine laughter sounded from behind Stephen. Brodie glanced over, as if distracted by it, and caught Anna's eye. His expression must have communicated panic; she excused herself prettily and came to him. The surprise on her face was comical when he took her hands and then, as if on impulse, pulled her into a very close, very intimate embrace. Guests stared or looked away, according to their inclinations, while he seemed to nuzzle the hair at the base of her neck and nibble at her earlobe. All who knew the Anna Jourdaine of old were stunned and amazed to see her not only accept these unsuitable public endearments but actually return them in kind, with no show of remorse except the deep pink flush staining her cheeks afterward. From across the room, her aunt was heard to make shocked clucking sounds.

"I—believe I'll have some punch," Anna declared breathlessly, backing up and giving her husband a stiff and peculiar little wave before moving off toward the sideboard.

With a twisted smile, Brodie watched her go. It was a moment before he heard Stephen say, "Well? How much, Nick?" His distaste was poorly disguised. "If it's not too much trouble, I'd like to be able to tell them first thing in the morning."

Brodie hooked his thumbs in the armholes of his vest, as Anna had told him Nick used to do. "Oh, sorry; I got sidetracked. Hog spring, was it? Well, let's see—she's to be a hundred and seventy-five feet long, isn't she?"

"A hundred and seventy-eight."

"Mm. Let's give her two and a quarter inches, then. They can dub the top block afterward, and fay it to the bottom of the keel. All right?"

Stephen nodded, satisfied. Brodie almost laughed his relief out loud.

After that, things got easier. People asked him

casual questions—how had he liked Italy, had he seen the ruins, how were his lodgings? He had no trouble answering; O'Dunne had spent no small amount of time preparing him and Anna for just such questions during the journey home, to insure that they told the same stories. Brodie chatted easily, noting that Nick's men friends were cordial but showed him more respect than warmth, as if they were afraid or unwilling to loosen up too much with him. His women friends, on the other hand, had no trouble showing warmth, or loosening up. He glanced around for Anna; she was surrounded by another group of eager welcomers. But she looked up and their eyes met, and they exchanged a quick message that said all was well. For now.

A small orchestra was tuning up in what looked to Brodie like another drawing room, attached to this room but cleared of rugs and furniture and all the knickknacks and bric-a-brac and folderol that cluttered this one. Jenny flounced up to him and took hold of his arm in a friendly grip. "Dance with me, Nick! We've been waiting all afternoon for you and Anna to come." She pulled on him playfully.

Brodie knew nothing about upper-class social protocol, but common sense told him he ought to dance the first dance with his wife. He said so.

"Oh, pooh! Anna hardly ever dances, you know that." She pulled harder, smiling up at him with winsome determination. "Come on, Nick. Why be so formal? If we start, then everyone can dance. Please?"

It would be rude to keep saying no. Smiling uneasily, Brodie let himself be led through the archway into the smaller drawing room, and he and Jenny began to dance a waltz.

"Oh," said Milly Pollinax, Anna's best friend, in a matter-of-fact tone, "Jenny and Nick are dancing." She raised a perfect black brow and looked across Anna's shoulder.

Anna turned slowly, remembering to widen her lips in a pleased smile at the last minute. "Yes," she agreed, on the same note. Jenny, she saw, was at her most animated, eyes sparkling with excitement, face flushed, talking and talking and talking. Brodie smiled down at her indulgently—*fondly*, Anna would have to say. She felt a peculiar coldness when Jenny moved her hand from his shoulder to the side of his smooth-shaven chin and said something that made him throw his handsome head back and laugh. He never laughed at anything *she* said, it suddenly occurred to her. At least, nothing she said deliberately. She turned toward Milly again. "How's George?" she asked, hardly knowing what she was saying. Milly's long pause finally captured her full attention, though not as much as her answer. "I've left him."

"What?" Her jaw dropped. She took hold of Milly's hands, seeing for the first time the pain in her friend's dark, lovely eyes, the lines of tension around her mouth.

"No one knows yet. Needless to say, your aunt would never have asked me to come today if she had."

"Milly, I'm so sorry!"

"I'm not. I'm happier than I've been in years. I only wish I'd done it sooner."

She didn't look happy to Anna. Someone was waving to her across the way. "We can't talk now. Where are you staying? I'll come and see you tomor—"

"No," Milly said firmly, pressing her fingers. "You can't come. Write to me if you—"

"What do you mean? Of course I'll come."

"No, Anna. Think for a second. I mean to divorce George. I'm about to become a fallen woman," she said on a grim little laugh. "Decent society will have to cast me out."

"Don't be absurd!"

"Your aunt will see to it that our friendship is finished. And she's right, because knowing me would only hurt you, your position in—"

"I can't believe I'm hearing this," Anna hissed, ready to shake her. "Tell me where you're staying."

"In Lord Street, but—"

"I'll come tomorrow." The words were barely out when she felt a too-familiar hand on her arm and turned to see Brodie grinning down at her wolfishly.

"Care to dance, Annie?"

She saw Milly's eyes widen a trifle at the new nickname. She considered turning him down, still piqued because she was his second choice, but quickly saw the folly in that. "Yes, I'd love to." She squeezed her friend's hand one last time. "Tomorrow," she repeated, and moved toward the dance floor with Brodie.

Other couples were dancing now. She stepped into his arms stiffly, endeavoring to hold herself away from him. "Nicholas didn't dance like this!" she whispered when he pulled her closer, so close that their bodies touched and she had to tilt her head sideways to see him.

His mouth curved in a smile and he raised one silky eyebrow. "He's a changed man," he murmured, sliding his thumb across her knuckles in a slow and suggestive rhythm. "Now he can't keep his hands off his wife."

"Or his wife's cousin," she blurted out, then bit her tongue. Another of his lazy smiles antagonized her. "Not that it's anything to me." To her amazement, he bent his head and kissed the tip of her nose. "What are you *doing*?"

"Acting like a bridegroom. Stop scowling, Annie, people will think we don't like each other."

"We don't. Oh, I might've known you'd try to take advantage of the situation," she seethed, trying with little success to keep her expression pleasant. "But I can assure you it'll do you no good."

He leaned in. "It's already doing me good." He chuckled at the look on her face as she realized his meaning. People watched them with fond, tolerant expressions; under cover of the music, their words were inaudible to all but each other. "Why didn't Stephen like Nick?" he asked abruptly.

"Stephen? He did like him." She frowned, and reconsidered. "Perhaps they weren't friends, but they got along fairly well. Why would you think otherwise?"

"A feeling. A strong one."

"Well . . ." Some devil made her say it. "Maybe Stephen was jealous."

"Of what?"

"Of you—of Nicholas. He asked me to marry him once."

"Your *cousin* asked you to *marry* him?"

His look of astonishment irritated her inordinately. "You find that hard to believe?"

"I certainly do."

"Well, thank you very much indeed." She almost jerked away, she was so riled.

A Special Offer For Leisure Historical Romance Readers Only!

Get Four FREE* Romance Novels

A $21.96 Value!

Thrill to the most sensual, adventure-filled Historical Romances on the market today…

FROM  LEISURE BOOKS

As a home subscriber to the Leisure Historical Romance Book Club, you'll enjoy the best in today's BRAND-NEW Historical Romance fiction. For over twenty-five years, Leisure Books has brought you the award-winning, high-quality authors you know and love to read. Each Leisure Historical Romance will sweep you away to a world of high adventure…and intimate romance. Discover for yourself all the passion and excitement millions of readers thrill to each and every month.

SAVE AT LEAST *$5.00* EACH TIME YOU BUY!

Each month, the Leisure Historical Romance Book Club brings you four brand-new titles from Leisure Books, America's foremost publisher of Historical Romances. EACH PACKAGE WILL SAVE YOU AT LEAST $5.00 FROM THE BOOKSTORE PRICE! And you'll never miss a new title with our convenient home delivery service.

Here's how we do it. Each package will carry a 10-DAY EXAMINATION privilege. At the end of that time, if you decide to keep your books, simply pay the low invoice price of $16.96 ($17.75 US in Canada), no shipping or handling charges added*. HOME DELIVERY IS ALWAYS FREE*. With today's top Historical Romance novels selling for $5.99 and higher, our price SAVES YOU AT LEAST $5.00 with each shipment.

AND YOUR FIRST FOUR-BOOK SHIPMENT IS TOTALLY FREE

IT'S A BARGAIN YOU CAN'T BEAT! A Super $21.96 Value!

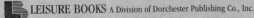 **LEISURE BOOKS** A Division of Dorchester Publishing Co., Inc.

"Steady as she goes," he said softly, holding on, pulling her even closer. "It doesn't surprise me that any man would want to marry you, sweet Annie. But I can't see you and your cousin together, that's all. He's not your type."

Unwillingly mollified, she relaxed slightly. "I didn't think so either," she admitted into the air over his shoulder. She remembered how much Stephen's proposal had surprised her. It had come soon after T.J.'s death. She'd turned him down gently, flattered but privately amazed that he could think of her in that way. She thought of him only as Cousin Stephen, older, remote, a rather formal man. She saw him now across the way, standing beside her aunt. They had the same faded reddish hair, the same upright posture, the same—stuffiness.

The dance ended. Instead of letting her go, Brodie joined his hands behind her back, keeping her in a loose clasp. "I like your father."

She had to lean back in his arms to see his face. The impropriety of this was making her squirm; she could feel the attention of the nearby guests on them again. "Please let me go," she muttered without moving her lips.

"What I like most about him is his generosity. When are all these people going to go away, Annie, so you and I can go up to your father's old room? Wasn't it thoughtful of him to give it to us?"

Her scowl faded; she almost smiled. "Indeed, yes. Father's a very generous man."

Now Brodie scowled. Something was wrong. She wasn't worried nearly enough.

Anna felt a sharp pressure on her arm and turned to face her aunt.

"Are you having a nice time, dear?" She drew

Anna away from Brodie as she spoke, smiling an
insincere apology.

"Yes, very. It was . . . kind of you to think of a
homecoming party." She wouldn't call it a wedding reception; it might lay her open to untimely
recriminations. Aunt Charlotte had forgiven her,
by letter, for eloping, but it seemed best to steer
clear of that subject for now.

"You're quite welcome. It was fortunate that the
Steubens of Bath happened to be passing through
town this week. But I don't believe you've spoken
to them yet."

That mystery was solved: this wasn't a party for
her and Nicholas at all, it was for the Steubens of
Bath. "No, I haven't seen them. Where—"

"You've been a bit wrapped up in other things,
haven't you?" The hand on Anna's wrist tightened
almost painfully. They were in a vacant alcove
between the two drawing rooms, with no guests
nearby to overhear them. Her aunt's voice
changed; she gave up all pretense of graciousness.
"What you do is out of my control now; you're a
married woman, and I'm only a guest in your
home."

"Oh, Aunt—"

"But I will say this anyway, out of a sense of
duty and for your own good." The massive bosom
expanded on a deep breath, and Anna dreaded
what was coming. "The behavior I've witnessed
tonight between you and Nicholas has shocked me
deeply. What might've been acceptable in that
libertine country you've just come from is quite
the reverse here."

"But—we're married!"

"What has that to do with anything?"

Anna blinked, at a loss.

"Do you suppose the bare fact of a wedding absolves you from any further responsibility to conduct yourself with propriety and decency?"

"No, of course—"

"If anything, you'd better take care to guard every aspect of your behavior even more closely than before."

"Why?" Anna cried in dismay. It didn't seem possible that she could be any more circumspect, any more rigid in her deportment than she had been in all the years before she'd married Nicholas. The very thought of trying made her go limp with depression.

"*Because you eloped.*" Aunt Charlotte gave her wrist a quick, vicious shake, and the anger in her eyes flared undisguised for an instant. "Three weeks before your wedding! Do you understand how that looks? Do you realize what people have been thinking—and in all likelihood saying?"

Anna swallowed, flushing hotly. No, she could honestly say she'd never given that aspect of her elopement a single thought. "I can't control what people think or say. I've done nothing to be ashamed of, and I won't be made to feel guilty because I'm in love with my husband." Her voice shook; she took a deep breath to steady it. "I've apologized to you for my hasty marriage; I thought you'd forgiven me. I'm sorry if anything I've done tonight has offended you or your friends, and I promise to take care that it doesn't happen again."

Her aunt's mollified face ought to have relieved her; instead it added fuel to the fire of a seething, sizzling anger that lay just below her embarrassment. A part of her wanted to murmur, "You're

right, Aunt, I'm so ashamed," while another—a
reckless, unfamiliar part—wanted to shout,
"Mind your own business, you hidebound, petty-
minded old prig!"

"Good," Aunt Charlotte purred, abruptly all
smiles and goodwill. She took Anna's arm in a
kinder grasp and steered her out of the alcove
toward the door to the hall. "Then we won't need
to speak of it again, will we? There's a cold supper
in the dining room, dear; shall we begin shepherd-
ing the guests in?"

"Yes, let's," Anna agreed grimly. "Otherwise
they'll be here all night."

Out of the corner of his eye, Brodie watched
them go.

"Well, Nick," drawled Neil Vaughn, smiling his
cynical smile and leaning against the wall for
support. The alcohol on his breath was stronger
now, although to Brodie's absolute knowledge,
Aunt Charlotte's blackberry punch was unadulter-
ated.

"Well, Neil," he returned in the same tone.
Anna hadn't been able to tell him much about
Vaughn; he'd only known Nick a few months, and
his past was unclear. His principal interests were
gambling and, if Brodie had correctly interpreted
Anna's highly oblique reference, woman-chasing.

"I've been seeing Jenny," Neil announced casually. "You don't mind, do you?"

"No, why should I?" But he thought he knew
why.

Neil shrugged, dismissing it as unimportant. He
took a sip from his punch cup. "So. Was the
honeymoon as drab as you anticipated?"

Brodie's hand tightened a fraction around his

own cup. "It had a few compensating features."

Neil expelled air from his lungs, his version of a laugh. "Really? Congratulations, my friend. They say it's the quiet ones who surprise you."

He managed an icy smile.

"I hope this doesn't mean you won't be joining me anymore at Mrs. Sprague's."

Now his smile wouldn't come at all. There wasn't a doubt in his mind that Mrs. Sprague ran a brothel. "Not at all," he said on a false chuckle. "But perhaps not in the immediate future."

Neil laughed again. "Name the day, my friend. The moment the charm of legalized copulation begins to pall, you let me know."

Brodie followed Neil's lazy, speculative gaze across the room to where Anna was guiding an elderly lady out into the hall, gentle-handed, smiling kindly at something the old girl was saying. He felt his body harden with suppressed violence, and wondered at himself. He had the strongest urge to drive a fist into Neil's bony, leering face.

"Come out with me for a drink after this is over, Nick."

"Not tonight, I'm dead on my feet." He tried to sound regretful. "Another time, soon." The prospect held no appeal. Vaughn disturbed him. He couldn't get the right rhythm with him, couldn't fathom what his relationship with Nick had been. And for once, he couldn't ask Anna.

Something made him look up. She was there, standing in the doorway. Hands clasped at her waist, watching him quietly across the nearly empty room. Patient, demure. Lovely. Neat and compact and competent in her plum-colored dress with the prim white collar. For a heartbeat in time

Brodie let himself think of what it would be like if she were really his wife. Something in his chest expanded, with fright. Because it would be so easy to belong to her. The easiest thing he'd ever done.

"Excuse me," he said to Neil, and went to her. Not smiling.

16

"I've laid out your gray morning coat with the black trousers for tomorrow, sir. And I'll take away your lounging suits and the checked paletot for cleaning, with your permission."

"The what? Oh, that coat thing. Right-o, Pearlman. It's Pearlman, isn't it?"

"Pearlman, yes, sir."

"That your first name or your last?"

"My last name, sir."

"What's your first name?"

"Ah, Andrew, sir."

"You used to be Sir Thomas's man, you say?"

"Yes, sir, before he became so ill."

"I see. Now Miss Fitch is his man, eh?"

The small, balding valet almost smiled, but caught himself in time.

Nick, Brodie recalled Anna telling him, had had one all-purpose servant, a fellow named Winslow who'd acted as cook, footman, butler, and valet.

He'd let him go just before the wedding, evidently expecting something better in the way of a "man" once he joined the Jourdaine household. "Well, Pearlman," said Brodie, "I've never had a 'man' before; what is it you do, exactly?"

"I, sir? Why—I *do* for you."

"Right, but what? What can I expect of you?"

"Well!" Pearlman seemed pleased to enumerate his responsibilities. "I take care of your clothes, all the cleaning and pressing. I make sure your dressing room is in order every morning, properly swept by the housemaid and so on, and that the fire is lit and burning cheerfully."

"Well, now."

"Yes, sir. I put your body linen on the horse before the fire, to air it properly."

"Good show, Pearlman."

"I lay out your cleaned and brushed trousers on the back of the chair, your coat and waistcoat, and always a clean collar. I see that your razors are set and stropped, and that the water's hot and ready to use."

"You mean to say you shave me?"

"If you wish it, sir."

Brodie considered. "I think I'll do it myself. No offense."

"None taken."

"Anything else?"

"I cut your hair every fortnight or so."

"Good, good. That about it?"

"I . . . select clothes suitable for the occasion. That is, if you yourself are indifferent to such things, of course."

"Oh, bloody good, Pearlman, that's the best news yet. Select away, my friend."

"Very good, sir," said the valet, coughing into

his hand. "And then if you're going out, I hand you your cane, gloves, and hat, and see you to the door."

"Do you, now? Well, that sounds fine. I'm tolerably easy to get along with, not too pricklish in the morning. I should think we'll rub along together all right."

"I'm sure of it, sir." They smiled at each other, Pearlman a bit shyly. "Well, sir, if there's nothing else, I'll say good night. Have you enough candle?"

"I think so. How do you turn that out?" Brodie pointed to the light in the ceiling over the bed.

"The gaslight? Right here, sir, this switch by the door."

"Good God. Amazing, isn't it, Pearlman? We live in an age of miracles."

"Yes, indeed. Well, good night, Mr. Balfour."

Brodie's smile faded. "Good night, Pearlman," he said, and watched the door close behind his new "man."

He put his hands behind his head and gazed up at the square wooden structure that projected over his bed, some kind of curtain-supporter, he supposed. If you pulled on this tassel thing at the headboard, you could draw two curtains around either side of the upper half of your body as you lay in bed. The question was, what the hell would you want to do that for? If it was the *lower* half of your body, he could see how that might, on occasion, be a—

A door closed suddenly beyond the wall to his left, and he sat up on his elbow. He could hear muted female voices through the wall and beyond the dressing room he and Anna were to share. What a foul, rotten trick. He knew now why the idea of them sharing Thomas's bedroom hadn't alarmed her: the wily old codger had a suite of rooms, one for himself and one for his long-dead wife, with a wide dressing room separating them. A mile-wide dressing room, it seemed to Brodie as he sat up and contemplated his bare knees under his nightshirt. Did men really wear these things? He thought he looked ridiculous with his hairy legs sticking out, like the wicked witch in a fairy tale.

The voices rose and fell, soft and alluringly feminine, while Brodie's sour gaze took in the details of his new room. He felt as if he'd fallen into one of those paperweights full of fake snow. He'd never seen so much *stuff*. Everywhere you turned there was furniture—tables, chairs, chests of drawers, an eight-foot-high wardrobe. Washstand, cabinets, a standing mirror, three-legged tables, chests, footstools, plant stands, even a sofa. The fireplace had a carved marble chimneypiece, iron grate, a brass fender, and a huge mirror that went all the way up to the ceiling. Every available surface had more stuff on it—pictures, photographs, vases, doilies, plants, pitchers, jugs, basins, bottles, vials. And thank God for the gaslight, because everything was so damn dark. Why had they painted the woodwork *brown*? Who had put this ugly red and green wallpaper on the walls? Why were the windows closed and curtained with layer after layer of flowered shrouds? Jesus Christ, a man could suffocate in here! He got off the bed—it was so high he had to use the damn wooden "step" to get down—went to the window, wrestled his way through the coverings to the sash, and threw it open.

Ah, fresh air. His view was of the garden in the back of the house. A wrought iron fence separated the spacious yard from the alley, where another gaslight on a pole shone discreetly, discouraging burglars. Suddenly he went stiff and his eyes narrowed; a moment later an unamused smile twisted at his lips. A man lounged in the shadows of the gaslight, and he was no burglar. As surely as he knew anything, Brodie knew he was one of Dietz's men, watching. Well, what had he expected? Dietz was no fool. He might trust him enough to let him into the Jourdaine household, but not enough to leave him on his own. Brodie was a sailor, and Liverpool was the biggest seaport in the world. Setting him free in it would be like handing him a few hundred quid, shoving him out of his cell door, and wishing him good luck.

He shook his head resignedly and took deep breaths of the clean night air. When he turned back, he could see himself in the cheval glass across the way. Looking ridiculous. He went to the bed. Pearlman had laid his dressing gown neatly at the foot. It was paisley, sort of blue and black, probably silk. He put it on. That was a little better. He told himself he didn't look quite so much like a man dressed up as a woman.

Anna's voice, subdued, sweet, came to him again through the two walls that separated them. He stared at the closed door to the dressing room—half hers, half his—and imagined what she might be doing in her room. Was she taking off her jewelry and setting it on her mirrored dressing table? Uncoiling her pretty hair and brushing it out? Sighing with relief as she unhooked her silly, useless corset. Stepping out of all those crinolines and petticoats. Unrolling her stockings. Pulling her chemise over her head and standing naked in the middle of the room, shaking her hair back—

Brodie was through the door, across the width of the dressing room, and pushing Anna's door open without knocking, all within the space of two and a half seconds.

Two startled female faces turned from their task—examining a stain on a puce satin petticoat—and gaped at him. One was Anna, depressingly fully clothed in nightgown, frilly robe, and slippers. The other was her maid; he knew her name was Judith, but Anna hadn't mentioned that she had the scowl of a tiger shark and a face like a boiled owl. She was hovering around her mistress now with a kind of Spanish vigilance that egged him on.

"Ladies," he said, with a fatuous bow. Anna raised her eyebrows and the maid dropped a perfunctory curtsy. He came farther into the room. They were standing beside the bed. "What's this?" He reached between them and fingered the petticoat they'd been studying. He could tell by the way they went stiff as marlinspikes that he'd committed some horrible breach of masculine etiquette. He held the satin to his nose and said, "Mmmm." The maid gave a little outraged gasp. He slid his arm around Anna's waist and rested his hand familiarly on the side of her hip. "You can go now, Judith," he said quietly, keeping his gaze on Anna's white neck where it disappeared into the collar of her nightgown.

"No!" Anna dropped her eyes to veil the anxiety and added with pretended calm, "No, stay, Judith; we hadn't finished what we were doing."

"Oh, sorry," he lied cheerfully, going behind her; "I'll just wait, then." He snaked both arms around her, clasped his hands together beneath her breasts, and rested his chin on top of her head.

There was a moment of silence. He remembered something. "Colored shoes are not considered consistent with good taste, you know," he mentioned. "However, delicate pink and faint blue each have their advocates."

Anna pulled down on his wrists as hard as she could while trying to keep her face tranquil for Judith's benefit. "What were you saying, Judith?" Each time she stopped her frantic pressure, he moved his hands a fraction of an inch higher. "The cream silk? Yes, I—I tore it. In Rome, I think, on an omnibus. We'll have to . . ." He pressed closer; she could feel every inch of him along her back and buttocks and thighs. "We'll have to take a piece of cloth from the . . . from the back, the inside, and make a . . ." He'd gotten a thumb inside her dressing gown and was stroking the bottom of her left breast. Her knees started to tremble. Judith had gone red in the face and wouldn't look at her. "A *patch*," she got out, then broke off again when he put his lips, and then his tongue, in the hollow place between her neck and her shoulder. She closed her eyes, just for a second. The working part of her brain finally grasped that Judith would be no protection, that there was almost nothing he would stop at while the maid remained with them, and that she would actually be safer without her.

So when Brodie murmured against her ear, sending little tremors to all of her extremities, "Now are you finished, love?"—she dragged her eyes open, drew a difficult breath, and said, "Yes, I'm—you—we'll talk in the morning, Judith. Good night."

"Night, Judith," echoed Brodie, his irrepressible grin a match for the look of dislike the maid threw him before she whirled and clumped out of the room, without a curtsy. "I don't think she likes me, Annie. Did I do something wrong?"

"Let go of me. Let go!" He didn't, and now he was running his tongue along her jaw and rubbing little widening circles on her stomach, humming with satisfaction. She put her fist in her hand and rammed her elbow into his side, causing him to say "Oof!" and let her go.

Brodie collapsed on the end of the bed, clutching his ribs dramatically, chuckling under his breath. She straightened her clothes and backed away, glaring. She opened her mouth to tell him what she would do if he ever tried anything like that again, then closed it. He called her threats dares, and she didn't have the nerve to tempt him to call her bluff. She watched in impotent silence as he patted the satin comforter on either side of his thighs and gave the feather mattress a few test bounces.

"I like your bed better than mine," he decided. "It's softer. But, Annie, I have to tell you, this is the ugliest house I've ever seen. How can you live in a room like this? You can't walk three feet in a straight line without running smash into some damn gewgaw or other."

"I might take that seriously," she bristled, "if it came from anyone else but a man who's used to sleeping in a hammock and eating out of a brass cooking pot. You wouldn't know a fine, respectable residence if it bit you, John Brodie, so don't you dare criticize my house!" In a corner of her mind a low voice buzzed, saying he was right and she knew it, had often thought it; its insistent echo only made her madder. "Now would you please go? I'm tired and I'd like to retire."

" 'Retire'? I'll make a deal with you. I'll leave as soon as you say you want to go to bed. Come on, say it. You can do it."

She ground her teeth. She wasn't afraid to say it, she was afraid of what he would say after she said it. Something vile, she hadn't any doubt.

"What's that?" he asked suddenly, pointing behind her.

She looked, and turned back. "That's my violin."

"You play the violin?"

His look of hidden hilarity irritated her exceedingly. "I'm learning. Is there something funny about that?"

"Absolutely not." But his tickled grin belied the answer. "I can't wait to hear you practice. How do you think it went tonight?" he asked without a pause, throwing her off. "I've been thinking it might not have been such a bad idea, your aunt's party. This way we got the worst of it over with all at once."

She settled one hip against her dressing table and began to fiddle with a perfume bottle, lifting the stopper out and putting it back, out and back. "Yes," she conceded, "I think you're right." It seemed he was going to behave himself. Speaking to him like this, alone, both of them in their night clothes, made her intensely uncomfortable. But there were things she needed to say to him right away, and she could see no immediate way out. "Actually, I think it went quite well. I was watching people's faces, and I saw nothing to indicate anyone having the least difficulty believing you were Nicholas." *As incredible as that seems*, her tone implied. "There were one or two things I wanted to mention, however."

Brodie folded his arms and waited. Even when she was insulting him, he loved to hear her talk. It was partly her voice, partly her upper-class accent, partly the words she used.

She was struggling for words now. She didn't want to tell him that he had a quality of repose, a quiet self-containment Nicholas had never had and that she found dangerously attractive. Nicholas had been restless, discontent, seeking. He'd wanted so much. Mr. Brodie didn't seem to want anything.

"Nicholas had an abundance of nervous energy," she began carefully. "He was hardly ever still. If he was sitting, he might drum his fingers or jog his foot up and down. Standing, he'd jiggle the change in his pockets or—or look around the room restlessly, even if he was speaking to you." Self-consciously, she stopped fidgeting with the perfume stopper and put her hands into her robe pockets. "Also, he—he didn't laugh at a joke quite as much as you. He wasn't a *hearty fellow*, you might say. Perhaps he—"

"Had no sense of humor?"

"I was going to say, perhaps he was more serious than you." Then again, maybe he had been humorless. She no longer knew. She had an idea that he hadn't liked people as easily as his brother, nor had he trusted them as readily. And tonight she'd made the further discovery that people warmed to Mr. Brodie much more quickly than they had to Nicholas.

Brodie stood up. "All right," he agreed, stuffing his hands in his pockets and twitching his fingers, "I'll try to act restless. And I'll try not to laugh so much, but you'll have to help me."

"I? How?"

"By not telling any more of those side-splitting jokes of yours, Annie. Sometimes you really kill me."

"Very funny." She pinched her lips together irritably. He moved toward her and she sidled away, going to the bureau. "Here's a book I'd like you to read. Keep it in your room—it's on web frames and side stringers, and Nicholas would've known all about that."

"I heard something about you tonight I didn't suspect," he told her, pocketing the book. "Why didn't you tell me you were an angel of mercy? I had to pretend I already knew it."

"What are you talking about?"

"'Anna's poor-peopling,' Jenny called it. She said you've been single-handedly feeding half of Lancashire for months during something she called the 'cotton famine.'"

She clucked her tongue. "What nonsense. I've given some time to an organization that's helping to feed textile workers, that's all."

"Why can't they feed themselves?"

"Because their factories are closed. The North won't let any cotton out of Southern ports in America, and without cotton there's no work in Lancashire. Eighty thousand people have no jobs."

Brodie's face softened. "It's wonderful of you to do that."

"No, it's not, it's necessary. What's wonderful is the attitude of the workers. You'd think they would support the South in the war and press for England to help end the blockade, but they don't. They're suffering the most, and yet they sympathize with the North."

"Because of the slaves," he guessed.

"Yes. For these people the war boils down to a contest for the destruction of slavery. I think it makes it easier for them to endure all their hardships." In surprise, she watched his face close, go completely blank, before he walked away from her. She gazed at his broad back as he stood beside onc of the bedposts, fingering the intricate swirls of carved wood. "Is something wrong?" So many seconds passed, she thought he wouldn't answer. But then he did, in a voice she'd never heard before.

"I saw a slave ship once. The captain was Danish, the ship was Spanish, the crew was every nationality under the sun. I was serving on an English merchantman, heading for the Horn and then San Francisco. I'll never know why, but the Spanish brig took us for the Royal Navy and threw all her cargo overboard before we could close with her."

Anna went white. "What do you mean?"

"We saw it start from half a mile away. At first we didn't know what they were—bags of something they'd been smuggling, we thought. Then we got closer. We saw hundreds of 'em, *hundreds*, being flung over the gunwales on both sides. Children. Women and men. We couldn't get there in time and they all drowned. All of them."

Imagining the horror, Anna pressed her fists to her lips and closed her eyes. "My God," she breathed. But the pain and fury were too sharp, too strong; she couldn't contain them. She thought of Brodie instead, of the life he'd led. What other human cruelties had he witnessed in the last fourteen years? What had they made him capable of? She shivered with an irrational fear, feeling his alienation, his separateness. It would be easy to allow her repugnance for the atrocities he'd lived through to color her feelings for the man himself, she realized. Because he was so different from the people in her tiny, civilized universe, his experiences so foreign. She knew nothing at all of his life, and it frightened her.

"Don't be afraid of me. I couldn't stand that."

She looked up, and saw that he was watching her. Had her face given her away, or could he read her mind? When he came toward her, she didn't move. "I'm not." She shook her head, whispering.

He didn't believe her. "I'm not a monster, Annie, I'm only a man. I've never touched a woman in anger. I would never, never hurt you."

"*I know that.*"

She did. So he'd been wrong—fear wasn't the cause of the chasm between them after all, the mile-deep gulf he'd seen in her eyes for a few seconds. It was something wider, stronger, truly unbridgeable. He hesitated, weighing the risks, and then he put his arms around her, fast, before she could slip away.

Anna held her breath, amazed, not because of what he'd done but because she could feel his strong arms trembling. Her hands crept to his shoulders and she let him hold her, even while she pondered how this could've happened and why she was letting it continue. He rested his cheek against hers. His hands were still; he didn't try to kiss her. She felt the flutter of his eyelashes on her temple, heard his unsteady breathing, and a deep longing rose in her. She wanted to protect herself and she wanted to give him everything. "Please go now," she said, her voice muffled against his shoulder.

He didn't move. It wasn't enough yet, he was

still starving, freezing cold, burning for her.

"Please." Now she was the one trembling.

Brodie tried to take the raw need out of his voice. "I want to kiss you good night."

"Why?" she cried. "What good will it do?" She felt his lips move against her cheek and suspected he was smiling.

"If you have to ask, you haven't done nearly enough kissing." He knew now she was going to let him, but she could never say the word "yes." So he stopped asking and drew back to look at her. The worry in her eyes calmed him down a little. He took his forefinger and brushed it with whispery gentleness across her upper lip. "This one," he murmured. "This one's my favorite." He leaned in and touched both of his to that one of hers, hearing her soft sigh. With the tip of his tongue he opened her mouth, and used it to prod her top lip between his, sipping gently, nibbling. He hadn't been going to touch her at all, but now he put his hand between them, over her heart, and felt its heavy racing. Anna tried to open her eyes, but she was drugged. His soft breath on her cheek warmed her. His mouth fastened to hers and the kiss deepened and deepened until there was nothing more it could be. Then it faded and blossomed into another, and another, and another. When they drew away, their breathing was harsh and seductive and their eyes were bleak with wanting.

Anna recovered first. She stepped away until she felt the reassuring solidity of the bureau at her back, and wrapped her arms around herself. She said "Good night" as soon as she could trust her voice.

It took Brodie longer. His blood and muscles and bones were in rebellion, daring him to leave her now. He meant to say good night, and was as surprised as she when he said instead, "It's better the second time, I swear it is." She knew exactly what he meant, he could tell from her face. "I know it scares you. Can you believe it scares me too? But it'll happen. It'll happen, Annie."

Threat, dare, boast, promise—she no longer knew what it was. But as she watched the door close behind him, a sinking, thrilling fear seized her that he was telling the simple truth.

17

Brodie stood on the top carriage step and took his first look at Jourdaine Shipbuilding. It was bustling and immense and intimidating, but he felt as if he'd seen it many times before because Anna's descriptions had been so colorful and accurate. To his left a tangle of masts, booms, and spars rose high above the waterline, and at the sight he felt an inner shifting, a sort of balancing because he was around ships again—as if he'd finally straightened a crooked picture frame that had been aggravating him. He jumped to the curb and turned to help Anna down, taking another surreptitious swipe at his head with his handkerchief at the same time. "What the hell is this stuff?" he muttered, frowning at the oily spot on the linen cloth. "Pearlman slathered it on me this morning."

"It's macassar oil. Gentlemen use it to keep

their hair neat. Nicholas used it," she added pointedly.

"Well, tomorrow he's giving it up. I smell like a rotten apple."

"You do not. And I think it looks rather nice."

He sent her an incredulous stare. "I look like an otter. And everything I put my head against gets greasy."

"That's why someone invented the antimacassar," she told him, almost smiling.

"The—aha!" He laughed as he made the connection. "Of course. First they invent something stupid, then something ugly to make up for it. We live in a wondrous age, Annie."

"Yes. Be that as it may, to your right are the buildings for the pattern shop, the foundry, the turnery, and the drawing office. The railroad spur runs behind them. We build some ships in those covered sheds, right in the water, and others, over there"—she pointed to her left—"are built on slips and launched afterwards. You can see the scaffolding from here. The deciding factor is size, generally speaking. The mould and sail lofts are over there, those painted wooden buildings." She took his arm and they began to walk toward a handsome brick structure in the center of the yard. It was the administrative office, she told him, where Nicholas had worked, along with Stephen, Aiden O'Dunne, and the other company officers. "You're to have Father's old office; that was settled before Nicholas and I eloped." She broke off to smile and wave at someone across the yard. "That's Jonathan Wall, he's in charge of the joiners and fitters. He's shy, he won't come over."

"Did Nick know everybody by name?" fretted

Brodie, beginning to perspire under his tobacco-brown frock coat.

"No, of course not. Just the foremen, mostly, and I've told you who they are."

He grunted. "Don't leave me for a second today, Annie, do you hear? You have to keep me from sticking my feet in my mouth."

She did smile now, and wondered why she wasn't more on edge. Brodie's obvious tenseness for some reason had a calming effect on her. And she was excited and happy to be back at work, even under these surpassingly peculiar circumstances. "Those men over there are steam hammer drivers," she said, motioning. "They're going to work today on *The Four Winds*."

"*The Four Winds*: an eighteen-hundred-ton steamer with a screw propeller, for Connor Shipping Lines of Aberdeen, to be used in the Baltic trade for miscellaneous cargo. She's about half finished."

"Excellent," she said, patting his arm.

Brodie beamed. "Have you got an office too? Is it right next to mine?" He leaned closer, leering a little. "Or is there a dressing room in between?"

Her smile faded. "No, I don't have an office."

He stopped. "Why not?"

"Oh—" She gave him the most obvious answer. "Because I don't work for the company. Technically."

"Technically? Annie, you work your behind off for the company."

She flushed and began to walk again. "That's the Acorn," she said quickly, "our local pub. Everyone eats lunch there. It's been here forever, before the docks were even—"

"Hold on, now. Tell me why you—"

"Hush! This man coming is Martin Dougherty, and he *will* speak to us. Do you know him?"

"Customer liaison. Helps with contracts. Bachelor, lives with his mother."

"His sister."

"Whatever. Hullo, Martin!" he called jovially, waving.

"Not quite so *hearty*," Anna hissed.

The first thing Brodie noticed about Martin Dougherty was that he wore a lot of macassar oil. He had white, white skin; he parted his shiny black hair in the middle and slicked it straight down on both sides. He reminded Brodie of a piano.

"How do you do, Mrs. Balfour?" Dougherty said formally. "Welcome back to you both."

"Hello, Mr. Dougherty. It's good to be home."

Brodie had no trouble with the small talk they engaged in for a minute or two. Then Dougherty asked him a question.

"Olufson won't settle for November after all and wants eight percent out of the escrow up front. What should I tell him?"

He felt rather than saw Anna go rigid, then sag a little. Olufson, Olufson. He put his thumbs under his arms and stared at his feet. Pieter Olufson, the Gander Line, a Danish outfit. Jourdaine was building them three barks for the South American copper-ore trade. One of them must be off schedule, and Olufson didn't like the delay. "Tell him he can have four percent, and his barkentine will come off by the first of October. I'll speak to Hardy and arrange it." Michael Hardy, the yard superintendent.

"Fine, I'll take care of it. Good to have you back, Nick."

"Thanks, Martin."

"Good day to you."

Dougherty walked away. Brodie reached unconsciously for Anna's hand, frowning, worrying the inside of his lips with his teeth. "Well? Was it all right? I forgot to jingle my change. Did I answer him right?"

Anna was quietly jubilant. "John, you were perfect, it's exactly what Nicholas would've said. Now, when you speak to Mr. Hardy, be a little abrupt; tell him you've given your word and he *has* to have the ship ready by October. And don't worry, he will." She pulled on his hand to get him moving. "Now let's hurry—Nicholas was never late for anything."

He let himself be pulled along, grinning, almost laughing with relief. By God, it was working! But that wasn't even the best part. The best part was that she'd finally called him John.

"This doesn't do you justice, Annie."

It was afternoon. The morning had been busy but blessedly uneventful, and lunch at the Acorn had held no unpleasant surprises. Now Anna looked up from the foundry superintendent's report to see Brodie smiling down at the framed photograph of herself on Nicholas's desk. "That? On the contrary, I've been told it's very flattering."

"Told by who?"

"Whom. Everyone—Aunt Charlotte, Jenny, Milly. No, not Milly—Milly said I looked like I was sitting on an anthill." She colored as soon as the words were out, belatedly perceiving their indelicacy.

Brodie laughed heartily, as she might've known

he would. "I like your friend Milly. I'm sorry I didn't get a chance to talk to her."

"Mm." Anna was sorry *she* hadn't gotten a chance to talk to her, when she'd gone to see her yesterday in her dingy Lord Street rooms. The footman had said Mrs. Pollinax was not at home. She wondered again if it were true, or if it had only been Milly's misguided way of protecting her. She'd left a note; if it went unanswered for long, she intended to take more aggressive steps to see her friend.

"Let me have it," she told Brodie, hand outstretched. "I'll take it home with me."

He cradled the photograph in his arms protectively and leaned back in Nicholas's chair with pretended alarm. "Oh, I couldn't part with it!" Her expression made him laugh. "I'm serious."

"But you just said it was ugly."

"I did not, I said it didn't do you justice. It doesn't show how pretty you are."

She got up from the corner of the desk, blushing foolishly, and handed him the foundry report. "You are an idiot. Here, read this; Mr. Ketchum is coming in the morning to—"

There was a light knock at the door, it opened, and Aiden O'Dunne stuck his head in. "Welcome home, Anna, Nick!" he said loudly. He came in and closed the door behind him. Anna embraced him; Brodie came out from behind the desk, hand out, grinning. There were low-voiced expressions of gladness and subdued backslapping. They felt like guilty conspirators, delighted to be safely together again. O'Dunne recounted an uneventful meeting in Southampton with Dietz and three Ministry officials, then asked how events were proceeding so far in Liverpool.

"Well, I haven't given the game away yet," Brodie grinned. "I think the trick is to keep moving."

"He's been wonderful, Aiden," Anna said. "No one suspects anything, I'm sure of it. You would hardly believe how easy it's been."

"Good, excellent. But don't relax your guard or become complaisant, either of you. This is a tricky business; all it would take is for one person to begin to—"

Another knock at the door. All three started nervously and glanced at each other. "Come in!" called Brodie after an instant's hesitation.

It was Stephen. Brodie had thought him a stiff, starchy sort of fellow at the welcoming party, but compared to his bearing at work, he'd been frisky as a new pup that night. His gray suit looked like someone had pressed it for him a few minutes ago, and he carried himself as if two strings from the ceiling were holding his shoulders up. He and Aiden shook hands with formal cordiality. O'Dunne assured him, when he asked, that his father in Scotland was much better, and then Stephen got down to business.

"This must be a mistake, Nick," he said, handing Brodie a piece of paper.

He glanced at it. "No, I don't think so," he said pleasantly. Seeing the veiled alarm on Anna's face, he handed it to her, then sat back down in the chair behind his desk.

"What is it?" asked O'Dunne.

Stephen told him. "It's a copy of a letter Nick's written to Horace Carter."

"Who?"

"An American businessman. While you were away, Carter wrote to us asking for a meeting.

Naturally I didn't respond."

"Naturally?"

"He says he wants to form a partnership with Jourdaine to build a line of luxury passenger ships." He turned toward Brodie. "I only put his letter in your stack of correspondence for your information. Surely you don't really intend to meet the man."

Brodie raised his brows. "Why not?"

"Because," Stephen answered, laughing, "we don't build passenger liners. Much as Anna might wish otherwise," he added indulgently.

Brodie leaned back in his chair and folded his hands across his stomach—then recalled himself and stood up. He began to pace between the desk and the window, jingling the change in his pockets. "Until a few years ago we didn't build motor launches, either," he said briskly. "I hope that doesn't mean we have to close the corporate door on the idea forever, just because it's something new."

"But what's the point of seeing this American? We're not forming any partnership with him," Stephen insisted. "It's a waste of time."

"Do you think so? I'll see him myself, then, so you won't lose any time."

Stephen looked nonplussed. "But why?" Suddenly he cast a speculative glance at Anna. He tried another laugh. "This is ridiculous. We've been negotiating with the Navy for the last six months, and we're finally on the verge of a major contract for warships. We've got no business—"

"Then now's the time to reconsider, isn't it? Before it's too late."

"Reconsider?" Stephen went still, except for a vein in his forehead that began to pulse. "You can't be serious. Passenger ships?" He almost spat the words out. "It's the wrong direction for us and you know it. Uncle Thomas agrees with me. *You* agreed with me, Nick. This is just Anna's—"

"Anna's father's agreement isn't as meaningful as it used to be."

The vein pulsed faster. "What is that supposed to mean?"

"Only that he's failing. Frankly, I was shocked when I saw him. You see him every day, you don't notice how changed he is."

"He's still the owner of this company."

"Of course. No one's disputing that." Brodie knew Anna was staring at him, trying to disguise her astonishment. He stopped pacing and sat on the edge of the desk; after a moment he remembered to bounce his knee up and down. "All I'm saying is that I don't see any harm in hearing the man's offer. The purpose of this company is to make money, after all. If we can make as much forming a partnership with a private citizen, that's got to be preferable to linking up with the damn government." He had an idea that Nick would've put that another way, but it was the best he could do on short notice. "Horace Carter says he'd like to meet with us when he's in the country in a couple of weeks, and I've told him yes. I'm sorry if it upsets you, Stephen, but I've made the decision and it's final. I hope you'll be with us—Anna and me—when we meet him."

Stephen's hands had balled into fists. He stood for half a minute, rigid with anger, and then stalked to the door. With his hand on the handle, he turned. "I know what you're trying to do," he got out, stiff-lipped, "but you won't get away with it. Uncle Thomas will hear of this, I can promise you. Tonight."

Before he could say more, the knob twisted in his hand, the door opened, and his sister tripped in, wearing a black hat with a rakish green feather. "Goodness," she trilled, laughing and breathless, "why is everybody so grim?"

18

"Stephen," Brodie called out before the door could close.

"Yes?"

"Shorter's old office next door—who's moving into it?"

"McGrath, at the end of the week."

"Let him keep his old one. Anna's taking it."

Stephen let out an incredulous and completely artificial laugh. "What?"

Jenny's jaw fell, while a small smile tugged at the corners of Aiden O'Dunne's mouth. Anna went perfectly still.

"Will that be a problem for you?" Brodie asked quietly.

A thick fog of hostility seemed to hover between the two men. The shade of purple Stephen had turned went poorly with his reddish-orange hair, and the vein in his forehead looked ready to burst.

"No," he said in a low voice, "that's not a problem. I'll arrange it."

"Thank you." Brodie nodded in dismissal, with no idea how much he resembled his brother in that one small, imperious gesture.

Anna stood with her hands folded, her wide-eyed gaze on Brodie across the room. She didn't know what she would say, but she badly wanted to be alone with him, to speak to him. His pale eyes fastened on her; the world seemed to narrow and focus and funnel until they were the only two in it. Aiden excused himself, but she hardly noticed. Finally it was Jenny's voice, almost strident, cutting through the loaded silence that brought her back to reality.

"I said, why don't you and Nicholas join Neil and me tonight, Anna? You can't have made any plans already. We're invited to the Swansons' card party. And afterward that terrible soprano from Bolton is going to sing. Remember her, Nick, last summer in Clyde Park? Lord, we laughed so hard!" She laughed again, remembering it, laying her hand on Brodie's sleeve. She was the pinnacle of fashion in a jade green silk walking dress and a black mantle, and she had the usual effect on Anna of making her feel old and eclipsed and boring. Her cousin was so lively and pretty, a shameless flirt, full of energy. Today, though, she seemed almost too gay.

"I don't think we can make it tonight, Jen," Anna began. "There's so much work to catch up on, by the time we finish it'll be—"

"Oh, pooh! It doesn't start till ten o'clock; you could come if you wanted to. Come on, Anna, there'll be people there who haven't seen you in two months. Nick, make her say yes."

Brodie wasn't sure what tack he should take, how Nick would have responded. "Well," he temporized, "I guess if it doesn't start until ten, we could—"

"I've just remembered," Anna cut in. "There's a lecture at Creighton Hall tonight and we were thinking of going. It was—in the paper this morning."

"Oh, Anna," Jenny cried, exasperated. She turned to Brodie. "What's it about?"

He hadn't a clue. "Um—"

"It's a professor from the University of Edinburgh, Dr. Robert Comstock," Anna said defensively.

"Yes, but what's it about?"

She could feel herself flushing. "A physiographical exploration of the geology of Lancashire."

Brodie bent his head.

Jenny laughed outright. "You can't be serious! This is too boring, even for you."

"Actually it was my idea," Brodie spoke up. "I had to talk her into it. I like rocks. Can't get enough of 'em. Come with us, why don't you? You and Neil. It starts at eight, doesn't it, Anna? You two could meet us there."

Anna had the most ridiculous impulse to weep, and another to go to him and put her arms around his neck.

Much to her surprise, Jenny agreed to accompany them. "Very well," she said with a brittle laugh, "although it won't be easy dragging Neil there. Don't blame me if he sleeps through it. Eight o'clock, did you say?"

"Wasn't it seven-thirty, Nicholas?"

"You're right, my love; I'd forgotten."

She blushed again, and realized that the endearment that used to annoy her so much now intrigued her.

"Then it's settled," said Jenny. "We'll see you this evening." She sailed out of the room, jaunty green parasol over one shoulder.

Anna leaned back against the closed door, pressing light fingertips against the wood panel behind her. She regarded Brodie in silence for a long moment and then said quietly, "Thank you."

Still perched on the edge of the desk, he made a business of pinching the creases in his trousers above each knee. "For what?"

"You know what."

He waved a hand and made a little grimace of dismissal with his lips.

She would be specific, then. "For giving me an office."

"Oh, that was long overdue, I just—"

"And for saving me from Jenny's ridicule. For once. All my life, you see, I've been . . . a bit of a joke to my cousin." His face softened; she hurried on, afraid he might pity her. "And most of all for writing to this man, Horace Carter. That was so kind of you." He started to shake his head, but she wouldn't be put off; she wanted him to know that she understood what he had done and why he'd done it. "It's nothing to you, but you knew what it would mean to me, how much I've always dreamed of Jourdaine building passenger ships instead of navy cruisers. And of course nothing can come of it, I know that—there's too much opposition to changing directions at this late date, from my father and others in the company besides Stephen. But, John, I'm so grateful to you for trying."

After a moment he stood up and moved toward

her. "It's nothing more than Nick would've done," he said evenly.

She didn't have to think about that for long to know it wasn't true. And she owed Brodie the truth. "No, he would not have. It wouldn't have occurred to him. And I could never have asked him."

He fought against a profound need to touch her. Her eyes were their warmest brown, her mouth soft and sweet with gratitude. A man ought not to take advantage of a woman's gratitude. He brought his hand to the side of her face and stroked the cool silkiness of her skin. Bent his head toward her.

There was a knock at the door. They moved in separate directions with identical self-conscious haste, and Martin Dougherty came in. He was full of news of Pieter Olufson and the necessity to speed up construction of the Gander Line's third barkentine. Neither of them heard a word he said.

"From the stratigraphy of the terrestrial crust we can see that, by far, the largest part of the area of dry land is built up of marine formations. From that, of course, we draw the inference that the land today is not an aboriginal portion of the earth's surface after all, but has been overspread by the sea in which its rocks were, by and large, accumulated."

Out of the corner of his eye Brodie saw Anna's jaws quiver as she swallowed an enormous yawn, and he smiled to himself in the darkness. On his other side, cousin Jenny shifted and squirmed, transfixed with boredom. Next to her, Neil snored audibly. So did the woman sitting behind Anna. On the far side of her was nothing but the wall.

The stage was set. Brodie made his move.

At first she thought he was stretching, that the long arm he put around her was temporary, accidental. By the time she realized its true purpose, it had begun to seem natural resting there across her back, the hand draped lightly over her far shoulder. The stroking of his fingers was gentle and gradual, even absentminded; it didn't alarm her. It distracted her, though. Instead of following Professor Comstock's enumeration of the earth's miocene, pliocene, and pleistocene strata, she found herself waiting, when Brodie's fingers stilled, waiting for them to move again.

Time passed. With vague alarm she realized she was going blind to the stout gentleman behind the podium, as every sense concentrated and focused on the engrossingly arbitrary pressure of that one fingertip moving, side to side, across her collarbone. She thought she could hear the velvety sound of skin caressing skin. Her lips slowly parted and her eyelids dropped, as if they had weights on them. It was as though she'd swallowed some narcotic drug. Was she imagining it or had his hand slid ever so slightly downward? Her own hands came unclasped in her lap. No, she had not imagined it. She had on her sherry-colored muslin with the square lace collar; this light-fingered fondling had begun above that collar, and now it was definitely inside it.

"A distinct type of mountain that has come about as a result of direct hypogene action is to be seen in the volcano," the professor intoned, pointing to a chart behind him. Anna's eyes almost closed; she breathed through her mouth. What ought she to do? She could jump up from her seat and hit Brodie over the head with her umbrella.

But to do that she would have to use her legs and arms and the muscles in her back, and at present that all seemed beyond her. "But while these subterranean movements have raised parts of the lithosphere above the level of the ocean, it may be seen that the detailed topographical features of the landscape are not principally attributable to these eruptions."

The woman behind them coughed herself awake, and Brodie's hand went still. Anna stopped breathing entirely. A moment later, soft snoring began again. And then there was no ambiguity, no other way to think of it or describe it: Brodie had all four fingers spread across the top of her left breast, and he was working them down with excruciating slowness toward the small part of her that had long since gone tight and hard with longing.

It seemed that all her body fluids were rushing downward and pooling somewhere in the vicinity of her lap. Was it possible for a person to melt, literally? The idea of concentrating on the professor's words had become laughable. She tried to shock herself out of her treacherous inability to move by dwelling on the fact that she was allowing Brodie to do this to her in *Creighton Hall*, of all places, and that if anyone saw them she would be disgraced. It didn't help. She was still paralyzed, and her mind still flashed with lurid and thrilling pictures of what might happen next if she didn't stop him, and then after that, and after that . . .

Somehow she made herself turn her head, and it was a dim relief to know her neck muscles were still working. Brodie's hard profile was not a comfort. Unlike her, he seemed utterly engrossed in the distinction Dr. Comstock was making between gneisses and schists. His hand had almost located its goal. Very slowly he turned and looked at her, and after that whatever she was going to say or do eluded her completely. His eyes burned with a hot, bright light in the darkness, and in their pale depths she saw the naked mirror image of her own need. All her will deserted her.

She dropped her gaze to his beautiful mouth and imagined kissing him of her own free will— just leaning over right now and putting her lips on his and kissing him. Was she inching toward him? Was she going to do it? At that moment his fingers closed over her nipple, and a slow, exacting torture began.

Her eyelashes fluttered; her mouth went dry. Was he using two fingers or one finger and his thumb? Some peculiar part of her wanted to know. With an effort, she kept her head from lolling over backwards. She had never known about this direct path between the breast and the—the vitals. Sparks ignited where his fingers gently pinched, setting a fire low in her belly, spreading lower. It was only by a miracle that she didn't moan or cry out.

As though he knew it, he moved his hand then and slid it slowly, warmly, to the side of her neck. His fingers tangled in her hair. Her eyes closed. She missed his hand on her breast, but they were going to kiss after all. She wet her lips. Then the applause began.

Anna's eyes widened in near-panic when he took his arm away, and her body became light and cool and empty. He was clapping. Surly and reluctant, the blood began to flow again in her veins. She started to tremble. The lights came up. "That is the last time, Anna, the *very last time* I ever let you talk me into coming to one of these things," Jenny whispered furiously. Anna unclasped her shaky hands and pretended to be looking for something in her purse, certain that if anyone saw her face they would know everything. Her mind was a jumble of guilt and confusion and embarrassment, while her skin still tingled and crawled with frustration. Brodie helped her to stand with a hand under her elbow. She couldn't look at him, even when he draped her shawl across her shoulders and tied a loop in front with the two ends. He offered his arm but she pretended not to see it, and somehow she got herself out of Creighton Hall unassisted.

"Drink?"

"Thanks," muttered Brodie, taking the leather-covered flask Neil Vaughn handed him and upending it, while keeping one wary eye on the two women who walked ahead of them. The night was misty but mild; they'd decided to send the carriage back empty and walk home. Anna was quiet, and may or may not have been listening to the voluble outpourings of her more animated cousin. The whiskey bit into Brodie's gut with just the jolt he needed, but only temporarily. No sooner had the warm sensation dissipated than he was thinking about her again. Remembering how it had felt to touch and excite her, and suffering from a painful mixture of remorse and randiness. He ought to apologize, not just for tonight but for everything; after all, his goal in life for the last two months had been to seduce her. But hypocrisy, at least, was not one of his vices. To say he was sorry would stick in his throat like the lie it was. No—he *was* sorry, it was just that—might as well be honest—he would do it all again in a minute. He couldn't seem to keep his hands off her. Part of it was her prim, ladylike ways and the pure pleasure he took in making her forget them. But it wasn't just that—it wasn't only that he liked the feeling of having power over her. The truth, strange as it sounded, was that he needed her. He wanted to soften her, to draw out affection and approval from her, make her care for him. He needed her to steady him. He wanted her strength.

"Listen, Nick, let me have twenty quid, will you?"

"What? Oh, sure." Brodie drew out his pocketbook and handed Neil the bills. The sight of so much cash in one place still amazed him. "That enough?"

"Right, thanks. It's just till the end of the month."

"Don't worry about it." The request surprised him—Anna had said Neil had plenty of money. He came from somewhere in Norfolk and his family was rich. Other than that, no one knew much about him. He didn't work; he'd shown up in Liverpool late last year, made a few friends, and stayed on because he had nothing better to do. He disappeared occasionally but always came back, full of stories about the high life in London or Brighton or Ascot.

Up ahead, Jenny was hanging back, waiting for them to catch up. When they did, she hooked arms with Brodie and Neil and skipped along between them, laughing, shaking her coy ringlets, full of some gay story Brodie didn't listen to. Anna went ahead, small and resolutely alone, swinging her closed umbrella like a scythe. He wondered what she was thinking, and what words he could possibly say to make her his friend again. In spite of everything, they had been friends, from time to time. The odd adventure they'd embarked on together made them allies of a sort, and sometimes he believed she saved him from embarrassing mistakes not only for the sake of the scheme but because she wanted to protect him. Because she was too decent to want to see anyone humiliated, even him. As rotten as he'd been to her.

He saw that she'd stopped under a huge shade tree beside a streetlamp, half a block up the hill ahead of them, with the lights of the city spread out behind her. She was resting her back against the tree, waiting for them to catch up. "There's Anna in her stopping place," Jenny observed at the same moment, still tripping along between them.

"Her what?" asked Neil.

"Her stopping place. You explain it, Nick."

Brodie said quickly, "No, you."

"It's where she always stops to catch her breath," Jenny obliged. "She's got weak lungs. She spent practically her whole childhood in bed. The doctors say she's better now, but no one really knows for sure if she's well. Nick?"

He'd stopped walking. He started again when Jenny pulled on his arm, looking up at him curiously.

He didn't speak until they reached Anna's tree. He took her by the arm and told the other two to walk on ahead without them. They did, as Anna started to protest. He seized her other arm too and loomed over her, blocking the way. "Why didn't you ever tell me?" he said in a strident undertone, pulling her close.

"Tell you what?"

"That you were sick!"

She stared in astonishment. "I'm *not* sick."

He felt like shaking her. He refrained when it came to him that this hot anger was for him, not her. He gentled his hands but didn't release her. "Jenny just told me."

"Told you what?"

"About your illness. She said this was your stopping place, where you rest on the way—"

"Oh, that." She shook her head, dismissing the subject. "It's nothing. I'm well now." His eyes were so fierce in the dim yellow light from the streetlamp, his features so grim, she found herself wanting to reassure him.

"What happened to you?" he demanded, moving his hands to the sides of her face, holding her with ferocious tenderness.

She never talked about it. She said it as simply as possible. "There was a fire in our house when I was a little girl. My mother was killed. Two of the servants as well. My lungs were damaged, and I—wasn't able to have a normal childhood. But now I'm completely healed. Truly I am."

Brodie remembered what Jenny had said, and kept it to himself that that might only be Anna's opinion. When she tried to pull away again, he let her go. She leaned back against the tree and stared at him solemnly. He felt a heaviness in the chest, as if his own lungs were aching in sympathy. "Annie," he murmured, "I'm so sorry."

"For what?"

"For everything. Mostly for what happened in Florence when I . . ."

He trailed off, but she knew exactly what he was referring to. The last thing she wanted from him now was pity. "You mean that if you had known I was an invalid as a child, you wouldn't have attacked me that day in the woods? But otherwise you would have?"

He ground his teeth. "No, that's not what I meant."

"What, then? Does it make it all right that tonight I was *sitting down* when you mauled me?" She turned her face away, afraid she would cry. Hypocrisy wasn't one of her vices, either: she couldn't put her heart into denouncing him for doing things that had given her such intense pleasure.

"I apologize for that, too."

She whirled to face him. "Why do you do it?" she cried, in desperate earnest.

Brodie gave a disbelieving laugh before he realized she was serious. "Not because of Nick," he told her, his voice gone hoarse. "You were wrong about that. It's you I want, not my brother's wife. You."

Their eyes locked, but only briefly. What she saw in the pale depths of his was too potent, too tough; she couldn't bear it. She jerked her gaze away and swept past him, starting up the hill at a half-run. He caught up to her in a second and slowed her steps forcibly, pulling on her arm. When she realized he wasn't going to say anything more, she stopped struggling and matched his gait, knowing he had set this slow, careful pace for her benefit. They went the rest of the way in a tense silence.

They found Jenny and Neil on the front porch, drinking lemonade. They said a quick good night and went inside, leaving them there. Anna had never acted as anyone's chaperone before, and had to consider the propriety of leaving her cousin alone with Neil Vaughn. Oh, heavens, she scolded herself a second later, it was only the front porch, what could possibly—But that speculation came to a violent halt when she recalled with demoralizing accuracy what had taken place in another public place not an hour ago.

"You're back," said a voice from the drawing room.

"Hello, Aunt Charlotte. Yes, we decided to walk, it was so mild. The lecture was . . ." She searched for the right word.

"Uplifting," Brodie suggested. Ah, now, damn it, he was doing it again, right after he'd made up his mind to stop teasing her.

Anna turned her face away, and saw her father. "Oh, Papa, you waited up," she exclaimed, going to him. He was in his wheeled chair, and Miss Fitch was sitting on the sofa beside him. Anna put her arms around him and kissed his cheek.

Thomas Jourdaine patted his daughter's hand absently and mumbled, "Hello, hello. Hello."

"Papa, did Stephen speak to you today about Horace Carter?"

"Stephen? Stephen?" The light brown eyes looked blank.

Anna shot a look of alarm at the nurse.

"He's tired tonight," Miss Fitch explained, standing. There was reproach in her tone. "We expected you an hour ago."

"I'm sorry, we—"

"Nick!" Thomas called out suddenly, imperiously.

Brodie was by his side in three strides. "Yes, sir." He leaned over so that his face was on a level with the old man's.

"Nick," Thomas repeated, smiling. One hand

reached out and touched Brodie's cheek, gave it a playful cuff. "Cut it all off, eh? Ha ha! Cut it all off." The hand dropped back to his lap and his eyes closed. He was asleep.

Anna folded her arms around herself and watched her father's nurse wheel him out of the room. Presently her aunt's voice brought her out of a cold reverie.

"A note came for you this evening, Anna. It's here beside me." Her hands were full of needlework; she gestured with her head to the small table by her chair.

Anna picked up the letter, resting on top of the latest *Englishwoman's Domestic Magazine*, and recognized the hasty scrawl on the folded slip of paper. Brodie followed her, and pretended an interest in the words Aunt Charlotte was embroidering with pink thread on a square of white linen. "'Virtue is like a rich stone,'" he read aloud. "'best plain set.' Ah yes. So very true."

"Bacon, you know," said Aunt Charlotte, smiling smugly.

Bacon? frowned Brodie. What did it have to do with bacon? "Where do you think you'll hang it?" he asked, glancing about. "This room seems pretty well finished." In fact, he couldn't see a square inch of bare space left anywhere. Everything was clutter and ornaments and flaring chintz covers.

"Under the globe, I think, beside the windows."

Which were always closed and curtained, with a monstrous aspidistra in front to block out the last of any stray light that might find its way in and fade the damned upholstery. At least it was a relief to know that Aunt Charlotte, not Anna, was responsible for the fabulous quantities of needlework and embroidery decorating the house, much of it useless, most of it ugly. What a mausoleum the place was. And at night, he'd discovered, the servants went around, for reasons he couldn't even begin to guess, covering all the furniture up with huge sheets, only to take them all off again in the morning. What could be the purpose? He'd have to ask Anna.

"Aunt Charlotte."

They both looked up, startled by the brittle sound of Anna's voice.

"This letter is from Milly. Is it true that she came to see me tonight and you sent her away?"

"Sent her away? Not precisely. I advised her not to wait, as I didn't know just when you'd return."

"Did you tell her not to come back?"

"I—Certainly not." She laid her sewing aside and sat up straighter, offended. "But we need to have a talk about Mrs. Pollinax." Brodie made a move to rise from the chair he'd taken opposite her. "No, Nicholas, I want you to stay. I'm sure you'll be interested in this." She favored him with a small smile, as if she knew he would be her ally. "Today I heard some unpleasant news about your friend, Anna, I regret very much to say. I pray it's only a rumor; but until the true facts are ascertained, I'm terribly afraid the acquaintance must lapse."

"Lapse," repeated Anna.

"Yes. This will upset you, my dear. I've heard that Mrs. Pollinax has left her husband and taken up residence in a cheap flat in Lord Street. It's even said that she means to divorce him. When I confronted her with this news, she did not deny it."

"I know about it. She told me herself."

Aunt Charlotte gaped. "You—! Why didn't you

tell me? If I'd known, I would never have invited her to your welcoming party!"

"Why? What has she done? What social crime has she committed except to leave a cold and uncaring man whom she doesn't love?"

Her aunt heaved herself up from her chair. "Are you being deliberately obtuse? Can you possibly be unaware of the sort of scandal this will cause?"

"Not unaware—indifferent. Milly Pollinax has been my closest friend for years. How can you expect me to let our acquaintance 'lapse' at the very time she needs me most?"

"But you must! Think, Anna. What if there's a court case, a public trial? To be associated with the woman in those circumstances—"

"What if the man she married is beastly to her? Must she stay with him all her life because to leave him would cause a scandal?"

"Yes!"

"No! It's absurd!"

"It's not absurd, and you are naive. Society is governed by rules, like it or not. Your friend is about to break one of the cardinal ones, and you'll be sullied along with her unless you distance yourself from her immediately."

Anna drew herself up very straight. Never in her life had she defied her aunt. Her hands twisted nervously at her waist, but her voice was steady. "I refuse," she said carefully, "to 'distance' myself from my friend because she's in trouble. I'm sorry if it upsets you, Aunt Charlotte, but Milly is as welcome in this house as she's ever been. I intend to invite her to tea tomorrow, and I hope you'll join us. But if you won't, then I must insist that at least you treat her with courtesy and respect while she's here."

"You? You must insist?" The older woman's face had turned blotchy with anger. "Because this is your and Nicholas's home, and my family and I are only guests?"

It was the second time she'd said that. She meant it as a dare, Anna knew, a manipulative trick to get her way. Breathless with her own daring, she decided to call her bluff. "Exactly." But then her nerve failed. "You know this is your home," she said in a rush, "and you and Jenny and Stephen will be welcome here forever. But—but I'm a married woman now, Aunt, and I must make my own decisions. In . . . consultation with my husband, of course." She risked a glance at Brodie; his face was a study, she couldn't decipher it.

"Surely you don't condone this, Nicholas," Aunt Charlotte said, facing him abruptly. "You of all people should understand the importance of social appearances."

"And what do you mean by that?" Anna moved closer, her voice rising.

Aunt Charlotte held her ground. "Only that Nicholas is a Jourdaine now, in spirit if not in name, and the value of appearances is often clearer to one who has risen out of one class into another."

Anna was shocked into speechlessness. Almost. "That's an *insufferable*—" she got out before Brodie stood up from his chair and went to her.

"I have married above me," he agreed mildly. "I'll spend the rest of my life trying to deserve your niece, Mrs. Meredith." He slipped an arm around Anna's waist and brought her close. "One of the things I particularly love about her is her loyalty. Milly can count herself lucky to have such a friend as Anna. And she can come here whenever she likes. She'll probably say no, but if she wants to she can live here. God knows there's enough room." He gave Anna a soft kiss on the temple. "Annie, I'm tired. Let's—" He stopped, and smiled into her wide, serious eyes. "Let's retire," he said softly. "Good night," he called over his shoulder to a silent Aunt Charlotte as he guided Anna out into the hall and toward the stairs.

En route they passed Jenny, as speechless as her mother. Anna had time to wonder how long she'd been standing there. She and Brodie climbed the staircase together, and at the landing she glanced back down into the dim foyer. Jenny was still there, staring after them. Wearing the oddest expression.

19

The horses pulling the hired hackney up the hill to Rosewood were straining by the time they reached the summit. The vehicle stopped, and Anna began to gather together purse, gloves, umbrella, and shawl. "Come inside and have something to eat," she said to Milly, who sat beside her. "You can go home with Reese later, in our carriage." It still rankled a bit that Aunt Charlotte disapproved of her destination so much that she'd all but forbidden the use of the Jourdaine family carriage and Anna had had to hire this one. But she supposed she'd grumbled about it enough today, and vowed to put it out of her mind. She looked across at Milly, who hadn't moved. "Aren't you coming?"

"No, I don't think so. I'm a little tired, I think I'll just go home."

Anna sat back against the moldy-smelling cushion and turned a sober gaze on her friend. "But I'd like you to come in," she said quietly.

Milly smiled. "I don't believe I will."

"Why?"

"I told you, I'm—"

"A little tired. Then you can rest in my room. I'll have some tea sent up. You can stay for dinner."

"And then spend the night?"

"Yes, if you like."

Still smiling, Milly turned her head to look out the carriage window. "This is such a pretty street," she said absently.

Distracted for a moment, Anna asked, "Do you think Rosewood looks like a public library?" Milly laughed, then narrowed thoughtful eyes at the enormous house of red brick and granite. When she didn't respond immediately, Anna had her answer. "It does, doesn't it?"

"A little, maybe. Now that you mention it."

Anna shook her head, dismayed but resigned to it. Then she returned to the former topic. "Well? Are you going to come inside and visit with me or not?"

Milly smiled gently. "I thank you for the invitation. And for your kindness and friendship."

"But?"

"But I must regretfully decline the offer." Anna made an impatient sound; Milly reached for her hand and held it. "Please don't be angry with me. Try to understand. I know what I'm doing."

"I'm not angry, I'm—"

"Hurt, then. I'm sorry."

"Milly," she cried, exasperated, "you're protecting me from something I don't want to be protected from, something I don't care about any longer."

"Then you ought to." She looked down. "I know, I sound like your aunt."

"Yes, you do."

"She's not wrong, you know."

"She *is* wrong."

Milly sighed, and pulled her hand away. "Let's not quarrel. Let me go home, Anna. I'll pay the coachman the extra shilling to take me to Lord Street." She started to fumble in her reticule, but stopped when she saw Anna's face. Flushing a little, she slid the money back into her change purse.

"Thank you," said Anna, stiffly. There was an uncomfortable silence. Then both women reached out to each other in a spontaneous embrace. "Oh, Milly," Anna said past the lump in her throat. "When you want to talk, do you know that all you have to do is tell me?" They were both blinking away tears, and patting each other's shoulders briskly.

"Yes, I know it."

"I just wish I could help you."

"I know."

They kissed. Anna gathered up her things again and got out of the hackney. She had a word with the driver, paid him, and waved her friend out of sight with a watery smile. Then she turned and went into her house.

"Anna?" came Aunt Charlotte's voice almost before she could close the door.

"Yes, I'm home."

"Come in here, please." The voice came from the dining room. It sounded no more peevish than usual, so Anna took her time unpinning her hat and hanging her shawl in the hall closet.

She found her aunt supervising the table setting

for the dinner party she would give tonight. She looked up from inspecting the polish on a silver serving fork to ask, "How were things at Maghull?" She made the word sound like "hell" or "darkest Africa"—which to her aunt, Anna reflected, were probably very much the same thing.

"Fine." Then, feeling perverse, she decided to elaborate. "We can make three hundred gallons of soup a day now, and we sell it for a penny-ticket per quart. Today it was beef with potatoes and kale." Aunt Charlotte's look of refined horror was very satisfying. Anna kept it to herself that she'd bought a thousand tickets today, and next week she would buy a thousand more; one of the relief societies she worked for would distribute them to the unemployed and destitute.

"I cannot understand you. You were not brought up this way."

"Let's not argue about it again, shall we? Tell me, where did you think of seating the Webbers? He's such a Tory, I don't think we should put him anywhere near Mrs. Butte-Smith, do you?"

She didn't listen to the answer, but sighed again over her aunt's bitter disapproval of her puny efforts to help the textile workers. For Aunt Charlotte and her friends, sympathy for the less fortunate was commendable only so long as it was confined to parlor charity. Actual personal contact with the poor was taboo, a social solecism arising either out of naiveté or hopeless ungentility. That she was engaged in these unsuitable activities with Milly Pollinax, the centerpiece in the unfolding social scandal of the summer, was for Aunt Charlotte the last straw, and for weeks she and Anna had been speaking to each other as little as possible.

A noise from behind the closed conservatory doors drew her attention; it sounded like her father—laughing. She sent her aunt a questioning glance. "He's there with Nicholas," she said shortly.

Anna put down the napkin she was folding. "Do you need me here right now? I'd like to say hello to Father."

"Go on, then."

"I'll come back in a few minutes to help you."

"Don't bother; Jenny can help me."

She expelled a silent sigh. "All right. Jenny's better at this sort of thing than I am anyway."

"Much."

They stared at each other, expressionless. Anna went toward the conservatory without another word.

Moisture had condensed on the glass; she couldn't see through it. She pushed open one of the doors and moved silently inside. They were behind a tangle of schefflera in the west corner of the greenhouse. The sinking sun sent long shadows through the brass-framed windows; the air was moist and pungent with the pleasantly bitter smell of wet earth. Anna went closer to the sound of Brodie's voice, drawn by the amiable intimacy of it. He was reading aloud. Their backs were to her, her father in his wheeled chair, Brodie on one of the wooden benches. They hadn't heard her come in yet, and she didn't speak. While she watched, her father's plaid lap robe slipped from his knees. Brodie saw, and got up to spread it over them again, tucking the flannel in at the sides with gentle hands. Absentmindedly, Thomas passed his palm over the top of Brodie's bent head. The two men smiled at each other. Then Brodie sat down and resumed reading.

"Hello," Anna said softly. She moved around her father's chair and kissed him.

He patted her cheek and peered up at her. "Hello, my dear. Been shopping, have you?"

Anna murmured something and straightened. She turned toward Brodie. He watched her expectantly, wondering—as she was herself—how she would greet him for her father's benefit. "Good afternoon, Nicholas." She held out her hand to him. Once the amusement in his eyes would have irritated her; now it warmed her and made her smile. And when he brought her hand to his lips and put a slow kiss on her knuckles, pulling away was the last thing on her mind. But finally it did occur to her. She drew aside and took a seat on the other bench a little distance away. "Please go on, I didn't mean to interrupt."

Brodie glanced at Sir Thomas. His eyes were half-closed already, his hands limp and open on his lap. Nevertheless, he opened the book and began again at the place where he'd left off.

After a few minutes Anna realized he was reading from *The Heart of Midlothian*. Scott was her father's favorite author—something that had always amused her in light of the fact that Thomas hadn't a sentimental bone in his body. Or had he? He'd changed in the months since he'd become ill. He was softer. Perhaps because he had nothing to fight for now, and no professional reputation to sustain, he'd allowed a gentler side of his nature to emerge. His physical health hadn't changed much since her return from Italy, but his mind was growing vaguer as the weeks went by. He spent his days outside in his garden chair, dozing in the midsummer sun or gazing out toward the river, rarely speaking. She would sit with him as Brodie did, sometimes reading to him but more often sharing his silence. Strangely, she felt closer to him now than at any other time in her life. He could not live much longer, she knew, and this time they spent together was precious to her. What it meant to him, if anything at all, she had no idea.

The low, deep rumble of Brodie's voice calmed her; she felt as relaxed as her father looked. Once she'd thought his voice sounded like Nicholas's, and the similarity had pained and distressed her. But no longer—now he sounded like no one but himself. In moments such as this she didn't feel as confused about her feelings for him. She liked him—she could admit she liked him—because he was kind to a dying old man. What was strange in that? But at other times things weren't nearly so clear. The wound caused by Nicholas's betrayal had healed to the point that she could think about it now. But the same thin scab which was making that ache bearable was also making it possible for her to think of Brodie in a disturbing new light. Her feelings were deep and complicated. In her heart there was a fatal and inevitable correspondence between the brothers, and letting go of one seemed to mean turning toward the other. But what folly, what imprudence—madness, really— to allow such thoughts!

But she wasn't allowing them, she reminded herself, she was fighting them with all her strength, constantly, rigorously, and still Brodie was the focus of almost every waking thought, and certainly every dream. Part of the problem was that she honestly didn't know what it was about him that drew her. They were worlds apart; except for the love of ships, what did they have in common? Nothing at all. But to think that his sole appeal might be physical attraction filled her with shame. She wasn't that kind of woman! So she welcomed these moments of kindness to her father that showed him to be a decent, normal person, the sort of man a perfectly normal woman might find agreeable. But they scared her too. Perversely, she almost wished she *were* in the grip of pure physical attraction, because anything deeper would be too terrifying to contemplate.

She rested her elbow on a corner of the planting table and propped her chin in her hand, watching him. The room was humid and warm; he'd thrown off his coat and waistcoat and rolled up his sleeves. The late sun glinted on his hair, enriching the copper highlights, ruddying his skin. For the hundredth time she thought of what had passed between them three weeks ago in Creighton Hall. He'd stayed away from her after that, to her unspeakable relief, but only for a little while. He'd never been so crude as to refer to the event in words, but no doubt only because he knew he didn't have to—it was seldom far from her mind. And after a few days—four to be exact—he'd resumed his pursuit of her, until now he rarely missed an opportunity to touch her. When he wasn't touching her, he was looking as if he were *going* to touch her, which was scarcely any better. But the worst was that she'd begun to rebuff him out of habit, not conviction. Certainly not repulsion.

And she found herself wondering for the first time about Nicholas's chaste courtship. His treatment of her had begun to seem, in retrospect, more bloodless than chivalrous. Why had he never attempted any of the things Mr. Brodie tried with her? Had it been gallantry—or indifference?

"Annie?"

She glanced up, startled.

"I think your cousin wants to speak to you."

She looked around and saw Stephen in the doorway, shifting impatiently from foot to foot. She hadn't heard him; her mind had been a million miles away. As she got up, Brodie reached out, took her wrist, and pulled her close to his side.

"See you at dinner, my love."

"Indeed." She tried for a dry tone, but the hand he slipped up into the sleeve of her gown began to stroke the inside of her elbow with soft, sure-fingered skill. A now-familiar weakness tingled through her and her stomach gave a not at all unpleasant lurch. "Dinner," she murmured inanely, and hurried out.

Stephen walked out in front of her, heading for the hall and then the drawing room. She was meant to follow, she guessed, and did so with sinking spirits. Relations were as lacking in cordiality with her cousin these days as they were with Aunt Charlotte. She wondered what unpleasant thing he wanted to say to her now.

When she caught up with him in the drawing room, he handed her a letter in an opened envelope. "It came to the office this afternoon," he informed her, stiff as always. "I took the liberty of opening it."

It was addressed, she saw, to Nicholas Balfour. Typically, Stephen had worked through the Saturday half-holiday; otherwise she or Brodie would not have seen this letter until Monday. She pulled it from the envelope and opened it curiously.

It was from Horace Carter. He was on a wedding trip in Europe with his new bride, was writing from London, and—unless he heard otherwise within the next three days—was planning to visit Liverpool and Jourdaine Shipbuilding on Tuesday afternoon at two o'clock.

She looked up. "So, he's really coming. I wasn't sure—it was hard to tell from his first letter whether he really meant—"

Stephen cut her off with a muttered word. A curse? If so, it was the first time she'd ever heard him swear. "I won't stand for this. I don't know what you've said or done to Nick, but I warn you that it won't work."

"Stephen, for heaven's sake—"

"It didn't matter when you were wasting your time, but now you're wasting mine and the company's, and I tell you I won't stand for it."

"What do you have against this?" she demanded, bewildered. "Why won't you hear the man out? All we've asked for is a meeting. I can't understand your opposition."

"And I don't care what you understand or don't understand. You're an embarrassment to me and to this family."

"Why?" she cried. "What have I done?"

"Nick's lost his mind—it's the only explanation I can think of. But Thomas Jourdaine still owns the company, thank God. Ill as he is, I don't think he'll sit by and watch a *woman* take his life's work from him and turn it into rubbish. I'll be at your bloody meeting Tuesday afternoon, you can count on it. After that, we'll see who's in charge of Jourdaine Shipbuilding." He spun on his heel and stalked out, leaving her alone.

Anna brought her hands to her face and stared straight ahead. The echo of Stephen's words swirled in her mind, endlessly repeating. Why was he so angry? Why? Was it simply that he couldn't stand being under the authority, even nominally, of a woman? And it must seem nominal to him, for Brodie was issuing all the orders at Jourdaine these days—after thorough and exhausting consultations with her and Aiden. Or was it that he was afraid a partnership with Mr. Carter would mean relinquishing some of his own power? She could ease his mind about that if only he would talk to her. But for weeks he'd been cold and remote, to her as well as to Brodie, even to Aiden, completely unapproachable behind a wall of reserve and discontent. His last words had held a threat, but she couldn't imagine what he might do. She needed to talk to Aiden; his lawyer's mind would see through this mesh of anger and emotion and discover a solution. Tomorrow, she decided. She would speak to Aiden tomorrow.

A light patter of footsteps sounded on the stairs, and a second later Anna's other cousin appeared in the doorway.

"I do not appreciate," Jenny announced, blue eyes snapping with ire, "your interference in my life, which is no business of yours whatsoever."

Anna sagged a little more. "Jenny, if this is about Neil—"

"Yes, it's about Neil! How dare you tell Mother you don't think he's a suitable companion for me? How dare you? Do you think that just because you're married now you can run my life?"

"Oh, Jenny, please listen. All I said to Aunt Charlotte was that I thought he might be a little old for you and that—"

"He's younger than Nicholas!" Jenny blurted.

"That's true, but what does it have to do with

anything? I'm older than you, and Nicholas—"

"You told her he drinks," she interrupted hastily.

"He does." She'd found that out from Brodie.

"Well, so? Everybody drinks. Men, I mean."

"But Mr. Vaughn drinks quite a lot, I'm told. As a matter of fact, I've noticed it myself."

"I don't care! It still doesn't give you the right to barge into my private affairs."

"I'm sorry, I was only—"

"Anyway," she cut in, lips curling, "I would've thought that *shipbuilding* would take up all your spare time these days, so you wouldn't have any left over to poke your nose into other people's business."

Anna's eyes narrowed in irritation. She spoke without thinking. "Perhaps if you occupied *your* spare time with something besides gossiping and changing clothes, you'd know how to conduct your social life with a little bit of common sense."

Jenny's mouth fell open. After a half-minute of speechless staring, she spun around—much in the manner of her brother a moment ago—and marched out of the room.

Anna sank down on the arm of the sofa. Hopelessness settled over her, heavy as a cloak. She thought of what Milly had said that afternoon—"You and Nicholas ought to go away together." Anna had laughed. "But we just got back from our honeymoon!" "You ought to go anyway, even if it's only for a few days."

She imagined it now, how lovely it would be. Longing to go somewhere alone with Brodie did not shock her very much anymore. Except for her father, he was the only person in the house who wasn't furious with her.

20

July sun shone wetly through the raindrops flecking the half-closed carriage window. Anna peered past them unseeing, her thoughts a thousand miles from the drying Liverpool streets and the distant mast-streaked waterfront toward which she was traveling. She was late for a meeting with Aiden and Mr. Brodie to prepare for Horace Carter's visit this afternoon, and her mind was occupied with ideas of what they should and should not say to the entrepreneurial American. The likelihood of anything substantive resulting from this meeting was minuscule, she knew, but she wanted to be prepared all the same.

The carriage rolled into the north yard of Jourdaine Shipbuilding and she alighted at the railroad tracks, as was her usual habit. She walked past a scattering of outbuildings toward the central office, glancing down at the diamond-studded watch pinned to her bosom. One o'clock. She hurried her steps. She was a familiar sight in the yard; the workers nodded or doffed their caps respectfully, accepting her presence here a great deal more easily than her family and friends had. The men had accepted Brodie too, thank God—and with more genuine warmth, she knew, than they had his brother. They'd respected Nicholas: Brodie they liked. He had an easy way with them, issuing suggestions instead of orders, calling them by their first names, laughing with them. She knew they remarked on the change in him, and it gave her a strange feeling to know they believed she was the cause. She wasn't, of course, but the notion secretly pleased her. Last week, when they'd done Brodie the singular honor of inviting him to play on their cricket team, she'd known his acceptance was complete. He'd been guilelessly delighted by the invitation, and his simple pride in it had touched her.

She heard men's voices as she neared her second-floor office. Odd, she thought, nodding to old Wilkins, the porter; she and Aiden usually met in Brodie's—Nick's—office, for appearance's sake. She pushed open the door.

Five men turned at her entrance. Four of them she knew—Brodie, Aiden, Stephen, and Martin Dougherty—so the fifth must be Horace Carter. Brodie confirmed it by introducing him. He was a big man, with bushy gray sidewhiskers and huge square teeth. He stuck out a great paw of a hand and gave hers a robust shake.

"How do you do?" said Anna. "I'm sorry I'm late—"

"You're not late, I'm early! You know what we Americans say, the early bird gets the worm." He grinned, enjoying her surprise. He wore a striped suit of brown and tan and gray, and a yellow carnation in his buttonhole.

"We have the same saying," she smiled back, recovering quickly. "Is your wife with you?" She took off her flowered hat, setting it on the shelf over the coat rack, and patted the thick chignon at the back of her neck for stray hairs.

"No, no, I've left her in London, seeing the sights. We're at some hotel called the Crown, fancy as all get-out. I thought I'd come down a little early and catch you unawares." The mischievous twinkle in his eye was childlike and inoffensive.

"So I see," said Anna. "Well, shall we all sit down?"

Carter, O'Dunne, and Martin Dougherty took seats. Stephen walked away to the window. Brodie held Anna's chair for her behind her desk, and she went to it with misgivings. He was making her the leader of the discussion, she realized, and she sent him a quick, searching look as he seated her. He gave her shoulder a secret squeeze and went to stand by the wall on the far side of the room.

Carter seemed puzzled by the maneuver too, but not put off. After a moment's pause he directed his attention to Anna, and plunged right in. "I've been checking up on you, Mrs. Balfour. You've got a first-class operation here."

She folded her hands on the desk top and gave a smiling, noncommittal nod.

"Nobody can find anything wrong with it, not even any rumors. That didn't surprise me, but a businessman's got to be thorough." He hitched his pants and stuck his thumbs behind his suspenders. "I want to hook up with you," he announced baldly. "I'm proposing an equal partnership on either side of the ocean, to build the biggest, fastest, fanciest line of passenger ships there's ever been."

Anna suppressed a quick, physical thrill of excitement and tried to compose her features. In spite of the flutter of nerves in her abdomen, she fixed Carter with her serious brown eyes and said, not altogether truthfully, "You have us at a disadvantage, sir. You've determined that we're respectable, competent, and solvent, but we know very little about you. Tell us why it would be to our advantage to do business with you." As lies went, it was more than a little white; they'd been checking up on Horace Carter for weeks. But she wanted to hear what he would say.

The big American glanced over at Brodie as if expecting something from him—an endorsement of his wife's words, elaboration on them, maybe approval. When nothing was forthcoming and Brodie remained blank-faced, Carter finally returned his full, somewhat surprised attention to Anna and cleared his throat by way of preamble. "Well, now, that's a fair request. I've been in the business of transporting goods of one kind or another for about thirty years, since I was seventeen and got a job on a canal boat in Albany, New York. When I was twenty, I bought the boat, and by the time I was twenty-five I owned fourteen more of 'em. When I sold out, I bought a piece of a railroad just getting started in Pennsylvania and Ohio. That turned out to be a pretty good investment"—here Anna's eyes widened slightly as the name of the railroad he'd come to own flitted across her mind—"and when I sold it twelve years later, I'd made what you might call a tidy little profit."

"Indeed." She admired his flair for understatement.

"Since then it's been boats that interest me. I've got merchantmen bringing molasses out of the West Indies, I've got fishing schooners in Nova Scotia, some whalers out of Rhode Island, steamers hauling lumber and coal and bricks all over creation." He put his hands on his massive thighs and leaned closer, his broad, uncomplicated face pinkening with intensity. "What I don't transport right now is people, and I'm anxious to change that. With you, Mrs. Balfour, and your husband, and your daddy's shipbuilding company. I want to see the greatest shipping line in the world spring up between our two continents. These are prosperous times. Your country's the richest in the world, and as soon as the North wins this war in mine, it's going to start coming up right behind you. There's going to be money to burn, and I don't see why you and I shouldn't stash away some of the ashes."

Anna smiled, enjoying his bluntness. His crassness, Aunt Charlotte would say. "And how do you envision this passenger line, Mr. Carter? What sets it apart from Mr. Collins's or Mr. Cunard's?"

He sat back and grinned at her, then threw a look at Brodie that seemed to communicate admiration for his choice in business partners. "I'll tell you what sets it apart. It's going to outdo both of 'em, that's what. Carter Lines will be first class all the—"

"Whose lines?"

Carter let out a great growl of a laugh and slapped his knee. "Whoops!" he chortled, actually blushing. "A slip of the tongue, nothing more! Been calling it that to myself when I think about it, is all. We can call it Jourdaine Lines if you want, only nobody'll pronounce it right." His sheepish grin was charming.

"Let's name the line later, then," Anna suggested, smiling back at him. "You were saying—?"

"I'm saying we're a perfect match. I can tell you're a woman who's got class. You're a first-chop, A-number-one corker, and I knew it the minute I saw you."

Brodie and O'Dunne chuckled at Anna's expression, and Brodie said, "Mr. Carter, you've got a keen eye, I can see that."

"Thank you," he said modestly, and turned back to Anna. "I see our ships as huge luxury hotels on the sea, Mrs. Balfour. We'll have steam heat in every room, salt-water plumbing, carpets in all the cabins, stained glass and mirrors everywhere. I want a barbershop with adjustable chairs, and I want brass spittoons shaped like sea shells. Great crystal chandeliers in the dining rooms, and food that outdoes Delmonico's. We'll have an ice room with forty tons of ice every trip, so the fruit never gets moldy. We'll put fresh flowers in the cabins every day. We'll have bands and orchestras, a different one every night, and a ballroom as big as a field. Servants to wait on you hand and—"

"We have the picture," Stephen interrupted suddenly, the undisguised hostility in his voice bringing everyone to attention. He'd been staring stonily out the window, the only clue to his mood the pulsing blue vein in his forehead. "Why don't you get to the point?"

"The point?" Horace repeated mildly. "I thought it was Americans who were always wanting to get to the point." He shifted back to Anna. "Another thing about Americans, ma'am, is that we're obsessed with speed. We nearly went crazy two years ago when the *Persia* crossed from New York to Liverpool in nine days and averaged fourteen knots. Carter-Jourdaine Lines can do better than that, because Jourdaine Shipbuilding has the power right this minute to build one of my floating hotels that'll do twelve and a half knots. In two years time—"

Stephen let out a derisive laugh, cutting him off. "Oh, that's wonderful—that way one only has to spend *eight* days on one of your vulgar bobbing bawdyhouses."

"Stephen!"

"It's all right," said Carter, sitting back and folding his arms across his barrel of a chest. "I'd like to hear what Mr. Meredith has to say."

"What I have to say won't take very long. I'll only remind you that four years ago the great Collins line went bankrupt. After the Congress cut back his subsidies and the public got sick of hearing about one disastrous shipwreck after another, the man lost his shirt. Two of his 'luxury liners' are being used as army transports now in your Civil War, and the rest were auctioned off for practically nothing. So much for your American obsessions with speed and opulence!"

When Carter didn't answer immediately, Anna spoke up. "In part I have to agree with my cousin," she said calmly. "This need for speed burns up coal, burns out engines, and punishes wooden hulls. Then frantic repairs have to be made between crossings, and sometimes they're not enough. Two hundred and thirty people died on the *Arctic*, a hundred and eighty on the *Pacific*—"

"And Collins lost his own wife and two daughters on one of 'em," Carter finished quietly. "I know it. I know that in the last twenty years thirteen transatlantic ships have gone down and two thousand people have died. In my country they tell us to be sure and make out our wills before we set sail. But that's the very reason I've come to you," he insisted, pounding his thigh with a meaty fist. "This line—Carter-Jourdaine, Jourdaine-Carter, I don't give a damn—will be built so that it has what you want, which is safety and economy, and what I want, which is speed and luxury. And every time it comes to a choice between speed and safety, I'll compromise, and I'm prepared to put that in writing. What it boils down to is that we want the same thing. You've got the technology to build it and I've got the money to pay for it." He spread his hands. "I tell you again, Mrs. Balfour, we're a perfect match."

"But we're ship *builders*," Brodie put in. "We don't know anything about running a line."

"You'll learn," Carter said cheerfully. "In the meantime, you build 'em and I'll run 'em. Not to boast, it's what I do best, and I've had a little bit of success at it."

There was a pause. Anna's eyes found Brodie's. Her outward calm didn't fool him; he could see the excitement snapping behind her sober brown regard. He sent her a warm, private smile, then watched her lips quiver as she struggled not to return it. Stephen had turned his back on them again and was staring out at the yard, his body as stiff and unmoving as the coat rack next to him. Martin Dougherty looked thoughtful. Aiden O'Dunne cleared his throat.

"Have you brought anything with you in writing, Mr. Carter? Any proposals or—"

"No, sir, I haven't. No offense, it didn't strike me as time for the lawyers just yet. I wanted us to talk first and see how we liked each other."

"Quite right," Anna heard herself saying, smiling at him. "How long will you be in Liverpool, Mr. Carter?"

"I'm leaving tonight, ma'am—Dora'd kill me if I stayed away another day. She's already mad that I'm here, on our honeymoon and all. But we'll be in London till the middle of August. If you're interested in doing business, we can talk about it again in a week or two." He winked at O'Dunne. "We might even let the lawyers in on it then, if we feel like it."

Anna glanced again at Stephen. He hadn't moved. She looked at Brodie. He was fingering his tie as he watched her, a look of expectancy in his pale gaze. She drew a deep, not quite steady breath. "I think I can say for all of us that we're interested in your offer, Mr. Carter. Naturally we'll need time to consider it, and when it comes time for formal proposals we'll have to study them carefully."

"Well, now, that's fine," said Carter, beaming. He stood up when Anna did. "I've never done business with a lady before," he admitted as they shook hands across the desk. "It ain't half as bad as I thought."

Anna laughed. "I'm sure you mean that as a compliment, Mr. Carter."

"No, no, it's Horace now. We're going to be partners, I can feel it in my bones, so you've got to call me by my first name."

"I'm not sure if we're going to be partners or

not," she returned, "but if it's to be Horace, then it must also be Anna. I insist on it." Carter grinned his approval.

Brodie pushed himself off the wall and came toward them, holding out his own hand. "What do you say to a tour of the yard, Horace? You've got plenty of time before your train."

"That sounds fine, fine! Maybe you'd like to come along with us, Mr. Meredith?" he added, with unexpected diplomacy.

Stephen turned around slowly. The sight of his face made everyone, even Martin Dougherty, stiffen with surprise. "As much as you might want him to be, Anna," he said in a low, hate-filled voice, his teeth bared, "Thomas Jourdaine isn't dead yet." Anna's head snapped back and she gasped. "That means you don't run this company and you don't make decisions for it."

Into the taut, thundering silence Brodie's voice sounded ominously calm. "That's true, Stephen. But neither do you. As a matter of fact, I do." Everyone except O'Dunne stared at him. "Sir Thomas gave me his power of attorney this morning. Show it to him, Aiden." Brodie's eyes locked with Anna's as O'Dunne went behind him and approached Stephen. This wasn't the way he'd wanted to tell her. What was she thinking? He couldn't decipher her still, somber gaze. He heard the door behind him open and then slam closed, and when he turned around Stephen was gone. Aiden stood uncertainly, folding his papers. Brodie broke the silence again.

"Well, let's go, then, shall we, before the men go off work. Anna, do you want to come with us?" She shook her head slowly, and still he couldn't read her mood. He had to force down an urge to go to her, to touch her and make her talk to him. "Well, then. We'll see you in an hour or so." He stepped back to let Carter precede him out the door; Aiden and Martin Dougherty followed behind. With the door half-closed, he sent her one last searching look.

"It's all right, John," she said in a murmur he could barely hear. "I'm all right. I'm glad it's happened."

But she didn't look glad, she looked close to tears. It took all his will power to close the door on her pale, troubled face and leave her alone.

21

Most of the day had been overcast, but a fresh wind was blowing the clouds away in time for the spectacle of the sunset. Anna's office window overlooked the shipyard and the river beyond. She watched as bands of color layered and sank behind the western shore, softening the air and tinting it in delicate shades of coral and ochre and old gold. She never tired of watching the passing of the ships on the busy river, slow and stately as clouds, moving out to sea on a fresh voyage or scudding gracefully home to port.

She turned away from the seductive glory of the sunset and sat back down at her desk. She had much to do, but her mind was preoccupied with thoughts of Horace Carter and his proposition. She started at a knock on her closed door. "Come in!"

It was Neil Vaughn. "Nick here?" he asked.

"No, he's out; I'm afraid you've missed him."

"Ah, too bad. Gone for the day, I suppose." He lifted an eyebrow at the remnants of orange sunlight in the window.

"Oh, no. He was giving someone a tour of the yard, and then afterward I think he was going over to the reflag docks." She smiled at his blank expression. "Where we reclassify ships." Still nothing. "Make repairs, get them seaworthy again so they can meet reclassification requirements." He nodded his understanding, but she could see his interest was only polite. What, she wondered, and not for the first time, had Nicholas liked about this man?

"Nick's a busy fellow, isn't he?" he said in his bored drawl. "I've hardly seen him since the two of you returned from Italy."

Something in his tone made her wonder if he resented her for that. She didn't answer.

"Give him this, will you?" He strolled toward her, pulled something from his pocket, and put it on her desk.

She saw that it was money. "Yes, I will." There was silence while she waited for him to go. Instead he sat on the edge of her desk and folded his arms. He looked thinner than the last time she'd seen him; his cheekbones jutted whitely, leaving sunken hollows of sallow flesh beneath them. Did Jenny find his gauntness attractive? Romantic? It was hard to believe he was younger than Anna herself. His teeth were stained brown and his breath had an odd and unpleasant odor. He put a bony elbow on his knee, propped his chin in his hand, and leaned in toward her. He stared intently out of his pale, wolf's eyes, as if he were seeing her for the first time. "You look different," he murmured. "I think marriage agrees with you, Mrs. Balfour."

She recognized the implication in his words and steadfastly ignored it. He didn't mean "marriage," he meant lovemaking, and he wanted her to know it. He was making an advance. A few men had flirted with her in the past, but Neil's blatancy was a first.

No, that wasn't true. There was no one in the world more blatant than John Brodie. What was the difference between him and Mr. Vaughn? Everything, she realized. But why? She pondered it while Vaughn continued to look at her as if she weren't a person at all but an object, some thing he could make use of for his private gratification. For him, she belonged to a class of objects—women— and she was indistinguishable from the others to the extent that he could use her.

With Brodie it was different. He wanted her as much—no, more, much more—but it was she, Anna Jourdaine Balfour, he wanted. When he looked at her, he saw her. *Her.* She didn't represent anything to him, she was only herself. She felt a light trembling in her chest at the thought, a subdued euphoria that thrilled and dismayed her.

She looked up at Neil. "I still have quite a lot of work to do," she said quietly, then waited.

Rather a long moment passed. At last he removed his black-clad thigh from the corner of her desk and stood. "Of course. I wouldn't want to keep the businesswoman from her work," he said, giving the word an unpleasant emphasis. Then he smiled. "Good night, brown eyes." He made a shallow, facetious bow and walked out.

Anna stared at the closed door, thinking how little she liked Neil Vaughn. After a minute she sighed and shook her head, forgetting him. She had work to do. She picked up a packet of papers Brodie had handed her yesterday—with great casualness, she recalled, asking her to take a look at it when she had a moment; no hurry, it was of absolutely no importance, just something to read when she had a spare minute. His very offhandedness piqued her curiosity.

She spread it out before her, four closely covered pages. At first it was indecipherable—strange sketches with arrows and keys and obscure marginal explanations. On closer inspection, she saw it was a rough, inexpert series of designs for a cargo carrier. But unlike any cargo carrier she'd ever seen. He'd moved the bridge and engine room aft, leaving an unbroken space for freight. It looked like an elongated steel box, with a forecastle for the crew sticking up at one end and a poop to house the engines at the other. It made her think of an enormous dachshund. She shook her head, smiling, studying it. She tapped a pencil against her teeth. Slowly the smile faded as puzzlement turned to attention, then understanding. Yes, she mused, now I see what you're thinking of. Her eyes narrowed critically. But could it work? The design provided a long, unobstructed bin for the ship's chief cargo, in this case iron ore. The shrewdness and simplicity of it intrigued her. It would have to be redrawn, of course, by an engineer; he hadn't even used drawing paper and his scale was hopelessly off. But the idea was sound. No, it was more than sound: it was revolutionary. By rearranging the vessel's three primary components, he'd increased cargo space by . . . she frowned, reckoning it . . . by about 25 percent. She looked straight ahead, unseeing. Good lord!

She glanced at her watch. Past seven o'clock; the yard whistle had blown over an hour ago. She had a hundred things to say to Mr. Brodie. He must have finished his tour with Horace Carter long before now. Even though the work day was over, he'd undoubtedly gone to the reflag dock to check on the progress of the *Alexandra*. If he had anything at all in common with his brother, it was a habit of working long hours.

Anna stood. She straightened her desk in the fading light, picked up her shawl from the back of her chair, and took a last fond look around her office. *Her office.* She hugged herself, taking in the warmth of the painted wood paneling, the bright new carpet, the flowers on her desk and on the table under the window. To her the room seemed feminine and businesslike at the same time. Aunt Charlotte would loathe it, loathe the very idea of it, were she to deign to pay a visit; but to Anna it was beautiful. And it was much, much more than an office. It was her personal symbol of freedom and escape and opportunity. She put her hands to the sides of her face just for a second, the better to contemplate the odd and astonishing fact that she owed its existence to John Brodie. Then she whirled around, pulled open the door, and hurried out to find him.

The *Alexandra* was a three-masted English cargo steamer, a light scantling vessel of wood and iron, about seven hundred tons, used for hauling nitrates. She needed new decking, most of her scarfs reset, and a great deal of new plating. She was surrounded by scaffolding in her shallow, inclined slip. Anna cast a practiced eye over her enormous side, noting that the shell platers and riveters had finished their work and the caulkers had begun water-testing some of her inner compartments.

The dock seemed deserted. It was growing dark. Had she missed Brodie somehow, passed him on his way back to the office? Just then she thought she heard a noise on the *Alexandra*'s deck. "Mr.—" she caught herself and trilled, "Nicholas? Are you there? Nicholas?" No answer. "Mr. Brodie!" she called in a low, conspiratorial tone, then made a face at herself. Of course he couldn't hear that. She tried calling "Nicholas!" again, but still there was no response. Amid the scaffolding a tall, sturdy ladder tilted from the dock to the top of the *Alexandra*'s bulwark amidships. Heights didn't bother Anna. She gathered up her skirts in her left hand and began to climb.

Negotiating the gunwale in a flaring crinoline was a task best accomplished without witnesses. She managed it fairly easily, and stood on the edge of what remained of the decking over one of the cargo holds directly below. Three thousand tons of the Mersey River had been pumped into the hold in order to test is watertightness. "Mr. Brodie!" she called across the blackish corrie at her feet, spanned by a thirty-foot plank. She heard a noise from the quarterdeck in the stern. "Mr. Brodie!" The plank was a yard wide, thick and strong. She hesitated only a second, then stepped up and set off across it toward the bridge.

It was when she was one step away from the precise center that she saw the drilled holes, perhaps a dozen of them, neatly bisecting the plank. She halted, unable to go forward, too frightened to step back. Horrified, she heard the crack of ripping wood and watched sharp white

splinters leap out across the dotted line. She
twisted sideways as she fell, to keep from striking
either half of the severed board. She didn't hear
herself scream.

The water hit her with a body-jarring smack
that forced the breath from her lungs. Flailing,
kicking, she fought back to the surface and gasped
a great chestful of air. She was only fifteen feet
from a wooden ladder built into the bulkhead, but
her skirts were dragging her down. She went under
long enough to rip feverishly at the ties of petticoats and crinolines under her dress; kicking free,
she struggled back to the top and treaded water,
panting and exhausted.

Through the water in her ears she heard her
name. When she looked up, she saw Brodie cata-
pulting off the deck high above, arms outstretched
in an ungainly swan dive. His impact almost
swamped her.

She spat out a mouthful of water and waited for
him. Seconds passed. His head bobbed up, seven
feet away. She saw him take one panicked gulp of
air before he disappeared again under water. The
truth struck her like a blow to the head. Brodie
couldn't swim.

She dove, her brain empty of everything but
horror, and thrashed through the heavy water
barrier between them. She could see his darker
outline in the blackness and reached out. She
caught a handful of cloth, hauled on it, scissoring
her legs, and pushed against the wall of water
toward the air. She caught a breath just before she
felt Brodie's hands on her hips, heaving her up
higher and then letting go. With an inward scream
she dove again. This time her panicky fingers
found his hair; she pulled up and backward with

all her strength. Her head hit the surface just before his.

"Go limp!" she shrieked into his ear from behind, away from his flailing arms. Somehow she got a grip around his chest. Hauling on him, she forced him to lie back on top of her. "Stop moving!" she yelled, just before his weight forced her under. She fought back, sputtering and spitting, her legs jackknifing to keep them afloat. She heard him choking as she dragged him sideways toward the ladder, her own breath coming in jagged, watery gasps. With the ladder an arm's length away, her strength gave out and she felt herself sinking. Brodie grabbed her shoulder and gave it a hard shove through the sluggish water. The effort pushed his own body back, away from her. Her fingers scrabbled against solid wood. She wrenched around and stretched her arm out to him, but he was too far away now to reach it. She watched him go under, and knew a bottomless despair.

Sobbing, crying his name, she hooked her feet around the rung of the ladder just below water level and extended her whole body toward him, arms and legs straining, muscles beginning to cramp from exhaustion. His head broke the surface, just out of reach. She felt something and gripped it hard. His wrist. She tugged and he flailed toward her, nearly sinking her. They reached for the ladder at the same second.

They collapsed against each other, gasping and coughing, holding as tightly as if the danger hadn't yet passed. They tried to speak, but weren't capable of anything beyond half-curses and choked-off whispers. Their heads rested against each other's wet shoulders, and when the ability to breathe normally returned, they remained as they were. The water calmed, grew still. Anna told herself she was still clinging to Mr. Brodie because she was too exhausted to move a muscle, even as she rubbed his back with the flat of her palm in long, slow, ardent strokes. He had his hand tangled in her dripping hair, holding the side of her face to the side of his. Minutes passed, and finally she felt called upon to speak.

"What the devil were you thinking of?"

Brodie smiled, and gave her hair a silent, secret kiss. He'd never heard her say "What the devil" before. "I was thinking of making an ass of myself. You're not going to rub it in, are you?"

She closed her eyes and remembered the hard, desperate feel of his hands pushing her, away from him, toward safety. "No," she whispered. "I'm not going to rub it in."

They rested against each other until the compelling peace between them began to feel dangerous. Anna knew the way to break it, but first she had to struggle through a profound unwillingness. "It wasn't an accident. Someone cut holes in the plank. It split when I got to the center."

Brodie pushed her back to look at her. She watched his face harden and his eyes turn opaque with fury. His hand on the back of her neck tightened painfully. As quickly as it came, his anger disappeared. "For me," he said as he realized it. "Not you—they meant to kill *me*."

Her mind swirled. Out of all the questions, one finally surfaced. "Why?"

He shook his head.

"Who knew you were coming here?"

"Half the yard."

She tried to think. "Who knew you couldn't

swim?" He didn't answer immediately. If she hadn't seen it with her own eyes, she wouldn't have believed it. He was blushing.

"Half the yard," he said again, but looking away and mumbling. "I mentioned it to Dougherty once and he went and told everybody. It was a big joke, the shipbuilder who couldn't swim. Well, Nick couldn't either," he noted defensively.

Anna said nothing, too tactful to point out that the *sailor* who couldn't swim was an even bigger joke.

"How is it *you* can swim?" he asked—somewhat accusingly, she thought.

"I had a doctor, years ago, who thought it might help me. He called it 'therapeutic.'"

He felt relieved that she'd brought it up. Since that night on the hill she had never discussed her old illness; he wanted to respect her reticence, but he had to ask. "How do you feel, Annie?"

"I'm fine now."

"I mean, how are you . . ." He felt awkward saying the words.

She realized what he was asking and hesitated, appraising herself, concentrating on how she felt. Then she laughed. "I'm cold and wet and tired, but otherwise I'm in perfect health. My lungs are as strong as yours. Which is just what I've been telling everyone for the last five years."

He wanted to kiss her. His relief was so strong, he couldn't hide it. He drew her into a soft hug, loving her smallness and warmth. "Let's go home," he murmured against her neck.

She pulled back, misty-eyed. "But—we have to tell Aiden what's happened. He thinks whoever killed Nicholas and attacked you in Naples were Union agents, trying to prevent the transfer of the

Morning Star. This proves it wasn't! It's someone in the company, John, it has to be. We have to tell Mr. Dietz—"

"Tomorrow's soon enough to tell Dietz and Aiden. Tonight we have to get you home and get dry."

"But they'll see us, ask a million questions, Aunt Charlotte won't let—"

"We'll sneak in the back door. We'll get cleaned up. Then we'll talk."

22

Brodie couldn't concentrate on his book or his newspaper. At every imagined sound in the silent, sleeping house, he looked up to see if Anna had finally come. Wet and chilled, they'd stolen into the house unobserved more than an hour ago. She'd offered him first use of the lavatory, because he would be quicker. He'd invited her to come to his room afterward—so they could talk. She'd frowned and pursed her lips, and told him to meet her in the library.

He touched tentative fingers to his throat. It didn't burn anymore, and the ache in his lungs was gone. It was as if almost drowning had happened to someone else. Clean and dry and warm, he might find the whole incident incredible except for one thing: the clear memory of his panic when he'd heard Anna's scream and seen her struggling in the black hold beneath his feet. And when the dank water had seemed to bury them and he'd known with a terrible, hopeless certainty that his life was ending.

He put his head back against the sofa and closed his eyes. Who had tried to murder him? Murder Nick, he corrected. Who was the masked man who had killed Nick on his wedding night, and who must believe now that he'd somehow survived the attack? Anna was right: this second attempt—third, if you counted Naples—proved that Aiden's theory of Union agents was preposterous. The *Morning Star*'s fate had been sealed weeks ago: she was either a cruiser called the *Atlanta* fighting in the American war or she was at the bottom of the sea, the victim of Dietz's superiors having taken the matter "under advisement." Brodie didn't know, nor did he much care. What mattered was who had killed Nick. Greeley had spoken of an accomplice at Jourdaine. Was the murderer that man? Had they fallen out over money—or had the accomplice feared exposure, and stabbed Nick to death to insure his own safety?

He heard a soft sound behind him and looked around. Anna stood in the library door, poised in diffident silence. He wondered how long she'd been standing there. She'd put on a loose-fitting gown the color of new ivory. And truly he was bewitched, for in the dim glow cast by the lamp beside him she looked both warm and insubstantial, a small and lovely ghost, beautiful but in danger of disappearing.

She clasped her hands and rested her temple lightly against the door post. She'd never seen the rust velvet smoking jacket he was wearing over his collarless white shirt. How handsome he looked in it. It contrasted with the color of his hair, which glowed like fiery dark copper in the lamp light. And on his feet he wore gray carpet slippers. That made her smile. The newspaper on his lap, the glass of brandy on the table beside him—there was no other word for it: he looked *husbandly*.

"Come in where I can see you, Annie."

After a second's hesitation, she took a few silent steps into the room, self-conscious, hands behind her back. She had to move carefully to avoid trampling the miniature model engine he had been building for the last week or so. It leaked alcohol on the carpet, and yesterday one of its numerous prototypes had caught fire. Aunt Charlotte had been furious. "What are you reading?" she asked, to break the intimate, returning silence.

"The *Daily Post*."

"Nicholas always read the *Courier*."

He smiled and wrinkled his nose. "Too stuffy."

She came closer, smiling too. "I suppose he was stuffy."

They both went still. There was no need to acknowledge it out loud: each knew these were the first unkind words about Nicholas she had ever uttered.

Anna looked away first. "And this—what's this you're reading?" She put one finger on the cover of a thick book lying beside him on the table.

"Marx. *The Communist Manifesto*."

She turned her head and fixed him with a long, penetrating stare. He returned it equably. "I remember asking you once if you could read." Her voice was steady but very quiet. "I don't believe I know you at all, Mr. Brodie."

His only response was to focus his light blue gaze on her more narrowly and run the fingers of one hand across his bottom lip, over and over.

Something fluttered in her stomach. She turned her back on him and did something she'd never done before. She went to the liquor cabinet and poured herself a brandy.

Brodie stood up and walked toward her slowly. "You were wonderful today, Annie. Carter couldn't stop talking about you all afternoon. I think he's in love with you."

She turned around, and suppressed a start when she saw how close he was. She took a sip of the brandy and closed her eyes as it burned all the way down. When she opened them, she saw that he was watching her throat. If she'd been naked, she couldn't have felt more exposed to him. "You're the one who was wonderful. I know what you're doing, and I know why."

He tilted his head. "What am I doing?"

"Pushing me forward. Making me—take the initiative. You wanted Stephen to see me in that role. Because of later, when . . ." Her voice trailed off.

"When I'm gone."

She reached behind her and set the glass down somehow without spilling any brandy. Then she clasped her hands again, to keep him from noticing that they had started to tremble. "It went well with Mr. Carter, don't you think?"

"Very well," he answered automatically. "I think a partnership with him can work. He's an honest man. An excellent businessman."

"Yes, I like him very much."

He stuffed his hands in his jacket pockets. Something told him she was paying no more attention to what they were saying than he was. And even though it was what they had come down for, neither of them wanted to talk about what had happened tonight on the *Alexandra.* "Annie."

"Yes?"

He took a breath, held it, and let it out in a rush. "I'm sorry about your father."

That wasn't what he'd been going to say, she was sure of it. "Never mind."

"It's not the way I wanted you to hear about it, the power of attorney. Aiden said it would be a good thing to do before the meeting with Carter, and I didn't—"

"It's all right, honestly, it's better this way. It had to happen sooner or later."

He felt relieved. "I thought you might think that I'd done it myself somehow, to swindle money out of your father or—"

"I never thought that. Never. Not for a second."

Their eyes met and held, and it was as if a kind of concussion jarred the space of air between them. In the aftermath, there was no sound except their shallow breathing. Anna reached backward again, this time to clutch the cabinet and steady herself. He watched her cheeks pale, in fear and acceptance. The need to touch her was like hunger; it made him weak, even as all the muscles in his body tensed and hardened. He took one hand from his pocket and reached out to the cream-colored rose in the center of her bosom. Her face flinched but she didn't move. He stroked the cloth flower lightly, just before his fingers clenched around it and he crushed it in his fist. Her lips parted on a silent gasp. He remembered everything about her mouth. He drew his breath in through his teeth and said, "Go to bed, Annie," in a raspy whisper. She didn't move, and he dragged himself back from her one step. "Go. Now."

All the color returned to her face in a violent

rush. She sent him one tormented look, darted around him, and raced out of the room.

For long minutes Brodie didn't move. He stared into the empty space where she'd been and asked himself what he'd done. Footsteps sounded in the hall. He whirled. Yes, this was the ending—that other was wrong, absurd. Of course, *this*—

It was Jenny. And one look at her face confirmed the truth of a suspicion he'd hoped was unworthy of her. And of Nick.

She stood in the doorway, tense and uncertain, before she spied him in the dimness and hurried over. Her hair was uncombed, her clothes seemed put on at random; he thought she looked as if she'd gone to bed and gotten up again.

Words tumbled out of her mouth, low, fast, and urgent. "We have to talk, I can't go on like this." He took a half step back. She reached for his hand and held it with both of hers. "I know what I promised, but it's too hard. Please, Nick, don't send me away."

"Jenny—"

"I can't do it anymore. Living in this house with you, seeing you every day—oh, God! Sometimes I think I'll explode if I can't touch you." Tears began to streak down her face. Her hands tightened and her voice turned into an anguished whisper. "Don't do this to me! I know you still want me—why are you pretending you don't?"

Brodie shook his head, eyes closed, hurting for her. "Jenny, don't. Don't, now, it's—"

"Please, please—"

She had her arms around his neck. She pressed against him with all her grief and passion; when she pulled his head down and kissed him, he stood still and let it happen. A thick, heavy hopelessness settled on his heart. He felt her desire rising, put his hands on her shoulders, turning his face away to speak, and saw Anna in the doorway.

She took a step farther into the room, then another. Her eyes were huge and cloudy with pain. *Run away, Annie!* he thought, but she didn't run. His body had gone ice-cold, and finally Jenny felt it and turned her head and saw her cousin.

She began to cry harder. "I don't care!" she flung at Anna hysterically. "He's mine! I had him before you and he still loves me, he's lying if he says he doesn't!"

Anna put both arms straight out when she saw Brodie move away from Jenny and start toward her. The pity in his eyes took the scalding pain out of her heart long enough for her to whisper, "*Tell her,*" just before she spun around and fled.

Jenny's hands were like claws on his forearms, her stubborn body a barrier between him and the door. "No," she begged, dragging at him, "don't go to her, stay with me!" She kept talking while Brodie listened intently to the diminishing sound of footsteps, and at last, the distant slamming of a door. His body sagged.

After a minute he realized Jenny had stopped talking. When he raised his eyes, she was staring at him as if she'd never seen him. *Tell her.* But he couldn't. To do that would put Anna in danger. He had to protect her, even if it meant hurting her cousin.

"Jenny." There was no gentle way to say it. "I'm so sorry for doing this to you. I didn't mean to, and God knows you don't deserve it. Everything's my fault." She just kept shaking her head. *Damn you, Nick*, he thought. "What was between us is over now. It has to be. You're better—"

"No!"

"Listen to me. I'm married now, Anna's my—"

"Liar! You said it wouldn't matter, you said we could still be together!"

Damn you to hell forever. "I'm sorry. But it's impossible now, we—"

"Why? What's changed? Tell me why!"

"Jenny, honey." Brodie drew a long, hard breath and told her. "I've fallen in love with my wife." Her whole body jerked backward. This was worse than anything. He reached for her—"God, Jenny"—but she flinched away and darted to the door. "Please wait," he called after her.

"Go to hell!" she hurled over her shoulder, her face contorted with pain. She lifted her skirts and ran.

He heard her in the foyer and then on the steps, taking them two at a time. Silence flowed back into the house. He stood in the black hallway for a long time, listening to the silence. Then he went upstairs to Anna.

Her door was locked and she wouldn't answer him when he spoke to her. He stopped trying the main door and went into his room and then their shared dressing room. "Annie, please let me in," he said through the dressing room door, also locked. Silence. He decided he could stand there all night, talking through the door, or he could wait until she was ready to see him. It was hard, it went against everything, but finally he stopped talking and knocking and went back to his room.

She heard him go, as she'd heard his every word and movement through walls and wood panels for the last five minutes, and turned her face into the pillow. She hadn't cried in a long time, and the first deep, racking sob was physically painful. The sound frightened her, it was so heartbroken; but the more she tried to stop, the harder she wept. She pressed the pillow to her mouth and gave herself up to it.

Always she'd known she was not beautiful, not desirable in the certain way some women are to men. But she had never experienced total personal humiliation. Inklings of Nicholas's treachery had come to her from Aiden, from a look on Brodie's face once, from the evidence of her own insecurities. She hadn't paid any attention. The miracle of what she'd thought was his love had shone so brightly, it had blinded her. But now the light was out and she yearned for extinction too, or at least invisibility. She supposed it was a mark of her sinful pride that even finding out he'd cheated her father's company hadn't hurt this much. It was *this* betrayal, this faithless breach of the trust of Anna Jourdaine that cut to the bone.

Oddly, Jenny's falseness didn't hurt as much. She didn't know what her cousin had shared with Nicholas, and she didn't want to know; but she felt strongly that Jenny was as much a victim of his dishonesty as she was. More, she didn't doubt that at this moment they were sharing the same agony. It was the sudden mental picture of her and Jenny crying in each other's arms that finally stopped her bitter tears and released her, once and for all, from Nicholas's hold.

She got up. Lying in bed and muffling sobs into a pillow suddenly repulsed her. She splashed water on her swollen face, then lit a candle and began to pace up and down between the window and the fireplace. What was it now? If Nicholas was exorcised, what dull, grinding pain had her heart in a vice? Intimations of the answer floated past, but she didn't reach out for them. Not at first. She felt so bruised, and she feared more suffering. But she'd never been more vulnerable, and in a matter of minutes she succumbed to the truth.

Something hurt worse than the idea of Jenny with Nicholas. She pressed the heels of her hands against her temples, her eye sockets, pushing it away, but it wouldn't go. The thing that hurt worse, that burned and blistered her very soul, was the idea of Jenny with John Brodie.

The cabbage rose pattern repeated on alternating diagonals, the colors every other flower—red, green, red, green, red, green. In between were curling bands of streamers or ribbons, red, green, white. Red, green, white. There were twenty-two columns of roses across the width of the room, twenty-eight across the length. Or twenty-three, if you subtracted the two and a half the closet door interrupted and two and a half the hall door—

Brodie leapt out of bed, mumbling obscenities at the wallpaper, and stalked to the door to twist out the gaslight. Feeling his way in the dark, he found the window and wrestled the curtains aside. Warm, fragrant air rushed in on the strong moonlight. He rested his palms on the sill and inhaled, eyes closed, face bathed in silver. He unbuttoned his shirt and dragged the tails out of his trousers. The night air felt soft and fresh on his overheated skin.

After a minute he turned his back on the sill and leaned against it, bare feet crossed at the ankles, arms folded across his chest. He wasn't much of a man for praying, but he thanked God now with all his heart, because Anna had finally stopped crying. He could not have stood it for one more minute. Just before it stopped he'd begun to look around for his shoes, so that he could put them on before he kicked her door in.

But the silence was almost as bad. He imagined her lying on her bed right now, staring at the ceiling, too exhausted to cry another tear. For the dozenth time that night he cursed Nicholas to hell. He cursed fate too, for its blindness and stupidity, because it had given Annie to the wrong brother.

As acutely as his senses were tuned to every sound from her room, he heard nothing until the dressing room door swung slowly open. She stood without moving in a slash of moonlight. He sensed her alarm when at first she couldn't find him. Then she saw him at the window and took one more tentative step forward. "Mr. Brodie," she said.

"Yes, Annie?"

"I've come . . . I've come to . . . I want us to make love."

23

He didn't speak. His arms came unfolded and he put them behind him; he seemed to be hanging onto the sill. Why didn't he say something? Time passed. She swallowed and got more words out somehow. "Did you hear me?"

He made a sound, something like a laugh but maybe a curse. "I heard you. Go back to bed." He saw her flinch, heard her indrawn breath. "Do you think I don't want you?" He threw his head back and cursed the ceiling. "Christ, Annie, I'm burning for you."

She smiled a sweet, aching smile. "Then—"

"But you shouldn't have come in here. I want you to go."

She shook her head steadily. "I don't want to go. And I don't believe you."

He looked at the ceiling again, this time for guidance. She thought she could hear him grinding his teeth.

"Listen to me, love," he said, with great control. "After I've gone you'll still have your name, your reputation. I'm not going to take that away from you, too. Don't you see, Annie? I don't want to hurt you."

She almost laughed. She put one hand on top of her head. "I don't believe this. You compromise me the moment we meet, you come close to raping me in a garden. You coldbloodedly seduce me in my own bed, you—you—*fondle* me in a public hall"—somehow that would always seem the worst—"and now, *now*—" she was sputtering with frustration—"you won't touch me when I ask you to because you want to protect my *reputation*?"

She stamped her foot, infuriated. "It's *my* reputation, I'll do with it what I want. Besides," she went on illogically, "no one would ever know. And *anyway*, everyone will think we've been intimate whether we have or not, so I might as well hang for a wolf as for a sheep!"

He let go of the sill and came toward her. He stopped when he saw in the relative brightness of moonlight that what he'd thought was her cream-colored dress was really her nightgown. "Oh, sweet Jesus," he murmured inaudibly, rooted to the spot six feet away from her. "Annie, love, the last thing in the world I want to do is hurt your feelings," he got out through his teeth. "But this isn't the way it should be. You're in pain because of Jenny and you think this will take some of it away. I can't let you do it."

He meant it, he was going to send her away. Her throat was so thick, she could hardly whisper. "This is not about Nicholas." *It's you.* But that she couldn't say; it would not come out of her mouth.

She waited ten more seconds. Then she reached down with crossed arms, seized two handfuls of cloth at the knees, pulled her nightgown over her head, and threw it on the floor between them, inside out.

The shaking started immediately. She wanted to look seductive, but it was impossible to keep from clasping her arms across her breasts, both to cover herself and to camouflage her trembling. She made herself look at him, even though the intensity of his pale blue gaze was scorching her. If he rejected her now, she would die.

He tried to look away, but he couldn't. Jesus God, he was only a man, and Annie was so beautiful. Once before he'd seen her naked, but he'd been too wrought up to appreciate it. She was so small and perfect, and her skin glowed like pearls in the light of the moon. Her hair was still damp from her bath; she'd pinned it up, but soft wisps had come down to touch the gracious curve of her neck. Her crossed arms flattened her pretty breasts in an unspeakably seductive way. Still, somehow he might have found the strength to resist if she hadn't turned her head just then, so that the moonlight picked out the two silver tear-trails on her cheeks. That was his undoing, and in two long strides he was beside her.

Instinctively, she shrank back. He froze. She smiled, but her eyes were fierce with panic. He didn't tell her to trust him, or that he would make it good; his body was burning, but he wouldn't entice her. The moment stretched into forever. At the last second, just before he opened his mouth to soothe her, to lie and say it didn't matter, she uncrossed her arms and stretched one small hand out across the foot of space that separated them.

It came to rest on his shirt and stayed there, warm and tentative, until she found the courage to move it to the side of his neck. With a quick sigh, she pressed into him lightly, letting her breasts brush against his hard, hair-rough chest. He embraced her, hard at first, then more gently as he recollected what he must do, how he must behave. Above all, he mustn't frighten her. But her nipples against his chest were like twin spots of hard heat branding him, and soon he wasn't sure who was trembling, she or he.

They kissed. A sliver of sound escaped her when he slipped his tongue into her mouth. Hers was shy at first, then curious, then brave, sliding across his lips like smooth, hot glass. Her fingers tangled in his hair and brought him closer. Her eyes were tightly shut, her muscles tender, alert.

"Annie," he murmured, caressing her, "slow down, Annie." It crossed his mind that she wanted it over soon because she was afraid. He backed her toward the bed as he placed little sipping kisses along her cheeks and her eyelids. "It's better," he whispered, pressing her against the high mattress with his hips, "when you go slow." If you can, he added to himself, then pushed her over backwards and lay on top of her.

Anna gasped. He opened her thighs and settled himself between them. In a flash, all her fear returned. She remembered how it had been before when he'd kissed her like this and—ah! used his mouth on her breasts like this!—and then he'd hurt her and made her cry. She stiffened, even as she acknowledged the peculiar part of herself that wanted him anyway, needed to have him, painful or not, in exactly the way she had before.

But he had other plans. He gentled her with soft, soft kisses while he moved lower, lower, until the dire inevitability of what he intended burst on her. She tried to sit up, but he pressed her back firmly, almost roughly, and then knelt between her legs. She fought his hands, opening her, but the first touch of his mouth finished her. She cried out in surprise, then gladness. She heard her own echo, shockingly loud, and cupped her hand to her mouth, muttering into it, "I'm sorry, I'm sorry."

Brodie stopped what he was doing and loomed over her. "You're sorry?" he said, shaking his head at her. "Annie, I don't care if you yell the house down."

She felt a wild laugh rising in her throat. It stopped when he put his lips on her again, and turned into a long, tortured groan. This couldn't be natural, this was some terrible perversion he'd learned in some wild, godless, uncivilized. . . . She forgot what the noun was supposed to be, lost her whole train of thought. She was melting, her flesh was turning into fire and water, she was a hot puddle of inarticulate wanting and the brink was nearing, nearing—

Gauging her perfectly, he stood up and pulled her against him, holding her.

Shocked speechless, she could only clutch at him, shaking, whimpering, mad and bewildered. He let her go and started to unbutton his trousers. She felt a cooling sensation in her stomach and looked away. In her peripheral vision she watched him shove his pants down and kick them off. Now he was in front of her again, standing quietly. She wasn't a coward. She looked at him.

"Dear God." She might have said it out loud. The room was silvery-dim, but even in the soft darkness she saw more than she wanted to see of his white hardness, upright, aggressive, daunting. He took one of her fluttering hands, then the other, and brought them to his lips. She suspected what he would do next, and she was right. But he was quick. Before she could react he closed her fingers around his thick maleness and held them there. Both of them stopped breathing. Within seconds Anna discovered he wasn't repulsive, he was hard and warm and exquisitely soft. When he took his hands away to hold her shoulders, she left hers where they were. Gentle, exploring. Utterly fascinated. Then she saw his face, so open and vulnerable and aroused, and the last of her fear evaporated. The lines of power shifted. In the passing of seconds, they became equals.

"Let's get in bed," he suggested.

They lay beside each other, kissing and touching, sighing softly, murmuring. "I want to kiss you everywhere," he whispered, making her quiver with excitement. "Do you like this, Annie?" He had his fingers tangled in her pubic hair, one knee nudging her thighs farther apart.

"I do, yes—ah! Ah!"

He'd slid his wet fingers into her and now he was stroking her, until she ground her teeth and clamped her hand down on his shoulder.

In a trice he was on her, easing into her, watching her face. She felt like buttered silk. "Annie," he murmured, over and over. He went slowly. "Am I hurting you?"

She just laughed. He put his lips on her throat and felt the vibrations, tongued them. Her heart was soaring. Hurt her? She wrapped her body around him and let the joy and relief envelop them both. Ah, the sweet closeness of this!

"Why did you come back?" he breathed against her mouth. "Tonight, in the library, after you left. Why did you come back?"

"To see you, just to see you. I had to see you."

They kissed passionately, and then they forgot to kiss. And Brodie forgot everything about timing and waiting and carefulness as he felt her tighten and burgeon around him. His heart opened. They reached their peak together, so natural, and for her it was an answer, perfect, the loveliest solution she could imagine.

"My mother's name was Elizabeth Brodie. She was Irish. When I was little, I thought she was very beautiful. Her hair was almost the same color as yours, Annie. But later, she looked like an old lady. She was thirty-six when she died."

"How did she die?"

Brodie's fingers tightened fractionally around the handful of Anna's hair he was stroking against his chest. "She worked herself to death. So Nick and I wouldn't starve."

She felt cold, and pulled the sheet up to cover them. She lay in the crook of his arm, her head on his shoulder, hand on his stomach. "Tell me about her."

"I've never talked about her to anyone before." He put his lips on her forehead. "I want to tell you."

She closed her eyes and waited.

"Her family wasn't wealthy, but they educated her as well as they could. She left home when she was eighteen and went to Wales to be a governess. The man who hired her was Regis Gunne, the Earl of Battiscombe. He lived in an old Tudor mansion in the river valley of the Clwydd. His wife was dead; he had a little girl. He was lonely. My mother fell in love with him, and he made her his mistress."

Anna's gentle, stroking hand went still. "Was he your father?"

"Yes. His daughter died soon, of a fever, and not long after that my mother became pregnant. She had twins, Nick and me, and we lived like a family in that big house until I was six. The earl would be gone for about half the year, to London to take care of his business affairs. He told everyone she was his housekeeper. There were no gentry neighbors around, no one to gossip about them except the servants. She lived as much like a wife to him as possible, with every comfort, and she brought Nick and me up to be gentlemen."

"And then?" she prodded when he stopped.

"And then—everything changed. I didn't know why until years later, when she was dying. She told me, but she never told Nick."

Anna sat up on one elbow, watching him.

"She got a letter from Regis one day, from London. It said he'd be coming back in a fortnight with his new wife. He'd made arrangements for us to move to a house in the village. Nothing would change—she'd still be his mistress, we'd still have everything we wanted. He'd visit as often as he could."

She looked away, hurting for him. "What did she do?"

"She left. That day she packed what we had and moved us out of the house. She tried to make it a game for us, an adventure. We were only six, but we knew how sad she was. We never saw her cry, but we knew."

"Where did you go?"

"To Llanuwchllyn. It's a little village at the end of Bala Lake. She got work as a spinner, and we lived in a cottage that was falling down and hardly big enough for one." He rubbed the back of her neck absently, combing her hair with his fingers. "It wasn't a good life," he said simply.

"Why didn't she go back to Ireland?"

"Because her family wouldn't have her."

"Oh God, John. And the earl never found you, never came—"

"He came once. I don't remember it; it's one of the things she told me later. He ordered her to come back. She refused. They had a bitter fight. He went away, and they never spoke again. Whenever he sent money, she sent it back. Then he had a son by his wife, a legitimate heir, and after that the money and the letters stopped."

Anna put her head on Brodie's shoulder again and held him, blinking tears from her eyes. "It must have been so hard."

"It was. It killed her. I've hated my father ever since."

She shivered, as if his body had chilled her. She drew him closer, to warm him, and put her lips on his throat. "Why didn't she tell Nicholas the things she told you?"

Now it was he who comforted her. His arms tightened around her; he chose his words carefully. "My father's abandonment hurt Nick more, hit him harder than me, Annie. We went so quickly from having everything to having nothing at all. My mother would never talk about it, never explain what had happened, even though he pestered her about it constantly. He hated the way we had to live, really suffered from it. He wanted so much. He wanted us to have everything again." He tilted her chin up gently. "I think she never told him who his father was because she was afraid he would go to him and ask him for things. Money. And she was proud—she couldn't have stood that."

Anna's eyes clouded; he was right, she knew—Nicholas would have wanted his father's money, regardless of what had happened between his parents. She bent her head to hide the pain she felt and didn't speak.

He held her while the silence expanded. "Are you sorry for him?" he asked at last. "Are you angry?"

"Yes," she answered, her voice muffled against his chest. "I'm angry and I'm sorry for him."

"But he turned himself into a gentleman, Annie, and I—"

She raised her head, cutting him off; her light brown eyes flashed fire. "You are more of a gentleman, John, than 'Nicholas Balfour' could ever have been if he'd lived to be a hundred."

"But he—"

"He was a thief and a cheat. His whole life was a lie. My love for him was childish and self-deluding, and his for me nonexistent."

"I can't judge him. I'm sorry he hurt you." He let his breath out in a weary sigh. "I miss him."

She lay quiet, feeling the thud of his heart under her hand. When she lifted her face again, there was no more anger in it. "Then I forgive him, with all my heart. For your sake."

Brodie pulled her close and kissed her. "You take all the pain away, Annie. You make me happy."

"I want to make you happy." She shut her eyes tight and whispered so he wouldn't know she was crying. Her heart felt swollen. She drew him down and kissed him again and again until they were both burning. His lovemaking was gentle at first, hers desperate. Then it consumed them. They forgot everything, past and future, as time and separateness ended. Afterward, humbled, he asked her for only one thing—that she be there beside him when he woke in the morning. She promised.

24

But she broke her promise. She awoke from a dream that she was naked, serving tea and cakes to the Middaughs in her aunt's drawing room. They were scandalized—"I'm fainting!" cried Constantia, covering her eyes—but Anna was powerless, trapped, inexplicably doomed to serving tea in the nude forevermore. Awake and staring, she felt Brodie's hand on her breast. There was no moonlight now, and the dark, heavy truth descended on her in full force and without mercy: she was lying in her father's bed beside a man who was not her husband. Still, when his sleeping fingers twitched, she felt an instantaneous pull in her loins and an urge to turn to him.

Footsteps—the rattle of a tray in the corridor. Anna leapt up, knocking Brodie's arm aside. "Wait," he mumbled to her speeding back as she raced naked across the room and into the dressing room, just as Pearlman knocked quietly and pushed open the door from the hall.

In the bathtub, she washed her toes dispiritedly and lay back in the sudsy water, moaning. Muscles whose existence she'd never even suspected were aching in the oddest way. Rather than recall all the interesting ways in which she'd acquired her aches and pains, she forced herself to confront the dreadful suspicion that she had fallen in love. It would be mortifying to admit that she had given herself to a man she did *not* love, and yet she'd have settled for that, gladly, over this other, much more horrible possibility. The thought of Brodie leaving was already so painful, she could hardly bear to think of it. If she loved him, she reasoned, it would be a hundred times worse. Although she couldn't imagine it being any worse. She covered her face with her hands and recalled last night's compelling order of events. For a few seconds she entertained the notion that she'd gone to him because she'd been desperate with jealousy over Jenny. But it was no comfort, because it wasn't true. She had gone to him because she'd wanted him.

She could see only one thing to do. If it wasn't already too late, she had to put an end to this weakness, this—physical enslavement to Brodie, because it would cripple her later, after he went away. Was that brave or cowardly? she wondered unhappily. Probably neither; just self-preserving. Would he be angry? She'd explain it so that he understood. If he really cared for her, he would see she needed to protect herself. She didn't want to hurt him—she would rather hurt herself!—but it seemed the best, the most sensible course. And if they both tried, surely they could—

All at once the door burst open—she hadn't

locked it; no Jourdaine would violate a closed bathroom door—and Brodie strode in. She let out a shriek and closed up in a ball. Then blushed, knowing she looked ridiculous.

"Feeling dirty, Annie? Couldn't wait to get clean?"

His snarling ferocity bewildered her. "That's not—" She broke off and jumped when he slammed the door shut with his foot. "What are you doing in here? Would you please get out so I can—"

"No." He came closer, knelt beside her. "What the hell are you doing?"

"I'm—What do you mean?"

"What are you *hiding*?"

She blushed again, but didn't unwind from her tight crouch in the bathtub.

He reached for her right hand, which was gripping her left shoulder, and started to pry her fingers away. She squealed and batted at him, splashing bath water everywhere. There was a tap at the door and Judith came in, carrying an armful of underclothes. She saw Brodie and braked to a halt, gaping.

"Get out," he snapped, standing up.

"No! Stay, Judith."

"I said get out."

"Stay!"

Brodie put one hand on Judith's shoulder, spun her around, and gave her a firm shove out the door.

Anna went purple with shock. "Damn you!"

It stunned them both.

Brodie's pale eyes narrowed; his mouth thinned to a grim line. He stuck his head out the door and called down the hall, "You're fired! Two

weeks pay and a surly reference, that's all you get!"
The second slamming of the door rattled the
windows.

Anna's fists balled with fury. She gave a choked
cry when he bent down and hauled her to her feet,
hands under her arms, drenching himself. He
stuck one booted foot in the tub and pressed her
back against the wall. His mouth cut off the
beginnings of a fine tirade and his slippery hands
slid everywhere, rough and urgent, exciting her
effortlessly. She felt the cold sting of the tiles on
her buttocks, the heat of his body against her
breasts and belly. Slowly his kiss turned unbearably sweet, and the sound of her name on his lips
melted her. Her wet arms crept around his shoulders.

"You can't get away from me," he growled
against her lips. "You're not allowed to show a
man salvation and then yank it out from under
him like a rug."

"Please," she whimpered, "you don't understand."

"I understand everything. But I'm not letting
you get away with it, I don't care how scared you
are. Christ, Annie, I want you right now, and
you'd let me. You would, and we both know it. But
I've got a meeting with Dougherty and I can't be
late. But if I didn't, I swear I'd lie down in this tub
and make you lie on top of me, and then I'd make
you come and come and—"

"Stop! Stop, oh God—"

He pulled her hands away from her ears.
"You're going to sleep in my bed again tonight,
and every night until they come and drag me
away."

"No!"

He took her hands away again, and pinned her wrists behind her back. "Like it or not, and for as long as it lasts, you're mine." He kissed her fiercely, pulled his dripping boot out of the tub, and left her alone.

"There you are, Anna. Where have you been all morning?"

"Oh . . . in my room."

Aunt Charlotte peered at her curiously, then went back to making unnecessary last-minute changes to the table setting.

Anna fingered a linen napkin for a moment, then asked in an offhand way, "Have you seen Jenny this morning?"

"Didn't you know? She left quite early and unexpectedly."

"Left! Where did she go?"

"She went to visit Helen Terry in Manchester."

"Helen? But—"

"The girl's been asking her to visit since they left school last year. Jenny was tired of saying no, and decided this morning to just go and get it over with."

"Oh. Did she—leave word, or say anything to you about . . ."

"About what?"

"Nothing."

Her aunt stared at her over the water goblet she was holding up to the light. "You don't intend to wear that to luncheon, I hope."

Anna looked down at her green dress. "This? I—Why not?"

"Have you forgotten the vicar is coming?"

"The vicar! Oh . . ."

"What is the matter with you today, Anna?"

She gave a little helpless laugh. "I don't know," she said, truthfully. "I can't seem to keep my thoughts together. I'll run up and change."

She moved listlessly down the hall toward the foyer, dragging her fingertips along the wainscot. At the foot of the staircase, she heard a noise at the front door. When she turned, Brodie came through, and stopped when he saw her. Streaming sunlight through the stained-glass window tinted his skin a beguiling rose and set the dark red in his hair on fire. His tall, straight body was beautiful, his face beloved. But it was the quiet, waiting hope in his eyes that undid her. Without a thought, she raced to meet him, her arms outflung, face radiant. She cut off his relieved laughter with an exuberant kiss, and hugged him until he lifted her up and twirled her around, two feet off the ground.

They held on, smiling into each other's eyes, until Anna remembered to ask, "Why did you come home? Is something wrong?"

"No, nothing's wrong. Aiden told me what you did, and then I had to see you."

"What did I do?"

"You hired a man to investigate Mary's murder for me."

"Oh." She made a move as if to turn away, but he kept her hands. "He wasn't supposed to tell," she muttered, coloring.

"I know, he let it slip by accident." He tilted her face up gently. "Thank you. No one's ever done anything like that for me before."

"You're welcome," she whispered, shy.

"Why didn't you want me to know?"

"Because—" she thought fast—"because I didn't want you to be disappointed if they don't find anything."

He smiled and shook his head. "I don't believe you, sweet Annie. You didn't tell because you were afraid I'd think it meant that you cared for me. You do, don't you?"

Before she could answer, he kissed her again, and then she couldn't speak at all. But finally, pressing against him, she pulled her mouth away to say, "I didn't tell you because I was afraid you'd take advantage. You see I was right." A new kiss began, deepened, started over again. The rightness of it, the impeccable wholeness she felt in being with him demolished her last scruple. Without regret, she gave herself to him, body and heart.

They jumped and turned together at a sharp knock at the door, and saw the solemn black outline of the vicar through the stained-glass window.

"Reverend Bury!" she cried in a whisper, breaking free.

Brodie swore. "We're not through." They were standing beside the door to the hall closet. Before she could react, he opened it and pulled her inside.

"What are you doing?"

"Shh."

A second later they heard the maid's voice, greeting the vicar, and then the sound of her footsteps as she left him in the hall and went to fetch her mistress. Anna stood stiff and silent, terrified of making a sound.

"Ah, Reverend Bury," trilled Aunt Charlotte, as Brodie slowly, slyly, began to unbutton Anna's dress. She gasped, and tried to sink her nails into his wrists. "My niece will be down in just a moment. Didn't Delia take your hat?" Anna froze. He had the whole front of her dress open and was unhooking her corset. What if Aunt Charlotte put the vicar's hat in the closet? "We were hoping Sir Thomas could join us, but he's not quite . . ."

He ripped open her chemise, muffling her shocked squeal with his mouth, scorching her breasts with his fingertips. Footsteps retreated into the drawing room—the room beyond the wall Anna's back was pressed against.

"Turn around."

"What?" Her knees were trembling, and not from fear of discovery.

"Turn around," he said, louder.

She could clearly hear the vicar's stiff laugh, her aunt offering sherry. Brodie turned her around. Then somehow, before she could think, he got both hands under her skirts and lifted them to her waist. "Oh my God," she moaned, and reached for the two coat hooks over her head.

"I knew you'd be wet, Annie," he murmured against her neck, nuzzling her, gloating.

The vicar was talking about next week's bazaar. "Why are you doing this?" she asked in a desperate whisper as he caressed her. The rustling sound of skirts and petticoats and crinolines sounded shockingly loud.

"Because you make me crazy. I can't keep my hands off you, can't stop thinking about you. Open your legs."

"Degenerate!" she breathed against the wall, but she opened her legs. "Oh—oh!"

"Shh," he warned, groaning, trying not to laugh, "don't let 'em hear us *now*." Through the wall, Aunt Charlotte was offering her back yard in August for the ladies' choir tea.

"I hate you, John Brodie," Anna said weakly, almost weeping.

"No, you don't, you like me. And you like this, admit it."

"I can't stand you and I can't stand—ow!"

"What? What is it?"

"My hair, you've got your—"

"Oh, sorry." He moved, untrapping her hair between the wall and his forehead. "Turn your head and kiss me."

"Anna! Anna?"

She froze again, but Brodie did not.

"Delia, go upstairs and see where my niece is."

"Yes, ma'am."

"Kiss me, Annie, give me your tongue."

"This is what you really came home for," she panted, "not to thank me but to—"

"Kiss me."

She did.

Dimly they heard the maid on the stairs, returning. "You might as well let go," Brodie said, with difficulty. "I can hold out much longer than you." A bald-faced lie if there ever was one, but she didn't know it. "Let go," he coaxed, stroking with the heel of his hand, then one soft, insistent finger. "Let go, sweetheart." In the instant when she decided to take his advice, the explosion started. She made a whimpering sound and went stiff. When she cried out, he put his hand gently over her mouth. She bit down, unthinking, and the extra sensation sent him over the edge with her. He muffled his own groan into her hair, pulling her tight against him.

". . . not in her room at all, ma'am. Judith hasn't seen her either."

He turned her around and held her, breathing hard, kissing her. "You hired Judith again," he accused, when he could speak. Her skin was damp and sweet, her hair tumbled around her shoulders. She didn't answer. "Are you angry? Did I hurt you?" He thought she shook her head. "Don't be mad, I couldn't help myself. I'll never do it again." A weak, disbelieving laugh was her response. He helped her dress, both of them groping at buttons in the dark. There were no more voices outside; Aunt Charlotte must have taken the vicar into the dining room.

He put his hands on either side of her invisible face and held her. She felt his breath, then his lips on hers, light as a whisper. "I know why you're frightened, and I don't blame you. If I were you, I wouldn't want anything to do with me either. Why you like me at all is a mystery to me. But you do." He paused, and moved his hands to her throat, lightly stroking. His low voice deepened. "Don't throw what we have away, Annie. I'm asking you to let me love you for as long as we've got. What difference does it make that it's not forever?" He felt her swallow, felt her hot tears on his fingers. "Please don't cry. It's not sad, it's good. Let it be good for as long as it lasts. I love you, Annie. I love you."

She took a deep, shuddering breath and told him. "I love you too."

Brodie closed his eyes, and his restless hands went still. She felt him trembling. She put both arms around him and they stood for countless minutes, lost in the sweet, sad ache of their love. She pulled away to wipe her face. "I never thought that I would tell you that," she whispered, snuffling, "in a closet."

A pent-up laugh, full of emotion, burst from him. She joined in it, and soon they were giggling and touching each other, trying to be quiet, trying not to cry.

"Say it again."

"I love you."

"I love you, Annie. When did you start?"

She tried to think. "I'm not sure. Last night? No, before. When you told my aunt that Milly could live with us. No, no, before that, when you were kind to Mr. Trout. No—I don't know! A long time ago, I think." She wanted to ask him when he'd started to love her, but she was too shy.

She kissed him instead, with a brand new tenderness that hurt his heart and took his breath away. "God, Annie, how can I leave you?" He felt her go rigid, and knew she'd misunderstood. "I have to go back to work," he explained, unable, like her, to speak of that other leave-taking yet.

"Oh," she breathed, relieved. "I wish I could see you." He chuckled. She heard him fumbling, and all at once the opening door brought light and cool air into their tiny, intimate den. They blinked at each other, not sure they liked this invasion.

"What will you tell your aunt?"

She laughed softly. "I can't even imagine." She began to straighten her clothes, her hair.

"You look beautiful. Perfect." He stilled her hands and kissed her again.

"Why do you think I'm beautiful?" It had been on her mind for a long time. "I'm not, but why do you think so?"

"Because you are. I don't have time to tell you all the reasons."

"Will you tell me tonight?" Then she blushed and looked away.

He took her in his arms, smiling. "Yes," he promised. "I'll show you. Run away now, Annie,

before they find us. I'll leave right after you."
When she didn't move, he realized he was still
holding her hands. "Go," he ordered, releasing
her. He watched her scamper across the hall to the
staircase. Midway up the steps, she turned and
blew him a kiss, laughing. But her face was still
wet from her tears.

25

Everybody said it was the prettiest day of the year. There wasn't a cloud in the sky, and the air smelled as fresh as new flowers. On Hadley Hill hardly a breeze stirred. The perfection of the midsummer afternoon was especially welcome because, for two years running, Jourdaine Shipbuilding's annual employees' picnic had been rained out.

"Look down there, between those trees. Can you see it, the custom house?"

"Yes, sir, I can see it."

"You weren't even born when they filled in the Old Dock to build it. Then they stuck the post office in there next to it, and the excise house. Everything's changed, boy. The city's tripled in size since I was your age."

"Yes, sir, I expect that's so." Aiden sent Anna a private smile above her father's head; she returned it, acknowledging his kindness. In fact, Aiden had been eight or nine years old when Old Dock had been torn down, but neither of them felt like correcting Sir Thomas today. He was the center of attention in his garden chair and lap robe, regaling a respectful cluster of workers and colleagues with unusually clear-headed reminiscences of the city and its past.

"When I was a boy, there were no mansions over there in Childwall or Allerton," he went on, pointing; "there was nothing but fields and pasture back then. Same with Everton Hill, although Toxteth had a house or two, now that I think of it. I remember when they started laying out the Mosslake fields . . ."

Anna spied Milly in the distance, toiling up the last few yards of the hill, and sent her a welcoming wave. She waved back, making a face of exaggerated exhaustion, and started toward a group of women who had begun laying out picnic food on long tables. Anna was glad Milly had come—she'd said she probably wouldn't. "Oh, but it won't be the same without you," Anna had protested; "you *always* come." Things were different now, Milly had tried to explain, but Anna wouldn't listen. It was good to see that her arguments had prevailed.

She felt a light touch on her elbow and looked around. Her heart did a familiar little dance in her chest. Brodie's fingers brushed her shoulder in a flicker of a caress. He smiled, and the warmth of it seeped into her bones. "Hello," she said, as if they hadn't spoken only ten minutes ago. She had an urge to touch his tousled, reddish-brown hair, blazing with streaks of gold in the sunlight, and another to bury her face in the open collar of his shirt and inhale the heady masculine scent of him. She did neither. But she saw his thin, sensitive nostrils flare and a private light flash in his beautiful eyes, and knew that he knew.

"If you're going to surrender, you have to give up your weapon."

"What? Oh." She smiled, and handed him the croquet mallet she'd forgotten she was holding. "How's our team doing?"

"Better since you left."

When he laughed at her expression of mock outrage, baring his straight white teeth, she felt a quaking in her stomach. "I stopped playing," she told him in a low murmur, "so I could look at you." Your long, handsome legs and your hard shoulders, wiry and muscular and controlled, and the way you move, without a single wasted motion . . .

His laughter faded. They watched each other for many wordless seconds, oblivious to all the sights and sounds around them. It felt like ages, not hours, since they'd made love. His wide mouth looked delicious; it made her tremble with weakness, as if she were starving. She heard someone call "Nick!" behind him, and dropped her eyes. "Come on, Nick, it's your turn!"

"Better go," she murmured.

"Rather kiss you."

"Me, too."

He drew a deep, not quite steady breath, turned, and trotted away.

She took a steadying breath of her own, deliberately avoiding Aiden's fascinated stare, and looked about for Milly. She wasn't with the ladies by the picnic tables anymore, nor with the mothers organizing children's games under the oak trees. She hadn't joined the croquet players nor the sober circle of matrons sitting on lawn chairs

under a canvas awning. She spotted the familiar
dark head striding off in the direction of the path
that led back down the hill, stiff-legged and
straight-armed, moving steadily but with a studied
lack of haste. Anna broke away from the group
around Sir Thomas and hurried after her.

"Milly!" she called.

Her friend halted but didn't turn around. "I
shouldn't have come," she muttered when Anna,
out of breath, reached her. "I knew it."

"What's happened? Has someone said something to you?"

Milly's face hardened and she didn't answer.

"Come over here with me, I've set out a blanket—" She slipped her arm through Milly's and
pulled her along gently, trying to read her expression.

"You're foolish to do this, Anna, in front of all
these people. You shouldn't even be seen with
me."

"*You're* foolish to even say such a thing," Anna
retorted, giving her a little shake. "We'll sit over
here, under this tree. No one will bother us. Who
spoke to you? What happened?"

"Nothing, it doesn't matter."

They sank down on Anna's plaid blanket, Milly
with her back to the others. Anna realized she
didn't want to talk about whatever hurtful thing
had happened, and stopped asking questions.
They sat quietly, Anna munching on cherries from
a black bowl and, feeling wanton, flinging the
seeds into the grass. From where they sat they
could see the estuary, and beyond it the distant
hills of Wales. The Great Heath spread out behind
them, the Pennines to the south. A part of Anna's
mind noticed that the leaves on the trees were a

deep, dark, heavy green, as if they were tired and almost ready to give up. Even the birds sounded grown-up and weary. Sadness, she knew well, lurked at the edges of her thoughts all the time, just out of sight. If she allowed it, it could obliterate her fragile joy. But she would not allow it.

"I've hired a lawyer," Milly said suddenly. "Did I tell you?"

"You said you were going to."

"His name is Mason."

"Is Mr. Mason a good lawyer?"

"It's—Mr. McTavish. Mason McTavish."

"Oh."

"Yes, he's a very good lawyer."

Anna couldn't help asking. "Did you tell him why you left George?"

Milly stared at her hands. "I did. I had to. He said I had to."

"I suppose so." In silence, she fought against feelings of hurt and disappointment because Milly had seen fit to confide in a stranger, a man, but not yet in her best friend.

"I wish I lived up here," Milly sighed, leaning back on her arms and gazing up through the branches overhead at the blue sky. "Far away from the city and the people. I'm so tired. If I lived in the country, I would start writing again. George wouldn't let me, did you know? It was . . . one of the things he didn't approve of."

Anna saw a door opening in the wall of Milly's reserve and took a chance. "Why are you so unhappy? Tell me about you and George." But one look at her friend's face—closed, retreating; embarrassed?—made her regret the impulse immediately. "I'm sorry, I shouldn't have asked, it's just that I care about you so much and I wish—"

"Oh, it's my fault! I can't—Anna, I just—I still can't talk about it. Not quite yet."

"Then we won't." She cast about quickly for another topic. "My father seems so much better today. Look at him, he's almost like his old self."

"How is he?"

"Not well, not really. Every day he's a little worse. He calls Jo—he calls Nicholas 'T.J.,' thinking he's my brother. And me. . . ." She laughed softly. "Sometimes I don't think he really knows who I am." A state of affairs not so very different from when he'd been well, if she wanted to be honest.

"When is Jenny coming back?" Milly asked, perhaps to distract her.

"I'm not sure."

"It's been rather a long visit, hasn't it?"

"Yes." And likely to be even longer, Anna guessed. She had wanted to write Jenny and tell her all was forgiven—she suspected that was what her cousin was waiting for; it would be like her to expect the first gesture to come from Anna—but Anna needed a little more time. The wound was still fresh, and she wanted her forgiveness to come from the heart. Jenny had been foolish and dishonest, but she was paying for it. What saddened Anna was that, no matter what happened, things would never be the same; they might forgive each other, but what had passed between them would never be forgotten.

"Oh, my. Will you look?"

Anna was already looking, and listening. About a dozen coatless and collarless men, Brodie among them, had formed a loose—very loose—semicircle beside the stream and were singing

"When Violets in the Valley Bloomed," in rather good four-part harmony.

"I had no idea Nicholas sang so well," Milly exclaimed.

Anna was thinking exactly the same thing. Brodie's voice came to her clearly over the others', a rich, strong baritone, perfectly pitched, with a warmth and vibrancy that inexplicably made her want to cry. Instead she laughed out loud. "Oh, my," she said, echoing Milly. The men had their arms around each other, their affection unabashed and undisguised. Their enthusiasm was a little stronger than the song warranted, and she suspected there was a bottle hidden somewhere among them. But no one was drunk; they were just happy. She felt a bittersweet happiness rising in herself, and shut her eyes to contain it. Oh, John, she thought. Oh, my dear.

"You love him very much, don't you?"

She looked into Milly's sad, soft face. All she could do was nod.

Brodie joined them a few minutes later. "What's this?" he said and picked up a small sketch from the blanket.

Anna snatched the sketch pad out of his hands. "Another failure." It was a watercolor sketch she'd done—of him. Until now her artistic efforts had concentrated on fruits and flowers and tentative landscapes. She ignored his speculatively raised brow and tucked the pad away in her purse.

"I hope this doesn't mean you're going back full-time to the violin." He sat down and planted a noisy kiss on her cheek, laughing heartily at her expression.

She blushed, anything but offended. She loved

his teasing. "It would serve you right if I did."

"How are you today, Miss Milly?"

"Very well, thank you. You were in fine voice, I couldn't help noticing."

"I was, wasn't I?"

Anna sat back and listened to their banter, at once delighted by their easy friendship and aghast that her best friend believed Brodie was her husband. The bizarre nature of the situation she'd gotten herself into sometimes seemed almost normal, but right now its unbelievable queerness struck her in full force.

"Uh, Nick, if you could, uh . . . could I speak to you for a second?"

The shy voice belonged to Max Paisley, Jourdaine's chief engineer. Anna smiled up at him; his Adam's apple bobbed in his skinny throat and he turned bright red. At designing sleek hulls and triple-bladed propellers he was a genius, but people, particularly women, rendered him inarticulate. Brodie scrambled to his feet and the two men walked off together a little ways.

"I'd better go," said Milly. "Thank you for inviting me."

"Oh, but you just got here," said Anna in dismay. "Don't go yet, you haven't eaten or—"

"I really must."

They held hands. "I'm sorry I made you come," Anna admitted, "because it's made you unhappy. It was selfish of me. I just wanted to see you."

"Nonsense, I wanted to see you, too."

"Will you come and visit me?"

"No."

Anna's face fell.

"But you could come and visit me."

"I will! Tomorrow."

"Not tomorrow, silly. One day next week. I'll send you a note."

"Milly—*damn* it!"

Both women's jaws dropped.

Then Anna started giggling. "Nicholas says it sometimes; I've picked it up."

"Good," said Milly. Mysteriously but fervently.

They kissed, and then Anna watched her friend walk away, head high, stylish skirts swaying.

"Christ, Annie, I almost understood what he was saying that time." Brodie shook his head in wonder and resumed his seat beside her.

She smiled. "You should have been an engineer."

"Should I?"

She saw her own sadness flicker for a second behind his pale blue eyes, and touched his cheek with her fingertips.

"Where's Milly?" he asked, more briskly.

"She . . . wanted to leave. I feel so—" She fluttered her hands in frustration. "She's hurting, and there's nothing I can do to help."

"You help by being her friend."

"But people are so cruel. People she thought were her friends have stopped seeing her, John, as if—as if she had a disease."

"Sweetheart." He took her hand and stared at it, lifting her fingers and bending them back and forth, one by one. "If I'd known what it was like for you in the beginning . . . if I'd had any idea how you live, how the rules work here and exactly what you risk by having anything to do with me at all—"

"Don't say you wouldn't have gotten involved."

"I wouldn't have. I can't stand to think of people treating you the way they treat Milly.

Except that, if they knew about us, it would be much, much worse."

She couldn't deny it. "I don't care, though, I wouldn't change anything. No—I would, one thing. I would have come to you sooner."

Brodie looked into her light brown eyes, grave and honest and shining with love. "I wish . . ." He made a fist of her hand and pressed it against his chest. "I wish I were a gentleman," he whispered. "For you."

She closed her eyes. "Don't you know that you're—" She broke off; the rustle of grass warned her their solitude was about to be violated. But she smiled when she saw it was Aiden.

"Hello," he said diffidently.

Brodie set her hand away quickly—guiltily. She sensed his withdrawal and stared up at him in surprise, then understanding. He was protecting her. Protecting what he'd once called in anger her "precious reputation." He cared more about it now than she did. She was moved profoundly.

She took his hand back and held on to it. "John doesn't believe he's a gentleman," she blurted out. "Have you ever heard anything more absurd?"

Brodie plucked at the blanket to mask his confusion. Why would she say such a thing to Aiden?

O'Dunne stuck his hands in his pockets and surveyed them thoughtfully. "I'm a lawyer, I hear all sorts of absurd things. Perhaps that's not so much absurd as ill-informed." They blinked up at him. "What is a gentleman?" he asked rhetorically. "Is it a rich man with a title? Not in my experience. I think a gentleman possesses the old-fashioned virtues, things like loyalty and courage, fair play and good sportsmanship. Honesty. He can acquire them by birth, which is easier but by no means a sure thing, or by behavior, which is harder. In the latter case, he makes himself into a gentleman using whatever tools he's been given, including his own knowledge, labor, and resourcefulness." He smiled, rocking back and forth a little on his toes. "If you're with me so far, John, I think you'll have to agree that you're as much of a gentleman as anyone on this hill today."

After a few speechless seconds Anna cried, "Hear, hear," with quiet fervor.

Brodie felt the flush on his cheeks and fought a cowardly urge to lower his head to hide it. "Thank you, Aiden," he said simply. "I won't forget that. You've been a good friend."

O'Dunne made a deprecating gesture, a suspicion of pink staining his own cheeks. They exchanged a few more words—commonplace, but charged now with self-consciousness—and soon he took his leave.

Anna smiled with satisfaction. "Put your head on my lap and take a nap," she suggested.

He quirked one eyebrow. "What?"

"I've always wanted to do that on a picnic with someone. A man."

He grinned. "What about your aunt? She'll think it's indecent."

Anna grinned back. "I know."

He laughed at her, but obligingly settled himself with his head in her lap, long legs stretching out past the blanket to the grass. He closed his eyes. She laid one hand on his chest and tangled the fingers of the other in his hair. They wore identical small, delighted smiles. She felt the strongest, deepest impulse to kiss him on the lips, and only the thrilling certainty that she could do it later, when they were really alone, held her back.

She spied her cousin Stephen across the way, standing with Martin Dougherty. They both had on the same clothes they wore every day to work. They looked stiff and hot and out of place, talking together beside a crumbling stone wall that bordered the stream.

Adjacent to them, her aunt sat in the center of a group of ladies whose husbands and fathers worked for Jourdaine. Most sat on lawn chairs but some, like Anna—the truly debauched—reclined on blankets. What would Aunt Charlotte have to say about *that* tomorrow? she wondered incuriously. Most of the women had brought their needlework, she saw; one was reading aloud from an improving book. Oh, but why go on a picnic at all, she thought bewilderedly, if you were only going to keep on with the same tedious occupations you engaged in at home every day and night of your life?

She and Brodie had been going out quite a lot—a new and exhilarating experience. How lovely to be allowed to go anywhere in the city, day or night, to concerts and dances and parties, even slightly risqué music halls, unchaperoned by anyone except the man with whom you were in love! She had never known such freedom, physical or emotional: it was a liberation of the spirit.

She'd never imagined what perfect companions they could be, either, or how complete their compatibility, in as well as out of the bedroom. It amazed her that she felt no guilt, and no real curiosity in the question "Is there something wrong with me?" when she looked at the ladies surrounding her aunt and tried to imagine any of them doing, much less enjoying, the things she and Brodie did in bed. The question had become irrelevant: if there was something wrong with her, she didn't care. It didn't matter.

But in her heart she knew there was nothing shameful or unnatural in their passion, just as she knew that the women she'd heard of who endured lovemaking in a kind of coma, with lights out, clothes on, and teeth gritted, were the victims of a lie more pernicious than any perversion she could think of. It *was* a conspiracy!

But to what purpose? she wondered, nibbling a blade of grass, resisting the temptation to tickle Brodie's nose with it. Why weren't all men like him? Wouldn't they rather their wives enjoyed themselves? It made no sense. And Brodie had told her, with a certainty whose origin she hadn't cared to question, that the same respectable, gentlemanly husbands who, along with their wives, laid down society's laws and enforced them so diligently—those very same husbands consorted on a regular basis with prostitutes. It was as if men had decided to enclose women in two separate and mutually exclusive categories: wives and whores. How strange! And how sad.

She was having an affair. There was no other word for it. It was a shocking, shameful word, one she had never, could never have associated with herself as recently as a month ago, and yet not a bone in her body regretted it. What she regretted was that it couldn't last forever. But that she wouldn't think about. She had made a deliberate choice not to worry about the future, even if it came tomorrow. What she had was now, this glorious present, a happiness she'd never envisioned for herself even with Nicholas—even in the ecstatic first days of their engagement when she'd believed that somehow, miraculously, he loved her and all her dreams had come true. This was different, better, out of the realm of her expectations, and it exposed the paltriness and naiveté of her childish hopes. Loving Nicholas had been the fantasy of a sheltered girl. Loving his brother was the fulfillment of a woman.

"What are you thinking about?"

"You." Always you. "I thought you were sleeping."

He smiled lazily. "Couldn't. I'm finding this particular pillow a distraction."

"Not comfortable?"

"That's not what I said."

They exchanged a slow look, full of meaning. The charm of touching but not touching was beginning to wear thin.

"Is it time to go home yet?"

"We haven't even eaten."

"What did you bring for us?"

"Cold roast beef, salad, some cheesecakes. Ginger beer."

"Mmm." He looked thoughtful. "We could take it home and eat it in bed."

She pursed her lips. "It's possible," she conceded.

"But people would talk."

"Without a doubt."

"They'd guess what we were up to."

"Unerringly."

"Would we care?"

"Not even remotely."

They rose as one and began, with the most unseemly haste, to fold the blanket.

26

"And God forbid that we should ever entertain a serious thought in our silly female heads," Milly said as Anna watered a fern in the conservatory. "They want us sweet and soft, tremulous, submissive. Dependent on them. Ignorant of anything requiring intelligence—politics above all. It's no wonder they flee to their clubs, to get away from the very women they've gone to such pains to create!"

"I beg your pardon." It was an unexpected male voice.

Milly stopped her agitated pacing, and Anna peered through the fronds of the potted fern. Her cousin stood in the doorway. "Hello, Stephen," she said amiably. "You're home early. I left a little early myself because—"

"I have to speak with you."

She straightened. "I wonder if it could wait. Milly and I were—"

"It can't wait."

"Oh, I see." She sent Milly a private look, a mixture of puzzlement and humorous apology.

Her friend returned a quick smile. "It's all right—I didn't realize how late it was getting. I must go, or Putnam's will close before I can get there. You needn't see me out, I'll just—"

"Don't be silly." Anna came around the long planting bench, wiping her hands on her apron. "Will you wait for me here, Stephen?"

He nodded shortly, moving away from the door so that the ladies could pass. "Mrs. Pollinax," he said, barely moving his lips.

"Mr. Meredith," said Milly, in a tone only Anna recognized as ever so slightly mocking.

"Don't mind Stephen," Anna murmured in the open front door; "he's not very nice to anyone these days." She took Milly's hands. "I'm glad you came to see me. I wish you would come more often."

"Perhaps I will—you cheer me up so. It's obvious that you're happy, and I've never seen you looking so wonderful. You're beautiful, Anna, there's no other word for it. I mean it," she insisted, laughing, when Anna made a silly face. "You positively glow. If I didn't love you so much, I'd be jealous."

"I love *you*. I only wish there were something I could do to help you to be happy."

"But you do help me. I can't imagine what I'd have done in these last weeks without you." They embraced, a little misty-eyed. "Now run inside, or your cousin will bark at you." Milly tied the huge bow of her spoon-shaped bonnet under her chin and strode off down the walk.

Stephen didn't bark at her. One look at his tense

face told Anna that for once he was more upset than annoyed. "Shall we go into the drawing room?" she asked tentatively, aware of his preference for formality on almost any occasion.

But to her surprise, he went behind her to the glass conservatory doors and closed them. "No, I don't want us to be overheard."

She stepped away, an instinct warning her that what he had to say was something she did not want to hear. "Is anything wrong?"

"Yes, you could say that."

He was silent, and after a moment she tried a little laugh. "Well, am I to guess or are you—"

"It's Nicholas."

She took hold of both sides of a wrought-iron planter, but kept her face empty of everything but polite interest. "Oh?"

"I tried to tell Uncle Thomas, but it was like talking to myself. Now I've come to you. Perhaps I should have spoken to Aiden, but above all I want to avoid a scandal."

"A scandal? Stephen, what are you talking about?"

He came closer. She saw that he held something in his hand, a piece of paper. "This will upset you," he said uncomfortably; "I don't know any other way to tell you."

"Tell me what?" She'd never seen him so ill at ease. She wasn't frightened any longer; she was terrified.

"Nicholas. . . ." He looked away uncertainly.

She put her hands to her cheeks. *Dear God*, she thought, *he knows.*

"I'm afraid Nicholas is embezzling money from the company."

Her first impulse was to laugh; the feeling of

reprieve was so strong, she felt giddy. "Oh, Stephen," she gushed, her hand over her heart, "you gave me such a fright."

His cool brown eyes measured her in surprise. "I'm in earnest, Anna; this is a deadly serious matter."

"Oh, but it's a mistake. You've misinterpreted something, that's all. Tell me about it." She folded her arms and smiled, masking her relief behind a look of exaggerated tolerance.

His lips thinned. "I've misunderstood nothing, except perhaps the full extent of your blindness. I'm sorry," he said, waving his hand, "that was unfair. Naturally you feel loyalty toward him."

"Naturally. Now will you please tell me what it is you think he's done?"

"He's stolen fifty thousand pounds."

"That is absolute nonsense." She got the words out in a long, unnatural interval between heartbeats. Stephen didn't respond, and for half a minute they stared at each other. To her dismay, Anna had to look away first. In the swift passing of an instant, her mind played out a scenario in which it was all true; she saw everything in detail —how he'd done it, why, and what would happen next. Then a curtain descended and the scene was blacked out. Denial set in.

"I found out by chance yesterday. Mr. Cannon at the bank mentioned in passing that Nick had withdrawn a sizeable amount of cash from one of the corporate accounts; he suggested we speak to his colleagues in the investment division about our plans for such a large sum. I pretended I knew what he was talking about."

"And then?"

"I went to Nick and demanded an explanation."

"And?"

"He denied it."

Her breath came out in a rush. "Well, then," she laughed shakily. "It's a mistake."

Stephen made an impatient sound. "The money is gone, Anna. It hasn't moved to another account, it hasn't been invested, it hasn't been used for any capital purchase. It's *gone*. And all Nick will say is that he knows nothing about it."

"Then he knows nothing about it! Stephen, it's a mistake. Why do you think he would lie?"

"Because of this."

He held out the piece of paper she'd seen before. She put both hands behind her back; fear returned as a fluttering in the chest. After a pause she forced herself to ask, "What is it?" her voice a ludicrous attempt at casualness.

"A bank note. Nick signed it. It's his handwriting."

Hope resurfaced. *Nicholas* had signed it, not John! One hand reached out, slowly, as if toward a sleeping snake. With unusual care, she unfolded the paper. The words went out of focus for a few seconds, then swam inexorably back. She read the date: July 20. A week ago.

This was Brodie's painstakingly practiced forgery. She remembered the day in Italy when she'd helped him master it.

She felt for the small wooden stool behind her and sank down on it. The humid air was stifling. She picked up a trowel and began to stab at the soil in a clay pot, dirtying her hands and sleeves and the front of her apron. The smell of rich, wet earth sickened her. Sweat beaded on her forehead and trickled down her sides. "There must be a reason. It's something he's done on his own. He'll tell me."

"I don't think so."

"Why?"

"When I confronted him with the note, he told me not to say anything to you about it."

Her hands went limp. She should say something defensive, belligerent, but no words would come. She was breaking up inside, and the pain was almost intolerable. Nicholas's betrayal had hurt, had cut her to the heart, but this was worse. This was like dying.

"It's a mistake!" she said again, all she could seem to focus on. "There's some reason he doesn't want us to know." But the only reason she could think of stared back at her with a monster's face, mocking her. She shook herself, like someone trying to wake up from a nightmare.

"You do know something about this, don't you? This isn't a complete surprise to you, I think."

Stephen's suspicion sent her a warning and forced her to think. She stood up. "I know nothing of it. You were right to come to me," she said, sounding confident. "Of course there's an explanation, but for now we won't speak of it to anyone, not even Aiden." Especially not Aiden. "Leave this to me, Stephen; I'll take care of it."

When she tried to move past him, he stepped in front of her. "Because it's a family matter, I'll give you a few days."

She stared. "What?"

"After that, I'll fight you. I want Thomas's power of attorney, and now I have something I can use to get it."

She felt the blood drain from her cheeks and

knew that, unless she got out quickly, she was going to faint. "You'll never get it—there is nothing to use!" She brushed past him and made it as far as the door.

"Be careful, Anna."

Holding on to the handle, she turned back. "I don't need to be careful. My husband has done nothing wrong!"

Stephen shook his head slowly, ominously. "Your father was a fool. He should have left Jourdaine to the Jourdaines."

In spite of everything, her chin rose. Her voice lost its note of weak bravado and turned resolute. "I am a Jourdaine." Behind a film of grief, her eyes flashed defiance.

Brodie hoisted his feet to the top of his desk and leaned back in his leather chair, fingers steepled over the gold watch chain across his stomach. Out of habit, his eyes came to rest on the photograph of Anna in the center of his desk, its oval frame and sober sepia tones somehow civilizing the chaos of papers and letters and reports strewn across it. She had on her schoolteacher's face—solemn eyes, serious mouth, no-nonsense chin—but now it swamped him with a wave of affection, pulled at his heart, and made him smile.

Next to the photograph was the glass paperweight she'd given him a few days ago. It was big and heavy, it took up a lot of room on his desk, but he would never consider moving it. The magnified figure inside was that of a sailor in full storm regalia—gumboots, oilskins, rain bonnet—his big hands gripping the spokes of a ship's wheel. When you turned the paperweight upside down, thick snow swirled. The sailor had a fierce, chiseled face, black hair plastered over his forehead, a pipe clenched between strong teeth—and pale blue eyes. It was the eyes, Anna had said, that made him look like Brodie.

He smiled. He gave the glass ball a little tap with his shoe and closed his eyes. She'd be pleased when he told her what had just happened, as pleased as he was, although the precise source of his pleasure would probably mystify her. Harry Stark and Will Random, mould and sail loft supervisors respectively, had just offered to sponsor him for membership in the Liverpudlian Men's Choral and Fellowship Society. If they had come with a citizens' committee to present him with a bucket of gold, he couldn't have been any happier.

The depth of his satisfaction intrigued him, taught him something about himself. He was a poor Welsh sailor, an undereducated, familyless bastard; social respectability for a man like him was a goal so far out of reach that he'd never set it, never even considered it. Before Mary died and he'd gotten himself arrested, he'd thought he was reasonably content sailing ships. Now he could admit that he'd hated the loneliness. A sailor made friends easily but not for long; whenever a voyage ended, he moved on to a new ship, a new skipper, new mates. And for Brodie, even among the friends he'd kept, a piece of him had always felt alien. He could see clearly now what he'd hidden from himself before, that the life he'd chosen didn't really suit him.

His new life did. He liked the men he worked with and they liked him—*him*, not Nick Balfour; time and again of late, he forgot he was playing a part and simply played himself. And the work challenged him, fascinated him. The better he understood it, the more he realized it was what he'd been born to do. Now to be asked by these men, these stalwart pillars of middle-class Liverpool society, to join their close-knit, masculine community—except for permanency, truly he was a man who had everything.

Permanency was an illusion anyway. Brodie would settle for today because he had no choice—it was all that had been given to him. In his heart he knew Anna's detectives would turn up nothing, and soon he would have to go away. He was no closer now than he'd been two months ago to learning the name of Nick's accomplice at Jourdaine; if someone hadn't tried to drown him a fortnight ago, Dietz might already have sent him back to prison.

But he wasn't going. No matter what happened, he wasn't going back to prison. It had taken a while, but he understood himself well enough now to know that he would rather hang than spend the rest of his life in a cell. And now he didn't think of his promise not to try to escape as binding. Dietz and the men who had forced him to give it believed they were extracting it from a murderer. But he was innocent; his promise had been coerced. He had no intention of honoring it.

Not that a lifetime in exile was very much better. What was it but another kind of prison? And now there were things for him to miss—a home, friends, work he loved. Anna.

Ah, Annie, Annie. He ought to feel despair, but it was impossible. He was too happy.

He didn't hear the soft opening of the door. A minute passed, and then something made him open his eyes and raise his head.

"You look . . . satisfied."

He smiled a slow, contented smile. "I am. Especially now." He held out his hand. She must not have seen it; she closed the door very deliberately and walked across the room to the window overlooking the yard. He watched her in silence, beguiled by the geometric slants of light and shadow on her face through the blinds. But gradually the stillness began to feel strained and unnatural. "Is anything wrong?"

She faced him slowly. "I see you're wearing your brother's watch."

He glanced down at the handsome chain under his folded hands. O'Dunne had given it to him. He'd worn it before today; hadn't she noticed it until now? "What's wrong, Annie?"

She didn't answer.

He got up and started toward her. Her eyes seemed to widen with each step he took. She was beautiful to him, a feast for his eyes, but now he noticed how pale she was. When he was beside her, he reached for her hand. It was cold, but it gripped his with a ferocity that amazed him. Then she pulled away.

He frowned, watching her poker-straight back as she stood beside his desk and stirred the papers on it jerkily. "I talked to Dougherty about that ballast problem you were telling me about," he told her, for the sake of something to say. "They were using shingle dredged up from the bay at Callao. That stuff breaks out of any box you can build for it and then rolls with the ship. Dougherty said—"

"I'd have given it to you if you'd asked me for it."

It was the sound of her voice that shocked

him—low and despairing and ice-cold—even before he understood the sense of her words. He flushed; his hands clenched into fists in his pockets.

She saw. Her lips trembled as they drew apart in a terrible smile. Her voice shook. "Yes, I've been speaking to my cousin. Did you think he wouldn't tell me?"

Brodie leaned back against the windowsill and crossed his ankles, hands still in his pockets. "What exactly did he say to you?"

She hated the fake nonchalance in his voice, the casualness of his pose. Was he going to lie? How much of a fool did he take her for? "Everything!" she cried. "I know everything. Except how you expected to get away with it."

"How I expected to get away with what?" he asked softly. "What is it you think you know, Annie?"

"Stop it. Please, please, just stop. I know that you're a thief and a liar, a hypocrite, a deceiver—I don't know the words to say what you are!"

Brodie felt the shredding of himself like tearing paper, slow, violent, and irrevocable. But what he said was, "Don't underestimate yourself."

She moved toward him, confronted him from the center of the room. "Is that all you can say to me?"

"No, not all. I could tell you you're wrong. Would it do any—"

"I saw the note, John. It's your handwriting—the money's gone!"

"Ah." He folded his arms stiffly. A muscle jumped in his jaw. "Then I guess that's it." *Tell her*, a gentler part of him urged. But there was so much anger now, so much trampled pride, and he wanted her to hurt as much as he did.

Anna's pride meant less to her, at least now. "Tell me anything," she begged, almost inaudibly. "Make me believe you."

Brodie pushed away from the window and came toward her. "Make you believe me," he said in a deadly quiet voice. "You want me to make you believe me?"

A chill raced through her. For the first time, she was afraid of him. He stood close; she could feel his breath on her face. In her ears, his question took on the dangerous cadence of a threat. Anger radiated from him in bright, shimmering waves. She wet dry lips and forced herself to speak. "Please. Tell me why."

"And if not? If I won't explain and I ask you to trust me, what then?"

"Don't do this. Don't make it a test."

"The test was over before you came in here. What do you say, Annie?"

"This is not fair."

"I'm waiting."

She clasped her hands together under her chin and whispered, "Did you take the money?" She thought his eyes would freeze her where she stood. Then he gave his answer.

"Yes."

Her body wilted. Through a haze she saw him move away, back to the window. "Why? Won't you tell me—" But then she knew. "You're going to escape."

He stood with both hands gripping the sill and looked at her across his shoulder. "Right again."

"Bastard!"

"Ah, that's good, Annie. You're coming right along." His smile was as ugly as a sneer. "Or maybe you meant it as a statement of fact, not a curse at all."

The first tears sprang to her eyes, but she bared her teeth in fury. "You won't get away with it, I'll expose you." But in the next breath, she cried, "What are you waiting for? Why don't you go, run away? Do you think if you stay you'll get *more* money out of my father? Between you and Nicholas, haven't you done enough? You've already gotten what you wanted from me, so why—why don't you—" But her voice finally broke. Tears streaked down her cheeks and she had to turn away, swallowing, fighting for control. If she let this pain overpower her, she feared she wouldn't survive.

"I didn't betray you."

She turned around. A terrible hope seized her. "Tell me," she choked. "Just tell me."

"I might have, before. Not now. Do what you have to do, but take your tears and get out of here. I can't stand the sight of them. Or you."

His eyes had gone lifeless in his white, stricken face. She had a fleeting, anguished sense that his wound went as deep as hers, but it passed. Or perhaps she buried it, under the crushing weight of hurt that was trying to suffocate her. There was one other thing she needed to tell him, but she couldn't think what it was. Was this all, then? Was it over? She felt blind. She wanted to see all of him, devour him with her eyes for the last time; but something in her mind, something besides tears, was preventing it. "Goodbye," she tried to say, but she was mute, too—the word wouldn't come out, wouldn't be uttered. She knew intense hate for him, and love just as strong. So this was all. She stopped looking at him and walked out.

27

"Nick's not in again today?"

Anna looked up from the delivery schedule she was trying to focus on and saw O'Dunne in the doorway. "Hello, Aiden. No, he . . . wasn't feeling well." Her fingers tightened around the pen in her hand as she contemplated the lie, and the cold contempt she felt for herself for telling it.

O'Dunne came all the way in and closed the door. "Is Brodie all right?" he asked in a low voice. "Is it anything serious? He's been out for three days."

"No, no, it's not serious, he's—just under the weather. Perhaps he'll be in tomorrow." Or perhaps tomorrow he would go away. For all she knew, he might already have gone.

"Anna? You're not looking well yourself, you know. Why don't you take the afternoon off? You've been working much too hard."

"I'm fine, Aiden, don't worry about me." But he

was right—she was exhausted. And she had a mirror; she knew what she looked like. Brodie's recent absence had given her a taste for what it would be like to work here when he was gone. Hard, hectic, challenging. Intensely lonely. And at the heart, empty.

She cleared her throat, and finally asked the question that had been on her mind for days. "Has there been any word from Mr. Dietz?"

"No, but it can't be much longer now. I'm surprised they've waited this long. If it hadn't been for what happened on the *Alexandra* that night, I think they'd have taken him back before now. He's turned up absolutely nothing."

She stared straight ahead. "And—I don't suppose you've heard anything from the man you engaged to investigate the death of Mary Sloane."

"No. But frankly, I didn't expect to." He laid his hand on top of her cool, stiff one. "Anna, I'm so sorry. I swear to you, if I had foreseen how this would turn out, I'd never have agreed to any of it."

"Nor I," she said.

"You're in love with him, aren't you?"

She pulled her hand away. "No. I'm not."

He smiled gently. Whether he believed her or not, she couldn't tell. "It'll all be over soon, my dear."

"Soon, yes." But there was no comfort in that, either. "Do you know, Aiden, I believe I will go home." She stood up, restless. "God knows, I'm not accomplishing anything here."

"Good, it's just what you need. Say hello to John for me."

"Yes, I will."

But that was another lie: she hadn't spoken a

word to Brodie in three days, and had no intention of starting now. But a feeling of incompleteness plagued her, intensifying the anguish she felt because of his betrayal. More needed to be said between them, it couldn't end like this, and yet she shrank from the pain a new confrontation would surely bring. Besides, he wouldn't speak to her. He wouldn't stay in the same room with her. He avoided the office in order to avoid her, and he was careful never to take a meal with the family if she was to be among them. If her aunt noticed his absences, she didn't comment on them. Neither did Stephen: he only watched, and waited.

The nights were the worst. Sleepless, weary to the bone, she would listen for a sound from his room—a cough, the creak of furniture, anything to assure herself that he was still there. Every morning she expected to find him gone, and every morning when she saw him she was overcome with a relief so vast it frightened her—then infuriated her, because of this madness inside that wouldn't let her foolish love for him die. In his eyes she saw anger too, quiet and scorching, and fretted because she knew of no reason for it. What had *he* to be angry about? Hadn't she given him every opportunity to explain anything he wanted? But there was nothing to explain—he was a thief, exactly like his brother. Fifty thousand pounds was a great deal of money, but her father's company—*her* company!—would survive the theft. What Anna honestly did not know was whether she would survive the theft of her heart.

She longed to confide in someone. Aiden was the only friend she had who knew their secret, and she couldn't tell him. She needed a woman. She needed Milly. And yet somehow she wasn't ready, in spite of everything, to confess to her closest friend that she'd been living a lie since her wedding night—no, before that, if she cared to include self-delusion. She would tell Milly everything one day, but not until Brodie was gone. Did that mean she was still protecting him? Or herself? She was too confused to know, too bruised to care.

At home, Brodie wasn't in his room. She knew it because the dressing room door was ajar; through it she could see Pearlman at work, industriously tidying the top of his master's bureau. "Where is Mr. Balfour?" she asked from the doorway.

"Outside, mum, with Sir Thomas. Since lunch, mum."

"Thank you, Pearlman."

She changed her dress. Why, she couldn't have said. Judith was nowhere, not expecting her mistress home at this hour. That was fine with Anna; she liked her maid almost as little as Brodie did. She recalled the morning he'd discharged her—then thrust the thought aside; it came with too many other memories. She put on a green and yellow flowered dress that flattered her, showed off her small waist. In the mirror she paused, contemplating her pale reflection, the faint but unmistakable blue hollows of fatigue and worry under her eyes. She bit her lips and pinched her cheeks, but the resulting color looked unnatural. Then she whirled away in disgust. What did she care what he thought of her? She went off to find him. To find her father, she corrected herself.

Brodie rolled Sir Thomas's chair two feet eastward, following the shifting slant of the afternoon sun. The old gentleman blinked thoughtfully but didn't speak. That wasn't unusual; they'd spent most of the afternoon in a comfortable silence, listening to birdsong and the hum of bees in the hedges. Brodie's head had almost stopped throbbing; his mouth no longer tasted like sour, wadded-up cotton. His recollection of the night before was imperfect, but he remembered the basics. He'd gone out and gotten blind drunk with Neil Vaughn.

The evening had started out innocently enough. They'd gone to Roe Street and potted at Victoria and Albert and Napoleon III in something called the "Royal Shooting Gallery." They'd moved on to taverns and dance halls; he vaguely recollected watching peep shows or *poses plastiques* at a "club" near the river. After that, his strongest memory was of when they'd stopped in an alley in Lime Street to relieve themselves against the wall, and Vaughn had offered him a puff on his pipe. It wasn't a tobacco pipe. And Brodie was drunk, but not that drunk. He'd traveled the world, he knew about the effects of chewing or smoking shredded coca leaves. He'd declined the offer, wondering if Nick would have done the same. A lot of his questions about Neil suddenly had answers.

But the basis of the friendship between Neil and his brother still puzzled him. Nick had been, at least outwardly, a pillar of the community, a self-made businessman—exactly how self-made had been his own ironic secret—who had married the boss's daughter and cultivated friends like Edwin Middaugh. Neil Vaughn, not to mince words, was a degenerate.

Later, much later, they'd gone to a brothel—although Brodie had no recollection of how he got there, only of arriving. He'd followed a girl upstairs. He remembered she had long black hair, straight as a stick. He remembered lying beside her, fully clothed, and her naked, struggling with his belt buckle. Then he'd passed out.

If John Brodie had done such a thing, they'd have taken his money and thrown him out in the street. But Nicholas Balfour was a gentleman. He'd been allowed to sleep it off in a whore's bed until dawn, then gently told to go home to his wife. They'd even given him a cup of coffee.

"Hello, Papa."

He jerked his head up. As usual the sight of her—small and lovely, and now tragic-eyed—twisted and wrenched at his insides. So he stayed away from her, only this time she'd taken him unawares. He wanted to look away, but he couldn't. The sun shot arrows of fire at her red-gold hair, defying and dramatizing the severe style she'd chosen. She was the most beautiful woman in the world to him, there would never be another, and merely looking at her caused him a pain he could scarcely endure. She bent to kiss her father's cheek and spoke softly in his ear. The old man smiled vaguely and nodded, staring off into space. Then she straightened her back and shifted her somber, wary gaze to Brodie. He stumbled to his feet. Without a word, he strode toward the house and didn't look back.

Why didn't he just take a knife and stab her in the heart? Anna thought hysterically. She murmured something to her father. He didn't seem to hear, but she left him anyway and marched toward the house with long, purposeful strides, arms swinging. She found Miss Fitch in her room, reading, and sent her outside to her father. Brodie she found in the library.

She almost stumbled over his model engine that

still sat on the floor. Gathering dust now—he'd abandoned it with all of his other work since the day she'd confronted him with the evidence of his theft. He was sitting in a chair by the open window, pretending to read a newspaper. His refusal even to acknowledge her tripped what was left of her temper.

"What are you waiting for?" she demanded, hands on hips, eyes blazing. "Why are you here? *Why don't you just go?*"

Brodie lowered the paper to his knee. The chill of his smile matched his eyes. He decided to tell her. "I'm waiting for the fourth of August." That shut her up. Confusion and apprehension flitted across her features. He liked confounding her.

"Why?" she finally asked.

Because I want to see the look on your face, Annie, just before I walk away. Aloud he said, "Why not?"

She flung away angrily and went to stand beside the bookcase on the far wall. The fourth of August was two days from today. Had he chosen to leave her then, the day of her twenty-fifth birthday, on purpose? If so, it showed a new dimension of cruelty she hadn't suspected. She made herself face him. "I know you don't care anything about me. But have you thought of what your sudden disappearance will do to my family, to the reputation of my father's company? Do you hate us all so much that you would take pleasure in ruining us?"

That made him mad, at the same time it made him want to comfort her. He stood up and moved toward her. It pleased him that the closer he got, the harder she pressed back against the bookcase, as if she'd like to merge into it. When he was standing in front of her he growled, "Don't worry about your precious reputation. I'll make sure it stays intact."

She wet her lips, frightened and thrilled by his nearness. "How?"

He ignored that. He had a question of his own. "Why didn't you tell anyone about the money? Why hasn't Dietz come to get me?"

She felt herself flushing and tried to move around him, but he leaned his arm against the shelf behind her, blocking her exit.

"Well? Why haven't you turned me in, Annie? You didn't even tell Aiden, did you?"

She started to tremble. She never thought he would ask her this. Bastard! Couldn't he take what she gave him and leave her in peace? Did he have to torture her, too? "Stephen will tell them. He said a few days, and then he would tell."

"But why not you?" he persisted, soft-voiced, leaning in. "Why not now?"

He knew why. And she was helpless, unable to lie, unable to do anything but stand, not meeting his eyes, and wait for him to kiss her. She wanted him to, longed for it. Was she moving toward him, subtly lifting her face? If he would touch her, she would be healed, if only for a moment. It would be worth it. Her eyes closed.

She heard nothing, but she felt a change in the air. When she looked he was halfway to the door, moving fast. "John," she cried, softly, hoping he wouldn't hear, praying he would. He didn't stop.

"But you must have been in love with him sometime, Milly, at least when you first married him."

"Of course I was. I thought he was a god—I loved him passionately! And I really believed he would rescue me from the tedium of my life at home."

"Was it so very bad?"

"You know it was—it was worse than yours before you married Nicholas. Nothing but endless visiting, call-paying, and card-leaving. Writing letters and reading out loud. Taking walks. Fancywork! Making shell boxes and seaweed albums and wax flowers—"

Anna laughed ruefully, remembering it well. "But to work, to do anything truly useful with your life, might make people think you needed the money."

"Horrors!"

"So the essence of gentility is to do absolutely nothing."

They shook their heads at each other, smiling grimly.

"Doesn't your aunt hate it that you go to the docks with Nicholas almost every day, and now you even have your own office?"

"Yes, she's appalled. She can't even talk about it."

"God, Anna, I envy you. You have everything—a wonderful husband who doesn't mind that there's work that you love. Children someday."

Anna tried to smile, but without success. There would never be children and she longed to tell Milly so, so that she could comfort her. She had no husband. And Nicholas's permissive attitude about her work had been the result of indifference, not tolerance.

She put her teacup in the saucer and set them on the table between her chair and Milly's, straightening her shoulders. The Lord Street sitting room was sparsely furnished but still cramped, the furniture old and unmatched. It was always damp and usually dark. What saved it from complete shabbiness were Milly's small, eccentric touches —the odd or humorous prints cut from magazines and pasted to the dingy walls, an Indian rug that hid all the sins of the lumpy old sofa, candles of every size and color lining the mantelpiece and the homemade bookshelf. There was no servant except for a girl who came for an hour or so in the afternoon to sweep and to bring Milly a meal from the pub down the street. But despite the discomforts and the dramatic difference between her friend's old life and this new one, today Anna noticed an excitement in Milly—not just nerves, but a real enthusiasm for living that she hadn't seen in her for a long time.

"What was it like in the beginning with you and George?" she asked diffidently, brushing the arm of her chair with her fingertips, staring down at her hand. "How did it feel to be in love?"

"You should know that," Milly smiled. "You've been in love with Nicholas for eight years."

Anna stirred restlessly. "Did you . . . were you . . . ?" How absurd to be this tongue-tied with her best friend. "Did you ever experience physical passion?" she asked directly, blushing a little but relieved now that the question was out.

Instead of answering, Milly stood and went to a cloth-covered three-legged table under the window. She opened a box and brought out a small yellowish object. Anna's mouth dropped open when she saw that it was a cigarette. "Want one?"

She shook her head, wide-eyed.

"It's an affectation." Milly struck a match against the brick mantel, lit the cigarette, inhaled, and blew out a big gray puff of smoke. "I don't really like the taste." She stood with her back to the fireplace, arms crossed, the hand that held the cigarette draped over one shoulder. "I was younger than you when I married George, and even more ignorant."

"If such a thing is possible."

"It's incredible, isn't it?" she exclaimed, distracted. "How utterly stupid women are about sex? But that's how they want us, I truly believe it. It gives them even more power over us. But anyway." She waved her cigarette in the air, as if to say she didn't want to get started on that subject. She took another deep drag, and didn't exhale this time. Anna stared, fascinated, as the smoke exploded fitfully from Milly's mouth and nose while she talked. "When we were first married, when we made love, I didn't enjoy it."

Anna nodded sympathetically, remembering her first time. Then she smiled in anticipation, recalling her second. "But then?"

"Then . . ." Milly flung the cigarette into the fireplace and turned away. "Then it got unspeakably worse."

Anna's smile dissolved. "Oh, Milly." She stood up uncertainly. Was this what had made her leave George? She went to her side. "Did he hurt you?" she asked, taking Milly's hand, brushing the dark hair back from her cheek to see her face. "Did he?"

"Yes. Sometimes." Her lips trembled but she was dry-eyed. "On purpose." She gave a short, bitter laugh. "I was so naive, I wasn't even sure, for *years*, that there was something wrong with him. I thought all men must be that way." She turned away again. "For all I know, they are."

Anna thought of Brodie and how, even at his most outrageous and impossible, he had always wanted her pleasure at least as much as his own. "They're not," she said, quietly but positively.

"I'm glad I told you," said Milly, brushing ash from her skirts and turning brisk. "I've wanted to tell you before now, so many times, but I felt ashamed." She jerked her head up. "Which is ridiculous—I'm not the one who's done something wrong!"

"Of course not. And you were right to leave him. He's a beast—you should have left him sooner."

"I should have. That's the one thing I am ashamed of."

"Does Mr. McTavish think there will be any trouble with the divorce?" Anna asked after a pause, to change the subject. She had an idea Milly wasn't ready to say more about what her marriage to George had been like, at least not right now.

Milly moved away and went to sit on the sofa. She draped one arm over the back and said, quite casually but looking away, "That's the other thing I've been wanting to tell you."

Anna raised questioning brows.

"Mr. McTavish isn't my lawyer any longer."

"No? But I thought you liked him."

"I . . . do like him. I like him very much. Indeed."

Anna blinked. After a moment she joined her friend on the sofa. "How much?" she said softly.

Milly's face was a study. In it Anna saw a clash of worry and excitement, hope and despair. "Mr. McTavish and I have become"—she traced the Indian rug pattern on the sofa with an apparently idle fingernail—"friends."

"Friends."

"Yes."

"Good friends."

"Yes." Finally she met Anna's fascinated stare. "I think I'm in love with him. He says he's in love with me, too. It was impossible that he could stay in my employ any longer as my solicitor under—under the circumstances."

"No, I can see that." She laughed in sudden delight and seized Milly's hand. "But how wonderful! I'm so happy for you! His name is Mason, isn't it? What's he like? Tell me everything." Milly slipped her fingers out of her enthusiastic grasp and stood up, as if she wanted to put distance between them. Anna frowned and finally asked, "What's wrong?"

Milly leaned against the fireplace mantel and folded her arms—defensively, Anna thought. "You may not feel quite so happy for me when I tell you what I've done. In fact, you—may despise me."

Through her puzzlement, Anna almost laughed again. "That seems exceedingly unlikely. What have you done?"

"I've—I've—been intimate with him. And I—am not sorry. I have no intention of marrying again, even though he's asked me to. But I'm not willing to give him up. Do you understand what I'm saying?"

"I think so," Anna said slowly, returning Milly's serious, intent gaze in kind. "You mean to take Mr. McTavish for your lover. Indefinitely."

"Exactly. So." Her tone turned brittle. "You don't know what to say to that, I can see. Now you know why I've been trying to protect you. This is a bit more than you bargained for, isn't it? If my relationship with Mason becomes known, your reputation will suffer almost as much as mine, simply because you've been my friend. I expect this means—"

"Milly, stop trying to make me angry. Come over here and sit down." After a few seconds, she came. Anna closed her eyes and rested her head against the back of the sofa. "I gather you're expecting me to condemn you for this. Pick up my things and walk out, never see you or speak to you again. Is that what you think?"

"You'd have the right. You've always cared more about convention than I have. You've lived your life by the rules. Your husband is respectability itself, your aunt—" She broke off, bewildered by Anna's sad laughter.

Anna faced her, not bothering to disguise her unhappiness. "Listen to me. I would be the last person in the world to judge you for the things you do because you love this man. The very last person. All I want for you is happiness. If Mason McTavish can give it to you, my advice would be to take it. While you can, in any way that's available to you."

Milly's eyes filled with tears. "Oh, Anna," she whispered, snuffling, fumbling for her handkerchief. "Thank you. I'm sorry, I didn't know what you would think, what to expect. I should have known you'd be like this. What would I do without you?"

The clock on the mantel struck twice. "Muddle through somehow, I expect." She stood up, blinking back tears of her own. "I don't want to leave. There's so much we need to talk about—such as why you won't marry a man you're in love with who wants to marry you. But I'll be late for my aunt's tea if I don't go now, and she's angry with me for so many other reasons already, I—"

"Never mind, you have to go. We'll talk again soon."

Milly stood up, and Anna gave her an impulsive hug. "Oh, I wish you didn't live here, I wish you would come and live with me!"

"How delighted your dear aunt would be."

"I don't care, Milly, not anymore. I honestly don't."

"I think you mean it. I hardly know you anymore, Anna. And I thank you, but I'll stay here. I'm growing rather fond of the place, to tell you the truth. I never knew how lovely it could be to live alone. If you will come to see me every now and then, I'll have everything."

They walked to the door together, arm in arm. "I have something to tell you, too," Anna said quietly. "Not today, but soon."

"I know."

She looked up. "You do?"

"I know something's troubling you. Is it Nicholas?"

Anna leaned her head back against the doorpost, poised on the edge of laughing and crying. She closed her eyes and nodded. "What I have to tell you will take a very, very long time."

"Is he treating you badly? I thought—" She hesitated. "It's just that at the picnic he was so nice, I liked him better than I ever have. I'm— surprised."

She took a shaky breath. "Oh, Milly." So it was to be crying. "I'd better go."

Milly held her arm. "Listen to me. I don't know what the matter is, but please don't make the same mistake I did."

"What did you do?"

"Because I didn't want to face it, for the longest time I talked myself into believing nothing was wrong between George and me."

"I don't think I'm doing that."

"Listen to your heart, not your head," Milly insisted, hardly hearing. "It's wiser. And it doesn't lie." Her grip on Anna's wrist was almost painful; her dark eyes glittered with intensity. "Do you understand what I'm saying? Protect yourself. Believe your feelings and act on them."

Anna looked away. "If I were to act on my feelings . . ." she began with a half-laugh.

"What?" Milly prodded.

"I would go to him now," she breathed, realizing it as she said it. I would tell him it doesn't matter about the money because I love him, I forgive him, and somehow I still believe he's a good man. Oh, but why did he have to take the money?

"Then go to him," Milly said firmly, smiling. "Is he still at home, still not feeling well?"

"No, he—was going to go to work this afternoon." Something she would not have known if she hadn't overheard him saying it to Stephen this morning. She'd wondered why he was going back; was it to see his friends one last time? Tomorrow was the fourth of August.

"Go and see him there, then."

"Oh, but I don't know—"

"Go. Trust yourself. Don't waste time, like I did. Then in a few days, come and tell me what happened."

The carriage let her down in the north yard. Two forty-five, her watch told her. Would he be in his office or somewhere on the docks? And what would she say when she found him? She set off purposefully, deciding she would figure that out when the time came.

A man was coming down the brick steps from her building, walking toward her. She blinked in disbelief and missed a step. It was Horace Carter. What in the world—?

"Hello!" he called, catching sight of her, too. They moved toward each other. "How d'you do!" he said heartily, seizing her hand in his beefy paw and shaking it. He was already perspiring in the warm August sun. "Didn't expect to see you today," he added, before she could say the same thing to him. He mopped his face with a huge handkerchief and led her by the arm to the patch of shade the building cast. "Things are moving along real well, Anna, smooth as silk."

"They are?"

"Yes, indeed. They'll go even faster now with your contribution. I've got to tell you, little lady, I like your style."

"Our—what? What contribution?"

"Why, your fifty thousand pounds! What is that in dollars, anyway? Notice I didn't say 'in real money.' Ha ha! Dora finally broke me of that."

"What—?"

"Matched with our fifty, it should make for a nice, smooth planning phase. I can't foresee any problems at all! Your husband's got as good a head for business as you do, and that, my dear, is a high compliment." He grinned engagingly. "I like the sound of this new kind of engine he and his engineers have been tinkering with, too. I don't see why—" He stopped, finally noticing her shock. Then he turned sideways and swore under his breath, turning red. He slapped his massive forehead twice with the heel of his hand in energetic chagrin. "Damnation! I forgot it was supposed to be a surprise, and here I've gone and spoiled it. Nick was going to tell you tomorrow. *Now* I remember! Listen," he said conspiratorially, looming over her, "he'll kill me if he finds out I let it slip. Do you think you could manage to act surprised?"

Anna was leaning on the wall for support. "Horace."

"Ma'am?"

"What exactly is the surprise?"

He grinned his big-toothed grin. "The surprise is—" he held out his hand again—"we're partners."

"Partners." She shook weakly.

"In Carter-Jourdaine Lines. We decided to put Carter first because it's alphabetical." He winked broadly, cackling. "But the first liner to come off the ways is going to be called *Anna*—we put that in the contract. It was Nick's idea. Hey, what are you doing?"

"Crying." She found her own handkerchief in her pocket and wiped her eyes. She couldn't get her breath, and she wanted so much to shout out loud and laugh for joy.

"Well, do you think you can?"

"What?"

"Act surprised."

She smiled shakily. "Oh, Horace, I don't think so. I think it would be best if I talked to him right away. Now, in fact." A giddy laugh bubbled up. She put her arms around his thick neck and hugged him. His startled look tickled her so, she planted a big, noisy kiss on his cheek. "Excuse me, I have to go now." And she darted away, leaving him staring.

"Is Mr. Balfour in or out, Jim?" she asked the porter at the front door.

"Haven't seen him go out, ma'am, so I expect hc's in. Nice to see him back!" he called to her as she dashed up the steps.

She'd have taken them two at a time if her skirts had allowed it. She was breathless when she reached the top. Please be in, *please*, she prayed, trying to see through the frosted glass of his door at the end of the hall. She didn't knock. She threw open the door and swept in.

And halted in her tracks. Brodie rose from a crouch in the center of the room. The slanting sun glinted on the paperweight in his right hand. One drop of blood fell from the glass ball—or was it his fingers?—onto the corpse at his feet. Martin Dougherty's skull was crushed and he was bleeding all over the carpet.

28

Brodie dropped the paperweight and started toward her. She took a fast step back. He saw fear in her eyes. "You think I killed him," he said.

At first she couldn't speak. Then she said, "No."

But all he heard was her hesitation. He shouldered past her and charged out into the hall. She heard him call to Aiden, then to the porter downstairs, shouting at him to run for a constable because a man was dead. In the seconds before the room filled with people, she found herself staring, past rigid fingers that covered her face, at the broken body sprawled on the floor. The familiarity of that leaden, intense, unreal stillness sliced through the curtain of forgetfulness she'd drawn months ago to conceal the full horror of Nicholas's murder. Through the jagged tears, memory shot back in blinding bursts, searing and burning, transfixing her. People jostled past; dimly she heard exclamations of shock and revulsion around her. The intensity of a stare brought her back, and she raised her head. Brodie watched her from the other side of the room, over the corpse. In his eyes she read bitterness and disillusionment and the beginnings of a terrible acceptance. She stepped toward him, drawn by a compulsion to console. She stopped when he moved sideways, literally recoiling from her.

At that moment O'Dunne put his hand on her arm and turned her. Over his shoulder she saw Stephen, white-faced, hanging back in the doorway, unwilling to come closer. "Are you all right?" asked Aiden.

"I—yes, I'm fine. I just got here. N-Nicholas found him."

O'Dunne's head swiveled toward Brodie, who was wiping blood from his hands on a handkerchief. The two men exchanged short, unreadable stares. "Come outside," O'Dunne urged; "you look as if you're going to faint."

She could have said the same to him. She looked back at Brodie. He'd turned his back to her and was talking in a low voice to Nigel McGrath and Tom Shorter. With a shiver of panic, she let O'Dunne lead her out of the room and into her own office next door. He spoke to her quietly, reassuringly, but she didn't hear. Brodie's face blazed in her memory, branding her mind's eye and blinding her to everything else, even the dreadful fact that a man was dead and someone had murdered him.

"Take this at once," she heard Aiden say to the boy who ran errands in the office; he handed him an envelope, and she recollected that a moment ago Aiden had been scribbling something on a piece of paper at her desk. "Number 19, Queen Street. Do you have that?"

"Yes, sir," answered the boy, and darted away.

"What is it? Who are you writing to, Aiden?"

O'Dunne hesitated a second, then said, "Dietz."

"Why? The police are coming. What does this have to do with him?"

"Stay here." He started for the door.

She stepped in front of him. "Tell me! It's about John, isn't it?"

"Yes, but it'll be all right. Dietz has to know."

She made a grab for his arm. "But why? Aiden, you don't think he did this!"

"I don't know."

"He didn't! He couldn't have! For what reason?"

"Stay here," he ordered, and left her.

She obeyed, for five minutes. But then she couldn't bear it and went into the hall to look for Brodie. She saw him in the open door to Stephen's office. She started toward him at the moment she heard the tramp of half a dozen heavy feet on the stairs. The police had arrived.

Confusion ensued for the next two hours. People continued to mill about, speaking in hushed voices at first, then louder as shock wore off and excitement set in. Two policemen questioned her. She told them what she'd seen, and heard the implication of her own words with a lurch of alarm. Where was Brodie? Sometimes she would catch a glimpse of him, always far away, always in a crowd, but he would never look at her. Once she found him alone, holding onto the railing over the second-floor staircase, staring down at the dark well below. She went to him quickly. "We have to talk," she said in a low, fierce voice. "Will you please talk to me?"

His eyes were empty this time, even of regret. "No," he said quietly. Politely. And he walked away from her into a room full of people.

Dietz came, with another man, one she'd never seen before, whose job seemed to be taking notes and not speaking. She led them into her office, where Dietz asked her all the questions the police already had. Then he asked them over again. "And you heard no voices, no sounds of arguing as you approached the door?"

"No, I've told you. The man was dead, John found his body."

"Mm," he said, and she was growing sick of the sound. His words and manner were noncommittal, but his very reticence terrified her. He crossed his long legs and smoothed back the iron-gray hair at his temples. "And how do you know that for certain, ma'am?"

"Because I know it!" She unhooked her hands from the edge of her desk and willed herself to relax. She needed to keep calm; now was not the time to give in to emotion. But she felt like screaming.

"And the paperweight was in Brodie's right hand when you entered?"

She let her breath out slowly. "Yes."

"And you know it was Brodie's paperweight because you gave it to him."

She didn't trust her voice; she nodded once.

The big man surged to his feet. "All right."

She popped up in his wake. What did "All right" mean? she wondered frantically, following him to the door. "What will happen now? What are you going to do?"

He looked down at her with something like kindness. "There's no need for you to worry, Mrs. Balfour." She almost sagged with relief before he continued. "No matter what happens, Mr. Brodie's identity will remain a secret, to protect you. If he's guilty, I promise you he'll hang as Nicholas Balfour."

She lost all color. "He's innocent!" she hissed as he opened the door to the hall. "Where is he? Tell me, I have to see him." She tried to move past him.

Dietz's hold on her arm was unexpectedly forceful, though his voice was still mild. "Not yet, if you don't mind. We have a few more questions to ask him first. Then you can see him. It shouldn't be long."

But half an hour later, when she threw her door open and raced out to find him, the constable in the hall told her he'd been taken to police head-quarters.

"Pearlman, are you telling me that he's not back yet?"

"No, mum, not yet."

"But it's after ten o'clock!"

"Yes, mum."

Anna unwound the light lace mantle from her shoulders and dropped it on a chair in the dressing room. She had come upon Pearlman in his master's room, turning the bedclothes down for the night. The valet searched her face discreetly, but he'd have let himself be sacked before he'd ask Mrs. Balfour what in the world was happening to her husband. Anna couldn't have told him anyway. News traveled fast; no doubt Pearlman already knew everything she knew. It wouldn't have surprised her if he knew more.

"Very well, that's all for tonight, there's no need for you to wait up."

"Very good, mum." The valet bowed politely and left the room.

Instead of going back to her room, Anna came all the way into Brodie's. Avoiding the mirror on the wardrobe door, she made a slow circuit of the room, letting her fingertips glide lightly over tabletops, curtains, the chest of drawers. The book on his bedside table was *Great Expectations*. Beside it was *Bell's*, his favorite sporting newspaper. His paisley dressing gown lay at the foot of the bed, neatly folded. The comb and brush on his bureau were spotless; a bottle of macassar oil was tightly stoppered and unused, but another bottle beside it was half empty. She picked it up and opened it. The scent that escaped unlocked a flood of memories. It was the cologne he wore sometimes, grudgingly, but more often since she'd told him she liked it. Without guilt, she opened his top drawer. Handkerchiefs and collars and the scant jewelry he possessed. A small box in the back. With a tiny stab of guilt now, she pulled it toward her and opened it.

And smiled. He'd said he'd given up smoking, but evidently it hadn't been a clean break. She took out a rolled cigarette and held it between her middle and index fingers, turning her hand to study the effect. She brought it to her nose and sniffed. Not pleasant, but not unpleasant. She put the tip to her lips and inhaled, blowing imaginary smoke up and out, the way she'd seen Milly do it this afternoon. An affectation, indeed.

Go to him. Trust yourself. She'd taken Milly's advice, but she'd been too late. Horace Carter's revelation had rendered her new faith in Brodie meaningless. She would live with that mistake for the rest of her life.

She replaced the cigarette in the box and closed the drawer. Restless, she crossed to the bed. Where was he? He couldn't still be at the police station! And if he was, what were they doing to him? She'd spent the last two hours at the Dougherty house in St. George Street, offering condolences on behalf of her family to Martin's spinster sister. The news of his death had arrived there before Anna, so at least she'd been spared that. Victorine Dougherty was a silly, flighty woman, but her grief was heavy and real. Anna had felt helpless in the face of it. It astonished and dismayed her to realize how little she had really known Martin. He'd worked at Jourdaine for as long as she could remember, although he was only middle-aged. With the friends and neighbors who had come to console his sister, she'd tried to dredge up memories of him, kindly or good-humored anecdotes about him for Victorine's benefit, but without much success. Once Brodie had told her Martin reminded him of a piano; she'd seen the resemblance, laughed at it. Mentioning it tonight hardly seemed appropriate. When she thought of him at all she thought of a serious, rather dour man, who had done his work competently and kept to himself, rarely socializing. But Victorine would miss him—he was all she had—and the financial stability of which Anna had privately assured her seemed paltry in comparison to her loss. Who could have killed him? Who could have had enough motive, enough passion to murder so viciously such a quiet, seemingly passionless man?

Not Brodie. She put out her hand to touch his dressing gown. Unable to help herself, she picked it up and held it to her bosom, breathing in the scent of him that lingered in its silky folds. Oh, my dear. My love. I've lost you.

Weeping now, she lay across his bed. Barely a week ago they'd lain on it together. She remembered the night she'd first come to him here, in his room, asking him to love her. He never would again. Memories were all she had now, all she would ever have. She closed her eyes and dreamed of him.

Morning light shone pale and grudging. She blinked in its surly gleam and sat up on her elbows. She was alone. The bed was still made; she was still in her clothes. Had he come, seen her, and gone away? The thought was wrenching, but an instinct told her it hadn't happened. Then where was he?

Her toilette was hasty and thoughtless. Judith was more silent than usual. I should've let Brodie discharge you, Anna mused as the maid buttoned her into a white lace chemisette and maroon silk skirt. It was too early for breakfast; she didn't want it anyway. She would check on her father— would he remember Dougherty? miss him at all?—and then quietly leave the house for the office. If Brodie wasn't there—her mind shut down; with a jolt of despair, she realized she couldn't think past the next hour or so of her life.

But Stephen was in the hall. Had he been waiting for her?

"He's been arrested."

She held onto the bannister, focusing intently,

willing herself not to shout out, not to cry. "What are you talking about?"

Stephen looked as if he hadn't slept at all; he still wore the clothes he'd worn yesterday. "Nick's in gaol. They're saying he murdered Dougherty."

"It's a lie," she said weakly. She was in the act of sinking, sitting down on the second-to-last step, when she saw her aunt come out of the drawing room.

She wore her nightgown under a brown satin robe. Night cream slicked the flaccid folds of skin on her face; her hair was plaited in a long gray braid over one shoulder. Anna had time to think she looked younger, she looked almost pretty, before her strident voice sent all thoughts flying. "This is what comes of marrying beneath you. I told Thomas, but he wouldn't listen. Now see what's happened."

John? She wanted, longed to say his name out loud, but she couldn't. "Nicholas?"

"He's been arrested!"

Somehow she came the rest of the way down the stairs, into the hall. "Where's Reese? I need the carriage."

"Are you out of your mind?" Aunt Charlotte put her hand out. Expecting sympathy in spite of everything, Anna let it rest on her arm until she felt the anger in it. Then she flinched away. "You can't go there!" her aunt cried, horrified.

"Please get out of my way."

"Anna! Think! He's in gaol for murdering that man. You can't go there. You have to begin to distance yourself from him. No one will think less of you—you were only married three months. You can have it annulled, no one—"

"Let me go!"

"Let her go," echoed Stephen. She sent him a grateful look, but his face froze her in motion. "I'll have it now," he gloated, grinning. "The power of attorney, everything. And there's nothing you can do. Go to him, what difference does it make? You deserve each other."

It took all her self-control not to strike him.

"If you leave this house, I'll move out. I mean it!" Aunt Charlotte's shiny cheeks were beet-red, her thickset figure quaking with indignation.

Anna's own fury brought a freezing-cold calm. "You won't have to. I'll move. Get out of my way."

But her aunt was rooted, immovable. In the end, Anna shoved past her, and something in her enjoyed the physical contact, the near-violence that finally propelled her aunt out of the way.

She walked to the police station, her mind in a chaotic whirl of worry and determination and residual anger. The eastern sun was in her eyes, piercing them. She was perspiring by the time she arrived.

"He's not here," a man in a uniform told her when she demanded to speak to her husband. Afterward, she couldn't remember what she said to him. She remembered waiting, and then another man, not in uniform, speaking to her. "Mr. Balfour's been released in Mr. Dietz's custody, ma'am." He said something about the Ministry, something about a different jurisdiction—she hardly heard. *Where was he*? "He should be at the docks by now, ma'am; he was going there this morning, he said, in case we needed him."

The docks! She hired a carriage in the street and told the driver to take her to the shipyard. Why hadn't he come home? She sat, numb with misery as the city passed unseen out the window, kneading her skirts with her fingers, blind with confusion. The need to see him was like a sickness now. It ate at her, scattering her thoughts. Her heart felt shredded. When she arrived at the north yard she ran toward the brick building in the center, oblivious to the workmen watching her, tipping their caps in amazement. She'd done this yesterday, an indistinct voice reminded her. But Martin Dougherty had been dead then and she'd been too late. This time she must not be. She raced up the steps, unnaturally aware of the dust in their corners, the grainy pattern of oak in the risers. Her hand shook when she reached for the knob of Brodie's door and threw it open.

29

"Get the hell out of here. Now!"

Anna stopped dead. Her eyes darted between the faces of the two men who stood at opposite sides of Brodie's desk, confronting each other. One was Brodie, the other was Aiden. The tension between them was thick, nearly visible. For a second she thought of yielding to Brodie's harsh command, then elected to ignore it. She closed the door and leaned her back against it, wide-eyed. "No, I won't. Not until you talk to me." She jumped when he hammered his fist on the desk and barked out a truly vile oath, but she didn't move from the door. She had never seen him so angry. "John, I'm not leaving. What is the matter? What's happened?" Brodie only glared. She thought she saw something else in his eyes besides antagonism: she thought she saw fear. "Aiden? Will one of you tell me what's wrong? I won't leave until you do."

The lawyer's face was harder to read. Fear was there too, but masking it were anger and wounded dignity. His hair, usually so neat, looked wild; the skin under his day-old beard was gray and pasty. "John has been making some interesting accusations, my dear." His voice was a failed attempt at humorous acceptance. "I suppose you may as well hear them."

"I want you *out*," snarled Brodie.

"What accusations?"

Aiden affected a laugh. "He seems to think I'm the one who murdered poor Martin, and he's giving me an opportunity to turn myself in. Evidently I'm supposed to feel thankful for this act of kindness, but somehow I can't summon up any gratitude. Churlish of me, I know, but—"

"Get out of here, God damn it," Brodie said, leaving the desk and moving in her direction.

"Will you stop saying that? I'm not going anywhere!" She planted her feet and folded her arms. Brodie halted in front of her, with a look that would have withered a less determined adversary.

"But you haven't heard the best part," Aiden went on before he could speak. "He also thinks I killed Nicholas." He laughed falsely a second time and shook his head at Anna, who had gone as pale as a ghost. "Of course he can't tell me *why* I murdered one of my best friends, a man I've known since—"

Brodie whirled on him. "Maybe for the same reason you killed Dougherty—because he knew too much about you."

Anna's confusion finally overcame her shock. "Explain this to me, John," she said weakly. "What are you talking about?"

"Why should I? You wouldn't believe me any-way. The best thing for you to do, Mrs. *Balfour*, is to get the bloody hell out of here. Go home!"

She tried not to flinch, but his anger was too potent. She swallowed and said again, as calmly as she could, "Explain it to me. I'm going nowhere."

He watched her for a long, tense moment, funneling all the antipathy and bitterness he felt into a malicious stare, but it didn't work. She wouldn't go. If he wanted her out, he would have to throw her out, bodily. That held no small appeal, but maybe, for now, it was better if she heard what he had to say. It concerned her as much as it did him, after all.

"All right," he agreed shortly. He went back to the desk and sat on the edge, a position from which he could watch both of them. "I had a conversation with Dougherty yesterday. About an hour before he died. He came to me wanting to know where his share of the money was. 'What money?' I asked. That made him mad. 'O'Dunne's got his by now, I'll bet,' he said. 'Where's mine? You said a month after Naples.' What do you think he meant by that, Aiden?"

O'Dunne looked scornful, but Anna noticed the perspiration on his forehead.

"Dougherty must have gone to you right after that," Brodie continued, not expecting an answer. "You didn't know he was in on it with Nick until then, did you? Must've come as quite a shock. Nick was good at keeping his crooked associates ignorant of each other. How did you get Dougherty into my office while I was out of it? That was a bright move. It made everybody think I killed him. Right, Annie?"

"Never," she whispered, shaking her head, her

wide-eyed stare intent on him. "I never thought that." She went whiter when his lips curled cynically.

"This is absolute nonsense," O'Dunne scoffed.

"What I can't figure out is why you killed my brother," Brodie continued after a few seconds.

"Oh, for—"

"You needed him. You needed each other."

"I didn't kill him!"

"Was it just for his share of the money? Or was it to shut him up so he couldn't tell anyone who his partner was? That's why you killed Dougherty, but you were about an hour too late."

"You're completely wrong." Aiden was sweating profusely now. He mopped his face, then stuffed his handkerchief back into his pocket. "You don't believe any of this, do you, Anna?"

She couldn't answer.

"It was you who hired the two thugs on the docks in Naples, wasn't it?" Brodie pressed. "What were they supposed to do, keep me from finding the *Morning Star*? They bungled that. You hired a pair of incompetents, my friend. They killed Billy instead of me, and they almost killed you."

"It's a lie, I haven't killed anyone! Anna—"

"What will Mr. Dougherty's records show, Aiden?" she asked suddenly, fearfully. "About the Dutch company that supposedly bought the *Morning Star*? Martin visited it in April. Did he really go there, or did it only exist on paper?"

"How did Dougherty account for the absence of any money from the sale?" Brodie pursued. "Must've been some pretty fancy bookkeeping. Dietz will be interested in looking at it, don't you think? Up to now he's only had your word that everything's on the level."

"It's preposterous!"

Then Anna remembered. "The telegram, Aiden —the one I sent after yours—I told them John had given the money up and saved your life. But what did yours say?"

O'Dunne couldn't seem to speak.

Brodie answered for him. "His said I tried to escape and he caught me. He advised them to send me back to Bristol immediately."

Anna sagged. "Oh, Aiden."

"Dietz has known about you ever since. He's been waiting for you to lead him to the third man. What he didn't reckon on was that you'd kill him."

O'Dunne looked back and forth between their bleak, suspicious faces. He reached again for his handkerchief. Instead he jerked out a pistol.

"Son of a bitch." Brodie stood up quickly and moved between Anna and Aiden.

"It's all true," Anna breathed, twisting her hands, appalled but not afraid. "My God, Aiden, how could you have done this?"

"Listen to me." The lawyer leveled the gun at Brodie's midsection with a hand that shook badly. "I had no choice, I swear it. It started a year ago when Nick sold the *Ariel* to the Confederates."

She put her hands to her face. "The *Ariel*," she echoed hopelessly. She'd wanted so much to believe Nicholas innocent at least of that.

"I learned of it, and he offered me money to keep quiet."

"How much?" Brodie snapped.

Color began to stain the dead gray pallor of O'Dunne's cheeks. "Twenty thousand pounds. I— took it. Greeley's superiors wanted more ships, but Nick decided the *Morning Star* would be the last." He faced Anna, pity mingling with the panic in his mild brown eyes. "You see, when T.J. died and Nick realized you'd inherit everything, he saw a better way to make his fortune. I'm sorry, Anna, but—"

"I know it. I've known it for a long time." It didn't even hurt now; it only made her sad.

"And you didn't know Dougherty was in on it, too?" asked Brodie, measuring the distance between himself and the gun. As long as it was pointed at him, not Anna, he could keep his own panic under control.

"I suspected, but I wasn't sure. Until yesterday."

"And then you killed him."

Aiden closed his eyes for a split second, and then he nodded. "I didn't want to, but I had to shut him up. The paperweight was lying there on the desk. He turned his back. I picked it up and . . ." He seemed to run out of breath.

"Smashed his skull in," Brodie finished, without a trace of sympathy. "What now? Kill us, too? Then what?"

The lawyer shook his head as if to clear it. "No one's going to be killed. Move away from the door, both of you."

Brodie grabbed Anna's arm and pulled her out of the way. Keeping his gun on them, O'Dunne went toward the door and opened it. He backed through and Brodie followed, step for step.

"Stop, John, I mean what I say. Stay here and you won't get hurt." Brodie kept moving. They were in the hall, O'Dunne backing toward the stairs, his pistol in both hands now to steady it. "I'm warning you! Stay where you are."

"You'll have to kill me to get out of here," Brodie told him, quite calmly. Anna cried out and tried to catch hold of his arm. He caught hers instead and shoved her away violently, not even looking at her.

"I'll shoot!"

"Shoot, then. Do you think I give a damn?"

Doors opened. People started out of their offices, then stopped and stared.

Aiden had almost reached the steps. Brodie was three feet away and closing. "God damn you, I'll kill you!"

"Stop!" Anna begged, distraught, blinded by terror. She made a grab for Brodie's sleeve, but he pushed her off again and shoved her against the wall.

"Shoot me," he taunted, reaching for the gun.

Aiden took a last step back, into thin air. Without making a sound, without firing a shot, he fell backward across six steps before his head hit the seventh. His body struck all the eight remaining. But it was the seventh that had killed him, by breaking his neck.

30

Anna pushed black soil around the roots of one half of the bamboo plant she was dividing, turning the pot slowly, pressing with gentle thumbs. The springy, three-leaved fronds were ever so slightly off-color, the tiniest bit more yellow-green than green; she made a mental note to allow more time between waterings in the future. When the pot was finished, she set it next to its fellow on the ledge in front of the wide, brass-framed windows and wiped her damp forehead with the back of one hand. The house was quiet; she could hear nothing except the restless, ceaseless fluttering of the finches in a cage hanging in a corner of the conservatory. She went to the glass doors that led to the dining room and pushed them farther apart. Still silence. No distant voices, no bustle of house-keeping. But that was not so strange: except for herself, Brodie, and a handful of servants, no one was home.

Aiden had been dead for three days. On the second day, to escape the awkward and undiminishing repercussions of the scandal, Anna's aunt had departed on an impromptu excursion to Brighton, taking Sir Thomas and his nurse with her; at the last minute, Stephen had decided to go with them. Anna had urged him to go. He needed time away from Jourdaine Shipbuilding, she'd told him, to sort out what he wanted to do. If he chose to stay, she wanted his complete support for the new partnership venture with Horace Carter. Stephen had been cool and abrupt, but he'd agreed to think it over.

That was yesterday. Ironically, a day later the worst seemed to be over: journalists no longer pressed for interviews, neighbors and friends had stopped dropping in to console or to gape, and police and Ministry officials were finally gone from the drawing room where they'd carried on their endless interrogations. Here in the sleepy late-afternoon stillness there were no more reminders, at least not visible ones, of the catastrophe that had rocked her family, her company, and the city's shipping community.

The sun was setting in the west window, reflecting splinters of yellow light against the tall glass. The humid air curled and frizzed the ends of Anna's hair, turning it into a reddish-amber halo. She went back to the potting bench and began to prune the pointed leaves of a palm in a claw-footed terra cotta jardiniere. She heard a timid mew and looked down to see Jenny's kitten sharpening its claws on the ruched hem of her skirt. Not really a kitten any longer, she saw; Ambrose was more of an adolescent now. And probably lonely, with no mistress to pay attention to him. She bent, put a hand under his chest, and brought him up on her lap. He curled in a ball and began to purr, and Anna thought for the first time in months of Domenico, the cat who had followed her everywhere at Casa di Fiori. He'd liked women better than men, she remembered with a smile; he'd ignored Brodie, and barely put up with Billy Flowers's clumsy, gentle-handed attentions. He hadn't let Aiden come near him.

She stroked the cat absently as she let her mind wander back over the familiar thought-path it had been pacing ceaselessly for three days. She'd known Aiden O'Dunne since she was ten years old. Fourteen years—no, fifteen. He'd been the age she was now when they had first met. She'd liked his quiet manner, the way he took her seriously, his unfailing kindness. Over the years she'd learned to love him, and to value his friendship above anyone's except Milly's. How could she reconcile the sober, generous friend she'd known with the man who had murdered Nicholas, and Billy, and Martin Dougherty? The man in a mask who had swung a poker and nearly killed her, too?

She couldn't. And yet it was true. But how was it possible, then, for human beings ever to understand one another at all? And why did she still grieve for him?

She raised her head, listening. Was that a sound, a thump, from somewhere in the house? Ambrose slept on; Anna must have imagined it. She lifted the gangly kitten down to the flagstones and went back to her work. But a moment later she paused again to listen. Again, nothing. She was being a fool. Brodie was somewhere in the house, carefully shut away from her—not by anything so crude as a locked door, but only because that wouldn't be necessary; he knew a closed one would serve the same purpose.

She was in a state of suspended animation, frozen in time, waiting for something to happen that would start her life again. She suffered from the painful and persistent feeling that she was being punished. Deservedly. But Brodie's careful politeness was worse than punishment, it was torture. It flayed her skin and cut to the bone. He would speak when spoken to, even agreeably; he would not fight. He was remote, courteous, almost courtly. She'd submitted to his treatment at first —after all, she thought humbly, it was only what she deserved. But she hurt so deeply, ached so wretchedly. When would it be enough? When would the debt be paid? And lately the rebellious thought had begun to intrude that the chasm dividing them was partly—*partly*—his fault. He could, after all, have told her the truth about the money at any time and ended the quarrel. But he was too proud. They didn't have time for his pride!

She had wronged him—she knew it, she had no will to deny it. He was an honorable man. The murder of Mary Sloane had called his honor into question, and she'd always thought that it injured him as much to be believed guilty of her death as it did to face the consequences of his conviction. She remembered his words when she'd told him, all those weeks ago in Rome, that she knew he could never have killed anyone—"Annie, you can't know what that means to me." But then she had accused him of stealing. She'd called him a thief, a seducer, a hypocrite—no better than his brother. For a man like Brodie, such words would be all but unforgivable. Now she was paying for them.

And there was so little time. Mr. Dietz had wanted to take him back to Bristol immediately after Aiden's death, saying the job was done, the bargain was finished. By what amounted to browbeating, she'd persuaded him to let Brodie remain until the man investigating Mary's death sent her his last report. He had written that he needed one more week to track down his final lead—a boy, who might or might not be the same boy who had handed a bottle of drugged wine to Brodie and Mary in the street. His letter was businesslike, straightforward, but between the lines Anna feared she could read an absence of enthusiasm. She suspected he wanted to be able to say he had tried everything before he gave up.

The time remaining—a day? a week?—was an illusion anyway. She knew Brodie had no intention of passively allowing himself to be incarcerated for the rest of his life for a crime he had never committed. He would try to escape. But when? He would not tell her, not even admit he intended it, when she asked. Why, for that matter, was he still here at all?

Brodie had asked himself the same question one time too many. Now he was through stalling, dithering, dreaming up half-baked excuses to stay another day, one more night. With an oath, he turned away from his bedroom window, where he'd been staring at yellow leaves flickering down from a pair of willow trees, and stalked to the eight-foot-high mahogany wardrobe. Behind its decorative cornice was a traveling bag. He took it down, standing on a chair, and threw it on the bed. He would not take much; but then, a sailor didn't need much. It troubled him that he was obliged to take anything at all from this house, but in that he had no choice: he owned nothing. He would take a few of Nick's things, then—but by God, nothing Jourdaine money had paid for.

He ought to have left before, days ago, as soon as Dietz had stopped asking him questions. It was crazy to stay; they could come for him any time, without warning, and haul him off to prison. At least he'd laid his plans. He owned papers now that identified him, under another name, as an A.B., or able-bodied seaman—it had seemed too risky to try for a fake mate's certificate—and he'd found out the departure dates of deepwater ships leaving the Liverpool docks in the next few days for Australia, South America, and the South Pacific. Now all he had to do was walk away. The time had come for the death of Nicholas Balfour, and with it the permanent disappearance of John Brodie.

What form would Nick's fatal accident take? he wondered. Maybe a sudden illness while he was away on some unexpected business trip. Or a shooting mishap on an impromptu hunting expedition. Or better, a quiet calamity at home, while there was no one about but a few servants. A fall down the steps. No—that might suggest Nick was drunk, and they'd want to keep his sterling reputation shining and spotless for Anna's benefit. He muttered another curse, flinging a shirt into the case. What did it matter how they killed him off?

He went to the high bureau and rummaged in the top drawer for his tobacco. He wished he had something to give Pearlman; if not money, then a memento, something to express his gratitude because he'd been a good and reliable "man." But there was nothing. He'd write him a note, then.

He caught sight of his reflection in the glass. As usual it arrested him, gave him pause. Who in the hell was this respectable-looking fellow in a standing collar and a silk tie? Christ, he hardly knew himself anymore. It wasn't just the clothes, either, or the careful haircut, the professional shave. It was—everything. He had to give Anna credit for that, anyway: by God, he *looked* like a gentleman. But he'd changed inside, too, and that was where the trouble lay. The basics were probably still intact, but quite a few things on the side weren't the same anymore. Things like expectations, and notions about how he ought to be living his one short life. Things that could get a man to thinking too hard and ruin his peace of mind. It was time to go back to being John Brodie, but he didn't know exactly who that was anymore. He'd lost himself.

Beside him the door to the hall opened slowly. He subdued a violent start when he saw that it was Anna. They surveyed each other, wordless and wary, for a moment before her edgy gaze shifted to scan the room. Her face paled, changed, and he knew she'd spotted the traveling case on the bed. He closed the bureau drawer with more force than he'd intended and moved away, putting distance between them. "Was there something you wanted?" He thought her hair looked like a soft cloud around her quiet, lovely face. He saw tension in the carriage of her shoulders, and determination in the set of her fragile mouth.

"You're packing," she observed with a stiff little wave.

He looked at the bed and smiled a bland, ironic smile, false in every way.

She made herself drop her twisting hands to her sides. The effort at control had drained most of the

color from her cheeks. She raised her eyes to
Brodie's blue ones, although the sight of him hurt
her, and spoke from her breaking heart without
weeping. "Don't go, John. 'Let me love you for as
long as we have'—that's what you said to me once.
That's what I'm asking of you now." Her voice
deepened, but she didn't cry. "Don't go. You're
the only man I'll ever love. I'm begging you not to
leave me yet. Stay until it's time. Mr. Dietz said a
week—"

The violent slicing gesture of Brodie's palm
through the air finally forced her to stop. He
pivoted away from her just for a moment; when he
turned back, his jaws were clenched and his eyes
were fierce. "Anna," he said, his voice a parody of
calm.

She shivered with dread. He had never called
her that before. She felt behind her for the door,
bracing herself.

"It's time to tell you. I was lying when I said I
loved you. I don't."

Her chin rose, but she could barely whisper.
"That's not true."

He anchored his eyes to a spot behind her left
shoulder. "It is true. I'm not the kind of man for
you anyway. You need someone different, better.
A woman like you—"

"Stop it, it's you I want! I'll go with you!" She
swallowed and made an attempt to speak quietly.
"You're still angry because I didn't believe you,
didn't trust you. I don't blame—"

"No," he said—truthfully this time. "I was
before, but not anymore."

"You are," she insisted. "And you should be. I
was wrong, but I swear I'll make it up to you. Take
me with you! I don't care where—America, Cana-

da. You have a place in mind, I know it. I'll go with you!"

He wore a stiff, peculiar smile, but his eyes were burning. "But I don't love you. I don't want you now. I only said it before because I wanted to take you to bed."

Everything went dark. She sounded hoarse when she tried to force her voice past the thick clot of misery in her throat. "If you're trying to hurt me, you're succeeding."

"No, I don't want to hurt you. I want you to know the truth."

His truth was going to kill her. "But—I—love you." She would say it anyway. Then tears overflowed; she didn't see his face blanch. Her hand found the doorknob at her back. She wasn't a coward: she'd have gone down on her knees to him if it would have changed anything. A paper-thin veneer of pride let her get the door open and squeeze through it before she started sobbing.

Eyes unfocused, Brodie listened to her hurried, shuffling footsteps. He waited to hear her door, next to his, open or close. It never did; she must have gone downstairs. He went to the bed and sat, holding onto the post. Silence rushed back, muffling everything except the pitiful bleat of a mourning dove in the garden and the sound of his own careful breathing. His skin felt fragile and too thin, too frail even to hold the hollowness inside him. He fought back a vivid fantasy of himself leaping from the bed and charging out after her. His mind played it over and over despite everything he could do, and he had to set his teeth and curl his fingers around the smooth wood to withstand it.

He'd done the right thing. She hurt now, but it

wouldn't last as long if she thought he'd used her. It was better this way. She would remember this day and the lies he'd told, and they would finally erase everything else, blot out all the sweetness that had ever been between them. Soon she would hate him, and after that she wouldn't think of him at all. He rested his forehead against the bedpost and waited, bleeding, for the will to get up.

A movement caught his eye. He looked up and saw her. Without a sound, she had come back. So she was going to torture him some more. All the same, his heart felt lighter just because she was there.

She hadn't bothered to disguise the ravages of her tears; her face was flushed and her voice came out gruff and sore from crying. She stood in the center of the room, eyeing him confidently, fearfully. "You're lying. You love me."

"No." He stood up.

"Yes, you do." She moved toward him steadily, and when she reached him she put her arms around him. "Don't go. Don't go."

If he could only hold her. It would just be for a minute. He lifted his hands to her shoulder blades. She murmured his name against his throat and he started shaking. "I'm not good for you, Annie, don't do this."

"There's nothing else I can do. Be honest. It's hard, I know, harder than running away. Stay with me."

He couldn't move, wanted no part of leaving her. "I love you," he sighed, defeated, into the subdued shine of her sweet-smelling hair.

31

Her own tears tasted salty on the skin of his neck. "Love me now," she whispered, embracing him. She stepped back and fumbled at the opening of her dress, taking too long, clumsy with impatience and leftover shyness. He stayed motionless with wonder until she said, "Will you help me?" and then he came out of his trance. His fingers were unsteady too, but he went slowly, folding soft cloth back from softer skin, entranced by the miraculous sight of his own hands against the pale flesh of her shoulders, her throat, her chest. With her eyes closed, Anna kissed his big palm and laid it against her cheek, dreamily slipping buttons out of the buttonholes of his shirt. They shed layers of clothing and reserve and caution; and after they were naked they felt as if they wanted to take more off, to strip away skin and flesh and bone if it could bring their hearts closer.

Oddly, there was no passion at first, only caring

and soft touching, giving and receiving. Half-spoken apologies and mumbled forgiveness. They knew now what they had, and understood that it was precious. With quiet sighs and low murmurs, they rested from turmoil in the temporary eye of peace.

But her skin was so warm, his breath so hot. His sleeking hands aroused her in a breathless moment and her whispered words fired him. They sank to the bed in a lover's knot of tangled arms and legs. She gloried in touching him, hearing his breathing change, feeling him tremble. Her innocence was gone but she didn't mourn it; she'd given it to him, and now she knew ways to make him sigh and shudder exactly as she did. His body was so different, hard-muscled and lean, shades darker than hers. His strength amazed her. She touched the sides of his face, caressed his mouth with her thumbs, watching his smile fade and his pale eyes cloud. He took her with a deep and drugging kiss, down, down, until she thought she would drown from it. Murmuring, she buried her fingers in his hair and took him with her, wanting them to perish together.

"Ahh," she said on a long sigh when he filled her, and they watched each other, fascinated, seeing their own sharp and heavy pleasure reflected back. They had known desire before but not like this, never like this. This was blind need, complete abandon, beating in their blood in time with the thoughtless imperative to give each other everything. Anna lost herself, did not know who she was. She felt fear, not of pain but of the unknown, where she could die, could disappear, be consumed—and she wanted it. Longed for it.

He was her lifeline and the instrument of her oblivion. At the end of this dire adventure, she knew he would save her.

He wanted to tell her how beautiful she was, how dearly he loved her, but words weren't possible. For one desolate moment he remembered that he must leave her, and in that flicker of time he touched her almost with violence. But she knew, and soothed him with her mouth, her soft fingertips. Then there was nothing but sensation, hot and exquisite, urgent, climbing. They grew frantic, rising and rising together. He was bursting; she knew she was dying. His fingers slipped over the damp flesh of her arms and they clasped hands, kissing. When the moment came, it was neither a death nor an explosion. It was a gift, a paradox of fury and peace that obliterated separateness and bound them to each other for this time and forever.

Afterward they lay in the dark, touching and whispering, full of thanksgiving, exchanging breathless compliments. Their bodies cooled; Brodie retrieved the rumpled coverlet they'd kicked to the floor and covered them with it. Thoughts of the past gradually filtered through the walls of their intimate cocoon, and then the need to apologize overtook them again. Anna started it. "Forgive me for not believing you, I'm sorry, I'm sorry. I hate the words I said. If I could take them back—"

"It's my fault, Annie, not yours. I don't know why I was so angry, it doesn't make sense to me now. You made a logical assumption—all I had to do was tell you you were wrong."

"Logical! It was absurd, and stupid and idiotic."

She gave him a little shake. "And you *did* tell me I was wrong, but still I didn't believe you. Anyway, I know why you were angry."

"Why?"

"Because you believed in me, gave me your trust, and I threw it back in your face." She started to cry, and brushed at the tears impatiently. "I betrayed you. I said I loved you and then I called you a thief, on the flimsiest of evidence."

"A signed and dated bank note is not that flimsy," he pointed out, his lips against her temple. "You only believed what you saw."

"But I shouldn't have, I should have known."

"How could—"

"It was my pride."

"*Your* pride?"

"I thought you'd used me, so I was hurt and angry and I couldn't think straight. It's all my—"

"Annie, it was *my* pride that got us into that pit, not yours. I couldn't stand it that you thought I'd steal your money. I *wanted* to hurt you—"

For a few more minutes they argued about whose fault everything had been. They indulged in an orgy of magnanimity, outdoing each other in forgiveness and high-minded blame-taking, and felt much better for it afterward.

Brodie lit the candles beside the bed. Golden light flickered on the canopy, the coverlet, Anna's soft skin. They found themselves talking about Aiden. It surprised them to learn that they both grieved for him. Now they could mourn him together, and they were glad; they hadn't known how much they'd needed each other for that.

"I just can't make myself believe he killed Nicholas," Anna said again, resting her cheek on Brodie's shoulder. "They were *friends*. Perhaps everyone has a potential for violence, but Nicholas wasn't killed in anger or fear or out of self-preservation the way Martin Dougherty was. It was murder, John, calculated and coldblooded." She looked up into his shadowed face. "I saw it, did you know?"

He nodded and gathered her closer, trying to ease the memory away. "I can't find it in me to hate him, either," he admitted. "It's strange. I knew they were using me for bait to lure Nick's killer out, but I didn't care. I wanted to know who it was much more than they did. I wanted to see him punished—maybe kill him myself." He stared intently at the long curl of Anna's hair in his palm. "But Aiden—I didn't want Aiden to die. Or even to suffer." He looked down into her serious brown eyes, hoping for an answer. "I don't understand it."

But she couldn't help him. "I'll miss him," she confessed, as bewildered as he.

Wind blew in the linden tree outside the open window with a dry, tired sound. She shivered, and he stroked the cool, smooth skin of her encircling arm, warming her. Summer was dying. Anna thought of all the smoky late afternoons to come, the perpetual cold gray of winter, the colorless Mersey slapping irritably at the docks. "Where will you go?" she murmured, shuddering, holding tighter. She felt him stiffen, then relax.

"Someplace warm," he said against her hair, trying to smile. "Maybe the tropics. I'll sit under banyan trees and eat figs and coconuts and bananas. Beautiful women with hardly any clothes on to wait on me. No worries, nothing but—Oh, sweetheart, I'm teasing," he said gently, seeing her expression.

"I know, it's not that." She smiled feebly.

"What, then?"

She moved her shoulders. "There's so little time. I have so much to tell you, and no time to say anything except that I love you."

They listened to the sound of that for a while. "I love you," Brodie echoed. Thcy kissed.

It would be so easy to give in to sadness. "What will you miss the most?" she asked. He looked at her, incredulous, and she smiled. "After me."

His answering smile faded slowly. "I was happy here. I wanted this life, even though I stole it. What I regret is that, after a little while, no one will remember me."

"That's not—"

"They'll remember Nick, the man they thought he was. No one will remember John Brodie."

Her throat hurt; she had to swallow hard to speak. "I will. Always, always."

"But I don't want you to," he whispered back, their faces touching, eyes shut tight. "Forget me quick, Annie. Let all of this go, like a dream."

"Oh, no."

"Listen to me. I want you to marry someone else. *Yes*. And have children, lots of them. I want it for you, darling—children running around the docks, getting in the way when you're trying to tell the platers where to weld the new seams on one of Carter's big ships. I want you to have everything, the best. Don't cry. Please don't cry now."

But she couldn't stop. "Take me with you," she begged hopelessly, pressing against him. She felt him shake his head, and despaired. She carried his hand to her lips. "Love me, then. Give me your baby."

He pulled away, stunned. "God, Annie!"

"Did you think it could never happen?" she asked, smiling softly through the tears.

He hadn't thought about it at all. He lay back against the pillow, rubbing his forehead, staring at the shadowy ceiling. "This—we can't—" His mind was a jumble. "I don't want—if you—" He stopped talking and tried to put his thoughts in order.

She leaned over him and took his hand back, kissed the knuckles, then pressed it to her breast. "Love me," she said again, easing his palm across her jutting nipple, shifting against him. "Let me love you."

"Wait, now—" He tried, not very hard, to snatch his hand back, but she held on. "Wait now, Annie. We can't, ah . . . we'd better . . . oh sweet Jesus."

Her free hand drifted down his chest, his stomach. She ruffled the hair on his thigh with the soft skin of her inner wrist. "How is the solicitor-general this evening?" she murmured silkily. Two weeks ago he'd taught her all the vulgar synonyms he knew for the male organ—eleven in all. "Solicitor-general" was really her second choice; her favorite was "Member for Cockshire," but she couldn't quite bring herself to say that one out loud. Brodie's chuckle turned into a long groan as she began to stroke the warm, thick length of him in the palm of her small hand. It was lovely to watch his face; it told her more clearly than words what pleased him best. An idea came to her. Raising up on one elbow, she put her lips to the satiny tip and gave it a soft kiss. It was a fine idea, she could see that right away. How interesting that they both had these small spots of identical sensitivity on their very different bodies. She thought

of a subtle refinement on her original purpose and
stroked him with the tip, then the flat of her
tongue. The effect was electric. "Does it hurt?" she
asked, pausing, worried.

His pent-up breath came out in an explosive
laugh. When he reached for her and pulled her on
top of him, she knew a mixture of thwarted
curiosity and nervous relief. But when he opened
her and eased inside her soft woman's place, she
knew nothing at all. She took him deeply, urged
him on with sweet, natural skill. It had never been
so intimate before. She made a curtain for them
with her hair and kissed him under it passionately.
She wanted his seed, his last gift, his baby. She
held back, held back—then couldn't any longer
and shuddered against him, weeping with emotion. And Brodie forgot about doubt and caution
and indecision, and gave her what she wanted.

The night slipped by so quickly. It was long past
midnight when they tiptoed downstairs to find
something to eat—the soul was replete but the
flesh was starving. They sat at the big oak kitchen
table in lantern light and ate the cold potato soup
and lobster salad that the cook had put back in the
pantry when they hadn't appeared for dinner.
They leaned against each other, still needing to
touch, to reassure. Every minute seemed precious,
every word extraordinary. They abandoned all
pretense that things would be all right, would work
out somehow, and freely confessed the anguish
they felt. They told each other their dreams, and
their bittersweet sadness deepened when they discovered that their dreams were exactly the same—
to live together in their own house, to have children, to watch their shipbuilding enterprise grow
and prosper. And Brodie wanted to be respectable.

She cried when he told her that. They clung together, not speaking, until the first bird sang and the sky began its treacherous lightening. Then they hurried back to their room, their bed—their island—to hold each other again.

Sleep became the new enemy; they fought it tenaciously, minute by minute, knowing what it would steal if they let it seduce them. They were exhausted from lovemaking, hoarse from speaking, and dizzy with fatigue, but they held on. Until they fell asleep.

Anna awoke a little after noon. When she saw that she was alone, she went sick with dread. In minutes she was dressed. The house was terrifyingly quiet; her hurried footsteps on the staircase sounded too loud. She found the hall empty, and passed into the dining room. Empty. "John?" she called—but softly, not only because it was dangerous to say his name here but because her panic was rising; if she called out loud and there was no answer, she would know that the very worst had happened.

There was no one in the conservatory. She went back to the foyer, across to the drawing room on the other side. Empty. Dear God. She heard a soft noise in the library, through the sliding doors. A servant? Oh please, please—

It was Brodie. He was standing over her father's big desk, scribbling something with a pen. He straightened when he heard her. They met in the middle of the room, and embraced as if they had been separated for weeks. "I thought you'd gone," she cried softly, pressing against him, stroking his back.

"No, no."

"Thank God. Please, don't—" She broke off in

shock. She'd put her hands inside his coat to touch him; her fingers closed around the warm hilt of a pistol at the small of his back, stuck inside his belt. She drew it out before he could stop her. The heavy black ugliness of it repelled her; she let him snatch it back and put it on the desk behind them. For the first time she noticed his clothes—Nicholas's oldest, shabbiest suit, no tie, no waistcoat. She took a step back. "You were leaving," she accused, wide-eyed. "You would have just written me a note. Not even said goodbye!"

He took her arms. "No." His mouth was a grim line. "I should have, but I couldn't."

"Then—"

"I was writing something to Pearlman. Just a note, thanking him. I couldn't have left without seeing you."

"Oh," she breathed, holding him, vowing that somehow she would get through this without crying.

He caressed her hair as he gazed out at the soft rain falling in the garden. "Are you disappointed in me because I'm running away?" She looked up blankly. "I gave them my word. I said I'd go back to Bristol when this was over. Now—"

"No, no, I couldn't bear to think of you being locked up!"

"But I made a promise."

"But you're *innocent*. Where is the justice? Your promise can't bind you to an unfair bargain. You have to take responsibility for their mistake."

He smiled with relief and hugged her; he'd worried that she would think him dishonest. But he couldn't have allowed himself to be locked up for the rest of his life for something he hadn't done, in a place less than two hundred miles from

Annie, no matter what principle was at stake. It was too much to ask.

He took hold of her cold hands. "Listen to me, now. As soon as I go, you must send a message to Dietz, telling him. Immediately. Do you understand?"

"No, John, you'll need time. I should wait at least a day—"

"No, I *won't* need time. Tell him right away so he'll think you knew nothing about it. Yes!" he insisted, squeezing her hands. "Besides, he'll have to think of a way to explain my death, Nick's death, and he'll probably want to say it happened away from the house, without witnesses. Not even you. So—"

"Where will you go?"

He reached up and touched her cheek. "It's better if I don't tell you."

She closed her eyes. "Oh, my God."

"Dietz will ask you a hundred questions— you'll have to convince him you don't know anything. It's better—"

"You won't tell me?" Helpless tears streaked down her face; she lacked the will to wipe them away. "Will you write to me?" He shook his head, and her heart broke.

"I can't," he murmured. "Too dangerous for you."

Their clasped hands grew slippery from the tears splashing down from her wet cheeks. She imagined the tie that bound them stretching, stretching until it snapped, leaving them alone and separate for the rest of their lives. It would be as if he had died. Or she had.

"Don't cry," he begged her. Unfairly—his tears were on the inside, and easier to hide.

"Take me with you."

He shook his head.

"Please!"

"No." She whirled around, angry, but he pulled her back. "This is where you belong. It's not as hard for me—I never had a home for long. But you have your family here, your work, all your friends."

"I don't ca—"

"If you came with me you'd hate the way you had to live—"

"I wouldn't!"

"—and before long you'd learn to hate me."

"Never!"

"Listen to me. We'd be poor, we wouldn't be respectable—"

"Respectable!" She spat it out like a curse. "I don't care anything about respectability." His expression of sad amusement galled her. "I don't! Society's rules, all the conventions—they're more of a prison for me now than the one you're escaping. Please, John, please—" She hated the pleading in her voice, but she couldn't help it.

"No," he repeated, firmly.

She shoved at his chest with her bunched fists, furious. She walked in a frustrated circle back to him and threw her arms around him.

Now Brodie's tears were on the outside, too. He held her tightly, feeling her heat, the beat of her heart against him. "It doesn't matter where I go because I'll always be with you, you'll always be in my heart. Be happy, Annie, live a good life. Be careful, too; don't let anyone hurt you."

She drew a choking breath. "I will always, always love you."

"You taught me everything."

"You taught *me*."

This was too hard. They drew apart at the same moment, and turned together at a noise in the doorway. It was the maid. Anna looked away; Brodie swiped at his face with his sleeve.

"You have a visitor, sir."

He swore incoherently. "It's probably Neil. I said I'd lend him some money. I've put him off twice already. I'll get rid of him."

But the maid handed him the engraved visitor's card, and instead of brushing past her he halted in his tracks and went dead white.

"Who is it?" asked Anna, clenching her hands, fearing the worst. Dietz.

"It's my father."

32

They heard it at the same moment—the slow, labored thumping of a cane on the wood floor. It dulled on the carpet, rang out again on the parquet as it drew nearer. Anna went to Brodie and took his hand. His face frightened her. "Are you all right?"

He didn't hear. His senses were concentrated on that deliberate and sinister thunk, thunk, thunk, and the sibilant shuffle that accompanied it. A lifetime of bitterness rose in his chest, but something even stronger pulled on a private, unused place inside.

The drawing room draperies were closed, the room was dim; they saw the shape coming toward them only as an indistinct, hunched form until it crossed the threshold and stood still in a splash of afternoon sunshine on the library floor. Even then, slowly swirling motes of dust in the brightness softened the outline and obscured the features.

Anna glanced at Brodie anxiously before leaving his side and moving toward the visitor, an uncertain smile faltering on her lips. "My lord," she said softly.

Regis Gunne, the Earl of Battiscombe, was an old, old man, white-haired and brittle-boned, thin as a rake, humped and bent and curved with arthritis. His skin stretched tight over the fragile, almost visible bones of his face, then sagged in countless folds and wrinkles around his birdlike neck. Gnarled, misshapen fingers of both hands held onto a black walking stick; stick and bowed legs made such a shaky tripod, Anna was afraid to offer her hand. She curtsied instead, and realized the gesture felt entirely natural.

"How do you do?" said the earl. His voice was gravelly but refined. "Please do pardon me for coming here without any warning, it was unforgivably rude, but I . . ." His words trailed off as he seemed to give up trying to pay polite attention to Anna and fixed his fierce old eyes on Brodie. His thin, nearly invisible lips opened and closed two times before he could get his next words out. "Nicholas? Is it you?"

Brodie was clenching his hands together behind his back. Hard-faced, unmoving, he answered. "No, I'm John. Nick's dead."

The earl seemed to stumble. Anna reached for his arm and steadied him. With gentle hands and slow steps she steered him to the leather sofa and helped him to sit. He clutched at his cane between his knees and closed his eyes, and his face paled to the color of beeswax. The paper-thin nostrils flared in and out with his quick breathing.

Anna flashed Brodie a look of alarm. His

granite-hard pose was crumbling; he moved toward his father slowly, drawn there by emotions more powerful than resentment or twenty-year-old anger, and lowered himself to the seat beside him. Anna stared at them, twisting her fingers, searching for a resemblance. She found it in the eyes, although the earl's were clouded with age, and in the high, proud forehead.

There was silence for a long moment. Regis lifted one hand and laid it with palsied lightness on the sleeve of Brodie's coat. "John?" he quavered. If he had a sparrow's body, at that moment his eyes were ferocious as a hawk's. "John," he repeated, staring down at Brodie's motionless hand. "My son."

The angry child in Brodie wanted to recoil, to shout out loud, to force this decrepit old man to cringe from the power of his rancor. Instead his hand surrounded his father's in the gentlest of clasps and then he carried the aged claw to his lips and kissed it. "Father," he whispered. Regis's arm stole around his son's neck. They embraced.

Anna stared at the floor and watched teardrops slap at the carpet and the toes of her shoes.

The earl pulled away to peer at his son; he couldn't take his eyes from him. "I've been trying to find you for so long. More than a year, John, you and Nicholas. The gentleman I hired told me you were in prison for—for killing someone. But when I went to the gaol, they wouldn't let me in. They said I couldn't see you."

"I never killed anyone."

Regis flicked a bony wrist in the air. "Of course you didn't," he said feelingly. And with that he dismissed the subject.

Brodie looked down, embarrassed by the un-manly tears that had filled his eyes so suddenly. But his father's lack of hesitation, his blind, in-stantaneous faith in his innocence moved him powerfully. He felt a feather-light pressure on his shoulder and looked up again.

"So. Nicholas is dead?"

"Yes, sir. Four months ago."

"He was ill?"

"No, he . . ." Brodie broke off, at a loss. "It was sudden. He . . . didn't suffer." He glanced at Anna, who had quietly taken a seat a little distance from them. Her face was full of sympathy. He wanted to ask her what in the world he ought to tell his father about Nick, and how best to explain his own presence in the Jourdaine home. The old man's mind seemed perfectly clear, but to tell him the whole complicated truth about everything would cause him too much pain.

"Thank God for that," his father was saying. "I have another son." Brodie nodded. "My late wife's boy, your half-brother." He shook his head grimly. "He's a grave disappointment to me, John. I couldn't leave everything to him; he'd only drink it away, or worse. Much worse. That's why I've been trying to find you. I've had people looking for you and Nicholas for so long, I had almost given up. This—this is like a miracle to me."

They were holding hands. Summoning all his courage, Brodie made himself ask the question that had tormented him most of his life. He kept his voice gentle, non-accusatory. "Father, why . . ." he stopped, started again. "Why did you send us away?"

The Earl of Battiscombe raised his chin and

looked off into the distance. His throat convulsed on a nervous swallow; restless fingers pressed a crease in his trousers above one pointed knee. "Because—" he had to clear his throat—"because I was proud and stupid." After that he couldn't speak, and Brodie had a glimmer of an understanding that he was hearing words his father had never spoken to anyone before, and perhaps had never admitted even to himself.

A movement in the doorway caught his eye. The maid again. He started to shake his head. "Mr. Vaughn is here to see you, sir—"

Anna stood up. "I'll speak to him, John," she said quietly. It was time to leave them alone together, and she was glad of the opportunity to steal away. "I'll have some tea sent in. Please make yourself comfortable," she told the earl, smiling; "this is your home now. Excuse me."

Brodie watched her go, and felt an ache inside that was almost intolerable. Leaving her had become obscene to him, a perversion of his best instincts. His father's words reclaimed his attention, but the lead weight on his spirit would not lift.

"I loved Elizabeth dearly, John, but I couldn't marry her. Or I thought I couldn't—today, heaven knows, I would do everything differently." He smiled his sad, thin-lipped smile. "But she was so low-born, and in my mind that made it impossible. And you boys were illegitimate. I was afraid of the scandal." He looked down, ashamed. "But I never thought she would leave me. I thought she would let me keep her, support her, that things could go on as they always had. I was . . ." he swallowed again and took a deep breath—"a little arrogant." He looked Brodie in the eye. "I was an ignorant son of a bitch." He saw his son's lips twitch, and it gave him the heart to go on. "But she was stubborn too, and that's the truth. She wouldn't take a penny from me, sent all my letters back unopened. When I finally found out where she'd taken you, I went there and tried to talk sense into her. Hah! Might as well have saved myself the trip. We said some ugly things to each other that day, John, words I'll regret till the day I die. After that, I never saw her again." His hand tightened on Brodie's; bitter sorrow bleared his old eyes, and in that moment Brodie forgave him everything.

"Then Edwina—my wife—became pregnant, had a child, and I tried to make myself forget. I was delighted to be having a son, the legitimate heir I'd wanted for so long. I turned my attention to my new family. And I'll admit, I was sick of being rejected by Elizabeth. But I never loved Edwina, and Neil was a disappointment almost from the hour he was born."

"Neil?"

"Your half-brother. Edwina spoiled him, but it was more than that." He sank back against the sofa tiredly and spoke with half-closed eyes. "He was a wild child, cruel, not—natural. I could tell you awful things. And he didn't grow out of it; if anything, he only got more beastly. I tried everything—cut off his allowance, even told him I would disinherit him as soon as I found my other boys." He smiled the smile Brodie was beginning to treasure, beginning to wish he knew ways to encourage. "My twins," Regis said softly. "My beloved sons."

"But you've only got one 'beloved twin' left, dear Father. In a minute, you won't have any at all. You'll just have me."

Neil Vaughn—Neil Gunne—stood in the doorway, grinning a ghastly brown-toothed grin. One hand was wrapped around Anna's shoulders; the other held a gun to her temple.

Somehow Brodie got to his feet. His body felt paralyzed, as if all the blood and muscle had washed out of him. Anna's white face reflected his panic back at him. "Let her go," he said in a croak, and Neil laughed.

"Oh, I don't think so." He lowered the gun slowly, dragging the barrel down her neck, her chest, until it lodged in the crease between her breasts. "No, John, I don't think so." He laughed again, and Anna shuddered, smelling his foul breath. "Are you surprised because I know your name? I've always known you weren't Nick. After all, I'm the one who put a knife in his heart." Anna gave a gasping sob, and his fingers threading her hair jerked her head back when she would have slumped forward in despair. "I thought I'd as good as killed you too when I slit your whore's throat, but you turned up again like a damned phoenix. Not this time, though, I don't think. This time I'll be more direct." His lips drew apart in a grisly smile. "Subtlety was my downfall the first time, but I've learned you can't trust someone else to do your work for you. Not even the hangman. Get away from my father."

Brodie had stepped in front of Regis, blocking him from Neil's gun. "Was it your thugs who tried to kill me in Naples?" he gritted out, not moving. His brain felt stuffed with cotton; all he could do was stall while he waited for an opening, a moment, a chance.

Neil nodded. "Stupid, incompetent dago pigs. All they succeeded in killing was your bodyguard."

"Three people are dead because of you."

"Five in a minute."

Brodie heard a buzzing in his ears. "Four. That's all you need. Let Anna go."

"Oh, sorry. Can't do it."

Regis used his stick to get to his feet. "Neil," he said, as if there were no breath in his lungs. "For the love of God—"

"Stop! Don't come near me, Father, or I'll have to kill you, too. And that would ruin everything. Your death comes a little later. At home, where it will look natural."

Brodie was sure he meant it, that he would shoot his own father without a thought. "Let Anna go," he said again, moving to his left, away from Regis. Neil pivoted, turning Anna with him, following with his eyes. He slid the gun up to her cheekbone, still holding her hair.

She closed her eyes, and felt a dangerous acceptance flood through her. It terrified her. Her arms were free. She sent Brodie a wild, beseeching look, praying he would understand and react. As if she were clenching her hands together in anguish, she cupped her right fist in her left hand. She took a slow, deep breath and drove her elbow into Neil's ribs with all her strength.

The gun went off in her ear, and she knew she was dead.

Then how could she see Brodie hurtle across six feet of space and crash to the floor with Neil in his arms? She screamed, clutching at her hair, watching them roll and roll over each other, bringing furniture down all around them. Another shot fired with an ugly muffled sound. The two men lay still. Anna screamed again when Neil stumbled to his knees, then his feet. Brodie lay still in a pool of his own blood.

She staggered toward him, sank to her knees beside him. Cradled his head in her arms, moaning. Rocked him in blank, mindless misery.

"You won't do it, old man."

Neil smiled at his father, who held a pistol—Brodie's pistol, which had fallen to the floor—in two quaking hands. Neil turned his gun and his smile on Anna. She heard the hammer cock. Goodbye, she said, or thought, into Brodie's white and lifeless face.

An explosion. Neil's body hit the floor with the force of a felled tree, and the room shook. Regis stared down at his dead sons.

33

"We're so terribly sorry for your loss, dear."

"You poor child, if there's anything we can do . . ."

"What a terrible tragedy. He was so young, and with so much to live for."

Mourners filed past the closed casket before speaking quietly to the veiled widow seated nearby with her family. She returned their condolences with a nod or a murmured word, a gentle squeeze of the hand; behind the heavy veil, friends and acquaintances thought they saw tears.

Cousin Stephen, dignified in black, greeted visitors and guided them to chairs in the Jourdaines' best drawing room. The widow's aunt sat by her side, upright and formidable, patting her hand in a bracing way from time to time. Next to her was Cousin Jenny, weeping softly into a lace handkerchief. Behind them the widow's best friend, Milly Pollinax, sat beside Mr. McTavish. From time to time she dabbed at her cheeks; strangely, though, her handkerchief was dry. Stranger still, behind the discreet screen of her lashes, there was a gleam of anticipation in Mrs. Pollinax's pretty dark eyes.

The smell of autumn hung on the light breeze that billowed the curtain in the open window. Late crickets piped in the shrubbery, and evening birds called out shrill good-nights from the willow trees. The sinking sun sent morose shadows across the polished floor, the polished casket. A servant lit candles. Mourners began to wonder whether there would be refreshments.

From the back of the room a low, uneasy murmuring began. Visitors in front were too well-bred to turn around, but they wanted to, especially when the restive hum grew louder. A man was threading his way between chairs and mourners, moving toward the casket. When he reached it, he stood with his head bowed, one hand resting lightly on the rich mahogany. His other arm hung from his shoulder in a black sling. The murmur turned into fierce, whispered questions. The widow stared fixedly through her dark veil at the man's back. He turned.

There was a collective gasp of astonishment. Cousin Stephen glided up to the newcomer and shook his hand, muttering sedately. A new whispered refrain started to circulate through the room: "The brother!" "It's the brother, they were twins." "This one's name is Brodie, I heard." "Illegitimate, you know." "Yes, but his father's an earl, he'll get all that money." "*Shh.*"

All eyes were glued, openly or covertly, on the rich earl's illegitimate son as Stephen steered him toward the widow. There were low introductions which, try as one might, no one was able to overhear. Soon after, the two men helped Mrs. Balfour to her feet and supported her out of the room. As she passed by Mrs. Pollinax, the latter seemed to wink. But that was impossible; she must have had something in her eye. The widow disappeared, and the whispering turned into a discreet din.

In the library door, Brodie leaned over and spoke low and confidentially into Stephen's ear. "I'd like to speak to my brother's wife alone for a few moments, if you don't mind."

"Oh, of course." Stephen looked faintly surprised; but he made a short, dignified bow and turned away. The door closed behind him with a solemn *click*.

Brodie turned toward Anna. The sight of her sobered him, tempered the euphoria he'd been straining to conceal for the last few minutes. Small and sad-looking, she was shrouded in black, the thick lace veil completely hiding her face. But in one quick, graceful movement she peeled the veil off, and he had a hasty glimpse of her face—laughing and joyful—before she tumbled into his arms.

"I missed you, I missed you so much! I thought you would never come. Where did Dietz hide you? How is your shoulder, how is your father? Why did it take you so long? Are you all right, are you healed? It's been weeks!"

"Days," he corrected, laughing, kissing and kissing her. He held her so tightly, she knew the answer to one question at least—he was healed. "My father is well," he told her. "He'll come tomorrow, for the funeral. He wants to have Nick's body moved to Denbighshire, near his home."

"You told him everything, then?"

"Everything." They held each other gently, letting melancholy slip through them, thinking of the old man's grief. "He wants to go to London afterward," Brodie said after a moment. "He wants me to go with him."

"To London? Why?"

"To see his lawyers. Annie, he wants to adopt me."

"Oh, John. I'm so glad." She cried against his shirt; he almost joined her.

There was a discreet knock at the door. "I'm sorry, Anna, but several of the guests are leaving," Stephen called quietly. "Would you and Mr. Brodie care to say goodbye to them?"

"Would we?" she whispered.

"I'd much rather stay here and console the widow." In the blink of an eye, he had three buttons undone in the front of her somber mourning gown.

"None of that," she admonished severely, removing his hand, which was at work on the fourth. "I'm in mourning for a year."

Brodie laughed out loud, a great, hearty guffaw. They clapped their hands to their mouths at the same moment, shushing each other, giggling. He pulled her into a close embrace so they could hear each other when they whispered.

"A year, John, it's obligatory. Aunt Charlotte would swoon if I shortened the mourning period."

"Better break out the smelling salts," he advised, nibbling at her lips. "I can't wait a year for this widow." She tasted so good; she was like a banquet after a forty-day fast. "Anyway, Aunt Charlotte may come out of her swoon sooner than you think when she finds out that your new suitor is about to become a marquis, and will one day be an earl."

"A marquis? Good heavens." She turned her head to the side, as if regarding him in a new light. "Yes," she agreed, "I should think that in itself might shave off six months or so from Aunt Charlotte's year."

Brodie growled, backing her up against the door. "I can't wait six months." He slipped both hands inside her bodice, and her head fell back. He put his lips in the soft hollow of her throat. Her pulse was racing.

She tried not to make a sound, but he was doing something with his thumbs, or perhaps it was his palms, that made it almost impossible. She loved the smell of his hair, the feel of the hard length of him pressing against her. "How long can you wait?" she gasped, eyes tightly closed, into the air over his shoulder.

"I can't wait another second." He slid his thigh between hers almost roughly and took her in a deep, wilting kiss.

"Anna?" Stephen sounded impatient. "Are you coming?"

Brodie thought he heard her say, under her breath, "Almost." He pulled back in amazement. She looked as surprised as he. "Annie, you made a joke," he exclaimed. "A *dirty* joke."

She broke into a delighted grin. "I did, didn't I?"

"Anna?"

"We're coming, Stephen!" She stood back and rebuttoned her dress, began to pin her veil on again. "We'll discuss this subject at another time, Mr. Brodie," she said briskly, albeit breathlessly.

"Oh, we will, Mrs. Balfour," he agreed, straightening his tie, tugging at his waistcoat. "Are you ready?"

"I certainly am." She shot him a wicked glance, full of meaning. He shook his head in wonder.

They cleared their throats, stiffened their shoulders. Tried to compose their faces. Brodie opened the door; she preceded him. With slow, solemn decorum they proceeded toward the foyer, where a knot of well-wishers waited to say goodbye. Anyone walking behind them for the first six paces, though, would have been shocked to see the future Earl of Battiscombe's palm resting, in a comfortable way, on the Widow Balfour's shapely behind.

PATRICIA GAFFNEY

Fortune's Lady

"Like moonspun magic...one of the best historical romances I have read in a decade!"
—Cassie Edwards

They are natural enemies—traitor's daughter and zealous patriot—yet the moment he sees Cassandra Merlin at her father's graveside, Riordan knows he will never be free of her. She is the key to stopping a heinous plot against the king's life, yet he senses she has her own secret reasons for aiding his cause. Her reputation is in shreds, yet he finds himself believing she is a woman wronged. Her mission is to seduce another man, yet he burns to take her luscious body for himself. She is a ravishing temptress, a woman of mystery, yet he has no choice but to gamble his heart on fortune's lady.

_4153-7 $5.99 US/$6.99 CAN

CATHERINE HART — Fire & Ice

Beautiful and spirited Kathleen Haley sets sail from England for the family estate in Savannah. On board ship, she meets the man who will forever haunt her heart, the dashing and domineering Captain Reed Taylor. On the long, perilous voyage, she resists his bold advances—until she wakes from unconsciousness after a storm and hears Reed's shocking confession. She then knows she must marry the rogue.

But their fiery conflict is far from over. Through society balls, raging duels and torrid nights, Kathleen seeks vengeance on Reed's brutal passions and his secret alliance with pirates. At last she is forced to attack the very man who has warmed her icy heart and burned his way into her very soul.

___4303-3 $5.99 US/$6.99 CAN